FOCUS ON THE FAMILY® PRESENTS

Adventures in ODYSSEY®

The Official Guide

A BEHIND-THE-SCENES LOOK AT THE STORIES, ACTORS & CHARACTERS

D1418352

Tyndale House Publishers, Inc.
Carol Stream, Illinois

FOCUS ON THE FAMILY® PRESENTS

Adventures in ODYSSEY®

The Official Guide

A BEHIND-THE-SCENES LOOK AT THE STORIES, ACTORS & CHARACTERS

by Nathan Hoobler and the *Adventures in Odyssey* team

Editor: Marianne Hering

Cover design: Josh Lewis

Interior design: Joseph Sapulich

Cover Illustration: Gary Locke

How-to-Draw Illustrations: Joseph Sapulich based on Gary Locke originals.

Illustration Credits—Pierre Babasin: 325 (*Clubhouse* magazine 10/97). **Scott Burroughs**: 369. **Dave Clegg**: 108 (*Clubhouse* magazine art), 325 (*Clubhouse* magazine 6/97). **Bruce Day**: xii, 68 (Whit at bottom), 71 (Connie's head on left), 90, 107, 112, 117, 120, 149, 504. **Gita**: 318, 356, (*Clubhouse* magazine), 364, 367 (*Clubhouse* magazine), 401, 404, 417. **Rick Hemphill**: 325 (*Focus on the Family* magazine 10/97, *Clubhouse* magazines 10/97 and 5/98), 339. **Beau Henderson**: 516-7 (book covers). **Robert Holsinger**: 325 (*Clubhouse* magazine 6/97). **Rob Johnson**: 520. **Joe LeMonnier**: 517 (map). **Karen Loccisano**: 108 (*Strange Journey Back*), 252, 514. **Gary Locke**: i, ii, x, 6, 17, 21, 24-7, 31-5, 41, 46, 69, 73, 76, 81, 88-9, 92, 95, 99, 100 (George and Jimmy), 101-4, 109, 113-4, 121-2, 125, 127-9, 133, 142, 146, 151-2, 154, 157-9, 162, 165, 173, 178, 183, 186, 205, 220 (Katrina filled in), 224, 228, 231, 235-6, 262, 266, 268, 284 (Boredom Buster), 294-5, 300, 303, 328, 338, 352, 359, 360, 366, 367 (Nose), 370, 373, 378, 382, 391-2, 397-8, 402, 408, 410-11, 414, 419, 422, 438, 442, 445-6, 448, 455, 463-4, 466-8, 471-2, 479, 484, 487, 497, 507, 510, 513, 528-30, 556, 562-3. **Rick Mills**: 325 (*Focus on the Family* magazine 10/97). **Joseph Sapulich**: 243. **Richard Stergulz**: 214, 306, 309, 316-7, 320-2, 331, 340, 343, 350, 355, 356, 474. **Keith Stubblefield**: 325 (*Clubhouse* magazine, 6/97). **Laura Stutzman**: 521. **Ludmilla Tomova**: 519. **Fred Warter**: 232, 256, 264, 270, 273, 276, 281-2, 289, 293, 298, 304, 524-7. **Phil Williams**: 394.

Library of Congress Cataloging-in-Publication Data

Hoobler, Nathan D., 1979-

    Adventures in Odyssey : the official guide / by Nathan D. Hoobler.
       p. cm. — (A Focus on the Family book)
    At head of title: Focus on the Family
    Includes indexes.
    ISBN-13: 978-1-58997-475-3
    ISBN-10: 1-58997-475-1
    1. Adventures in Odyssey (Radio program)   I. Title.   II. Title: Focus on the Family.
    PN1991.77.A38H66 2008
    791.44'72—dc22

Printed in the United States of America

16 15 14 13 12 11 10 09 08
 9 8 7 6 5 4 3 2 1

To Mark Drury, for starting my adventure

Contents

Contents

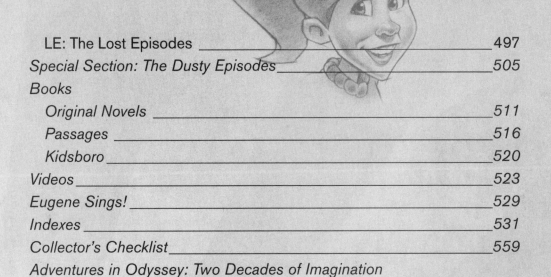

Adventures in Odyssey: Two Decades of Imagination

Acknowledgments: Thank You . . .

To Dave Arnold, Marshal Younger, and Paul McCusker
For reading many drafts of hundreds of pages, thousands of names, and hundreds of thousands of words. And for being the best bosses anywhere.

To Marianne Hering
For being a detailed, kind editor. And for the chocolate.

To Josh Lewis, April Birtwistle, and Callie Wilburn
For finding, scanning, and taking hundreds of photos. And for inventing the title "production monkey."

To Carol Rusk
For getting permission for every name and detail. The book wouldn't be over 500 pages without you.

To Josh Shepherd and Kellie Vaughn
For making this book happen. And for allowing it to weigh as much as a bowling ball.

To Sam Bailey, Sarah Benson, Tiffany Carter, Jacob Isom, Ruthie Kreidler, J. B. Lewis, Chris Poon, Elisa Poon, Jonathan Schultz, Susan Squires, and Corey van der Laan
For giving thoughtful suggestions and goof alerts. And for being the best fans in the world.

To Norman Beck, Elisabeth Hendricks, Amy James, Jean Stephens, and LeeAnn Toyer
For checking each and every episode for accuracy.

To Jeff Rustemeyer, Linda Howard, Joseph Sapulich, Kimberly Hutson, Lois Rusch, and the entire team at Tyndale House Publishers
For creating and designing a beautiful book.

To the entire *Odyssey* Cast and Crew
For the interviews and the memories. And for making it all possible.

To, you, the reader
For opening this book. If you read every word of it, it will only a take a few months.

Whit unveiling a new invention

Introduction

"Why don't you get the whole family together and join us for another adventure in Odyssey?"

I first heard those words when I was eight years old, and, like listeners around the world, my family joined *Adventures in Odyssey* for hundreds of adventures. We couldn't get enough. We listened to *Odyssey* on the radio, we watched the *Odyssey* animated videos, and we read the *Odyssey* novels.

As I got older, I wanted to find out everything about *Odyssey*. But I couldn't keep all the details straight because the series had so many wonderful stories. *What was the first episode in the Blackgaard saga? What was the show where Richard Maxwell talked about having a sister? Which episodes had themes of "obeying your mom and dad"?* (Sometimes I really needed to listen to those episodes a few times in a row.) The real question was this: *How do I organize all this information?* In college, I created one way—a fan Web site!

After I posted the site, an unexpected thing happened. I started getting E-mail from the writers, producers, and sound designers of the show. It was like a *Star Wars* fan getting a personal letter from the creator, George Lucas. I was thrilled! Before long, I started chatting online with Mark Drury, one of the sound designers of the show. He suggested that I come out for a summer internship at Focus on the Family and work with the *Adventures in Odyssey* team. After I recovered from a near-dead faint, I thought that was a great idea. I came out during the summer of 2000 and wrote my first script under the caring eyes of Paul McCusker. What a dream come true!

Being involved with the *Odyssey* team made me realize that the great episodes that go out on the radio, on video, and in novels are only *half* the story. What happens behind the scenes during the creation of the show is filled with just as much excitement and conflict, just as many twists and turns, and just as much drama and intrigue as your favorite *Adventures in Odyssey* tale.

But what fun are all those great behind-the-scene stories if no one knows about them? It would be like Whit creating an incredible new invention, but never unveiling it. Why not create a book that allows readers to follow the story of *Adventures in Odyssey* both through the stories in the fictional town and through the stories

of the team that creates that town every day? That's what the *Odyssey* team thought, and our 20th anniversary provided the perfect opportunity.

So now you hold in your hands an adventure that is 20 years in the making. It's *Adventures in Odyssey: The Official Guide*!

Even when I was eight years old, *Odyssey* tapes were in my cassette-tape player.

But before we begin, a few quick notes.

With a book longer than the M volume of the encyclopedia, we wanted to save space where we could. So "BTS" doesn't mean

Bureau of Transportation Statistics, Bug Tracking System, or even Bangor Theological Seminary. BTS is short for "Behind the Scenes," and it's here that you'll find those stories of the creation of each show, from the creators, writers, producers, actors, and sound designers. You'll also see the word "Foley" in many of the BTS and Sound Bites. Foley, named after sound-effects pioneer Jack Foley, describes the live sound effects that the sound designers create. When you hear Bernard pulling that squeaky squeegee across a pane of glass, that's the work of a sound designer doing Foley.

We reference many movies, books, and TV shows that have inspired *Odyssey* stories. Just because we mention some of these media doesn't mean that we recommend them for our readers. Of course, we hope that God is truly the inspiration for our work. We give Him the glory for all the success the show has had . . . though we don't want to blame Him if we make an error.

Also, be careful when reading about albums and episodes you haven't heard. We tried not to include spoilers, but in some cases, we couldn't talk about the episodes without giving away endings.

And finally, did you notice that I used the word "we" in the previous paragraph? We told the behind-the-scenes story of *Odyssey* from a team perspective, so the "we" means everyone who was involved in its creation or who worked on a particular episode. So if you read a story from album number 1 that uses the word "we," don't think I was somehow around for those decisions. Remember, I was eight when *Odyssey* began! So "we" means "we" in the *Odyssey* team sense of the word.

And . . . well, the rest you'll just have to figure out as we begin this adventure.

—Nathan Hoobler

"Would you like to join us? Then get ready! Because you never know what could happen when you have an adventure in Odyssey!"

Character: Whit

Birthplace: Aberdeen, Scotland
Something you may not know about Whit:
He doesn't own a television set.

How Adventures in Odyssey Began

Adventures in Odyssey has aired for over 20 years with more than 640 episodes, making it one of the longest-running radio dramas in history. The radio show has also led to the creation of 17 videos, nearly two dozen novels, plus video games, music albums, and more. Hundreds, maybe even thousands, of stories have been told in the world of Odyssey. So where did all these stories get their start? To get the answer we talked with a man who was there from the beginning—Steve Harris.

Steve worked at Focus on the Family in the 1980s as head of the Special Projects department. Special Projects was a research and development team that worked on the early versions of many Focus on the Family radio programs, including Adventures in Odyssey.

Q: Back in the 1980s, Focus on the Family Special Projects team wasn't doing radio drama. What made the team decide to produce one?

SH: Around Thanksgiving 1983, the leaders of the broadcast team needed to decide what to do for the *Focus on the Family* Christmas broadcast. For years, we'd been repeating the show of Dr. Dobson reading "Helen's Buggy," his favorite Christmas story. It was a fine show, but we were all getting a little tired of doing the same thing.

I said to my teammates, "Hey, how about we produce a radio drama?"

There was a long pause. Then the other two said, "Uh . . . what other ideas do we have?" The more we talked about it, however, the more everyone liked the idea, so we decided to give it a shot.

Q: How did you put that first drama together?

SH: I had some contacts with the Jeremiah People, which is a Christian performing-arts group. Dennis Shippy worked with them. Dennis was asked to write the original draft of the Christmas script. He developed a basic story that dealt with a husband and wife who got caught up in the holiday rush. I rewrote and adapted the script, which came to be called "Spare Tire." Chuck Bolte, then director of Jeremiah People, played the husband. Chuck suggested we hire D. J. Harner to play the wife.

We produced that show with a magnificent, state-of-the-art, four-track reel-to-reel tape recorder, which I think should now be in a Smithsonian museum. "Spare Tire" aired on December 17, 1983.

Q: What was the reaction to "Spare Tire"?

SH: It was enough of a success that Dr. Dobson said, "This is great! Can we do four of these a year?" It would have been great if we hadn't had so many other projects to do. We didn't actually have time to do another drama until almost two years later.

Q: Is that when you produced "House Guest"?

SH: Right. That one was about a father who lived at his grown daughter's house for a while. I based the script on my own experience when my dad stayed at my house after his heart-bypass surgery. We needed someone to play the father, and Chuck gave me the name of Hal Smith. Chuck had worked with Hal on a Christmas program years before and wanted to work with him again. Of course, I remembered Hal from *The Andy Griffith Show* [1960–1968]. I called the number

Timeline: The Abbreviated History of *Adventures in Odyssey*

November 23, 1985
"House Guest" airs. (First Focus radio drama featuring Hal Smith.)

January 5, 1987
First *Family Portraits* drama ("Whit's Visitor") airs on the *Focus on the Family* daily broadcast.

November 21, 1987
First *Odyssey USA* episode ("Whit's Flop") airs on 200 radio stations.

December 17, 1983
"Spare Tire" airs. It is the first *Focus on the Family* radio drama.

July 23, 1986
"Gone Fishing" airs. (Another foundational drama.)

August 10, 1987
Radio drama "Tilly" airs; it was based on the book by the then unknown author Frank Peretti.

April 23, 1988
Name changes to *Adventures in Odyssey*. First episode to air: "The Quality of Mercy."

thinking I'd get his agent, but Hal himself picked up. I guess he'd given Chuck his home number.

We had a wonderful conversation, and Hal wanted to work on the program. While we were recording "House Guest," I learned my lesson about working with Hal. When you book Hal Smith for a recording session, if you need one hour of voice tracks, you book a two-hour session; one hour to get the voice tracks done—because he knocks those out no problem—and an hour for him to tell stories about his experiences and his career.

Q: You worked with Hal again on the next drama, didn't you?

SH: That's right. It was "Gone Fishing," a story about a guy who pretended to be sick so he could skip work and escape his life by going fishing for a day. While he was fishing, he met a wise man who set him straight about a few things. It was just Chuck and Hal for most of the show, which was great.

Q: Most of these shows had only two or three people in them, so they were fairly simple, right?

SH: At first, yes. We had a limited pool of talent to draw from in those early days and an even more limited budget. Then in 1986, I received several copies of a homespun radio program by a little-known author by the name of Frank Peretti. I was very touched when I took the time to listen. It was a sweet story

Actors Hal Smith and Chuck Bolte recording "Gone Fishing"

May 1988
First retail package (*Odyssey USA*) released.

December 10, 1988
In "Connie," Connie becomes a Christian.

Summer 1989
Chick-fil-A puts *Adventures in Odyssey* booklets in its kids' meals.

March 3, 1990
In "By Any Other Name," Bernard first appears in *Odyssey*.

June 18, 1988
The Barclays first appear on *Odyssey* in "Family Vacation."

March 18, 1989
Whit unveils his greatest invention in "The Imagination Station."

July 8, 1989
Dr. Regis Blackgaard arrives in *Odyssey*. ("The Nemesis")

August 5, 1991
Adventures in Odyssey starts airing daily on stations around the country.

called "Tilly." I called Frank and asked him if I could adapt his script and produce it for the Focus on the Family broadcast. He said, "Sure." This gave me a chance to raise the bar dramatically. I expanded the quantity and quality of sound effects, many of which were original, rather than from records or CDs. The show benefited from the best musical score we had received to date from my composer friend John Campbell.

The show went on to become (and remains today) one of the most popular *Focus on the Family* broadcasts ever. So it was obvious that radio drama was around to stay. Later, Frank Peretti turned the script into a novel, and a made-for-television production was done in 2003 by Love Life America.

Q: What made Focus decide to go from producing individual dramas every once in a while to doing an ongoing series?

SH: During an interview on the Focus on the Family broadcast, author Bruce Wilkinson commented to Dr. Dobson that it wasn't enough for Christians to complain about the poor programming on radio and TV. He presented the challenge to do something about it.

Not long after, Dr. Dobson and the vice presidents came back from a leadership retreat with a new mandate: Create a children's radio drama series. It was up to us to take it from there. The best part of my job back then was that we got to do things we had never done before. We made up the rules as we went along.

So, we needed to flesh out the details of whatever this new series would be. I started by searching for staff members who could help me work on the day-to-day production. We placed ads in several newspapers like the *Los Angeles Times*, and in response we received a stack of demo scripts that was literally several feet high. I read each one of the scripts and found very few that demonstrated the sense of imagination I was looking for. However, about three-quarters of the way down the stack, I found a script that someone had sent us that was an unproduced episode of *The Twilight Zone* television series [1985–1989]. Finally, a premise with promise! The story demonstrated

September 1991
First Adventures in Odyssey video released: *The Knight Travelers*.

Summer 1992
First novel released *Strange Journey Back*.

January 8, 1994
Eugene meets his future wife, Katrina. In "Truth, Trivia, and 'Trina."

September 3, 1994
"Gone . . ." airs. Whit leaves. Jack Allen comes to town.

October 1991
Focus on the Family moves from Pomona, California, to Colorado Springs, Colorado.

June 27, 1992
Harlow Doyle first appears in *Odyssey* in "Harlow Doyle, Private Eye."

January 27, 1994
Hal Smith passes away.

November 5, 1994
Tom Riley elected mayor of Odyssey in "Tom for Mayor."

a flair for the unusual, interesting characters, and, most important, a sense of values. This guy named Phil Lollar wrote it.

I called Phil in for an interview and saw right away that we didn't see eye to eye on everything, but praise God for that! You'll see elements of both of our points of view

Focus on the Family magazine, January 1987. An article about *Family Portraits* airing on the daily broadcast

in the blueprints of Odyssey. So we brought Phil on and also hired another writer, Susan McBride.

Once we had that team in place, we started brainstorming what became known as the

Family Portraits series. It was a test-run series of 13 episodes that would air Mondays on the *Focus on the Family* broadcast. If we survived that test, the idea was that we would go into full-scale production and spin the series off as an entirely new program.

Q: Did anyone think you were crazy to try a radio drama in the era of television?

SH: There were a number of reasons to suspect our sanity. Many people were skeptical that we could get children in the 8- to 12-age group to listen to the radio. There weren't very many existing programs in the genre, and the ones that did exist were very different from the style and tone we wanted. Also, we discussed how the program would be funded in the long term since the typical support model on Christian radio involved asking listeners for donations.

I had a lot of confidence in radio and, fortunately, Dr. Dobson shared that belief. As long as he didn't think we were crazy, we were okay.

December 3, 1994
Jason Whittaker moves to Odyssey. ("A Name, Not a Number")

September 2, 1995
In "The Time Has Come," Eugene becomes a Christian.

January 13, 1996
"Pokenberry Falls, RFD" features the Barclays leaving for Pokenberry Falls.

Summer 1996
First *Focus on the Family Radio Theatre* production released. (Charles Dickens's *A Christmas Carol*)

December 24, 1994
"Unto Us a Child Is Born" airs. Stewart Reed Barclay is born.

October 7, 1995
"The Final Conflict" airs. The album *Darkness Before Dawn* is finished. Dr. Blackgaard dies.

May 18, 1996
Paul Herlinger steps in as the voice of Whit in "The Search for Whit."

November 2, 1996
"Home, Sweet Home" airs. Whit returns to *Odyssey.*

Q: How did you brainstorm the ideas for this new series?

SH: The emphasis (especially at the beginning) was on the "storm" and not so much on the "brain." Susan was generally agreeable, but Phil and I had some of the most wonderful creative arguments you could ever imagine. We debated every conceivable angle about the format, audience, and characters. We felt that if this series could stand up to the pounding we were giving it, the series would stand up to years of use.

November 1987–*Focus on the Family* magazine—
"Coming Broadcast" November 2 is "Whit's Flop"

Of course, at the time we had no clue that the show would last as long as it has. We were thinking maybe a couple of years. But even a couple of years is a hundred episodes if you do one every week, and we knew we needed a solid foundation for the show.

All of us were passionate about the program and wanted it to be successful. The creative process through which we gave birth to the program wasn't always easy or quiet. But, then again, neither is the human birth process. As a mother could tell you, the baby was worth it.

Q: You could have created any kind of drama. Why did you decide to set it in a small town?

SH: I was excited about doing a show with a special environment or setting, where there's a large ensemble cast. Several great TV shows did this, like *M*A*S*H* [1972–1983] and *The Andy Griffith Show*. We needed an environment that was narrow enough to be familiar to people and feel like home. Yet I also wanted the setting to be big enough that there

January 1997
Adventures in Odyssey goes on vacation and takes a break from production. Re-airs the best of *Adventures in Odyssey*.

November 1997
The Complete Guide to Adventures in Odyssey released.

November 29, 1997
"New Year's Eve, Live!" is recorded in Colorado Springs, Colorado, to celebrate *Adventures in Odyssey*'s 10th anniversary.

March 6, 1999
Tom Riley opens the Timothy Center. ("Opening Day")

September 6, 1997
Production resumes with "For Whom the Wedding Bells Toll." Jack Allen and Joanne Woodston marry. Eugene and Katrina Shanks get engaged.

November 8, 1997
Margaret Faye elected mayor of Odyssey. ("The One About Trust")

May 23, 1998
In "The Graduate," Connie finally graduates from high school.

October 1999
First Passages book—*Darien's Rise*—is released.

wasn't a story idea that would come down the road that we'd have to say, "Sorry. Doesn't fit the format."

So I came up with the idea of creating this mythical place that was somewhere in the United States. East, west, north, south—it didn't matter. Just somewhere that all these adventures could happen.

Q: *Odyssey* was different in tone and style than many Christian programs. How did that feel come about?

SH: Our first rule right up front was that you don't talk down to kids. That's something we had seen again and again, and it frustrated us. Programs like that bothered me even when I was child. It seemed like "talking down to kids" was even more prevalent in Christian writing.

I knew enough children to know that they're asking tough questions. They're going to school in a social environment where they're bombarded all the time. They see unhealthy adult relationships portrayed on TV. They have problems at home. They're wrestling with real stuff. So we wanted our show to have an element of reality. We wanted kids to listen to it and feel respected.

Q: But you weren't writing just for kids.

SH: No. We wanted this program to appeal broadly. Children don't listen alone. We knew of other children's programs—both radio and television—that parents would listen to or watch with their kids and feel like screaming because the shows were so corny.

So we made a point of packing in little tidbits of humor that maybe 5 percent of the audience would get—primarily adults. A great example of that type of humor is the Warner Bros. cartoon series from the 1940s and 1950s. The cartoons were shown in theaters, and they had all kinds of political, social, and pop-culture references that flew right over the kids' heads, but the adults loved them.

December 18, 1999
A Look Back celebrates a millennium of *Adventures in Odyssey* episodes. (See sidebar in *The Lost Episodes*)

April 1, 2000
Official Web site launched at WhitsEnd.org.

May 26, 2001
Wooton Bassett's first appearance at Whit's End.

January 26, 2002
Eugene and Katrina finally tie the knot and promptly leave the show for several years. ("Plan B: Missing in Action")

February 7, 2000
"Mandy's Debut" recorded live at National Religious Broadcasters' convention in Anaheim, California.

December 2, 2000
"Opportunity Knocks" airs. The Novacom saga series of action-adventure shows begins.

January 5, 2002
Whit's End Connellsville opens in "Grand Opening."

July 7, 2002
"Exit" airs. The Novacom saga ends.

Q: Many radio dramas—even those produced now—are very simple productions. There might be a generic audio background and a few footsteps here and there for sound effects, but that's it. Why did you decide to be so elaborate with *Odyssey*?

SH: Because we knew that radio is far more visual than television could ever hope to be. If you want to see something in a movie, it has to be visually represented in some way. Television can't hold a candle to the power of the imagination. We wanted to set kids' imaginations free, and so we knew we had to make our productions awesome.

Q: How did you create that level of quality on a four-track tape recorder?

SH: It was difficult at first. We were bouncing intermediate mixes back and forth between different machines. We had to get very creative. It got to the point where we adopted the famous motto: "We the willing . . . have done so much, with so little, for so long, that we are now qualified to make anything out of nothing."

Q: So, *Family Portraits* aired for 13 weeks on the *Focus on the Family* broadcast. How successful do you feel your audio drama test was?

SH: It was a mixed bag. Outside producers and directors were brought in to do most of the work after the writing was done, and, frankly, some of our best stuff got lost in translation. On the plus side, the test gave us the chance to develop the basic blueprints for both the town of Odyssey and the show. It was also a good, creative "shakedown cruise," which gave us an opportunity to test ideas and see what worked and what didn't.

Q: You said that the goal was to spin off *Adventures in Odyssey* as a separate program in its own timeslot. How did that decision get made?

SH: I think Dr. Dobson and the leadership at Focus on the Family responded to the listener reactions and decided to launch the program. We received 4,965 letters about *Family*

July 13, 2002
"500" airs, a show celebrating 500 *Odyssey* episodes.

January 25, 2003
The Washington family first appears in "The Toy Man."

December 2003
Gold Audio Series begins.

April 2, 2005
"A Most Intriguing Question" airs. Eugene returns to *Odyssey* with much fanfare.

July 25-27, 2002
"Live at the 25" recorded at 25th anniversary of Focus on the Family in Colorado Springs, Colorado.

November 22, 2003
Connie almost gets married. ("Something Blue")

Fall 2004
Adventures in Odyssey video games released. ("The Treasure of the Incas" and "The Sword of the Spirit")

October 15, 2005
Eugene learns that his long-lost father, Leonard, is alive. ("Prisoners of Fear")

Portraits, and 4,771 of them were positive. But even after that response, it took awhile for the *Odyssey* program to be approved.

Q: When did you start working on the series itself?

SH: Focus gave approval for *Odyssey* to go into production just three weeks before the first episode was supposed to air on the radio. We were doomed from day one. For the first month, Phil Lollar and I were putting in 80-hour work weeks. It was ridiculous.

Q: How did you get back on track?

SH: We hired a few people. Writer Paul McCusker had submitted a few episodes freelance for us, and we brought him on full time. About that time, Susan McBride left the staff. And then Chuck Bolte left the Jeremiah People and came on as executive producer over the entire show. Phil and I had been writing many of our scripts together. One of the first things Chuck did was to make us write shows separately so we could work faster.

Q: You worked with *Odyssey* for the first two years. How did your time there come to an end?

SH: After Chuck came on board, my job at Focus on the Family grew more and more administrative and less creative. It was time for me to take what I had learned at Focus on the Family and apply it in other contexts.

Not long after leaving the staff, I ran into Dr. Dobson at a local restaurant. I took that opportunity to tell him personally how grateful I was that he gave me the chance to do things I never would have been able to do anywhere else. Many of the things I can do well are the result of his investment in my personal and professional life. (On the other hand, the stuff I mess up isn't his fault!) Seriously, I owe him and other leaders at Focus on the Family a debt of gratitude that I can never repay.

December 3, 2005
Connie starts writing a book. ("Tales of a Small-Town Thug")

March 10, 2007
Eugene Meltsner discovers that he has a brother, Everett. ("The Top Floor")

March 1, 2008
Odyssey considered for Best Small Town in America. ("Suspicious Finds")

Summer 2008
Adventures in Odyssey: The Official Guide released.

December 16, 2006
The Washington family become foster parents to a girl named Kelly. ("The Chosen One")

September 29, 2007
Leonard Meltsner leaves for Africa. ("A New Era")

June 2008
First Kidsboro novel released— *Battle for Control.*

September 2008
50th album released: *The Best Small Town.*

Episode Information

The first 13 dramas set in the town of Odyssey aired on the *Focus on the Family* daily broadcast in 1987. These episodes laid the foundation for future *Odyssey* dramas. These dramas are known as the *Family Portraits* Series.

FP1: Whit's Visitor
Original Air Date: 1/5/87
Writer: Steve Harris
Sound Designer: Bob Luttrell
Scripture: Malachi 2:13-17
Theme: The effects of divorce on children
Summary: Whit finds eight-year-old Davey Morrison in his basement. Davey wants to move to escape the pain of his parents' divorce.

FP2: Dental Dilemma
Original Air Date: 1/12/87
Writer: Susan McBride
Sound Designers: Steve Harris & Bob Luttrell
Scripture: Psalm 27:1
Themes: Teasing, dealing with fear
Summary: Middle-schooler Mark Forbes plants fear in the heart of his younger sister, Emily, as she anticipates her first dental appointment.

FP3: The New Kid in Town
Original Air Date: 1/19/87
Writer: Phil Lollar
Sound Designers: Steve Harris & Bob Luttrell
Scripture: Proverbs 18:24
Theme: Making new friends
Summary: Whit meets a 13-year-old girl named Shawn Walker who is new to town and has no friends.

FP4: No Stupid Questions
Original Air Date: 1/26/87
Writer: Susan McBride
Sound Designer: Bob Luttrell
Scripture: Proverbs 18:15
Themes: Respect for the handicapped, the value of seeking knowledge
Summary: Young Meg Stevens asks a constant stream of questions, which annoys a cranky man named Chris Gottlieb.

FP5: You're Not Gonna Believe This . . .
Original Air Date: 2/2/87
Writer: Phil Lollar
Sound Designer: Bob Luttrell
Scripture: Proverbs 18:7; 22:1
Theme: The importance of a good reputation
Summary: Fourteen-year-old Budgie Wentworth III exaggerates the truth, which makes it hard for his cousin to believe anything he says.

FP6: My Brother's Keeper
Original Air Date: 2/16/87
Writer: Paul McCusker
Sound Designer: Bob Luttrell
Scripture: Proverbs 12:18
Theme: Sibling conflict
Summary: A boy named Phillip Callas wants to get rid of his younger brother, and his wish might come true—permanently.

FP7: **While Dad's Away**
Original Air Date: 3/2/87
Writer: Phil Lollar
Sound Designer: Bob Luttrell
Scripture: Malachi 4:6
Theme: Absentee fathers
Summary: Whit tells the story of Mike Brettman, a vice president for a local company, whose job keeps him from seeing his family.

FP8: **The Letter**
Original Air Date: 3/9/87
Writer: Steve Harris
Sound Designer: Bob Luttrell
Scripture: Ephesians 6:1-4
Theme: Communication with teens
Summary: A teen named Stacey, who is talking on the phone with a friend, gets into an argument with her father after he takes away the phone and hangs up on her conversation.

FP9: **A Different Kind of Peer Pressure**
Original Air Date: 3/16/87
Writer: Steve Harris
Sound Designer: Bob Luttrell
Scripture: Romans 12:2
Theme: Peer pressure
Summary: Richard Hudson is upset when his 14-year-old daughter, Blair, gives into peer pressure.

FP10: **In Memory of Herman**
Original Air Date: 3/23/87
Writer: Phil Lollar
Sound Designer: Bob Luttrell
Scripture: 1 Peter 3:1-2
Themes: Life after death, salvation
Summary: Amanda and Vic Hardwick are a married couple who disagree about Christianity. Amanda is convinced that she must persuade Vic to accept the gospel so he won't go to hell.

FP11 and 12: **A Member of the Family, I and II**
Original Air Date: 3/30/87 & 4/6/87
Writers: Susan McBride & Steve Harris
Sound Designer: Bob Luttrell
Scripture: Exodus 20:12; Proverbs 3:11-12; Ephesians 6:4
Themes: Discipline, family conflict
Summary: When Whit's grandson, Monty, arrives for a summer in Odyssey, they are in for more trouble—and healing—than they expected.

FP13: **A Simple Addition**
Original Air Date: 4/13/87
Writer: Susan McBride
Sound Designer: Bob Luttrell
Scripture: Romans 12:10
Theme: Sibling rivalry
Summary: Elementary-schooler Nicky is upset that his baby sister is taking his parents' attention away from him.

The *Family Portraits* Package

All About Chris

One of the most difficult casting problems at the outset of *Adventures in Odyssey* was who would host the show. The team wanted a host who could land the program and drive home the biblical point in a gentle way, but they were facing a serious production deadline. The first drama, "Whit's Flop," had already been recorded and was slated to air in a few weeks. The script for the introduction and closing of the show had already been written.

Steve Harris remembers:

We tested several dozen voices for the host. But with each one, it took only five seconds for Phil and me to realize this voice wasn't going to make it. As the deadline got closer, there was a point where "alive and breathing" would get the job done.

Bob Luttrell suggested that I contact Chris Anthony. Bob wrote her phone number down, and five minutes later, I dialed this number. This nice lady answered. I asked her if she could be at the studio in an hour. She said she'd just gotten up and needed time to get ready. I said, "It's radio!"

Do I sound like I was desperate or what?

An hour later, Chris walked into the studio. We handed her a script, and when she read there was the instant warmth, the happiness, and the perfect feel we wanted for our host. We made the decision to hire her in about 10 seconds. That was the fastest casting decision we ever made.

Since the scripts for the host were not written with any particular voice in mind, Steve went back and rewrote them to fit with Chris's personality, and they recorded them a few days later.

December 1987 *Focus on the Family* magazine: An article about *Odyssey* in a new time slot.

March 1988 *Focus on the Family* magazine, insert: A resource description of the first album, *Odyssey USA*.

This girl, Aubrey Shepard, represents just one of more than 1,500 characters created for *Adventures in Odyssey*

Actor Chris Anthony, host of *Odyssey*

Writer, Inventor, Teacher, Town Sage: The Creation of John Avery Whittaker

The town of Odyssey needed a central character, but creators Steve Harris and Phil Lollar clashed over what that character should be like. Steve wanted someone whom kids could get to know and trust. "I wanted to make it so, when he spoke, kids would listen and feel comfortable with what he had to say. That he had the right to be heard."

Steve imagined that the character would be grandfatherly, warm, and gentle. Phil, on the other hand, wanted him to be edgy and mysterious . . . the kind of person who has things going on behind the scenes that no one knows about. Phil remembers, "I had just reread C. S. Lewis's Chronicles of Narnia

series (for about the fifth time) in which Aslan, the Jesus figure, is described as 'good, but not tame.' That's what I wanted most for this person."

Steve and Phil created a character who was a blending of the two ideas. He was both grandfatherly and mysterious. Both Steve and Phil were excited about what the character could become. There was only one problem—a name! They came up with many possibilities for a name, but none of them seemed suitable. "The one unanimous thing was that we hated all of them," recalls Steve.

After several days of disagreement, Steve called Phil and Susan into his office and said they weren't leaving until they had named the character. Steve remembers, "We went to the one resource book you go to when you're looking for a name—the phone book. We started looking. We started with the letter A and worked our way to the Bs. The character's name is Whittaker; it starts with the 23rd letter. Does that tell you a little bit about our day?"

When Steve and crew stumbled upon "Whittaker," they paused. "Everybody looked at each other and nobody hated it, which was a big step in the right direction," says Steve.

There was a difference of opinion on whether it should be a first or last name. They decided it should be a last name, which meant that they still needed a first name. Phil Lollar noticed a package of labels with the company name—Avery. Phil remembers, "It was unusual, but still easy enough to remember and say. Not only that, it was the last name of one of my favorite animators—Tex Avery!"

The character was named Avery Whittaker and the job was done . . . or so they thought. The more the group thought about it, the more they realized that "Avery" sounded a little formal for a first name. So "John" became his first name and "Avery" became his middle name.

John Avery Whittaker. "It was kind of a mouthful," says Steve. "But if we could call him 'Whit,' it would fly."

Shortly after, Phil went to his office and wrote an entire life history of John Avery Whittaker. It was so thorough and detailed, that even after more than 640 episodes, some bits and pieces have never been revealed. Phil remembers, "A lot of the details of Whit's life—his rural upbringing, his World War II experiences, his love of books, his academic career, his quiet wisdom, his strong Christian beliefs—were inspired by my father, Dale Lollar."

But who should play this amazing character? The team didn't need hours of brainstorming or discussion for that one. Hal Smith, the man who had worked on several of the early Focus dramas must play Whit.

The Blueprint

Creators Phil Lollar and Steve Harris created a hand-drawn blueprint for Mr. Whittaker's ice-cream shop, Whit's End, before the series began. Steve says, "We had to know how long it would take to walk from the ice-cream parlor to the library. That was important."

Despite the blueprint, the team was hesitant to actually show the drawing to listeners. Paul McCusker remembers, "To me, Whit's End was like the wardrobe in The Chronicles of Narnia. You didn't know how far this thing went or how many worlds were yet undiscovered."

Naming the Town

The town of Odyssey was given its name when Phil Lollar saw the book *United Nations Journal: A Delegate's Odyssey* by William F. Buckley (1974). The town was based partially on Phil's childhood memories of Klamath Falls, Oregon.

Naming Whit's End

The name Whit's End was inspired by the Algonquin Round Table, a group of writers and actors from New York City in the early 1900s. The members of the group were often called wits and said to be at their wit's end.

Secret Rooms at Whit's End

Secret Room or Passage	Where It Is	Episode in which it was discovered or revealed
A secret room with a fully dressed skeleton	In the basement behind a cabinet	The Case of the Secret Room
A secret computer room	Behind a bookcase in Whit's office	A Bite of Applesauce
A hidden room with a pipe organ built in	The attic at Whit's End	The Treasure of Le Monde!
A servant staircase	Behind a door in the kitchen to the secret computer room	Hold-Up!
A tunnel to the woods in McAlister Park	The basement of Whit's End	Hold-Up!
A second tunnel	The basement of Whit's End	The Underground Railroad

Whit's Best Friend: The Creation of Tom Riley

John Avery Whittaker was a great character, but "no man is an island," according to the popular meditation by John Donne (1572–1631). Whit needed a supporting cast of characters around him. The next character the team discussed was a contemporary for Whit. "We needed a friend whom he could knock ideas around with and reveal what was going on in his thought processes," says Steve Harris.

The team decided it should be an older farmer who had lived in Odyssey since he was born, unlike Whit who had moved to the town later in life. Steve remembers, "He was a gentle man who demonstrated Christian virtues at their best without getting overbearing—a quiet man whose faith was real."

They named the character Tom Riley. Bob Luttrell recommended Walker Edmiston to play the part. Bob had worked with Walker on the Salvation Army's radio drama *Heartbeat Theater*.

Walker based his performance on several characters played by the late actor Tom Poston, such as George Utley on *Newhart* (1982–1990). "It wasn't that Tom was dumb or stupid," says Walker. "He lived a simple life. He was aware of the emotions and the needs of all of his friends. But if he had to sit down at the kitchen table and figure out how much grain he had sold, it took him a little longer."

Walker also relied on his longtime friendship with Hal Smith. "There was an automatic, built-in bond between us. We'd worked together for 20 years before we started on *Adventures in Odyssey*."

Meet the Cast

Chris Anthony—*Host*

Chris is the voice of hundreds (or thousands!) of toys, including Barbie.

Q: What is your favorite *Adventures in Odyssey* episode?
CA: One of my favorites is "The Imagination Station" [album 5] when Digger Digwillow meets Jesus. I love when Digger talks about looking into Jesus' eyes.

Q: How is your real-life personality like the "host" Chris's personality?
CA: Both Chris and I love kids. When I'm with a group of people, I usually end up talking to the kids rather than to the adults.

Q: Are you really that happy?
CA: I'm a pretty happy person. God has blessed me a lot in my life. When I'm doing the show, I'm *really* happy. The best way I can describe myself is like a helium balloon. If you push that balloon under the water, it'll go down, but it always pops back up. And the helium in my balloon would be the Lord.

Q: What inspires you?
CA: God, my husband, Jerry, and my daughter, Kelsey, because they're all very creative.

Q: What has working on *Odyssey* meant to you?
CA: Sometimes when I'm working on the show, I picture myself in a big comfy chair talking to the kids and sharing the Lord with them. I've been doing voice-over for more than 20 years, and *Odyssey* has been the most rewarding. Nothing compares!

Katie Leigh—*Connie Kendall*

Katie's voice can be heard as Baby Rowlf on the television program Muppet Babies *(1984–1990), "Honker" Muddlefoot on* Darkwing Duck *(1991–1995), Sunni on* The Gummi Bears *(1985–1991), and Alex on* Totally Spies! *(2001–present). She's also the voice of the hungry kitten in* Babe: Pig in the City *(1998).*

Q: What is your favorite *Adventures in Odyssey* episode?

KL: I really liked the ones driving to Washington, D.C., with Joanne Allen [*In Hot Pursuit,*" album 41] because I had made the exact same driving trip in real life just a few weeks before. It was like reliving my vacation only with more adventure and not as much humidity.

Q: How are you like—or not like—your character?

KL: I am like my character in almost every way except I'm older. It's a little scary sometimes. Right after I went on a missions trip to Peru in real life, we recorded a CD-ROM game where Connie and Whit go to Peru! I hate darkness, and I can't stand it when the curtains or blinds are shut. There was a show where Connie said that exact same thing. However, I would never wear green leggings! Ever!

Q: Would you like to share any special *Odyssey* memories?

KL: I remember when I cried so hard during the recording of one of our scripts that Marshal Younger got me some jelly beans to help me feel better.

Q: What inspires you?

KL: God, love (same thing, right?), really good writing, and being able to make people laugh.

Connie Kendall

Will Ryan—*Eugene Meltsner, Harlow Doyle, Officer O'Ryan*

Will has played numerous voice roles in the entertainment business, including the sea horse in The Little Mermaid *(1989), Papa Bear in* Looney Tunes: Back in Action *(2003), and Petrie in* The Land Before Time *(1988). The Emmy Award-winning producer, lyricist, and composer also voiced Tigger and Rabbit on the long-running* Welcome to Pooh Corner *television series (1983–1995).*

Q: What is your favorite *Adventures in Odyssey* episode?
WR: Although I tend to gravitate toward those episodes in which Eugene sings and plays ukulele (or which involve vehicular instruction), my favorite episodes are usually the ones we're about to record.

Q: How are you like—or not like—your character?
WR: Like Officer O'Ryan, I enjoy driving around with the siren on. Not unlike Harlow Doyle, I'm amazed at almost everything . . . And, like the character Eugene Meltsner, I play ukulele and the Humanatone.

Q: What are your hobbies?
WR: Refereeing pie fights. Selecting special jelly beans to cheer up Katie. And appearing as America's Favorite Radio Cowboy on radio, television, and personal appearances. And making new music recordings.

Q: What inspires you?
WR: In acting, it's watching the rest of the cast work. They're so great!

Q: What is your favorite word?
WR: Contrary to the question's presumption, my favorite word is probably not the familiar pronoun "what."

Photo courtesy of Mammoth Motion Pictures

Eugene Meltsner

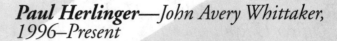

Paul Herlinger—John Avery Whittaker, 1996–Present

Paul Herlinger has produced scores of television documentaries and public-affairs programs for 25 years. He has narrated dozens of PBS documentaries, commercials, and films, including The Sixties: The Years That Shaped a Generation *(2005).*

Q: What is your favorite *Adventures in Odyssey* episode?
PH: It's a toss-up between "Clara" [album 28] and "Silent Night" [album 45]. Both shows are not only very touching emotionally, but they also give Whit a lot more dimension.

Q: How are you like—or not like—your character?
PH: I'm similar to Whit in that I like people and enjoy being with them, but I couldn't dispense as much good advice as he does.

Q: Would you like to share any special *Odyssey* memories?
PH: It was quite daunting to pick up where Hal Smith left off. My special memories are those of being accepted by my fellow cast members as we recorded more and more *Odyssey* shows! I felt as though I was being taken into a warm and caring family!

Q: What inspires you?
PH: Hearing my wife, Ilona, tell stories about her escape from Europe in World War II.

Q: What has working on *Odyssey* meant to you?
PH: It has given me a chance to work in the profession I started in as a high school kid and still love most . . . radio! At the same time, I work with a lot of extremely talented and dedicated people in producing programs that have so much meaning for so many people.

Mr. Whittaker

Dave Madden—*Bernard Walton*

Dave was a series regular on television's
Camp Runamuck *(1965–1966),* Rowan
and Martin's Laugh-In *(1968–1973), and*
Alice *(1976–1985), but is most well known
as Reuben Kincaid, the manager for* The
Partridge Family *(1970–1974). He also voiced
the ram in the animated classic* Charlotte's
Web *(1973).*

Q: What is your favorite *Adventures in Odyssey*
episode?
DM: That's what I'd like to know . . . How do
you figure after 20 years, I'd remember a favorite episode? I don't remember what I had for
lunch yesterday!

Q: How are you like—or not like—your character?
DM: I'm not like my character at all. I hate
washing windows. I almost never get angry or
frustrated. My wife says the secret to my longev-
ity (and I really have longeved) is that I never get
upset. Do you understand?! NEVER! So stop
bugging me about it.

Q: What are your hobbies?
DM: Magic and photography . . . although I never
photograph magicians. I wonder why that is.

Q: What inspires you?
DM: You do . . . and I'm not really sure who's reading this!

Q: What is your favorite word?
DM: "It" is my favorite word. I find I'm using it constantly!
Although I almost never write about it.

Bernard Walton

Alan Young—Jack Allen

Alan wrote, produced, and starred in The Alan Young Show *(1950–1953), first on radio and then on television. (The television show earned him a star on the Hollywood Walk of Fame.) Alan starred in many movies, including* The Time Machine *(1960), but is best known as Wilbur Post in the popular 1960s television show* Mister Ed. *He voiced Scrooge McDuck in* Mickey's Christmas Carol *(1983) and* DuckTales *(1987–1990).*

Q: What is your favorite *Adventures in Odyssey* episode?
AY: My favorite is always the last one that I did.

Q: How are you like—or not like—your character?
AY: I've known Jack for so long. I'd like to be as patient as Jack.

Q: What are your hobbies?
AY: Scuba diving and animal welfare.

Q: What inspires you?
AY: My faith.

Q: What is your favorite word?
AY: Gratitude.

Q: If you could have another job besides acting, what would you do?
AY: I've never thought of doing any other work. I started when I was 13 years old, which was about 15 to 20 years ago . . . or so.

Q: What has working on *Odyssey* meant to you?
AY: It's such a delight to work for a show that is so well written and so clean. It's like a nice warm bath.

Townsend Coleman—Jason Whittaker

In addition to being the voice of NBC for nearly two decades, Townsend has appeared in a plethora of cartoons and films. He is Corporal Capeman in Inspector Gadget *(1983–1986), Michelangelo in* Teenage Mutant Ninja Turtles *animated series (1987–1996), and the title character in* The Tick *(1994–1997). He was also the voice of the red 7-Up dot in commercials.*

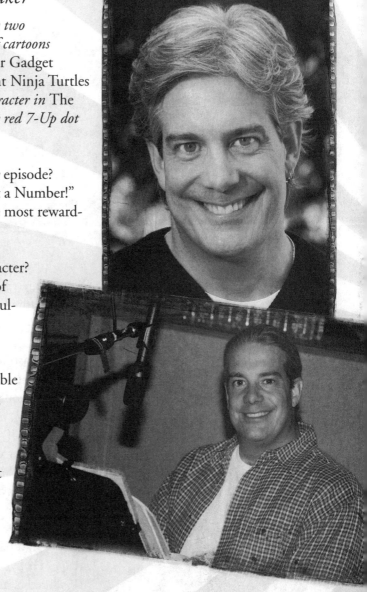

Q: What is your favorite *Adventures in Odyssey* episode?
TC: That's easy… my first one, "A Name, Not a Number!" [album 22]. It was the beginning of one of the most rewarding and fulfilling jobs I've ever had.

Q: How are you like—or not like—your character?
TC: I think I have a good deal of Jason's love of adventure and intrigue. I can also be a bit impulsive and impatient. But only a bit.

Q: What inspires you?
TC: Humility, real and true. A genuinely humble person is someone I really look up to and long to be like.

Q: What is your favorite word?
TC: "Spizerinctum." Yes, it's a real word and it means energy or vitality.

Q: What has working on *Odyssey* meant to you?
TC: I love reading the letters from appreciative listeners. To be a part of something that has made such a positive impact has been a true joy for me.

Jess Harnell—*Wooton Bassett, Bennett Charles*

Jess has voiced thousands of cartoons and movies. He is the voice of Wakko on Animaniacs *(1993–1998), Arnold on* Totally Spies!, *and Ronaldo Rum on* Biker Mice from Mars *(1993–1996). He also voiced Ironhide in* Transformers *(2007).*

Q: What is your favorite *Adventures in Odyssey* episode?
JH: "Nothing But the Half Truth" [album 42]. It was genuinely funny and it said a lot about being yourself.

Q: How are you like—or not like—your character?
JH: I'm more like Wooton than I'm not. I'd like to think that I'm like Wooton in that I'm perpetually childlike.

Q: What inspires you?
JH: Good attitudes, people who make me think, and, of course, God.

Q: If you could have another job besides acting, what would you do?
JH: Singing. I still do quite a bit of it. There's an old saying, "He who sings prays twice," and I believe that.

Q: What has working on *Odyssey* meant to you?
JH: I've done a variety of projects in all kinds of media, and *Adventures in Odyssey* comes to mind, along with *America's Funniest Home Videos* and *Animaniacs,* as shows that can be enjoyed by all ages and all kinds of people. I love the fact that I get to be on a program with such positive messages. And at the same time, it's good entertainment! On top of that, I get to play a character that I'm really fond of. I consider Wooton a friend.

Corey Burton—*Cryin' Bryan Dern, Walter Shakespeare, and many more*

Corey's movie voices include Captain Hook in Return to Neverland *(2002), Moliere in* Atlantis: The Lost Empire *(2001), and various characters in* Aladdin *(1992),* Hercules *(1997), and* A Goofy Movie *(1995). His television credits include Ludwig Von Drake in* House of Mouse *(2001–2002) and Dale on* Chip 'N Dale: Rescue Rangers *(1990).*

Q: What is your favorite *Adventures in Odyssey* episode?
CB: "Top This!" [album 24]. It was the funniest and most interesting exploration of the Bryan Dern character.

Q: What are your hobbies?
CB: Audio "tinkering," and I suppose—in recent years—writing (of the hopefully informative variety, for my Web site's interactive message board, or the occasional interview like this).

Q: What inspires you?
CB: Great works of creative genius—particularly those of Walt Disney and his remarkable staff who made wonders like Disneyland and the greatest animated classics of all time.

Q: If you could have another job besides acting, what would you do?
CB: Audio engineering and sound design, most likely. That's what I did before establishing a full-time career as a voice actor/announcer.

Walter Shakespeare and Bryan Dern

Q: What has working on *Odyssey* meant to you?
CB: Great fun. And keeping radio drama alive. A rare and delightful opportunity to do what you might say I was cut out for (certainly prepared for, in my fundamental training): Being a real radio actor, in the classic tradition established in the 1940s.

Rodney Rathbone

Steve Burns—*Rodney Rathbone, Robert Mitchell*

Steve costarred in the television miniseries Centennial *(1978), the movies* Casey's Shadow *(1978) and* Lifeguard *(1976), and the television shows* Westwind *(1975) and* Blinded by the Light *(1980).*

Q: What is your favorite *Adventures in Odyssey* episode?
SB: "Aloha, Oy!" [album 19].

Q: How are you like—or not like—your character?
SB: I am nothing like Rodney except when I feel like bugging my own kids . . . which they hate. I am not like Mitch, but I do love Katie.

Q: What has working on *Adventures in Odyssey* meant to you?
SB: Being a part of it in even a small way and getting to work with very talented directors and actors has made my life fuller. It has also filled my kids' lives with great, fun times in the studio.

David Griffin—*Jimmy Barclay*

Q: What is your favorite *Adventures in Odyssey* episode?
DG: Probably "Someone to Watch Over Me" [album 10]. Getting to see Hal Smith's amazing vocal range in person always fascinated me.

Q: How are you like—or not like—your character?
DG: I'm probably like him in my sense of humor and knack for finding creative ways of getting into trouble. I'm also devoted to my family. But I don't wear baseball caps, and I've never been in a coma.

Q: If you could have another job besides acting, what would you do?

DG: I would love to run a charity that brings the arts to disadvantaged youth.

Q: What has working on *Odyssey* meant to you?
DG: When I was recording, I realized that I was good at something and had found something I love to do. Other kids had sports . . . I had acting. As the years have passed, I am finding a new reward for that early work: my interaction with the fans.

David Griffin

Jimmy Barclay

Kendre Berry—Marvin Washington, 2004-present

Kendre has appeared as Jabari Wilkes on Girlfriends *(2006–2007) and Backpack Boy on* Ned's Declassified School Survival Guide *(2004–2007).*

Q: What is your favorite *Adventures in Odyssey* episode?
KB: "A Christmas Conundrum" [album 45]. It really gets me in the Christmas spirit and makes me want to give.

Q: How are you like—or not like—your character?
KB: I would say that Marvin and I are alike in the fact that Marvin is a go-getter and never takes no for an answer and never gives up when times get rough. Marvin does things like sleep with his clothes on and a stick of gum in his mouth so he wouldn't have to dress or brush his teeth in the morning. All this just to get a few more minutes of sleep! I would have never thought of that!

Q: If you could have another job besides acting, what would you do?
KB: I would definitely be a music producer. I write songs and compose music so I hope to make a career out of that also.

Marvin Washington

Earl Boen—*Edwin Blackgaard, Regis Blackgaard*

A veteran of hundreds of voice roles, Earl has been heard on the TV animated series Kim Possible *(2002–2006) and movies* Clifford's Really Big Movie *(2004) and* Atlantis: The Lost Empire *(2001). Earl is also the voice of LeChuck in the* Monkey Island *video games.*

Q: How are you like—or not like—your character?
EB: I'm not at all like Regis. Like Edwin, I enjoy "chewing the scenery" as an actor when that's the appropriate style of acting.

Q: What inspires you?
EB: A really good golf shot. Nailing a difficult scene on stage, on a movie set, or behind a microphone.

Q: What has working on *Odyssey* meant to you?
EB: I enjoy being in the closest thing to old-time radio that I will experience. I grew up listening to shows on the radio, so it's fun to, at last, be a part of a classic genre. Also, I like being a small part of something that aims to impart some moral values in an entertaining way to young people growing up in a morally decaying society.

Sage Bolte—*Robyn Jacobs*

Q: What is your favorite *Adventures in Odyssey* episode?
SB: I think the episode that sticks in my mind the most is "Karen" [album 3]. The script was written based off similar events that had touched my life when a friend of mine died of cancer when we were about nine years old. I remember what grace and grit she displayed throughout her battle. I also remember a surprising peace about death after that— that death wasn't scary or strange.

Q: How are you like—or not like—your character?
SB: I am stubborn like Robyn, and quite honestly, they didn't have to do too much script writing with giving me an attitude—that was real!

Q: What are your hobbies?
SB: Unfortunately, I don't have much time for hobbies. I am finishing up a Ph.D. and working full time as an oncology social worker. So, my life is full of paper writing and studying. I guess studying could be a hobby—although I should probably enjoy the hobby!

Q: What has working on *Odyssey* meant to you?
SB: *Odyssey* was so much of my childhood. It was on in the car when we were driving. It was what I listened to on my way to sleep. It was what kept my sister and me from fighting in the backseat on road trips. And it provided discussions with my family that were really important. Now, *Odyssey* is part of my own family, and I love it!

Courtney Brown—Tamika Washington

Q: What is your favorite *Adventures in Odyssey* episode?
CB: "Odyssey Sings!" [album 45]. That was the most fun to work on and the most entertaining to watch.

Q: How are you like—or not like—your character?
CB: Tamika is very assertive and sure of herself, and I'd like to think I sometimes act that way too. However, she also tends to get a little bossy sometimes, and I'm like that only when I play Monopoly.

Q: What inspires you?
CB: When people do things with integrity, or simply make someone's day a little better, it makes me feel as if there's an enormous amount of hope in the world.

Tamika Washington

Q: What is your favorite word?

CB: So far, my favorite word is "intense." I enjoy declaring very mundane things "intense."

Q: What has working on *Odyssey* meant to you?

CB: *Odyssey* was my first real acting job. Whenever I go to a new studio, I always reflect on my studio time at *Odyssey*. Working there has been an honor. It means the universe to me!

Christopher Castile—*Zachary Sellers, Nick Mulligan*

Christopher played Mark Foster on the long-running television series Step by Step *(1991–1998) and Ted Newton in the* Beethoven *movies (1992, 1993). He also voiced Eugene Horowitz on* Hey Arnold! *(1996).*

Q: What is your favorite *Adventures in Odyssey* episode?

CC: I enjoyed "Sounds Like a Mystery" [album 43] because of the other actors involved. Kenneth Mars [the voice of Holstein and Chief Quinn] is one of my all-time favorite actors.

Q: What inspires you?

CC: At the risk of sounding corny, I am inspired by things that "flow." Nothing is more beautiful than watching a tennis player who plays with such ease and rhythm. But I wouldn't limit that to sports; thought works very much the same way. I love reading or hearing someone who can make difficult ideas easy to understand. It is great to be able to see people at their best, when things are working with great synchronicity. But what is even more inspiring is thinking where these things come from: God. One's ability to do something well and really capture something's essence to me means that they are tapping in to how God intended something to be.

Q: What has working on *Odyssey* meant to you?

CC: Working in a sound studio is infinitely more fun than working on a movie set or on a television show because you can sit there and read the script. I hate memorizing lines! I am glad that I have been given the privilege to work with people who are passionate about what they do and passionate about spreading the word of God. *Odyssey* and Focus on the Family have given me the chance to participate in a wonderful vision: using radio to spread the good news and good family values.

Aria Curzon—*Mandy Straussberg*

Aria voices Ducky on The Land Before Time *video releases and television show (1998, 2000–2007) as well as the Cornchip Girl in Disney's* Recess *(1999). She also appeared in the movie* Treehouse Hostage *(1999).*

Q: What is your favorite *Adventures in Odyssey* episode?
AC: Well, there is "The Great Wishy Woz" [album 35], of course. And "Worst Day Ever" [album 35]. I also really enjoyed any episodes that featured me with Travis Tedford, Scarlett Pomers, and Lauren Schaffel, because they were all my friends. But everyone on *Adventures in Odyssey* is a friend!

Q: How are you like—or not like—your character?
AC: I am like her because I am a Christian, I like writing, and I am fairly sensitive to others in the way that she is. I like school, but where she is quite the studious one, I take a more relaxed approach to school.

Q: Would you like to share any special *Odyssey* memories?
AC: I finally learned "My Little Mandy" on the ukulele from Will Ryan at a recent recording session! That was great!

Q: What inspires you?
AC: Mostly other people who do things I would love to do, or who achieve great things, even when they face difficulty. Then, of course, there are my family and friends, who give me daily inspiration, and my faith, and others whose lives are examples of strong faith and a close walk with God.

Q: What has working on *Odyssey* meant to you?
AC: Wonderful people, fun, and interesting stories to portray, and a lot of good memories. A family really. Not your typical Hollywood project!

Gabriel Encarnacion—*Lawrence Hodges*

Q: What is your favorite *Adventures in Odyssey* episode?
GE: I'll always love "Aloha, Oy!" [album 19] for several reasons. It was the only three-part episode I did; it was fun to interact with the same actors over several recording sessions. And it was the only episode that featured my real-life mom in one scene.

Q: What inspires you?
GE: Knowing that what I'm doing is making an eternal difference and that I'm contributing to something bigger than I am.

Q: What is your favorite word?
GE: I enjoy words that are fun to say, like "serendipity," "Piccadilly," or even "banana."

Q: What has working on *Odyssey* meant to you?
GE: I look back fondly on my time with *Adventures in Odyssey* as one of those "dream come true" moments. I wasn't into acting or anything like that, so when the opportunity came up to do it, I was really excited. What kid wouldn't want to be part of a show they love? I'm excited about introducing it to my boys when they get older.

Brandon Gilberstadt—*Jared DeWhite*

Brandon played Justin Taylor on 100 Deeds for Eddie McDowd *(1999–2002).*

Q: What is your favorite *Adventures in Odyssey* episode?
BG: "The Spy Who Bugged Me" [album 30]. It started showing Jared's somewhat "interesting side," I guess you could say. And I always like acting as if I'm crazy, so it was a fun show to do.

Brandon Gilberstadt

Q: How are you like—or not like—your character?
BG: Like Jared, I never just believe what I am told.

Q: What are your hobbies?
BG: Reading up on history and on current events.
I think it is important to know where you come from
and what events occurred that shaped the world.

Q: What inspires you?
BG: My dad. He is a living testament that if you try your
hardest and never give up, anything is achievable.

Q: What is your favorite word?
BG: Mellow.

Jerry Houser—Ben Shepard, Jellyfish, and many more!

*Jerry has been the voice of one of the
Keebler elves and the Pep Boys since
the 1980s. He voiced Bamm-Bamm
on several* Flintstones *television
specials (1993) and Sandstorm on the*
Transformers *television show (1984).*

Q: What is your favorite *Adventures in
Odyssey* episode?
JH: "Always" [album 45]. My own son
was leaving for college at the time.

Q: How are you like—or not like—your
character?
JH: Ben is a family guy and family is really important
to me. There's definitely a "wack factor" to me, just like Ben.

Q: What inspires you?
JH: I appreciate when people know what they're doing and
they do it well. You go to a restaurant and you have a waiter
who has really embraced what they do and it really alters your
experience there.

Q: What has working on *Odyssey* meant to you?
JH: In this business, I love anytime you have the opportunity to do something worthwhile. So much here is commercialism, and that's okay. But it's nice when there's the opportunity to work on something that has more meaning than just selling soap.

Danielle Judovits—*Aubrey Shepard*

Danielle plays Shadowcat on the television series Wolverine and the X-Men *(2008). She has appeared on the television series* Picket Fences *(1995),* Hey Arnold! *(1996), and* The Batman *(2005–2007).*

Q: What is your favorite *Adventures in Odyssey* episode?
DJ: "Always" [album 45], where Aubrey went off to college. I remember reading the script and thinking back on my own experiences and how I felt a lot of the same emotions.

Q: How are you like—or not like—your character?
DJ: Like Aubrey, I'm really close with my family.

Q: What is your favorite word?
DJ: My word of the moment is definitely "facetious." It means joking around or being sarcastic. I try to use it as often as possible to stump my friends. I love the looks on their faces when they have no idea what I'm talking about!

Q: What has working on *Odyssey* meant to you?
DJ: Working on *Odyssey* is especially rewarding compared to other jobs I've done because I know it affects so many lives every day. What could be more rewarding than that?

Mark Christopher Lawrence—*Ed Washington*

Mark's movie roles include The Pursuit of Happyness *(2006),* The Island *(2005),* Christmas with the Kranks *(2004), and* Crimson Tide *(1995). On television, he has appeared on* Seinfeld *(1992, 1994),* Coach *(1997), and* My Name Is Earl *(2006).*

Q: What is your favorite *Adventures in Odyssey* episode?
MCL: "The Toy Man" [album 39], because it is the episode in which the Washingtons were introduced and my first experience with this magical show.

Q: Would you like to share any special *Odyssey* memories?
MCL: My fondest memory happened one morning before we started work. I am notoriously early. Marshal Younger was gathering with his crew to pray, and he invited me in. That made me really feel like I was part of the *Adventures in Odyssey* family.

Q: What inspires you?
MCL: First and foremost, the love of God. That love inspires me to put my best foot forward in all that I do. Also, my beautiful wife, Rebecca, inspires me to continue pursuing my dreams even in times of great difficulty. Finally, my competitiveness pushes me constantly.

Q: What is your favorite word?
MCL: My favorite word is "grace," because the grace of God ensures my salvation.

Q: What has working on *Odyssey* meant to you?
MCL: Over the years I have enjoyed being involved with the show because there are so few outlets for family values. It warms my heart to see that there are people in the industry who are like-minded and not afraid to show it.

Donald Long—*Jack Davis*

Q: What is your favorite *Adventures in Odyssey* episode?
DL: "The Day Independence Came" [album 2]. It was a great experience to be in studio with such a large number of incredibly talented actors.

Q: How are you like—or not like—your character?
DL: I can be hardheaded and stubborn at times. Jack Davis is a little more of a risk taker than I am.

Ed Washington

Donald Long

Q: What inspires you?

DL: Without a doubt, I am inspired by the love and sacrifice demonstrated by Jesus Christ.

Q: What has working on *Odyssey* meant to you?

DL: I have enjoyed being a part of such a successful and spiritually uplifting show! Meeting the people involved in the creation of a show like *Adventures in Odyssey* and seeing how it comes together have been a great joy for me.

Genesis (Mullen) Long—*Lucy Cunningham-Schultz*

Q: What is your favorite *Adventures in Odyssey* episode?

GML: All of the Blackgaard episodes. Recording the episodes with the high level of intensity written into the scripts was fun and challenging.

Genesis Long

Q: How are you like—or not like—your character?

GML: I'm kind of a Goody Two-shoes like Lucy is, and I don't like to be in trouble. Lucy is a little more outgoing than I am.

Q: What is your favorite word?

GML: Joy. It is something I strive for each day.

Q: What has working on *Odyssey* meant to you?

GML: I am thankful that I was able to be a part of a ministry that has touched so many children.

Maggie Malooly—*June Kendall*

Maggie has guest starred in many television series, including CHiPs *(1978),* The Waltons *(1977),* Gunsmoke *(1975), and* The Brady Bunch *(1970).*

Q: What was your favorite character to play?
MM: The Scottish mother of John Avery Whittaker in "Thank You, God" [album 3]. It was fun, and a surprise, because I didn't realize that I would be doing a Scottish accent throughout the entire story until I arrived at the recording studio! But the accent r-r-r-rolled out quite well. Must be my Celtic genes.

Q: What inspires you?
MM: Integrity, character, truthfulness, and kindness.

Q: If you could have another job besides acting, what would it be?
MM: I did have another job. I reared four children and loved them unconditionally. It was a lot harder than acting!

Maggie Malooly

Q: What has working on *Adventures in Odyssey* meant to you?
MM: I loved being in the life of my dear, delightful, spontaneous, pretend daughter, Connie. It was a joy to work with Katie, a true professional and a fine woman. Personally, I liked the idea of being a mom to all the kids who listened.

Corey Padnos—*Trent DeWhite*

Corey voiced Linus in several Charlie Brown television specials (2000, 2002, 2003). He also voiced George Little in Stuart Little 3: The Call of the Wild *(2005).*

Q: What is your favorite *Adventures in Odyssey* episode?
CP: My favorite episode is "Called On in Class" [album 42]. It's funny to hear Trent squirm through fictional flashbacks over giving an oral report, but I enjoy the moral of the story that avoiding your fears is never

the answer. Around that time, I actually entered a speech contest, and that episode really inspired me. I won the contest.

Q: How are you like—or not like—your character?
CP: Trent and I both tend to find ourselves in unusually awkward situations. We both also daydream constantly. I wish I had Trent's metabolism so that I could eat at an ice-cream shop every day.

Q: What has working on *Odyssey* meant to you?
CP: The *Odyssey* team has been like an extended family. I remember, not too long ago, when my voice changed (literally, the morning of the taping of an *Odyssey* episode). Sure, I was concerned that I would be out of a job, but I was more concerned that I would never see these people again. I'm a better voice actor and, moreover, a better human being because of my experience with *Odyssey*.

Chad Reisser—Monty Whittaker-Dowd, Digger Digwillow

Q: What is your favorite *Adventures in Odyssey* episode?
CR: "The Imagination Station" [album 5] held special memories for me. I was 13 years old at the time, and I remember thinking that show stretched my acting abilities. I specifically remember doing the monologue about observing the crucifixion several times, with the director attempting to get more emotion out of my little barely-teen psyche. I guess they were successful!

Q: How are you like—or not like—your character?
CR: With Digger Digwillow, I'd have to say that the biggest difference between us would be the whole time-travel thing. I've never done that. I have a strange thing with *Adventures in Odyssey*—with the exception of Digger, or Monty, I always seemed to get cast as the bad guy. What is it about me?

Q: What inspires you?

CR: Great writing. That's actually the thing that makes me the most excited about *Adventures in Odyssey*: It's always been smart. Sadly, so often within the church we dumb things down to the lowest common denominator. This, in my ever-so-humble opinion, does not at all reflect how Jesus taught. [He taught] in parable and mystery, drawing out and challenging the listener to search for the real meaning rather than just shoving it in people's faces. I have always, even as an adult participant, thought the *Odyssey* scripts were smart, creative, and funny, while always preserving and pointing towards scriptural truths.

Lauren Schaffel—*Liz Horton*

Lauren played Becca on Still Standing *(2004–2006) and various voices, including Lucy, on several Charlie Brown television specials (2002).*

Q: What is your favorite *Adventures in Odyssey* episode?

LS: My favorite episode is "The Case of the Disappearing Hortons" [album 40]. In this episode, the listeners finally got some insight into Liz as a person and gained some understanding of her personality issues. I was able to see the human side of Liz, who is not just a mean bully, but instead she is a person struggling to deal with many problems in her family and her life.

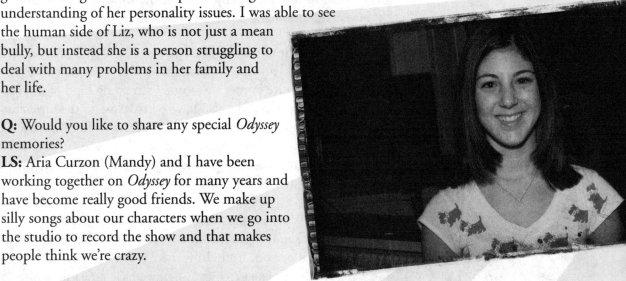

Q: Would you like to share any special *Odyssey* memories?

LS: Aria Curzon (Mandy) and I have been working together on *Odyssey* for many years and have become really good friends. We make up silly songs about our characters when we go into the studio to record the show and that makes people think we're crazy.

Q: What inspires you?

LS: I am inspired by viewing masterpieces of art like the works of Degas, Monet, and Michelangelo. I am also inspired by working with a director or teacher who is truly passionate about what he is doing and believes in his actors. I am inspired by seeing the faces of the audience when I am performing and seeing them smile.

Q: What is your favorite word?
LS: I like the word "flabbergast" because it is silly and funny sounding. I also like the word "discombobulated" for the same reasons.

Q: What has working on *Odyssey* meant to you?
LS: Working on *Odyssey* has been a wonderful enrichment to my life and my career. I started working on the show when I was 10, and ever since the very beginning, I have always felt as if the people on the show were one big family. I've enjoyed watching Liz grow up while I've grown up with her.

Liz Horton

Fabio Stephens—*Curt Stevens*

Q: What is your favorite *Adventures in Odyssey* episode?
FS: "Have You No Selpurcs?" [album 9]. Curt was always into lots of mischief. I enjoyed that the show had a positive message about being a person of honor.

Q: How are you like—or not like—your character?
FS: I had a blast playing someone that was quite the opposite of me. I was not a scheming kind of kid like Curt. He and I also have pretty close to the same last name. Production needed a last name for him and they called to ask me if he could be called "Stevens." My real last name is actually spelled "Step*h*ens," but I figured it was close enough.

Q: What inspires you?
FS: Lately, I am inspired by fearlessness. Fear can cripple a person. And sadly, there was a time when that had happened to me. When we have a relationship with the Creator, we have nothing to fear.

Q: What is your favorite word?
FS: Hope. In life it seems like we never end up exactly where we want. But having the hope in God and hope that He has a great future in mind for us/me seems to make everything okay.

Q: What has working on *Odyssey* meant to you?
FS: *Odyssey* gave me an amazing, professional, creative outlet in my early years of acting. At the time, it also gave me a great sense of right and wrong as I was touched by the content of every show that I was a part of.

J. Karen Thomas—Elaine Washington

J. Karen guest starred on Judging Amy *(2003) and appeared in* Ally McBeal *(1998–1999) and* City of Angels *(2000).*

Q: What is your favorite *Adventures in Odyssey* episode?
JKT: Each adventure is so uniquely satisfying. I couldn't pick just one favorite episode. That would be like saying one of my kids was my favorite.

Q: How are you like—or not like—your character?
JKT: We both have a strong sense of spirituality, gratitude, and we are both no-nonsense and very observant. Even when Elaine doesn't comment on something, you always get the feeling that she knows everything that's going on. How am I different from Elaine? Hmmm . . . I'm prettier. And my two "children" are furry.

Q: What inspires you?
JKT: Gathering with like-minded people at my church to celebrate God and the beauty of life.

Q: What is your favorite word?
JKT: YES! My favorite word is YES because it's always full of possibility, openness, and discovery.

Q: What has working on *Odyssey* meant to you?

JKT: Working as a voice-over artist is not something I dreamt of as a child. When I heard voices on the radio, they seemed real to me. I never thought about them as being separate from the character. The combination of an actor's voice and a listener's imagination creates magic. Working on *Odyssey* has allowed me to create that magic!

Janet Waldo—*Joanne Allen, Maureen Hodges*

Janet has been in the voice-over business for more than half a century. She played daughter Judy on The Jetsons *(1962-1963, 1985-1987), Josie on* Josie and the Pussycats *(1970–1972), and Mrs. Slaghoople on* The Flintstones *(1963–1966).*

Q: What is your favorite *Adventures in Odyssey* episode?

JW: I have enjoyed all of the episodes I've been in, but I think my favorite was "The Decision," [album 28] where Joanne was first introduced. It was great fun to establish the relationship with my dear friend Alan Young, who plays my husband.

Q: How are you like—or not like—your character?

JW: Joanne is very upbeat about life and is basically an optimist—I like to think I'm like her in those respects. She is very important to her husband, Jack, helping to run their antique shop, but I feel certain Joanne is a better businesswoman than I am! She adores her husband, as I did mine.

Q: Would you like to share any special *Odyssey* memories?

JW: I remember doing a show shortly after 9/11, and we all arrived for the session deeply shaken and devastated by the tragedy. But before we started, someone suggested that we pray together, which we did. One of the writers spoke, offering a spontaneous prayer. I found that experience both heartbreaking and very comforting.

Q: What inspires you?

JW: I'm inspired and sustained by my inner joy—it (almost) never fails me! My capacity for joy is a God-given gift for which I am so grateful.

Q: What has working on *Odyssey* meant to you?

JW: I'm always happy to get a call to work on *Odyssey*, not just because the scripts are well written and the actors exceptional—but because of *all* the people involved. They are caring, considerate, entertaining, and fun to be with.

Back row, from left: Walker Edmiston, Chuck Bolte, Paul Herlinger, Townsend Coleman.
Front row, from left: Chris Anthony, Aria Curzon, Katie Leigh.

From left: Coordinator Carol Rusk, Dave Arnold, Jonathan Crowe, Nathan Hoobler, Kathy Buchanan, Bob Hoose, Christopher Diehl, Marshal Younger, Nathan Jones

Meet the Crew

Steve Harris—*Cocreator, producer, writer, director, sound designer (1987–1988)*

Q: What is your favorite *Adventures in Odyssey* episode?
SH: No question about that one. It was "Gifts for Madge and Guy" [album 1]. Phil Lollar and I wrote that one together in my office, and I can't remember ever laughing that hard. Our sides ached, and at times we had trouble breathing.

Q: You were involved in *Adventures in Odyssey* for the first year. What's your opinion about how the stories and the characters have been developed since you left?
SH: When our children grow up and leave home, we watch them begin lives of their own. We're proud of their accomplishments, even though the credit rightfully belongs to them. That's exactly how I feel about *Adventures in Odyssey*. It's my little baby, all grown up. The people who succeeded me are all wonderful, gifted, hard-working professionals. I believe that they have taken the program to heights I might never have been able to achieve.

Steve Harris

Phil Lollar—*Cocreator, writer, director, producer, voice of Dale Jacobs (1987–2000)*

Q: What is your favorite *Adventures in Odyssey* episode?

PL: "Someone to Watch Over Me" [album 10]. It was based on a teleplay I wrote for the new but short-lived version of the old *Twilight Zone* series. The original revolved around the idea that for a completely paralyzed man, sleep would be a welcome escape from reality—he would be able to move, jump, run, and have all sorts of adventures. The worst thing that could happen to him would be waking up. *The Twilight Zone* didn't want it, so I twisted, turned, and pulled the idea a little bit, and came up with what turned out to be one of our most popular episodes ever, thanks in a large part to Dave Arnold's incredible production.

Bob Luttrell—*Sound designer (1987–1995, 2000–2005)*

Q: Which *Adventures in Odyssey* episode is your favorite?

BL: "Fairy Tal-e-vision" [album 43]. I enjoyed the challenge of having to re-create all of the different types of TV programs that were used in the show.

Q: Who is your favorite *Adventures in Odyssey* character?

BL: Connie. When she was a new Christian, she would say and ask things that most people would think twice before saying out loud.

Q: What inspires you?

BL: Being with other creative people.

Q: If you could have another job, what would you do?

BL: I'd be a mattress model in a department-store window.

Chuck Bolte—*Executive Producer (1988– 1996), voice of George Barclay*

Q: What is your favorite *Adventures in Odyssey* episode?
CB: "Our Best Vacation Ever" [album 5] because it showed that you don't need a lot of money to have a fun family vacation. Also "It's a Pokenberry Christmas" [album 31]. I can't remember having more fun recording in the studio.

Q: How are you like—or not like—the character of George Barclay?
CB: Probably my greatest similarity is that George had a very open, fun, and honest relationship with his children. Yet George, like me, was far from the perfect Christian father. Sometimes he wouldn't make the best decisions, but his intentions were always good. Where we differ is that I have absolutely no desire to become a pastor. I have the deepest admiration for those who are called to minister in this way . . . but zero desire to pursue such a vocation. And trust me, the world, as well as the church, is a better place because of it!

Q: What has working on *Odyssey* meant to you?
CB: I can say without reservation that being involved with *Odyssey*, particularly since its inception, has meant more to me than any other thing I have done in my professional life. The fact that God has seen fit to use *Odyssey* in such incredible ways in people's lives over so many years is humbling and rewarding beyond words. When individuals continue to come up to me and share the stories of how *Odyssey* has eternally affected their lives or the lives of their children, I am simply awed at what God has done. All of us involved in *Odyssey* were, and are, very creative people, but we simply couldn't have conceived how many shows we would actually produce, how many different manifestations of the original radio idea would be produced, how many lives would be touched through it, and how many

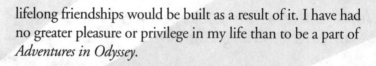

lifelong friendships would be built as a result of it. I have had no greater pleasure or privilege in my life than to be a part of *Adventures in Odyssey.*

Paul McCusker—*Writer, director, producer, executive producer (1987–1998; 2000–present), voice of Philip Glossman*

Q: What is your favorite *Adventures in Odyssey* episode?
PM: This is always a hard question to answer. But lately, as I've been listening to the episodes again with my kids, I've developed a particular affection for "Best Intentions" [album 16], probably because all the characters were so very true to themselves, and it still makes me laugh out loud. The performances and production were perfect.

Q: What inspires you?
PM: On my own, probably movies, music, and litera-ture. But I'm also inspired by ongoing interaction with other people—like the *Odyssey* team.

Q: What has working on *Odyssey* meant to you?
PM: I don't know how to answer this in a single paragraph. Participating in *Odyssey*—in a program that seems to have impacted so many lives in so many different ways—is as humbling an experience as I could ever have. It has shaped everything I know about writing and formed my relationship with God in the deepest possible ways. And to work with such a talented team makes me believe I'm one of the most blessed men on earth. And to think, I nearly turned it down to work as a book editor.

Dave Arnold—*Sound designer, writer, director, producer, executive producer (1988–1998, 2005–present)*

Q: Who is your favorite *Adventures in Odyssey* character?
DA: It's impossible to say because different seasons have different highlights for me. In the early years, Whit was my

Dave Arnold

favorite. I just wanted him to adopt me (and I knew he wasn't real!). Later, Eugene came into a particularly exceptional period. At times, I enjoyed characters like Bernard or Katrina or Officer Harley or kids like Jared or Lawrence. Even smaller roles like Holstein and Blackgaard. Right now, I'd say Wooton is spectacular.

Dave Arnold

Q: What inspires you?
DA: Elemental things. Wind through trees, people's faces, music, a dream.

Q: What has working on *Odyssey* meant to you?
DA: Fulfillment. Creative opportunity. The joy of being a part of something of value, something that will outlive you.

Marshal Younger—Writer, director, producer (1992–present)

Q: How did you come to work on *Adventures in Odyssey*?
MY: In 1992, I was doing graduate work at Regent University in Virginia, and I wrote a radio drama called "Making the Rain Stop." Another student, the producer, put it together, adding music and sound effects to the voice tracks. He was hoping for a job in sound design, and he sent the finished product to Focus on the Family. Paul McCusker called him and basically said, "The production doesn't work, but who wrote the script?"

Eventually, Paul and I talked, and I wrote my first script, "The Living Nativity" [album 16]. Five episodes and one year later, I was brought on as a staff writer.

Q: What *Adventures in Odyssey* episode is your favorite?
MY: "A Lesson from Mike" [album 31]. I think it is the most important show I've written, with the best lesson.

Q: Who is your favorite *Adventures in Odyssey* character?
MY: Wooton. I like how he doesn't quite make sense, except in his own mind. I like his heart, especially for children.

Q: What inspires you?
MY: My kids; writers C. S. Lewis, Aaron Sorkin, and Garrison Keillor; the Bible story of Joshua; the 1995 Cleveland Indians.

Q: What has working on *Odyssey* meant to you?
MY: I really don't feel like I'm good enough to have been a part of something so tremendous. Which tells me that God is behind it. And there's nothing better than being a part of something that God has inspired and blessed.

Mark Drury—*Sound designer (1992–1998)*

Q: How did you come to work on *Adventures in Odyssey*?
MD: I was working for Disney when I got an offer to work at Focus on the Family in the Youth Culture department. The problem was that the job was only part-time. Thankfully, there was also a part-time position available with *Adventures in Odyssey*, so Focus combined the two jobs to make one full-time position. My first *Odyssey* assignment was going through all two hundred or so episodes that had been recorded and replacing the old California address at the end of the show with the new Colorado address. Just as I finished the job, we found that there had been some confusion, and I had to replace all the addresses *again*! After a few years with *Odyssey*, I was hired full-time as a sound designer.

Q: What is your favorite *Adventures in Odyssey* episode?
MD: It's a tie between "The Underground Railroad, III" [album 24] and "It's a Pokenberry Christmas" [album 31].

Q: Who is your favorite *Adventures in Odyssey* character?
MD: I've always had a crush on Connie. I just love her "realness" in terms of being unguarded in who she is and what she says, which sometimes gets her into trouble. I can relate to that!

Q: If you could have another job, what would you be?
MD: A fighter pilot, who just gets to fly fast but not shoot things.

Q: What has working on *Odyssey* meant to you?
MD: A rare privilege to work with some neat and talented folks in the creation of a "world"— the town of Odyssey with all its amazing characters— that has offered hope, encouragement, wisdom, and entertainment to countless thousands for two decades.

John Beebee / John Fornof—Writer, director (1998–2006)

Q: How did you come to work on *Adventures in Odyssey*?
JF: In the summer of 1992, I got to meet Paul McCusker (then *Odyssey* producer). We hit it right off, and I started sending him story ideas. Over four and a half years I kept sending ideas (only because God and my mom kept encouraging me to do so)! Finally, Paul invited me to a writers' conference. Hey—exciting! But after I bought my plane ticket, they ended up canning the idea of bringing in new writers. Hey—bummer! I called Paul and explained my dilemma—here I was, stuck with a nonrefundable ticket. Paul said, "Come on!" Hey—exciting again! That was January 1997. I got my first assignment—"Tornado!" [album 30]—which aired in March 1998.

Q: What is your favorite *Adventures in Odyssey* episode?
JF: "The Great Wishy Woz." [album 35].

Q: Who is your favorite *Adventures in Odyssey* character?
JF: I love the "relatability" of Connie, the kidlike perspective of Wooton, the wisdom and warmth of Whit, and the quirky intellect of Eugene.

Q: What inspires you?
JF: Okay, fasten your seatbelts for this one: God. He's the One who gives me heart and perspective. And talk about creativity! I'm also inspired by the people He puts around me.

Jonathan Crowe—Sound designer (1998–present)

Q: Which *Adventures in Odyssey* episode is your favorite?
JC: For drama, it's "Saint Patrick: A Heart Afire" [album 31]. There is a magic about the episode that made me feel like I was really part of the story. For comedy, it's "Odyssey Sings!" [album 45]. In that episode, I had lots of freedom to try unusual production experiments, like recording a live band.

Q: Who is your favorite *Adventures in Odyssey* character?
JC: Bernard Walton—I think he's a very lovable curmudgeon of a character.

Q: What inspires you?
JC: Good programming or production that is well done. I'm also inspired by good writing and speeches.

Q: If you could have another job besides your current one, what would you do?

JC: Audio documentaries—especially a series that documents the uniqueness of people's lives, like the stories that are shared in *Guideposts* magazine.

Q: What has working on *Odyssey* meant to you?
JC: *Odyssey* has been one of the most challenging, stretching experiences in my professional life. I really appreciate the commitment to excellence and creativity in this show. Personally, it's been very touching to receive letters from people who were "raised on *Odyssey*," and to think, now they're looking forward to raising their own families with our programs.

Al Janssen—Producer, executive producer (1998–2000)

Q: Which *Adventures in Odyssey* episode is your favorite?
AJ: My favorite episode is the story of "Telemachus" [album 32], the martyr whose heroic actions ended the gladiator fights in Rome. It introduced a vitally important subject, that of suffering for our Christian faith even to the point of death. My work now takes me around the world to serve the church where she is persecuted. In many places, Christians pay a high price to live out their faith. Telemachus is one of the heroes of the faith who can inspire us to stand firm today in the midst of suffering.

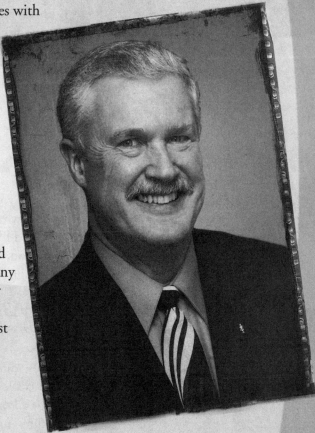

Q: Who is your favorite *Adventures in Odyssey* character?
AJ: Lucy Cunningham-Schultz. Her gentle spirit combined with her great love of literature make her especially endearing.

Rob Jorgensen—*Sound designer (1999–2004)*

Q: What is your favorite *Adventures in Odyssey* episode?
RJ: The Plan B series [album 37]. Those four episodes were compelling from every aspect: writing, acting, and production.

Q: Who is your favorite *Adventures in Odyssey* character?
RJ: I enjoyed a wonderful personal relationship with Paul Herlinger in the years I worked in *Odyssey*, so I have very fond feelings for his character, Whit, in the show. But Wooton remains my favorite character because of his zany innocence and the compelling depth of his past.

Q: What inspires you?
RJ: I love the history of radio, and old microphones especially enthuse me. I enjoy researching, repairing, and collecting microphones from the 1930s, 1940s, and 1950s.

Q: If you could have another job besides your current one, what would you do?
RJ: I'd like to own a coffee shop in Cannon Beach, Oregon. Coffee and the beach are an unbeatable combination.

Kathy Buchanan—*Writer, director (1999–present)*

Q: How did you come to work on *Adventures in Odyssey*?
KB: I came into *Odyssey* almost by accident. I was looking for a job where I could get medical insurance so I could go skiing [and be covered if I got in an accident]. I'd never heard a single episode, and I certainly had too busy of a life to be consumed with a "kids' show." I applied for several jobs at Focus and reluctantly took the *Odyssey* job when it was offered to me. My first assignment was to get acquainted with the series. I took my first album—*Signed, Sealed, and*

Committed [29]—home that weekend and I couldn't stop listening. From then on I always had albums playing in my car and I fell totally in love with the show.

Ironically, the job that I really wanted when I was interviewing was offered to me the day after I accepted with the job with *Odyssey* . . . and it was too late to switch. I remember being so frustrated at the time, thinking I'd taken the wrong job. Now I can't imagine what life would have been like without being a part of *Odyssey*—I'm so thankful.

Q: Who is your favorite *Adventures in Odyssey* character?
KB: Although Bernard and Wooton are my favorites because they offer so much comedy, Connie has endeared herself to me. It's been fun to see her grow and have her wrestle with some of the same questions about God and her life that I had. She has depth and heart and energy, and she's never boring. And the outfits she wears are to die for . . . if only I could look that fetching in green stretch pants.

Q: What inspires you?
KB: Books and the beauty of nature.

Nathan Hoobler—*Writer, director (2000–present)*

Q: Who is your favorite *Adventures in Odyssey* character?
NH: My favorite character by far is Eugene. He's such a complex and fascinating individual. But my favorite character to write for is Edwin Blackgaard.

Q: What inspires you?
NH: Hearing from fellow listeners. It seems that every time I get sick of writing, listeners will stop by or E-mail me about how *Odyssey* has been an influence on them, on their kids, or on their friends. Then I pray, "Okay, thanks, Lord. That was the inspiration I needed." And I go back to work.

Nathan Hoobler

Q: If you could have another job besides your current one, what would you do?

NH: I would find a way to get paid to listen to *Odyssey* full-time. There's got to be a way to make money doing that! Oh, wait . . . I do that now!

Q: What has working on *Odyssey* meant to you?

NH: It was awe-inspiring and overwhelming coming into *Odyssey* after being a fan for so many years. *Odyssey* was probably the biggest influence on my life outside of my parents. Now, working for the show, I can see how God uses it in other lives besides mine. With more than 640 episodes, I can't wait until we hit 1000 shows . . . or 2000! Imagine how thick a book like this will be then!

Bob Hoose—*Writer, director, producer (2002–present)*

Q: Who is your favorite *Adventures in Odyssey* character?

BH: I love the character of Mr. Feldstein. Sure, you probably couldn't stand listening to him star in a whole show (without fear of somebody developing a hernia), but I sure do find that particular Corey Burton character hilarious.

Q: What inspires you?

BH: Creative thought. I'm always excited by someone's ideas. It's a wondrous way that God has created us in His image.

Q: If you could have another job besides your current one, what would you do?

BH: I guess moving to a little town and working in a soda shop might be cool. Hey, if Connie can still be a teenager there, maybe I can too.

Q: What has working on *Odyssey* meant to you?
BH: From the first voice-over I did with the show more than 20 years ago, I've loved the incredible cast and inspiring shows. Radio theater is, unfortunately, an all-but-dead art form. I'm grateful to have been a small part of one of the last surviving shows. *Odyssey* is a quality, heartwarming example of the craft.

Bob Hoose

Glenn Montjoy—Sound designer (2001–2006)

Q: What is your favorite *Adventures in Odyssey* episode that you worked on?
GM: "Snow Day" [album 36]. Rob Jorgensen and I did lots of Foley in Cheyenne Canyon, Colorado. Very unique.

Q: Who is your favorite *Adventures in Odyssey* character and why?
GM: I'm gonna say Tom Riley. I like that he's very down to earth and can relate to everybody he comes in contact with. Everybody knows a Tom somewhere or another.

Q: What has working on *Odyssey* meant to you?
GM: It's interesting to see how far the program has come in the last 20 years. It's wonderful to be a part of a program that's had an impact on so many lives, including mine.

Nathan Jones—*Sound designer (2004–present)*

Q: What is your favorite *Adventures in Odyssey* episode?
NJ: "B-TV: Temptation" [album 49]. I love the fast-paced humor and endless possibilities in sound design fun.

Q: Who is your favorite *Adventures in Odyssey* character?
NJ: Wooton. Just about anything could happen when he is in proximity.

Q: Do you care to share any special memories?
NJ: My favorite thing is when we do playback and everyone gets to laugh or cry. This tells me that I've done my job right.

Q: If you could have another job, what would you do?
NJ: I would record and produce songs for music artists full-time.

Q: What has working on *Odyssey* meant to you?
NJ: *Odyssey* has helped me grow as a professional both artistically and socially with the team.

Christopher Diehl—*Sound designer (2006–present)*

Q: How did you come to work on *Adventures in Odyssey*?
CD: I learned about Focus on the Family through my wife, Angie. She was friends with the *Odyssey* guys and heard that there was a position opening. I came in to interview for the position, only to be led into a dark room, asked to sit in a chair with a spotlight shining on it. The interviewers (who shall remain nameless, but who bore a striking resemblance to Jonathan Crowe and Mark Drury) commenced to "interrogate" me. After perspiring a bucketful, I finished the interview and was offered the job.

Q: Who is your favorite *Adventures in Odyssey* character?
CD: Wooton. At first, you think he is just a silly guy with a really cool and wacky house, but every once in a while you catch the glimpse of wisdom that he keeps hidden.

Q: If you could have another job, what would you do?
CD: Something that involves working with my hands and creating something, preferably outside.

Q: What has working on *Odyssey* meant to you?
CD: It has given me a sense of joy to know that what I am working on is affecting the kingdom of God by ministering to kids and adults everywhere. It is also a huge responsibility.

Character: Connie

Quote: "Sorry, I'm late!"
Something you may not know about Connie:
She was an extra in a movie shot at her
school in California.

Album 1

The Adventure Begins

The First Album?

What is the first album of *Adventures in Odyssey*? It has come in many different packages, for many different reasons. Initially we created a 13-episode collection for *Odyssey*'s predecessor, *Family Portraits*. It included all of the episodes that aired on the Focus on the Family daily broadcast as a test run.

When the program got its own time slot, the entire series, along with the first collection of episodes, was called *Odyssey USA*. The series was renamed five months later, and yet another "first" collection was created—*Adventures in Odyssey*. Unfortunately, that album contained the character Officer Harley (see "The Trouble with Harley" sidebar at the end of this chapter), and Officer Harley's episodes were withdrawn. As a result, the earliest *Adventures in Odyssey* episodes were unavailable for a couple of years.

In 1991 we temporarily fixed the problem by creating an album called *The Early Classics*. But it created a new problem since it included episodes such as "The Trouble with Girls" that were out of chronological order (see notes on *The Lost Episodes* album).

Finally, when we embarked on the Gold Audio Series, we were able to restore the proper chronology of the episodes and replace the "out of sequence" shows with two that had never been included in albums before ("A Member of the Family" and "A Change of Hart").

Episode Information

1: **Whit's Flop**
Original Air Date: 11/21/87
Writers: Steve Harris & Phil Lollar
Sound Designers: Bob Luttrell & Steve Harris
Scripture: Romans 8:28
Theme: The importance of failure
Summary: Davey Holcomb, a young boy with a reputation for making mistakes, learns there's a positive side to failure.

2: **The Life of the Party**
Original Air Date: 11/28/87
Writer: Paul McCusker
Sound Designer: Bob Luttrell
Scripture: 1 Samuel 20
Theme: Friendship
Summary: Craig Moorhead's middle school friends like having him around because he makes them laugh. But then Craig faces a problem that isn't funny at all, and his friends aren't so friendly anymore.

4: **Connie Comes to Town**
Original Air Date: 12/12/87
Writers: Phil Lollar & Steve Harris
Sound Designer: Bob Luttrell
Scripture: Philippians 4:11-12
Theme: Being content
Summary: Even though teenager Connie Kendall has just moved into Odyssey, she can hardly wait to go back to California . . . and 10-year-old Bobby has secretly made up his mind that he's going with her.

5: **Gifts for Madge and Guy**
Original Air Date: 12/19/87
Writers: Phil Lollar & Steve Harris
Sound Designer: Bob Luttrell
Scripture: Matthew 1:18-25; Luke 2:1-20
Theme: Giving
Summary: Mr. Whittaker tells a "fractured" version of a famous Christmas story, starring an unusual couple named Madge and Guy.

6: **The Day After Christmas**
Original Air Date: 12/26/87
Writer: Paul McCusker
Sound Designer: Bob Luttrell
Scripture: Matthew 25:31-46
Theme: Caring for the poor
Summary: Annie McNeal, a young girl who is already bored with her Christmas presents, wanders into Whit's End looking for something to do.

Whit

7: Promises, Promises

Original Air Date: 1/2/88
Writer: Phil Lollar
Sound Designer: Bob Luttrell
Scripture: Romans 3:23
Theme: The folly of making promises you can't keep
Summary: Connie makes a resolution to be more patient no matter what, which turns out to be far more difficult than she imagined.

10: Nothing to Fear

Original Air Date: 1/23/88
Writer: Paul McCusker
Sound Designer: Bob Luttrell
Scripture: 1 John 4:18
Theme: Dealing with fear
Summary: Shirley Ziegler is afraid of just about everything. But when a real emergency comes up at Whit's End, she is forced to face her worst fear.
PARENTAL WARNING:
The nightmare scene and the scene in the basement at Whit's End may be too intense for younger listeners.

12: The Tangled Web

Original Air Date: 2/6/88
Writer: Phil Lollar
Sound Designer: Bob Luttrell
Scripture: Proverbs 12:22
Theme: Lying
Summary: Connie reads the story of Jeremy Forsythe, a boy who tells his mother a fib about some missing money. Both Jeremy and Connie learn that one lie leads to another.

17 and 18: A Member of the Family, I and II

Original Air Dates: 3/12/88 & 3/19/88
Writers: Steve Harris & Susan McBride
Sound Designer: Bob Luttrell
Scripture: Exodus 20:12; Proverbs 3:11-12; Ephesians 6:4
Themes: Discipline, family conflict
Summary: When Whit's grandson, Monty, arrives for a summer in Odyssey, the family finds they are in for more trouble—and more healing—than they expected.

19: Recollections

Original Air Date: 3/26/88
Writer: Phil Lollar
Sound Designer: Bob Luttrell
Scripture: Galatians 6:9
Themes: Fighting for your convictions, making good out of bad circumstances
Summary: Whit's best friend, Tom Riley, tells Connie the story of how Whit's End was created amid tragic circumstances.

27: A Change of Hart

Original Air Date: 5/21/88
Writer: Paul McCusker
Sound Designer: Bob Luttrell
Scripture: 2 Corinthians 3:18; 5:16-17
Themes: Salvation, living a changed life
Summary: Freddie Hart is constantly teased by his middle school classmates. But when he switches schools, he finds that his troubles follow him.

"Whit's Flop"

Actor David Griffin, voice of Jimmy Barclay

Behind the Scenes: Whit's Flop

"Whit's Flop" was the first *Odyssey USA* episode and the first *Focus on the Family* daily broadcast drama program that aired in its own time slot. In this show, listeners got a short tour around Whit's End, and we introduced the Train Station, the Inventor's Corner, Whit's workshop, and the displays.

Goof Alert!

In "Whit's Flop," Whit says that Davey knocking over the backstop was a coincidence. However, it's clear from later episodes such as "A Single Vote" (album 3) and others that Whit does not believe in coincidences.

BTS: The Life of the Party

The original title of "The Life of the Party" was "The Tears of a Clown," which was also the name of a hit Motown single by Smokey Robinson and The Miracles. It featured the debut of two actors who would later take on different and more prominent roles—David Griffin (later Jimmy Barclay—album 2) as Freddy, and Will Ryan (later Eugene—album 3) as Bill.

Sound Bites

When we were recording "The Life of the Party," we accidentally misquoted the Bible by having a character say, "What you reap, you shall also sow." With careful editing, the sound designers fixed the line to its correct rendering, "What you sow, you shall also reap." When you listen to this episode, see if you can tell.

The Eternal Teenager: The Creation of Connie Kendall

Once *Family Portraits* had finished its test run on the *Focus on the Family* daily broadcast and *Odyssey* was approved as its own series, the team knew it had to do more work on the characters for the show. Producer Steve Harris met with Hollywood writer Joe Glauberg,

Connie Kendall through the years

who'd worked on television shows such as *Happy Days* (1974–1984) and *Mork and Mindy* (1978–1982), and they worked on developing new characters. Steve remembers: "One of the big things that came out of our brainstorming was the need for another main character—a high school student who could act as a foil for Whit. Connie Kendall was born right on the spot, name and all.

"We had worked with Katie Leigh on *Family Portraits* and knew she would be perfect for the part. In fact, much of Connie's

Actor Katie Leigh, voice of Connie Kendall

character was written with Katie in mind. At the time, we intended to begin our brand-new drama series with the episode 'Connie Comes to Town.' However, when we called Katie in for the session, her son, Adam, was four days old, and she couldn't make it to the studio. She advised us to recast the part. We couldn't imagine anyone other than Katie playing the role of Connie, so we delayed Connie's introduction to a few shows later and recorded the program at a later date. Katie has played Connie for over 20 years now!"

BTS: Connie Comes to Town

In "Connie Comes to Town," Whit tells Connie to pick up a uniform, but uniforms at Whit's End are never mentioned again. Perhaps Whit changed his dress code.

My Take: Paul McCusker

I originally wrote "The Day After Christmas" around a nostalgic idea of Whit and his memories of Christmases past. But Chuck Bolte wisely insisted that kids wouldn't relate to an adult's memories. So I began to think about what happens to kids at Christmas, how they quickly go through their toys and are often bored by the end of the day. Steve Harris suggested the storyline about a cranky elderly woman named Mrs. Rossini, which gave a much better focus to the idea. Ultimately I liked the character of Mrs. Rossini so much that I created another one like her in "An Encounter with Mrs. Hooper" (album 5).

Cut Scenes

The first airing of "Promises, Promises" featured Connie losing her patience when Tom Riley and Officer Harley couldn't make up their minds on smoothie flavors. Because Officer Harley had to be replaced, we recorded a new scene in which Connie loses her patience when some kids are trying to figure out a riddle about an electric train.

Sound Bites

The "Promises, Promises" conversation between Whit and Tom (about reading a Robert Louis Stevenson book) originally appeared in the first *Family Portraits* episode, "Whit's Visitor."

BTS: Nothing to Fear

"Nothing to Fear" was the first episode that garnered a large negative reaction. It featured a nightmare scene with a mouse named Luther (played by Hal Smith) that proved to be a little too scary for a lot of children—which was ironic, considering the episode was intended to help children *deal* with fear.

Sound Bites

In "Nothing to Fear," Shirley's mother was played by Janna Arnold, wife of sound designer Dave Arnold.

BTS: The Tangled Web

The first script for "The Tangled Web" featured Jeremy Forsythe refusing to accept an award; instead the 11-year-old broke down and confessed to a lie in front of the entire town. However, in later drafts the ending was changed so Jeremy accepted the award on stage and never confessed. This drove home the point that even an undiscovered lie can create damage.

Family Portraits album

Odyssey USA album

The first *Adventures in Odyssey* album

The Early Classics album

Sound Bites

When we first recorded "The Tangled Web," we hadn't cast Maggie Malooly as Connie's mother. When Connie called her mom at the end of the show, no voice was heard on the other end of the line. Later, we needed to go back into the show and take Officer Harley out of an earlier scene. Since we had to make that change anyway, we decided to add Maggie at the same time saying hello when Connie called home.

BTS: A Member of the Family

"A Member of the Family" introduced Whit's family—his daughter, Jana, and grandkids, Monty and Jenny. We also learned that the Whittakers had moved to Odyssey shortly after Whit's older son, Jerry, died in Vietnam. It was also the first time that Whit's younger son, Jason, was mentioned. We learned that Whit made many mistakes while raising his children, which was in contrast to the kind and gentle way he treated kids at Whit's End. This flaw made him seem more real, approachable, and not quite so perfect.

BTS: A Member of the Family

D. J. Harner played Whit's daughter, Jana. Hal Smith and D. J. Harner also played father and daughter in the *Focus on the Family* daily broadcast drama "House Guest."

Fillmore Recreation Center

BTS: A Member of the Family

"A Member of the Family" originally aired as a *Family Portraits* episode and featured a Whit's End employee named Jimmy (voiced by Bob Luttrell). When we brought the show back to air on *Odyssey USA*, we replaced Jimmy with Connie (Katie Leigh).

BTS: Recollections

"Recollections" revealed the history behind the creation of Whit's End. It was also the first time we met the weasely city councilman Philip Glossman, who would play a major part in the later "Blackgaard Saga." Glossman promoted an offer from the Webster Development Company, which we later learned was owned by Dr. Blackgaard. We also established that Whit was a middle school teacher and that he is, in fact, quite wealthy.

Also in this show, Tom told Connie that the city council put off the vote on the Fillmore Recreation Center for a month. Much later, in "Clara" (album 28), we found that Whit's childhood friend, Jack Allen, took Whit to Nebraska for that period and that Whit almost adopted a daughter.

My Take: Paul McCusker

"Recollections" was one of the few episodes that Phil Lollar wrote but didn't direct because the recording date fell during his family vacation. I remember his last words to me: "Don't let them ruin my show." Chuck and I were particularly worried about the death-bed scene—that it might come off with too much melodrama. It didn't, thanks mostly to the great skills of our actors. And, in the end, the show wasn't ruined at all, but became an *Odyssey* classic.

In fact, the only thing that *didn't* work about the episode was the voice of Philip Glossman. I was coerced into playing the part, probably because no one else would do it, and we had no idea that he would turn into an ongoing character. I don't particularly like the sound of my voice and would rather not work on that side of the microphone.

BTS: A Change of Hart

"A Change of Hart" was the first *Adventures in Odyssey* episode that didn't have any of our regular characters in it. We were anxious to prove that the *Odyssey* concept was broad enough to accommodate a variety of stories and characters, even those that didn't involve Whit, Tom, or Connie. This show also marked

Paul McCusker and Dave Arnold in the studio

the first appearance of executive producer Chuck Bolte as Dr. Julius Schnitzelbonker. (By the way, his name came from a German restaurant in Silver Spring, Maryland, that Paul McCusker's family frequented.)

The Trouble with Harley

Officer Harley (played by Will Ryan) made his first appearance in "Lights Out at Whit's End," an episode that is buried in the archives. Harley was a bumbling policeman and the producers loved him for his comic potential, but not everyone felt the same way. After parents complained that he gave a bad impression of law enforcers, Dr. Dobson insisted that Officer Harley disappear from the show.

Producer Steve Harris remembers, "At the time, we were working day and night to get the program on schedule. I'm sure my fatigue contributed to my temporary frustration with the decision to take Harley out of the show. In hindsight (there's nothing like 20 years of experience to change your perspective!), Dr. Dobson was absolutely right. We needed to be proactive in teaching respect for legitimate authority. Looking back, I can see that God definitely had His hand in that whole situation."

So Officer Harley eventually left the show during its first year. Some of his shows, such as "Doing Unto Others," "Bobby's Valentine," and "Missed It by That Much," were later rewritten, retitled, and rerecorded without Harley (see "The Officer Harley Remakes," album 8). Others (including "Addictions Can Be Habit-Forming") were dropped completely and never aired again. In a few shows like "Promises, Promises" and "Rumor Has It" (album 3), we replaced his voice with another character or simply cut the scenes in which he appeared. Finally, a few traces of Harley remain in shows such as "Gifts for Madge and Guy" and "Recollections" where he was not a main character. Officer Harley originally appeared in "The Tangled Web." He was replaced by a well-meaning neighbor who had gone to a private detective school. This foreshadowed our permanent replacement for Harley—a private detective named Harlow Doyle (album 14).

Careful listeners will find brief cameos by Officer Harley in "Peace on Earth" (album 3) and "A Thanksgiving Carol" (album 12). Finally, Eugene calls Harley on the phone in "Curious, Isn't It?" (album 8).

By the way, when "Peace on Earth" first aired as a special on the *Focus on the Family* daily broadcast, Dr. Dobson noticed the appearance of Officer Harley at the end and good-naturedly exclaimed, "Hey, I thought we got rid of that guy!"

Album  Stormy Weather

Introducing the Barclays!

The Barclay family debuted in *Stormy Weather* beginning with "Family Vacation." The family's first names come from the movie *It's a Wonderful Life* (1946). In that classic film, originally made in black-and-white, Jimmy Stewart played George Bailey and Donna Reed played Mary Bailey—thus, Jimmy, George, Donna, and Mary.

David Griffin had played many characters for the first few months on the program. With this show, we decided it was time to lock him into the character of Jimmy Barclay, whom we hoped would encapsulate all the best aspects of the other characters he had played. David remembers: "When I first heard that I was going to play only Jimmy Barclay from this point forward, I was kind of offended. I had been playing so many characters, and I wondered if I had done something wrong so that I had to play the same guy again and again. I shouldn't have worried since Jimmy turned out to be the best character ever!"

In 1988, *Adventures in Odyssey* ran a promotion asking listeners to suggest a place for a great family vacation. Florida won out, so the Barclay family headed in that direction . . . though they never quite made it there.

The Barclays became the central family on the series for nearly a decade. They starred in many episodes that we called "fly on the wall" episodes. These episodes inspired people to write Focus on the Family saying, "When I heard this show, I was convinced you had a microphone in my house, because it sounded just like my family."

Episode Information

31 and 32: **Family Vacation, I and II**
Original Air Dates: 6/18/88 & 6/25/88
Writer: Paul McCusker
Sound Designer: Bob Luttrell
Scripture: 2 Corinthians 13:14; Hebrews 10:25
Theme: Family togetherness
Summary: The Barclay family of four takes off for a Florida vacation, but they get stranded when the car breaks down.

33: **The Day Independence Came**
Original Air Date: 7/2/88
Writer: Phil Lollar
Sound Designer: Bob Luttrell
Scripture: Proverbs 28:16; Acts 5:29; 2 Corinthians 3:17
Themes: American history, freedom, our Christian heritage
Summary: Irwin Springer, a middle-schooler interested in history, takes a wild journey back to the American Revolution, where he meets Nathan Hale, George Washington, and other men who shaped the United States.

34: **Stormy Weather**
Original Air Date: 7/9/88
Writer: Paul McCusker
Sound Designer: Bob Luttrell
Scripture: Psalm 103; Ecclesiastes 4:9-12
Themes: Courage, faith, friendship
Summary: Connie is frustrated with life in Odyssey and wants to move back to California. When a violent storm hits the town, she finds out she appreciates more in Odyssey than she ever realized.

35: **V.B.S. Blues**
Original Air Date: 7/16/88
Writer: Phil Lollar
Sound Designer: Bob Luttrell
Scripture: Daniel 3; Hebrews 4:12
Themes: Sharing your faith, God's provision in tough situations
Summary: Young troublemaker "Mugsy" Mumford crashes counselor Ned Lewis's vacation Bible school production of "The Fiery Furnace."

36: **Kids' Radio**
Original Air Date: 7/23/88
Writer: Paul McCusker
Sound Designer: Bob Luttrell
Scripture: Hebrews 10:36
Themes: Perseverance, commitment
Summary: Whit and the crew start a radio station in a back room of Whit's End. Of course, the station is run by kids, for kids!

37 and 38: **Camp What-A-Nut, I and II**
Original Air Dates: 7/30/88 & 8/6/88
Writer: Phil Lollar
Sound Designer: Bob Luttrell
Scripture: 1 Samuel 16:1-13
Theme: Building character
Summary: Donny McCoy looks younger than his 10 years. He journals about his many adventures that happen at Camp What-A-Nut.

39 and 40: The Case of the Secret Room, I and II
Original Air Dates: 8/13/88 & 8/20/88
Writer: Paul McCusker
Sound Designer: Bob Luttrell
Scripture: Matthew 6:24; 1 Timothy 6:10
Themes: Greed, justice
**Summary: The discovery of a secret room in Whit's End leads
Mr. Whittaker to a baffling case of robbery and murder.**
PARENTAL WARNING:
This is a mystery about an old murder. It contains subject matter
that may be too intense for younger children.

41: Return to the Bible Room
Original Air Date: 8/27/88
Writer: Paul McCusker
Sound Designer: Bob Luttrell
Scripture: The book of Jonah; Ephesians 6:1-3
Themes: Obedience, Bible story of Jonah
**Summary: Two kids, Jack Davis and Lucy Cunningham, meet the
biblical Jonah before finding themselves on a ship in a storm and
then in the belly of a great fish.**

42: The Last Great Adventure of the Summer
Original Air Date: 9/3/88
Writer: Phil Lollar
Sound Designers: Steve Harris & Dave Arnold
Scripture: Proverbs 23:24
Theme: God's protection, Dad as a hero
**Summary: Young Terry Johnston and his father (CIA codename:
Catspaw) take a sudden and dangerous journey around the world while
being pursued by a master criminal.**

Behind the Scenes: Family Vacation

Middle-schooler Donna Barclay was played by Azure Janosky. Dr. Dobson was friends with Azure's family and recommended Azure for a role on *Odyssey*. The casting of the Barclay parents proved more problematic. Roger Scott played George Barclay for "Family Vacation," but in all future episodes, executive producer Chuck Bolte took over the role. Mary Barclay proved even more difficult to cast. In the first episode, Maggie Malooly took on the part. Later, we decided that Maggie was ideal to play Connie's mother, and so Patricia Albrecht took on the role of Mary for four episodes. For a variety of reasons, she was replaced with Patti Parris, who maintained the character until 1992 when the role passed to Carol Bilger.

The Barclay family: George, Mary, Donna, Jimmy

Sound Bites

If you listen carefully when George turns on the radio in "Family Vacation," you can hear the announcer say that *Focus on the Family* is coming up and the station's call letters are KFOF.

BTS: Family Vacation

Donna insisted that Chester was an axe murderer who will "put us in his freezer in plastic sandwich bags." This line generated a few critical letters and phone calls to Focus on the Family from people who didn't appreciate Donna's particular brand of overstatement.

My Take: Paul McCusker

The name of the small town—Hopwood—is named after the place where my mother's family lived for years. My grandfather was a barber there and much loved by all the townspeople. His name was Chester, which I used for the character who helped the Barclays in "Family Vacation."

A Rose by Any Other Name . . .

In the beginning, there was *Family Portraits*, which aired on the *Focus on the Family* daily broadcast (see "How *Odyssey* Began," chapter 1). That name worked for a short test run when the show was an all-encompassing family program. But none of us thought it worked for the long term, especially since we were narrowing the target age range to 8 to 12 years old. It also didn't have the sense of wonder and excitement that we were hoping for.

A few well-meaning contributors wanted to call the program "The Children's Radio Playhouse of the Airwaves." The team decided that was too grown-up. How about "Odyssey"? No, it simply wasn't enough

Whit as Ben Franklin

(and that name was used in many other products and programs). Then came *Odyssey USA* and the team knew it was on the right track. The first 22 episodes were produced with that name.

However, we thought Canadian stations might complain that the name was too exclusive to America. The team brainstormed new names for days. Title suggestions included "Whit and His Friends," "Whit's Place," and simply "Whit's End." Finally, the vote went to . . . *Adventures in Odyssey*.

BTS: The Day Independence Came
This episode presented *Odyssey*'s first historical and time-travel adventure. The team initially wanted to take a more comedic approach to our nation's founding, but executive producer Chuck Bolte suggested a more serious approach.

This episode also generated some surprising negative mail centered on the prayer spoken by George Washington. A few questioned its historical accuracy. But writer Phil Lollar had taken the words from Washington's own prayer journal.

Sound Bites with Dave Arnold
"The Day Independence Came" signaled a new direction for the production of *Odyssey*. Bob Luttrell went much deeper in his layering of sound design, approaching the show more like a motion picture. It was the first time the production team used submixes.

With a submix, we mix sections of the sound design (such as the Redcoats' voices and footsteps in the background) before mixing it back into the other elements of the scene. We had to do that here because we ran out of tracks on our machine. Especially noteworthy was the scene where Nathan Hale and Irwin Springer jumped into the water to escape the wasps. Their voices blended perfectly with the water sound effects.

BTS: Stormy Weather

"Stormy Weather" was originally titled "A Stormy Afternoon" and featured an entirely different climax. Instead of Whit's being hurt by a breaking window, he rescued Connie from the branches of a fallen tree—putting Connie in the hospital instead. June Kendall, Connie's mother, made her first appearance in this episode.

Goof Alert!

In "Kids' Radio," Sherman tells Whit that five vacuum tubes work. Then we hear three break, and Sherman says only one works now. Perhaps he was was a little weak on math.

Sound Bites

The chemistry in the "Kids' Radio" studio between actors Donald Long (Brad) and Joseph Cammaroto (Sherman) was so good that we later paired the two actors up as Jack and Oscar in "Connie Goes to Camp" (album 5).

BTS: Camp What-A-Nut

We wanted an episode for Jimmy Barclay to continue the summer journal that he began in "Family Vacation." However, actor David Griffin was on a real-life vacation, so the part was changed to Donny McCoy. Also, Whit talked about the origin of the name "What-A-Nut" in the show, referencing how the land was constantly flooded and smelled like a swamp. His explanation later became the basis of the episodes "The Ill-Gotten Deed" (album 6) and "Called On in Class" (album 42).

Actor Joseph Cammaroto as Oscar

Cut Scenes

The first draft of "The Case of the Secret Room" featured the character Percival Fenwick waving a gun and threatening Whit, Tom, and the others. Writer Paul McCusker remembers how producer Steve Harris told him the gun part was too violent and had to be cut. Initially Paul didn't know how to fix the show, fearing that the idea would have to be scrapped. Only after a lot of thought did he come up with the idea of using a knockout dart, which he conceded was far more imaginative than a gun.

Sound Bites

Actor Earl Boen, who later voiced Regis and Edwin Blackgaard (album 5), made his first *Adventures in Odyssey* appearance in "The Case of the Secret Room," playing Police Inspector Howards. He had previously appeared in a *Family Portraits* drama titled "A Different Kind of Peer Pressure."

My Take: Paul McCusker

"The Case of the Secret Room" is the source of two of our favorite stories about Walker Edmiston (who plays Tom). During the recording of the scene where Whit and Tom are supposed to lift a large wardrobe, Hal Smith thought we had begun recording and dutifully started making all the grunting sounds one would expect when lifting anything heavy. After a few moments of this, he stopped—after which Walker paused and said, "Ready when you are, Whit." The production team was so tickled by that moment that it became one of Tom's catchphrases and appeared later in "The Other Woman" [album 28] and "Stars in Our Eyes" [album 43].

The second Walker moment came at the end of a particularly suspenseful scene where Tom and Whit discovered a skeleton in a secret room (see opening illustration). Walker—who was a huge fan of old-time radio dramas, and knew all of the sound tricks used in them—suddenly howled like a wolf to evoke the classic feel of intrigue. The team thought it was hilarious and often required Walker to howl in later recording sessions for mysterious or comedic effect.

Actors Walker Edmiston and Hal Smith having fun in the studio

Goof Alert!

In "The Case of the Secret Room," Whit says "I haven't done this much digging since I was in the Army." However, as made clear in "Rescue from Manatugo Point" (album 6), Whit was in the Navy.

Sound Bites

In "Return to the Bible Room," the "crowd" of sailors heard in the background throughout the storm scenes was performed by only three actors: Hal Smith, Walker Edmiston, and Will Ryan. They performed several takes of the scene, using different voices each time. Then, in postproduction, we layered these takes on top of each other to create the crowd.

BTS: *The Last Great Adventure of the Summer*

Portions of this episode were inspired by the classic Alfred Hitchcock film *North by Northwest* (1959). The show ended up being a complete departure from our usual *Odyssey* adventures, and its popularity ensured that spy stories would have their place in *Odyssey's* future. The show was Dave Arnold's first entry into postproduction for *Odyssey*. Steve Harris and Dave began working on the program together, but Steve got too busy. So Dave produced the entire program, and it became another breakthrough in our sound design. The success of the action scenes involving the train and the showdown on the roof pointed the way to even more complicated action scenes.

The Beginning of Kids' Radio

Our love of old-time radio inspired this episode, and Kids' Radio became a story-telling device for many years to come. Though Whit shut the station down at the end of the program, it returned in another form in "The Big Broadcast" (album 9). The station's call letters proved to be a source of consternation over the years. Is it *Kid's* Radio, *Kids'* Radio, or KYDS radio? After the first episodes aired, we learned that KYDS are the call letters of a real radio station in Sacramento, California. Out of respect for that station, we stayed away from those letters and simply announced future programs as "Kids' Radio."

Kids' Radio logo

Character: Eugene
Quote: "To borrow the colloquialism . . ."
Something you may not know about Eugene:
He was nicknamed "Short Stuff" in
high school.

Album 3 — Heroes

Greetings and Salutations! The Creation of Eugene Meltsner

The album *Heroes* marks the debut of one of *Adventures in Odyssey*'s most memorable characters: Eugene Meltsner. Eugene was inspired, in part, by a listener who wrote in to suggest that we create a character like her dad—brilliant, but always losing his keys. We also wanted to create another character for the incredibly talented Will Ryan, who had appeared as a variety of characters in previous episodes. Steve Harris remembers, "My biggest disappointment about losing Officer Harley was the prospect of losing Will. He was too talented and too much fun to work with to let slip away." Just as Katie Leigh brought so much to the character of Connie, Will Ryan inspired much of Eugene's character—even down to playing the ukulele and being very precise about grammar.

Paul McCusker came up with Eugene's name from the masthead of *European Travel and Life* magazine. While searching for a name for this new character, he picked the first name from one column of the magazine's editors and the last name from another column. That Eugene is also Paul's middle name is entirely coincidental—or so he assures us.

When Eugene first walked through the door in "Connie," he was primarily a comical character, but soon proved his mettle in all sorts of situations, from serious and heart-wrenching to poignant and sincere. He also became a perfect foil for Connie, then Tom Riley, then Bernard Walton. Whit's End was never the same after Eugene appeared!

Episode Information

20: Mike Makes Right
Original Air Date: 4/2/88
Writer: Paul McCusker
Sound Designer: Bob Luttrell
Scripture: Proverbs 16:18; Matthew 20:25-28
Themes: Pride, handling power, dealing with bullies
Summary: After putting Odyssey's biggest bully in his place, young Mike Caldwell discovers the dangers that can result from becoming a hero.

29: Rumor Has It
Original Air Date: 6/4/88
Writer: Paul McCusker
Sound Designer: Bob Luttrell
Scripture: James 3:5-12
Theme: The dangers of gossip
Summary: The Kirban family is new to Odyssey, and rumors about them abound. In spite of young Lucy Cunningham's caution, a curious boy named Jack Davis is determined to reveal the truth.

43: Back to School
Original Air Date: 9/10/88
Writer: Paul McCusker
Sound Designer: Bob Luttrell
Scripture: Ecclesiastes 3; Hebrews 13:8
Theme: Making new friends
Summary: When middle school starts in Odyssey, a girl named Leslie has to adjust to changes in friends . . . and friends who change.

46: The Shepherd and the Giant
Original Air Date: 10/29/88
Writer: Phil Lollar
Sound Designer: Dave Arnold
Scripture: 1 Samuel 16–17
Theme: The Bible story of David and Goliath
Summary: Connie tries out Whit's new invention—the Environment Enhancer—and witnesses an encounter between a young man named David and the giant Goliath.

47: A Single Vote
Original Air Date: 11/5/88
Writer: Phil Lollar
Sound Designer: Bob Luttrell
Scripture: Matthew 22:21
Themes: Voting, civic duty, participating in democracy
Summary: Whit tells a story about the difference a single vote can make.

48: Heroes
Original Air Date: 11/12/88
Writer: Paul McCusker
Sound Designer: Dave Arnold
Scripture: Hebrews 7:26
Theme: Hero worship
Summary: Superstar basketball player "Lightning" Livingston opens a sports store in Odyssey, but a scathing exposé reveals more than megafan Jimmy Barclay wanted to know.

49: Thank You, God
Original Air Date: 11/19/88
Writer: Phil Lollar
Sound Designer: Bob Luttrell
Scripture: Romans 8:28; Ephesians 5:20
Themes: Thanksgiving, salvation, making the best of a bad situation
Summary: At Thanksgiving dinner, Whit tells the story of how his stepmother changed his life.

Eugene

50: **Karen**
Original Air Date: 11/26/88
Writer: Paul McCusker
Sound Designer: Dave Arnold
Scripture: Psalm 23
Theme: Dealing with death
Summary: Donna Barclay tries to cope when her best friend, Karen Crosby, becomes ill with cancer.
PARENTAL WARNING:
This story is about the sickness and death of a young girl. While told sensitively, the episode contains subject matter that may be too intense for younger children.

51 and 52: **Connie, I and II**
Original Air Dates: 12/3/88 & 12/10/88
Writer: Paul McCusker
Sound Designers: Bob Luttrell & Dave Arnold
Scripture: John 3:16; Romans 5:8
Theme: Salvation
Summary: While visiting California, Connie encounters some old friends who remind her of how different she was before coming to Whit's End. Meanwhile, Eugene Meltsner starts working at Whit's End and promptly changes how the shop works.

53: **The Sacred Trust**
Original Air Date: 12/17/88
Writer: Phil Lollar
Sound Designer: Bob Luttrell
Scripture: Matthew 5:33-37; 1 John 2:29
Theme: The folly of making promises you can't keep
Summary: Lucy Cunningham and her friend Heather have promised to keep everything they tell each other a secret. But this arrangement gets Lucy in trouble when she has to decide if she should keep the secret.

54: **Peace on Earth**
Original Air Date: 12/24/88
Writer: Paul McCusker
Sound Designer: Dave Arnold
Scripture: Luke 2:1-21; John 14:27; Philippians 4:7
Themes: The peace of God, the reason for the season
Summary: Whit finds himself overcommitted on Christmas eve, and the Barclay family wakes up to a surprise on Christmas morning.

Eugene revamps Whit's End in "Connie"

Actor Will Ryan as Eugene during the late 1980s

Sound Bites with Dave Arnold

"Mike Makes Right" was the first time we asked someone other than John Campbell to compose a music score. John was busy and recommended his good friend Martie Echito, a professional music mixer, for the job. Martie mixed a lot of John's music in those days and was familiar with the style we needed. He did a fabulous job. He went on to write

Eugene by artist Bruce Day in the late 1980s

scores for many future *Odyssey* shows as well, including most of the shows produced in 1989 and 1990. We all felt that the fight-scene music that Martie composed for this show was one of the best cues done to that point. When Martie sent us the score for this show, just for fun he included an *Odyssey* song, complete with lyrics. Unfortunately, we never found a place to use it.

My Take: Paul McCusker

There's a golden rule we've always tried to follow with our radio dramas: "You must remember that your audience is blind, but must never be made to feel that way." A radio fight scene reminds listeners that they can't see what's happening. In "Mike Makes Right" we overcame that problem by having the character of Freddy play ringside announcer in order to provide the blow-by-blow description of the fights.

Cut Scenes
Officer Harley originally appeared in the final scenes of "Rumor Has It." We saved the show from the great-Harley-episodes-purge by replacing him in the final scenes with a "normal" policeman, who was played by Chuck Bolte.

Behind the Scenes: The Shepherd and the Giant
The success of "The Day Independence Came" (album 2) and "Return to the Bible Room" (album 2) inspired us to do more programs where the characters interacted with historical and biblical figures. However, we needed a better way to get them back in time than getting hit on the head with a book as in "The Day Independence Came." So we decided it was time for Whit to invent a machine that would accomplish that.

Our first solution was an invention called the Environment Enhancer. In "The Shepherd and the Giant," Connie used it to learn about a boy named David. Ultimately, the Enhancer seemed limited, so we searched for a new invention—one that appeared within only a few months.

BTS: Rumor Has It
This episode marked the first appearance of Jack Davis and Lucy Cunningham, played by Donald Long and Genesis Mullen. Jack and Lucy were good friends in *Odyssey*. In real life,

Actor Genesis Mullen recording a show as Lucy

Don and Genesis were too. They later fell in love and in 1993 became husband and wife. Though Don played several characters over the years, Genesis's voice didn't change, and she played Lucy until 1996. The characters appeared together (and actually got engaged) many years later in "The Triangled Web" (see album 50).

BTS: A Single Vote
An unusual story inspired us to write about how one vote made the difference in the statehood of Texas. The section of the story about one senator changing his vote and making Texas a state is completely true. The rest of the story, however, is fiction.

Goof Alert!
In "Thank You, God," Whit says that when he was young, his family "moved to Raleigh, North Carolina, where my father . . . taught at Duke University." Duke University is in Durham, not Raleigh.

BTS: Heroes

"Lightning" Livingston's name was originally "Lightning" Johnson, but we changed it because it sounded too similar to the name of famous basketball player Magic Johnson. We also thought "Lightning" Livingston had a better, alliterative ring to it.

Sound Bites with Dave Arnold

The original actor that we recorded for "Lightning" Livingston in "Heroes" didn't work out, so we later recorded Focus employee Bill D'Anjou in the role. Bill's voice was just right—husky, athletic, warm. The show was a real nightmare, though. Having to cut out every one of the original actor's lines from a reel-to-reel tape and then splice Bill's lines in so that they sounded natural was not an easy chore. Then again, I shouldn't complain too much. Bob Luttrell had to replace all of Tom's nephew's lines in "Thank You, God" when the actor we'd chosen for that part didn't work out!

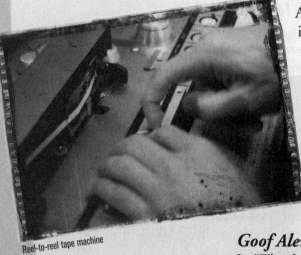

"Lightning" Livingston and Odyssey kids

Reel-to-reel tape machine

Cut Scenes

As Whit, Tom, and others recounted their blessings in "Thank You, God," Tom's wife, Agnes, told a story about how she had broken her leg. While Agnes was in the hospital, a helpful volunteer named Jenny Whittaker attended her. Jenny, Whit's wife, invited Agnes to church, where she met her future husband, Tom. This bit of background story had to be cut for a time, but we included it in a bonus feature on "The Pact" (album 39).

Goof Alert!

In "Thank You, God," Professor Harold Whittaker says, "There are no need for lights." To be grammatically correct he should have said, "There *is* no need for lights." I guess he wasn't a professor of English.

BTS: *Thank You, God*
This episode marked the one-year anniversary of *Adventures in Odyssey* and was aired concurrently on the *Focus on the Family* daily broadcast. It also introduced the name of Connie's mother—June Kendall.

BTS: *Karen*
"Karen" was loosely based on a true incident that happened to a friend of Sage Bolte, daughter of executive producer Chuck Bolte. Coincidentally, Sage played the voice of Karen.

Actor Maggie Malooly, voice of June Kendall

BTS: *Connie*
This episode marked the end of Connie's spiritual journey to becoming a Christian, which had been woven through the first year's shows. It was also the first time we used flashbacks of previous episodes, which enabled us to relive Connie's spiritual journey.

My Take: *Steve Harris*
The salvation scene at the end of "Connie" was one of those magical studio moments. After creating the character of Connie from scratch and putting all those scripted words in her mouth, she felt much more like a close friend than a fictional character. Hearing her part played so well by Katie Leigh, I literally got choked up during the recording session. Since I was there when Connie was "born," I came out of the studio feeling as if a close personal friend of mine had accepted the Lord.

Sound Bites with *Dave Arnold*
In the early days, we would often use dialogue from previous episodes for crowd backgrounds. If you listen closely to the first few scenes of "Peace on Earth," you can hear dialogue from Shirley and Jake in "Nothing to Fear" [album 1], and Leslie and Cindy in "Back to School," to name a few.

Art by fan J. Hanies, age 10

My Take: Paul McCusker

Chuck Bolte came up with the idea of the Barclays being burgled at Christmastime, but I couldn't figure out how to make it into a whole episode. Then I decided to spend part of the episode dealing with Whit and the Christmas hustle and bustle he was experiencing. That's why "Peace on Earth" may feel like it's actually two different stories—the first half focusing on Whit, the second half on the Barclays.

I also thought it would be fun to include everything that evoked Christmas. So you'll hear sleigh bells jingling, music playing, ornaments clinking, firewood burning, punch pouring, and even snow crunching.

This episode also showcased Tom, the one character who could keep Whit accountable when he was making a mistake. This is an element of their friendship we would later play out in episodes like "The Mortal Coil" [album 16] and "The W. E." [album 36].

Sound Bites with Dave Arnold

After I coproduced "The Last Great Adventure of the Summer" [album 2] with Steve Harris, I got my first big postproduction assignment—"The Shepherd and the Giant." It came with many obstacles. To my knowledge, this is the only show that used music from a stock library, a company that sells prerecorded music. It was also a biblical epic, introduced a new invention, and required processing and sound ideas that hadn't been done on the show before. Some of the challenges included chopping off Goliath's head—I used a machete on a cantaloupe—and altering the voice of actor Walker Edmiston to make it sound like the huge giant Goliath. I remember thinking, *If the team likes this show, I'll believe that I can do anything.* After they heard it, they all stood up and graciously applauded. It was the kindest thing they could have done. I felt accepted and confident that I could do the job into the future.

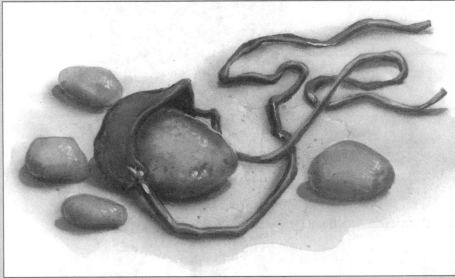

David's slingshot from "The Shepherd and the Giant"

Character: Tom Riley
Quote: "Howdy!"
Something you may not know about Tom:
His father was a country doctor and farmer.

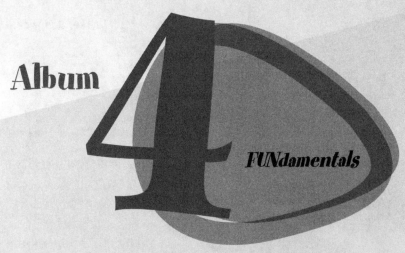

Album 4

FUNdamentals

The FUNdamentals of the Faith

Connie's salvation had been a key storyline throughout the first year, climaxing in the episode "Connie" (album 3). Now that she had become a Christian, we thought a series of 12 episodes that explored the basics of the Christian faith would be appropriate.

We intended to center all the episodes on Connie, but executive producer Chuck Bolte strongly suggested that a more balanced approach was needed—which is why Connie appears in some shows, but other characters are featured in others.

The challenge of capturing the essence of Christianity forced the production team to come up with some rather inventive storytelling. Whit took a "fractured fairy tales" approach. Jimmy Barclay lived out the prodigal son. We saw our first glimpse into Tom Riley's childhood. And a bunch of body parts got together for a story about the importance of church attendance.

FUNdamentals pointed the way for even more innovation to come, such as the development of the Imagination Station.

Episode Information

56: By Faith, Noah
Original Air Date: 1/7/89
Writer: Paul McCusker
Sound Designer: Bob Luttrell
Scripture: Genesis 6–9; Hebrews 11:7; 1 Peter 1:8-9
Themes: Faith, the Bible story of Noah
Summary: Whit tells Jack Davis and Lucy Cunningham a humorous version of the story of Noah.

57: The Prodigal, Jimmy
Original Air Date: 1/14/89
Writer: Phil Lollar
Sound Designer: Dave Arnold
Scripture: Luke 15:11-32; 1 John 1:9
Themes: Repentance, forgiveness, the biblical parable of the prodigal son
Summary: Jimmy Barclay decides that he has had it with the rules around his house and abandons his chores to spend an afternoon at the arcade.

58: A Matter of Obedience
Original Air Date: 1/21/89
Writer: Paul McCusker
Sound Designer: Dave Arnold
Scripture: John 14:15; 1 John 5:3
Theme: Obedience
Summary: A young Tom Riley is given the job of taking medicine to a sick woman—but he has to endure traveling with his pesky sister while remembering the specific instructions for the journey.

59: A Worker Approved
Original Air Date: 1/28/89
Writer: Phil Lollar
Sound Designer: Bob Luttrell
Scripture: 2 Timothy 2:15
Theme: The importance of Bible study
Summary: Middle-schooler Robyn Jacobs is embarrassed when she doesn't know the answer to a simple Bible question. Whit and Connie encourage her to find ways of studying the Bible.

60: And When You Pray . . .
Original Air Date: 2/4/89
Writer: Paul McCusker
Sound Designer: Bob Luttrell
Scripture: Mark 11:24
Theme: Prayer
Summary: When Jimmy Barclay prays for a bike—and gets one—Donna Barclay begins to wonder how prayer works.

61: The Boy Who Didn't Go to Church
Original Air Date: 2/11/89
Writer: Phil Lollar
Sound Designer: Dave Arnold
Scripture: 1 Corinthians 12:12-31
Theme: The importance of regular church attendance
Summary: Jack Davis participates in a unique play about the BODY or the "Brotherhood of Dutiful Youth."

62: Let This Mind Be in You
Original Air Date: 2/18/89
Writer: Paul McCusker
Sound Designer: Dave Arnold
Scripture: 1 Corinthians 11:1; Philippians 2:5
Theme: Being Christlike
Summary: Whit leaves Connie and Eugene in charge of Whit's End for the weekend with the instruction to "run the shop like I would run it."

63: A Good and Faithful Servant
Original Air Date: 2/25/89
Writer: Phil Lollar
Sound Designer: Bob Luttrell
Scripture: Psalm 24:1
Theme: Stewardship
Summary: The Barclays get a budget for the first time, and so Jimmy and Donna must learn how to handle their finances.

64: The Greatest of These
Original Air Date: 3/4/89
Writer: Phil Lollar
Sound Designer: Dave Arnold
Scripture: John 15:12; 1 Corinthians 13
Theme: Unconditional love
Summary: The trouble starts when Robyn Jacobs is paired with slow learner Oscar for the middle school science fair, but the trouble peaks when their model volcano malfunctions.

65: Bad Company
Original Air Date: 3/11/89
Writer: Paul McCusker
Sound Designer: Bob Luttrell
Scripture: Psalm 1:1-4; 2 Corinthians 6:14
Theme: Choosing friends wisely
Summary: Connie attends a Bible study with a questionable leader, while Donna hangs out with a girl who may not be honest.

68: Choices
Original Air Date: 4/1/89
Writer: Phil Lollar
Sound Designer: Dave Arnold
Scripture: Romans 14:23; 2 Timothy 1:7
Theme: Dealing with authority, standing up for your faith
Summary: Lucy is in a dilemma when her science teacher asks her to do a report on evolution.

69: Go Ye Therefore
Original Air Date: 4/8/89
Writer: Paul McCusker
Sound Designer: Bob Luttrell
Scripture: Matthew 28:18-20; Mark 16:15; Luke 24:46-48
Theme: Witnessing, evangelism
Summary: After being inspired to witness like the apostle Peter, Connie decides to evangelize her mother and her friends at school.

Young Tom Riley in "A Matter of Obedience"

Behind the Scenes: By Faith, Noah

In this episode, we presented a Bible story as a humorous skit. Some listeners didn't appreciate the story, so it was a long time before we tried to make a Bible story funny again.

Jimmy with his father, George Barclay

BTS: The Prodigal, Jimmy

We usually record each actor on his or her own microphone and add sound effects later. However, for the final reunion scene between Jimmy and George, actors David Griffin and Chuck Bolte recorded on one microphone and actually hugged each other. We thought this change gave the scene a warmer feel.

Sound Bites with Dave Arnold

I created all the sound effects for the arcade in "The Prodigal, Jimmy" from scratch. No actual arcade games were harmed. After the special noises were created, I had to place the sound effects so they would complement the vocal sounds that David Griffin made in the studio.

Sound Bites

The young actors who played brother and sister Tom and Becky Riley in "A Matter of Obedience" are also siblings in real life, so the bickering between them came naturally. Also, even though Whit doesn't appear in this show, actor Hal Smith does—as the old man in the woods.

My Take: Paul McCusker

"A Matter of Obedience" was inspired in part by C. S. Lewis's *The Silver Chair* and its message about obedience. Tom and Becky's journey in this episode parallels the journey of Jill and Eustace in the Lewis story. Many

years later, sound designer Dave Arnold and I teamed up to work on *The Silver Chair*. As part of the Radio Theatre series, all seven Narnia stories were produced.

BTS: A Worker Approved

Robyn Jacobs makes her first appearance in this episode and was played by Sage Bolte. When Robyn's sister, Melanie, later appeared,

Actor Sage Bolte, voice of Robyn Jacobs

she was played by Sage's sister, Erin. The affable character of Oscar also first appeared in this episode, but he was never given a last name on the radio show. Readers of the *Adventures in Odyssey* novels will know that his last name is Peterson.

BTS: And When You Pray . . .

Here we featured the first and only appearance of Grandpa Barclay, played by Walker Edmiston. Despite the Barclays' many adventures, we only heard from their relatives twice—Grandpa Barclay in this episode and cousin Len in "Castles and Cauldrons" (see album 8).

Connie and Robyn in "A Worker Approved"

BTS: *The Boy Who Didn't Go to Church*

For many years this was the most popular script requested by churches. It makes a lot of sense since the show was about the importance of church attendance.

BTS: *Let This Mind Be in You*

This is one of the earliest programs to feature Connie and Eugene engaging in playful banter. Actors Katie Leigh and Will Ryan had worked together for years on television programs like *The Gummi Bears*. Their chemistry in the studio was so good that it set the course for many future episodes featuring Eugene and Connie's good-natured bickering.

BTS: *A Good and Faithful Servant*

The financial plan George and Mary implemented for their kids was based on a plan devised in Ron and Judy Blue's 1988 book *Money Matters for Parents and Their Kids*. This episode also introduced "Zappazoids," a video game and movie franchise used in many future episodes, including "The Meaning of Sacrifice" (album 11) and "The Mailman Cometh" (album 41).

Donna Barclay in "And When You Pray . . ."

BTS: *Bad Company*

Whit's flulike symptoms recorded in this episode were very real. Actor Hal Smith was ill the day we taped, but, like a true professional, he showed up to work anyway. The original script called for Connie and Whit to talk at Whit's End, but because Hal's voice was so noticeably affected, the team changed the script in the studio to have Connie delivering chicken soup to Whit's house.

Sound Bites with Bob Luttrell

In an early recording session—we can't remember which one—we were taping Chris Anthony's wrap-ups, which included scriptures. One verse was in 1 Kings. Phil Lollar wrote down the reference as it appeared in his Bible—with a Roman numeral "I." And that's the way Chris read it. "In *eye* Kings, it says . . ." Phil and I started laughing, and, of course, teased Chris. "Hey Chris, read your Bible lately? Where in the Bible is *eye* Kings? Could you find that for us?"

Sound Bites with Dave Arnold

One of the many challenges we face when producing *Odyssey* is creating unique sound effects for strange and varied objects that the writers come up with. In the show "The Greatest of These," Robyn Jacobs builds a model volcano with her friend Oscar, who makes it erupt. Well, as you can imagine, no sound effects library on the planet carries the sound of a model volcano erupting. So, I created one. A mix of generators, straws being blown through a bottle of hair gel, glops of mud, and other foley combined to make the right sound. Not many people get paid to make a mess. I always said, "I can't believe I get paid to play." I still can't believe it.

BTS: Go Ye Therefore

Actor Steve Burns plays Connie's friend Robert, paving the way for another character he would play many years later—Connie's love interest, Robert "Mitch" Mitchell.

Album 5

Daring Deeds, Sinister Schemes

Odyssey's Nemesis: The Creation of Dr. Regis Blackgaard

In the early days of *Adventures in Odyssey*, Connie Kendall acted as a foil to Whit as she challenged him about his Christian beliefs. Once Connie became a Christian, the writers looked for new ways to present opposing points of view. They eventually decided that Whit needed a true nemesis, someone who would stand for everything Whit was against.

Our first version of the character was a subtly evil gentleman named Jonathan Dark, whose name and personality were based loosely on Ray Bradbury's Mr. Dark in the 1962 book *Something Wicked This Way Comes*. As writing began on an episode originally titled "The Arcade," the character took on a life of his own and became more overtly evil. He was named Janus Blackgaard (with "Janus" referring to a two-faced Roman god, and "black-guard" being an Old English word for scoundrel or villain). Finally, the name was changed to Regis Blackgaard, and his arrival ("The Nemesis") changed Odyssey in ways no one expected. You can see Regis in the illustration for "The Nemesis" at left: He's the man standing on the hill.

The following episodes chronicle the full story of Dr. Regis Blackgaard:

A Bite of Applesauce	Tom for Mayor	The Return
Eugene's Dilemma	A Name, Not a Number	The Time Has Come
The Nemesis	A Code of Honor	Checkmate
The Battle	Small Fires, Little Pools	Another Chance
One Bad Apple	Angels Unaware	The Last Resort
Waylaid in the Windy City	Gathering Thunder	The Final Conflict
The Homecoming	Moving Targets	Blackgaard's Revenge
A Rathbone of Contention	Hard Losses	

Episode Information

66 and 67: The Imagination Station, I and II
Original Air Dates: 3/18/89 & 3/25/89
Writers: Phil Lollar & Paul McCusker
Sound Designers: Dave Arnold & Bob Luttrell
Scripture: Mark 11:1-10; 14:12–16:13
Theme: The crucifixion and resurrection of Jesus Christ
Summary: With the help of Whit's new invention, young Digger Digwillow travels back in time to witness the death and resurrection of Jesus Christ.

72: An Encounter with Mrs. Hooper
Original Air Date: 5/13/89
Writer: Paul McCusker
Sound Designer: Bob Luttrell
Scripture: Colossians 3:12
Theme: Compassion for the elderly
Summary: On a trip to a nursing home, Donna Barclay meets the stubborn and cantankerous Mary Hooper and learns a lesson about compassion.

73: A Bite of Applesauce
Original Air Date: 5/20/89
Writer: Paul McCusker
Sound Designer: Dave Arnold
Scripture: Genesis 3
Theme: Disobedience
Summary: Against Whit's express orders, Eugene and Connie tamper with a top secret computer room—and the mysterious program Applesauce is unleashed.

74 and 75: Connie Goes to Camp, I and II
Original Air Dates: 6/10/89 & 6/17/89
Writer: Paul McCusker
Sound Designers: Dave Arnold & Bob Luttrell
Scripture: Proverbs 6:16, 18; Philippians 4:8
Themes: Disobedience, setting our minds on Jesus
Summary: Connie writes to her mom about her wild week at Camp What-A-Nut and about a difficult decision involving Lucy Cunningham.

76: Eugene's Dilemma
Original Air Date: 6/24/89
Writer: Paul McCusker
Sound Designer: Bob Luttrell
Scripture: John 15:13, 17
Themes: Doing what's right, responsibility, standing up for your friends
Summary: Eugene starts working at the college computer department with 11-year-old Nicholas Adamsworth and gets caught up in a grade-changing scheme.

77 and 78: The Nemesis, I and II
Original Air Dates: 7/8/89 & 7/15/89
Writer: Phil Lollar
Sound Designers: Bob Luttrell & Dave Arnold
Scripture: Psalm 46:1
Theme: Trusting God in times of trouble
Summary: The mysterious Dr. Regis Blackgaard arrives in town to open an "amusement house" for children. When it seems he won't win the city council's approval to build, he resorts to questionable methods to open his shop.

79: Our Best Vacation Ever
Original Air Date: 7/22/89
Writer: Phil Lollar
Sound Designer: Dave Arnold
Scripture: Ephesians 6:1-4
Theme: Family togetherness
Summary: The Barclays take the best vacation they've ever had—without leaving Odyssey!

83 and 84: The Battle, I and II
Original Air Dates: 8/18/89 & 8/26/89
Writer: Phil Lollar
Sound Designers: Bob Luttrell & Dave Arnold
Scripture: Romans 8:18, 28, 31
Theme: God's protection in times of trouble
Summary: Dr. Blackgaard's quest to steal Applesauce reaches its peak as he and crony Richard Maxwell take control of the computer at Whit's End.

Whit displays the Imagination Station

My Take: Steve Harris

Ever since the series began, we toyed with ways of telling biblical and historical stories. The idea of some sort of time machine had been discussed for months. I love time travel (you tell me there's a movie out on time travel, and I'm there!), but I was worried that it would be too fantastic for *Odyssey*. Then Chuck came up with the idea of imagination . . . it all happens in the imagination. It was like a door opening. I said, "Yeah! Absolutely! That's exactly how it has to be done!"

Clubhouse magazine March 1997

From the book *Strange Journey Back*

Q & A: Sound Designer Dave Arnold

Q: "The Imagination Station" contains the voice of Jesus. Since He wasn't available to record the part in person, how did you find a voice that was suitable?

DA: The team tried for weeks to find the right voice. It was much easier to find actors to play the roles of Peter and Judas, but to find the voice that spoke the universe into existence—that's tough. It was getting close to recording time and all the people they auditioned lacked one element or another. Finally, we resorted to trying out staff members for the role. They asked me to try. Although I wasn't keen, I eventually agreed, and for some strange reason they cast me in the role.

Q: How did you feel playing the part?

DA: Awkward. It's still hard for me to listen to that episode. But it was also an honor.

Use Your Imagination: What Does the Imagination Station Look Like?

The Imagination Station is Whit's greatest invention, though there wasn't always agreement either among the characters or among the team members about what it looks like. Digger described it as "one of those old time machines in the comics," but in "A Prisoner for Christ" (album 6), Nicholas stated that it looks like "a hot water tank lying on its side." In "Elijah" (album 6) Robyn says it is like "the front part of a helicopter, except you can't see inside." Early videos and novels made the Imagination Station look like a phone booth. Newer illustrations show it to be more like a spaceship in design.

However it's been drawn or described, we all agree that the best picture of the Imagination Station is the one you imagine while you're hearing the program.

Behind the Scenes: The Imagination Station

Much of this story is seen from the perspective of a character named John Mark. Biblical tradition teaches that John Mark wrote the gospel of Mark and accompanied Paul on his first missionary journey. Some biblical scholars also believe that John Mark's home was the location of the Last Supper for Jesus and His disciples.

The episodes were also inspired in part by two British works. C. S. Lewis's character of Digory in *The Magician's Nephew* (1955) inspired the name of Digger Digwillow. Dorothy Sayers, known best for her mystery novels, also wrote a radio drama about Jesus called *The Man Born to Be King* (1941–1942), which inspired parts of these episodes.

Jesus and Digger Digwillow

Sound Bites with Bob Luttrell

Creating the sounds for the Imagination Station was a real challenge. We wanted something very different so the Imagination Station wouldn't sound like anything that people had heard before. The metal-on-metal squeaks and shakes when a person steps into the invention and rickety vibrations when it is "landing" were created with a squeaky old typewriter table. We still use this same table in the Foley room for the Imagination Station. (Jonathan Crowe, sound designer, is making the sounds of the Station in this photo.)

Sound designer Jonathan Crowe

My Take: Chuck Bolte

"The Imagination Station" was a significant breakthrough in both its writing and its audio design. During the playback the episode's message and emotional power really hit home for all of the creative team. I remember us sitting there in awe of not only what was created but also of the potential spiritual impact this show could have on kids for generations to come. And, to our humble joy, that potential has been realized.

Goof Alert!

"An Encounter with Mrs. Hooper" features the introduction of Richard Maxwell. For many years, this episode was included in album 6 while all of Richard's schemes with Dr. Blackgaard were included in album 5. This led many listeners to ask questions about the chronology. For the "Gold Audio" release, we fixed this gaffe by including the "Mrs. Hooper" episode back in album 5 where it belonged. (We moved "Heatwave," which was not connected to the Blackgaard saga, to album 6.)

Goof Alert!

Eugene repeatedly calls Connie by her first name in "A Bite of Applesauce." However, for many years after he would insist on calling everyone by his or her last name except in very rare cases.

BTS: An Encounter with Mrs. Hooper

Richard Maxwell (voiced by Nathan Carlson) makes his first appearance in this episode. Richard proved to be a popular character in the series. In fact, almost 20 years later, fans still write in to request his return. Richard mentions his sister, Rachel Woodworth (heard in "Bad Company," album 4), but we never explained why they had different last names. Richard's family is only mentioned again briefly when he returned to Odyssey in "The Homecoming" (album 10). Every appearance from Richard always raises a new question about his loyalties and intentions.

Actor Nathan Carlson, voice of Richard Maxwell, 2004

BTS: A Bite of Applesauce

Careful listeners will find parallels between "A Bite of Applesauce" and Genesis chapter 3. Connie and Eugene seem to play out the same actions as Adam and Eve when they are told not to touch the "forbidden fruit," and they are given the penalty of being "cast out of the garden" when they do. Letters arrived in unprecedented numbers in reaction to Whit's firing Connie and Eugene from Whit's End.

In this episode we first ventured into Whit's association with the Intelligence Agencies, centered on computer programs. Like "The Last Great Adventure of the Summer" (album 2), these elements proved to be very popular with listeners and paved the way for future action-adventure shows.

Sound Bites

In "Connie Goes to Camp," Mrs. Neidlebark is actually played by John Eldredge, the well-known Christian author who was a Focus on the Family employee at the time. John did a Julia Child/Miss Piggy voice for the character. Few know that before becoming a successful writer, John loved acting and even created a one-man show about the Christian abolitionist William Wilberforce.

BTS: Connie Goes to Camp

The story about the goat-man in part one generated criticism from parents who said that it scared their children. Writer Paul McCusker included the story because it was a popular campfire story he'd heard as a youth.

Sound Bites with Dave Arnold

"Connie Goes to Camp" provided some interesting production problems. One was the arrow. I searched high and low for a good comical arrow sound but couldn't find one. I couldn't use the *real* sound an arrow makes because, quite honestly, it's boring. People expect to hear Hollywood arrows. What I mean by that is a more dynamic or overblown sound effect that grabs your attention. So, I created the sound from scratch. For the *whoosh* of the arrow, I blew through a small metal tube, for the impact I threw a pocketknife into wood, and to create the *doiiiing* of the impact, I slapped a coil doorstopper back and forth. Oh yeah, and the goat-man? Bob Luttrell and I did that voice together.

Regis Blackgaard

BTS: Eugene's Dilemma

Early scripts for "Eugene's Dilemma" featured Richard Maxwell demanding that Eugene change his grades in the college computer system. When Eugene refused, Richard planted a computer virus at Whit's End and threatened to deploy it if Eugene didn't change the grades. In the end, Richard's plan was thwarted when he spilled the plan to a couple of FBI agents (who turned out to be friends of Whit!).

Sound Bites

Actor Dick Beals played Nicholas Adamsworth in "Eugene's Dilemma." Far older than he sounds, Dick has provided the voice for many young characters through the years, including Speedy Alka-Seltzer (1951) in television commercials and Davey in the 1960s *Davey and Goliath* television series. Hal Smith played Goliath the dog and Davey's father in that same series.

Actor Dick Beals, voice of Nicholas Adamsworth

My Take: Earl Boen

When I was cast as the voice of Regis, I was coming off a very busy period of acting and had been sick with a bad cold. In that state, it was a lot easier to speak in my lower register, giving a softer and more menacing tone. I also thought that a quiet villain might be more interesting than a loud villain.

Actor Earl Boen, voice of Regis

BTS: Our Best Vacation Ever

This episode introduced the WOD-FAM-CHOC-SOD, one of the signature drinks at Whit's End.

My Take: Chuck Bolte

"Our Best Vacation Ever" is one of my favorite Barclay family shows. The idea was clever and required a lot of vocal work creating "physical" reactions, too—like Mary going down the water slide, the water fight, etc. The ultimate result was a fun show with a very practical message—that you don't need a lot of money to have a fun family vacation. In fact, we even received a number of wonderful responses from people who actually did some of the crazy things we portrayed in that show, like going camping in your living room.

By the way, an interesting behind-the-scenes fact about this show is one of the last-minute changes we made. As the Barclays began their vacation, a playful food fight broke out as they pelted each other with oatmeal, eggs, toast, and even pancakes and syrup. At the last minute, we decided that wasting food—even as a fun family event—wasn't a good message to send to kids. We decided on a water fight instead, which was just as much fun, but not nearly as messy.

Barclay family water fight

BTS: The Battle

The first draft featured Jimmy Barclay as the one hurt in the Imagination Station, not Lucy.

Cut Scenes

As Lucy was racing back to Whit's End to warn friends of the impending disaster in "The Battle," several scenes were recorded with her on the bus going across town. We cut these scenes to pick up the pace of the story.

Goof Alert!

In "The Battle," Whit says that Applesauce was broken into "on two separate occasions." In fact, Blackgaard and Maxwell broke into Applesauce only once. We can't account for the second time Whit is referencing . . . unless some *other* nefarious party was after the program, too!

How Does the Imagination Station Work?

Is the Imagination Station really a time machine, is it a virtual reality simulator like the holodeck on *Star Trek*, or is it simply a machine that stimulates your imagination? It was decided early on that the Imagination Station was not a *true* time machine because time travel isn't possible in our world. We agreed that the Station had to stimulate the imagination somehow. How? We determined that we would never say because too much explanation can work against the freedom of our listeners' imaginations. For example, in the image from "The Imagination Station," we see that Whit and Eugene are peeking into Jesus' empty tomb—we could never explain that!

But that didn't stop us from exploring a few deeper philosophical questions about the machine. One such question was this: Could a person actually feel pain in the Station? We answered that with George Barclay in "Moses: The Passover" (album 14). Next: Could a blind person imagine that he could see, or might a paralyzed person imagine he could walk? That was answered in "A Touch of Healing" (album 24). Could someone from history actually step out of the Imagination Station and into the present? We got to see just that in "Isaac the Chivalrous" (album 13). Those questions and more continue to fuel the fun we have with Whit's greatest invention.

From "The Imagination Station"

Album

Mission: Accomplished

The Treasure of Le Monde!

"The Treasure of Le Monde!" first appeared in 1990 as a two-part story in *Focus on the Family Clubhouse* magazine. It was later loosely adapted into the *Odyssey* video *The Caves of Qumran.*

In the illustration on the left, Whit, Connie, and Robyn Jacobs have just discovered a secret room with an old pipe organ in the attic at Whit's End. This is one of the best aspects of Whit's End—it has never been fully explored. This isn't the only program where hidden rooms or passageways have been revealed. In "The Case of the Secret Room" (album 2) Whit discovered a hidden room in the basement. In "A Bite of Applesauce" (album 5), we learned of a secret computer control room in Whit's office, and in "Hold Up!" (album 12), we explored a servant staircase from the kitchen to Whit's office. Additionally, Jack Davis discovered a tunnel leading from the basement in "The Underground Railroad" (album 24). The great thing is that even Whit didn't know about some of these secret places. Think of Whit's End like the wardrobe leading to Narnia . . . you never know what you'll find behind a door!

Episode Information

28: The Price of Freedom
Original Air Date: 5/28/88
Writer: Phil Lollar
Sound Designer: Bob Luttrell
Scripture: Ecclesiastes 3:1, 8
Themes: God's control, patriotism, the price of freedom
Summary: A teacher maligns 10-year-old Kirk McGinty's war hero father and the war he fought in. Kirk's mother and Whit and step in to set things straight.

80: A Prisoner for Christ
Original Air Date: 7/29/89
Writer: Phil Lollar
Sound Designer: Bob Luttrell
Scripture: The book of Philemon
Themes: The Bible story of Onesimus, forgiveness
Summary: Whit sends Nicholas Adamsworth on a journey to meet an escaped slave named Onesimus and an apostle named Paul.

81: Good Business
Original Air Date: 8/5/89
Writer: Paul McCusker
Sound Designer: Dave Arnold
Scripture: 2 Thessalonians 3:6-12
Themes: Honesty, a worker is worth his or her wages
Summary: Robyn Jacobs thinks she can earn money the "easy" way by starting her own business, but she soon learns it's not so easy after all.

82: Heatwave
Original Air Date: 8/12/89
Writer: Paul McCusker
Sound Designer: Bob Luttrell
Scripture: Romans 12:2
Theme: Using your imagination properly
Summary: Bored during a summer heatwave, Jack Davis turns into a private detective to uncover the mystery of an oddball kid with an armload of lumber.

87 and 88: Elijah, I and II
Original Air Dates: 9/30/89 & 10/7/89
Writer: Paul McCusker
Sound Designers: Bob Luttrell & Dave Arnold
Scripture: 1 Kings 17:1–19:2
Themes: Gods' sovereignty, the Bible story of Elijah, Queen Jezebel, and King Ahab
Summary: Robyn and Jack journey in the Imagination Station to meet Queen Jezebel, King Ahab, and a powerful prophet named Elijah.

89: That's Not Fair
Original Air Date: 10/14/89
Writer: Phil Lollar
Sound Designer: Bob Luttrell
Scripture: Romans 6:23
Themes: Fairness, God's grace
Summary: Connie, Oscar, and Robyn complain to Whit about how they are being treated unfairly. Whit pulls some strings to show them what it's like to be treated with absolute fairness.

90: But, You Promised
Original Air Date: 10/21/89
Writers: Diane Dalbey & Phil Lollar
Sound Designer: Dave Arnold
Scripture: Colossians 3:9
Theme: The consequences of lying
Summary: Robyn leaves her bike unlocked at the mall, and it is stolen. She lies to her parents about her carelessness to keep from getting into trouble.

91: A Mission for Jimmy
Original Air Date: 10/28/89
Writer: Paul McCusker
Sound Designer: Bob Luttrell
Scripture: Romans 10:14-15
Theme: Supporting missionaries
Summary: Jimmy Barclay is annoyed when he's put in charge of raising money for church missions. His attitude changes after he has a dream that gives him a glimpse of what it's like to be a missionary in a foreign country.

92: The Ill-Gotten Deed
Original Air Date: 11/4/89
Writer: Phil Lollar
Sound Designer: Dave Arnold
Scripture: Romans 12:19-21
Themes: The folly of revenge, Odyssey's history
Summary: Middle-schooler Calvin is fed up with his brother, so Whit tells him the story of another pair of brothers—Horace and Grover McAlister, who fought over land their father left for them in his will.

93: Rescue from Manatugo Point
Original Air Date: 11/11/89
Writer: Paul McCusker
Sound Designer: Dave Arnold
Scripture: Psalm 90:12; Psalm 39:4; 2 Peter 3:8
Theme: God holds the future
Summary: A mysterious letter reminds Whit of a remarkable adventure he had in the South Pacific during World War II.

94: Operation: Dig-Out
Original Air Date: 11/18/89
Writer: Paul McCusker
Sound Designer: Bob Luttrell
Scripture: Isaiah 40:28-31; Galatians 6:7-10
Themes: Spreading the gospel, doing good
Summary: An elderly British gentleman named Reginald Duffield arrives in Odyssey to keep a promise he made to Whit many years ago after a World War II battle.

102: The Treasure of Le Monde!
Original Air Date: 2/3/90
Writer: Phil Lollar
Sound Designer: Bob Luttrell
Scripture: Proverbs 28:25
Theme: Greed
Summary: Robyn and Connie find a hidden attic at Whit's End and stumble upon a forgotten mystery involving an old pipe organ, a greedy professor, and "the greatest treasure."

The Treasure of Le Monde!

Whit's End

Tinkering with the Imagination Station

The following are modifications to Whit's greatest invention.

Episode	Change or Modification
Elijah	A second door is added, accommodating two people in the Station at the same time.
Lincoln	Whit creates a remote control, enabling users to fast-forward through the adventure.
Saint Paul: The Man from Tarsus	Participants become characters in the adventure, automatically dressed in appropriate clothing. Two people can enter the adventure from the control room.
The American Revelation	An entirely new machine is built, modified to hold up to 10 people. A scanning chamber is added, enabling the user to scan a book or painting.
The Imagination Station, Revisited	Another new machine is built, using passageways and doors to give travelers a variety of adventures.

Behind the Scenes: The Price of Freedom

The War Memorial, created in this episode, appears in several later episodes including "East Winds, Raining" (album 12) and "Gathering Thunder" (album 25). This show, aired for Memorial Day 1988, received the most positive response of any shows in our first year. Many war veterans wrote in to tell us how the episode affected them and to thank us for remembering their sacrifice.

Sound Bites with Bob Luttrell

The guys loved to tease me about how I said the line "'He's motion-n-n-ing us forward'" in the dream sequence in "'The Price of Freedom.'" It was all good-natured . . . at least I think it was.

BTS: Good Business

Dale Jacobs (voiced by *Odyssey* writer/director Phil Lollar) makes his first appearance in this episode. Dale would later be identified as the editor of *The Odyssey Times*, the town newspaper.

BTS: Elijah

"Elijah" marked the first appearance of actor Fabio Stephens as Benjamin. He would later play the mischievous Curt Stevens.

My Take: Paul McCusker

The intention of "Good Business" was to play up Robyn's desire to get money without working for it. Yet, all of her efforts to get out of working to make money actually created more work for her. Having learned an important lesson, she gives up her start-up business and lets her workers have all the money they

The Odyssey Times

THE ONLY ONE WE'VE GOT | Vol. 1 No. 3 | ALWAYS (Free)

"Adventures in Odyssey": Captured In Print

by Campbell Freed
Times Staff Writer

First, the citizens of Odyssey listened in their lives were chronicled in dramatic episodes on cassettes featuring John Avery Whittaker (better known as Whit). Then came the animated videos. Now, Whit and his friends at the ever-popular "discovery emporium" called Whit's End can be found in a new series of novels just released by Focus on the Family Publishing.

Written by "Adventures in Odyssey" scriptwriter Paul McCusker, these generously illustrated books contain original new stories about Mark Prescott, a young boy who moves to Odyssey after his parents separate. Hurt and lonely, Mark faces the difficulty of making new friends, feeling accepted and coping with the many changes in his life. It isn't easy for him and he has to learn some difficult lessons as he encounters Whit's Imagination Station, an unwanted "girlfriend," a "whodunit" mystery, a mysterious gang and a secret cave.

"I was quite impressed," John Whittaker said after reading the books. "They're a lot of fun. And I think young people will relate to

figure out how the author knew I once kept the Imagination Station in the basement."

Tom Riley, who is mentioned in the first novel, said that he was particularly pleased with the book's sensitive handling of Mark's broken home. "It's about time somebody dealt honestly with that sort of problem in a book for young people," he said. He added that "they're realistic, but the author never loses sight of a basic Christian viewpoint."

"I like the pictures, too!" one younger reader was overheard saying. Well, actually, it was my youngest daughter.

Best read in order, the first three books in the series are: *A Strange Journey Back*, *High Flyer With a Flat Tire* and *The Secret Cave of Robinwood*. Look for them at your local Christian bookstore and at Frapp's Books & Dry Cleaning, with a new location now open at Trickle Lake Mall.

Mark and his problems. They'll also find a good dose of hope weaving throughout, which is rare in a lot of books they read now. Though I can't

Disciplinary Action Taken At Camp

Increase in Pranks and Rule-Breaking at Camp What-A-Nut

There has been an increase in disobedience, misconduct and insubordination at this year's Camp What-A-Nut, according to a report issued by the camp's board of directors.

"We're alarmed by what appears to be an upward increase of an alarming trend," said Joseph LaGard, director of the camp. "When one compares this year's figures with last year's, it's very clear what's happening. Last year, we only had to send one child home early for blatant disobedience of camp rules. This year we had to send three children home early."

When asked what sort of rules were being flagrantly broken, LaGard

explained that the most common problem was children breaking out of their cabins after "lights out" each night. "We also had one instance of theft this year, which is unprecedented. And one child was caught reading a book behind the equipment shed when he should have been at archery practice."

LaGard attributes these problems to the overall decline of moral values in society and a very liberal attitude towards child discipline by most parents.

Weather:

Today we can expect more seasonal weather with a high pressure system bringing the expected unpleasantness with just the right ... here's a chance of rain in some parts of the city, but not enough to worry about if you dress properly. As the day progresses, temperatures will drop suddenly in both Celsius and Fahrenheit bringing surprising wind.

Rathbone Wrecks

Rodney Rathbone, 15, received a broken collar bone when the car he was driving careened off the road and smashed into a sign post in the early hours of Sunday morning.

Allegedly driving without a driver's license, Rathbone was heading south on Walker Street in his father's car when he lost control of the vehicle and hit the stop sign at the intersection of Walker and Edmonton. Rathbone broke his collar bone when he collided with the steering wheel on impact.

Police spokesmen explained that the accident occurred when Rathbone took his eyes off the road in an effort to change stations on the radio.

Rathbone denied this, claiming that he wasn't listening to the radio but was trying to fix the cassette tape in the player. "It was eating my tape," he said. "It was one of my favorites, too."

Police will charge Rathbone with driving without a license and are expected to fine him for the cost of damages to the stop sign.

Bart Rathbone, the victim's father, reported that "Rodney is in stable condition ... for now."

Evolution Debate

Students from McCallum Junior High and Odyssey High School will participate in a debate over the merits of the Theory of Evolution vs Creationism at the Odyssey High School gymnasium during the half-time break in the wrestling championships next Tuesday night.

Sponsored by the Right to Know Campaign in both schools, the debate will center on whether mankind was created by God or evolved from apes, with both sides planning to bring conclusive proof for their arguments.

The concessions stands in the gymnasium will be open during half-time for those who don't wish to watch the debates.

An issue of Dale Jacobs's *The Odyssey Times*

generated. Some listeners wrote to complain that the episode seemed to endorse socialism at the expense of a capitalistic spirit. We agreed that the point of the story could be clearer, so we rerecorded several scenes where Robyn's dad explains what was wrong with her attitude, if not her actions.

Goof Alert!

Instead of using the red button to start the Imagination Station adventure in "Elijah," Jack Davis is told to push "the flashing white one." Writer Paul McCusker explained that it was part of Whit's changes to his invention, but future shows restored the button to red. Also, the prophet Obadiah eats

rabbit meat, a no-no because the meat was considered unclean and forbidden under Old Testament law.

BTS: That's Not Fair

Focus employee Dave Lipson played Fred Zachary, a teacher with a particularly bad speech habit (he repeatedly used the phrase "Uh . . . whatchacall" as sentence filler). Some listeners didn't think he was a good role model as a teacher and wrote to complain. So the team avoided using the character in future episodes. Writer Paul McCusker also explained that Zachary's verbal hiccup was based on the speech patterns of Paul's wedding photographer.

BTS: But, You Promised

The first draft of this episode was about Robyn making promises she couldn't keep, hence the title. Subsequent drafts changed the focus to dishonesty. Unfortunately, the title remained and actually has nothing to do with the episode. For this reason, and others, the show was held back from release for many years.

BTS: A Mission for Jimmy

The original idea for "A Mission for Jimmy" centered on a dream Whit had about the difficulties of being a missionary. We changed the main character to Jimmy to present a kid's perspective on being a missionary.

Sound Bites with Bob Luttrell

For "A Mission for Jimmy," we couldn't find the sound effects of a jeep on a bumpy road. None of us knew anyone who had a jeep, and there were no bumpy roads in the concrete jungle of Los Angeles. So Dave Arnold and I went to an unpaved field in the back of the Focus on the Family parking lot, disconnected two spark plugs from my 1987 Chevy Sprint, and raced the car over the ruts and through the weeds. Dave Arnold hung out of the passenger window and held the microphone down near the wheels as I drove purposefully over potholes and brush. The old car was never the same after that day, but hey—we got the right sound effects!

My Take: Paul McCusker

After I finished "A Mission for Jimmy," I handed the script to the staff of *Enfoque a la Familia*, the Spanish language broadcast at Focus. They translated the lines into Spanish and helped with our casting. This gave the episode a more authentic feel.

Sound Bites

Katie Leigh voices the young boy Malanga in "Rescue from Manatugo Point." Katie also used a similar tone when she overdubbed the voice of the young maharaja in the film *Indiana Jones and the Temple of Doom* (1984).

BTS: Operation: Dig-Out

Whit's long-lost friend's name is Reginald Duffield. Duffield is the maiden name of Paul McCusker's wife, Elizabeth. Elizabeth, a native of Great Britain, made sure that the British accents in the show were kept authentic.

Sound Bites with Dave Arnold

My biggest studio error came during the recording of "Rescue from Manatugo Point." We recorded Hal Smith's narration bits separately from the drama sections. I was the only person in the control room, and Phil Lollar was in the studio with Hal. Forty minutes into the recording, I looked back at the tape deck (we recorded everything on analog tape at the time), and saw that I hadn't enabled the record heads. A bead of sweat instantly came across my brow. If the record heads aren't enabled, all that happens is that the reels turn, but nothing is actually recorded. I asked Hal and Phil to hold on. Praying that a miracle occurred and somehow the audio magically got onto the tape, I rewound the reel and listened. Nothing. The entire 40-minute session had been for naught. Beet red from embarrassment, I had to confess to the guys about what happened. Although I could see frustration on Hal's face, he just started over and never said one unkind word.

Clubhouse magazine: "The Treasure of Le Monde," 1990

Wonderworld Tree House

"Heatwave" introduces listeners to the Wonderworld tree house, a prominent location in later shows such as "Someone to Watch over Me" (album 10), "Wonderworld" (album 15), and "Grand Opening" (album 37). Wonderworld was not the only tree house built in Odyssey. Years later, Wooton built one in his backyard. Also in this show, we find the name of another book that Whit wrote: *A Guide to Using Your Imagination*.

Album

7

On Thin Ice

Named by You!

This collection was the only one named by our fans. We held a contest on WhitsEnd.org, the official *Adventures in Odyssey* Web site, to come up with a name to match the picture (see left). We received more than 1,300 entries, with finalists including "There's Always a Catch" and "Winter Wonderland." Bethany from Spicer, Minnesota, submitted the winning title, "On Thin Ice." Congratulations (again) to her!

The image depicts a scene from the episode "Ice Fishing." Phil Lollar started working on that script at the same time that Paul McCusker was working on "Scattered Seeds." Paul remembers: "Somewhere along the line we realized that we were both stuck on our shows. I discovered that Phil had some good ideas for how to finish 'Scattered Seeds,' and I had some ideas for finishing 'Ice Fishing.' So we swapped scripts. When it came time to do their credits, we decided to blend Phil's mother's maiden name, Campbell, and my mother's maiden name, Freed. And so Campbell Freed became a new writer for *Odyssey*."

Episode Information

Art by fan Wilson C., age 9

86: Isaac the Insecure
Original Air Date: 9/23/89
Writer: Paul McCusker
Sound Designer: Bob Luttrell
Scripture: Psalm 139:14; Luke 16:15
Theme: Overcoming insecurity
Summary: Young Isaac Morton doubts himself when he is assigned to do a report with the much more popular Jack Davis.

95: The Very Best of Friends
Original Air Date: 12/2/89
Writer: Phil Lollar
Sound Designer: Dave Arnold
Scripture: 1 Corinthians 15:51-57
Themes: Anger, dealing with death
Summary: On the anniversary of her friend Karen's death, Donna Barclay struggles over the loss of her close friend.

96: The Reluctant Rival
Original Air Date: 12/9/89
Writer: Paul McCusker
Sound Designer: Bob Luttrell
Scripture: Matthew 5:43-48; Philippians 2:3-4
Theme: Treating others better than yourself
Summary: Whit's grandchildren, Monty and Jenny, arrive in Odyssey for Christmas. An orchestra leader discovers Jenny's exceptional musical ability, which leads to Jenny's rivalry with another musician.

97: Monty's Christmas
Original Air Date: 12/16/89
Writer: Paul McCusker
Sound Designer: Dave Arnold
Scripture: Malachi 2:16
Themes: The effects of divorce on kids, the importance of strong families
Summary: The Whittaker household tries to get into the holiday spirit, but 10-year-old Monty has trouble overcoming his heartache about his parents' divorce.

98: The Visitors
Original Air Date: 12/23/89
Writer: Phil Lollar
Sound Designer: Bob Luttrell
Scripture: Matthew 25:31-46; Luke 2:1-7; Ephesians 2:10
Themes: Charity, sacrifice
Summary: The Barclay family's Christmas celebration is disrupted by the arrival of three unexpected "guests" in their back shed.

99: The Barclay Family Ski Vacation
Original Air Date: 12/30/89
Writer: Jeff Parker
Sound Designer: Dave Arnold
Scripture: Luke 1:17
Theme: Family relations and togetherness
Summary: While on a ski vacation with her family, Donna gets a crush on her ski instructor.

100: Ice Fishing
Original Air Date: 1/20/90
Writer: Campbell Freed
Sound Designer: Bob Luttrell
Scripture: Psalm 139:13-14
Themes: Self-esteem, you are unique
Summary: Monty feels as if he's in competition with his gifted sister, Jenny, so Whit, Tom Riley, and Eugene take him on an ice fishing trip to Summit Lake.

101: Scattered Seeds

Original Air Date: 1/27/90
Writer: Campbell Freed
Sound Designer: Dave Arnold
Scripture: Matthew 13:1-23
Theme: The parable of the sower
Summary: Connie deals with nothing but trouble when she tries to direct a church play called "Scattered Seeds."

103: Front Page News

Original Air Date: 2/10/90
Writer: Paul McCusker
Sound Designer: Dave Arnold
Scripture: Acts 5:1-11
Theme: Escaping responsibility
Summary: Middle-schooler Curt Stevens ropes Oscar into a scheme to get out of gym class by joining the school newspaper. Their first assignment? Interview the gym teacher!

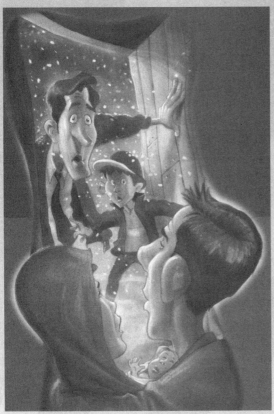

George and Jimmy Barclay plus three from "The Visitors"

104 and 105: Lincoln, I and II

Original Air Dates: 2/17/90 & 2/24/90
Writer: Phil Lollar
Sound Designers: Bob Luttrell & Dave Arnold
Scripture: Romans 13:1-5
Themes: Civil War history, Abraham Lincoln
Summary: Jimmy Barclay takes an Imagination Station adventure to see President Lincoln and the end of the Civil War.

108: Isaac the Courageous

Original Air Date: 3/17/90
Writer: Phil Lollar
Sound Designer: Bob Luttrell
Scripture: Joshua 1:6-7, 9; John 15:13
Theme: Courage
Summary: Isaac Morton is determined to join teenage bully Rodney Rathbone's gang—the Bones of Rath—to prove his courage.

128: One Bad Apple

Original Air Date: 9/15/90
Writer: Paul McCusker
Sound Designer: Bob Luttrell
Scripture: Genesis 1; 2:15
Theme: Taking care of the environment
Summary: Tom Riley's apples are causing people to get sick. While trying to find out why, he discovers a chemical company is polluting his land.

132: Thanksgiving at Home

Original Air Date: 11/17/90
Writer: Paul McCusker
Sound Designer: Bob Luttrell
Scripture: 1 Chronicles 16:8
Themes: Thanksgiving holiday, being thankful
Summary: The Barclay family's Thanksgiving holiday takes an unexpected turn when the flu hits their home, and Donna and Jimmy decide to fix dinner all by themselves.

Actor Parley Baer, voice of Reginald Duffield

Focus on the Family magazine December 1995

Behind the Scenes: The Very Best of Friends

This episode contains the last appearance of Reginald Duffield (voiced by Parley Baer). We had originally intended on using him as an ongoing character, but we realized that we were stretched to give time to the characters we'd already established (including two other wise elderly gentlemen). We also had other characters for Parley to play, including Connie's Uncle Joe.

BTS: Isaac the Insecure

Isaac Morton is introduced, and this episode started a miniseries of episodes bearing his name in the titles.

Goof Alert!

In "The Reluctant Rival," Whit tells Monty that he'll be staying in "Uncle Jerry's old room." But in "A Member of the Family" (album 1), Whit says that the Whittaker family moved to Odyssey after Jerry died.

Additionally, "The Reluctant Rival" was the first time that we'd seen or heard anything about Whit's daughter and grandchildren since "A Member of the Family." We saw Whit being uncharacteristically defensive as he dealt with Jana's emotional troubles.

Sound Bites

Tiffany Brissette plays Jenny Whittaker-Dowd. Television fans may know her as a robot on the science fiction television series *Small Wonder* (1985–1989).

BTS: Monty's Christmas

Whit tells Monty that he finished an Imagination Station program on Jesus' birth. Connie and Eugene experience that adventure the next year in "Back to Bethlehem" (album 10).

Eugene in "Ice Fishing"

BTS: The Visitors

This episode was translated into Spanish and aired on *Enfoque a la Familia*. It was also adapted into story form and published in the December 1995 edition of *Focus on the Family* magazine (illustration at left).

BTS: The Barclay Family Ski Vacation

This story was written by Jeff Parker, who also plays the role of Robb, the object of Donna's crush.

Sound Bites with Dave Arnold

I'll never forget the trouble I had creating the sound of skiing in the middle of a Southern Californian heat wave. Nevertheless, the show must go on, so for "The Barclay Family Ski Vacation," I borrowed a set of skis, then created my own snow by shaving ice cubes over a cheese grater. It took a long time, and the "snow" melted pretty fast in our sound-effects room, but I made it work the best I could, given the circumstances.

BTS: Ice Fishing

"Ice Fishing" helped establish the course of Eugene and Tom's adversarial yet friendly relationship, which played out in future shows.

Why Do Kids Leave Odyssey?

After "Scattered Seeds," Whit's grandchildren disappeared and were never heard from again. We often get requests for their return. However, listeners may not understand one of the strange realities we live with in *Odyssey*: changing voices. Connie Kendall has aged only a few years since *Adventures in Odyssey* began. She started out at 15 in 1987, and graduated high school in 1998, but that's because actor Katie Leigh, who is *not* a teenager, still sounds the same now as she did when she first appeared. But our other kid characters are usually played by actors who are the same age as their characters. They grow up and their voices change. We soon realized that if those original characters came back, their voices would sound *older* than Connie's and highlight the weirdness of our world. So, in general, when actors begin to sound too old for our audience, we simply let them fade away from the show or gave them a send-off, as we did with the Barclays. And *that's* why the Whittaker-Dowd children have not been heard from.

Sound Bites

Eugene's ukulele was first featured in "Scattered Seeds." Will Ryan, an accomplished player, often brought his uke to the studio to play old-fashioned ditties with Walker and Hal between takes. It made sense to add the ukulele to Eugene's character. Eugene's musical career took on a life of its own and eventually led to several musical albums—*Eugene Sings!*

Ukulele Jam! Eugene's Music in Odyssey

Episode	Songs
Scattered Seeds	Oh! Susanna
A Day in the Life	Sumer Is Icumen In
Caroling, Caroling	Seasonal Felicitations
Third Degree	The Blue Danube
B-TV: Thanks	I'm Glad I'm Me (sung by Harlow Doyle)
New Year's Eve, Live!	Out with the Old Year; Annum Novum
B-TV: Redeeming the Season	The Holly and the Ivy; O Tannenbaum; Silent Night
Odyssey Sings!	Red River Valley; Have You Ever Been to Odyssey?

BTS: Front Page News

In this episode, we introduced the character of Curt Stevens, played by Fabio Stephens. (Fabio previously played Calvin in "The Ill-Gotten Deed," album 6). Unlike Jack, who was recklessly mischievous, Curt was mischievous in a conniving way. Curt always looked for the easy way out, which usually meant he had to work twice as hard.

BTS: Lincoln

"Lincoln" was the first time the Imagination Station was used for a historical adventure rather than a biblical one. Walker Edmiston did an impression of actor Raymond Massey (1896–1983) for the voice of Abraham Lincoln.

BTS: One Bad Apple

This story was originally written with Tom and Bernard investigating Edgebiter Chemical. However, when actor Dave Madden wasn't available, Curt Stevens was substituted in at the last minute. This episode was controversial for some listeners who thought it blamed big business for the world's environmental problems, which wasn't our intent. However, due to these concerns, the episode was unreleased for many years. This was unfortunate because the Edgebiter scandal figured prominently in the later episode "Tom for Mayor" (album 22). When people heard that show without first hearing "One Bad Apple," they missed much of the back story.

Art from the cover of *Eugene Sings!*

Odyssey's Resident Bully— Rodney Rathbone

Rodney Rathbone and the Bones of Rath made their first appearances in "Isaac the Courageous." Rodney is voiced by Steve Burns, who (like Katie Leigh) sounds much younger than he is. For this reason, Rodney has stayed in his teens for many, many years.

Actor Steve Burns recalls: "Chuck Bolte brought me in to do the voice of a kid named Howie in 'The Prodigal, Jimmy' [album 4]. I tried a voice that I imagined for a little gang kid. The team liked the voice, but Howie never made another appearance. Almost a year later, they brought me back to do the same voice for another character—Rodney Rathbone. And now I've been doing Rodney for 18 years. It kind of painted me into a corner because no matter what other voices I used, Rodney always got in somehow."

Actor Steve Burns, voice of Rodney Rathbone

Character:
Bernard Walton
Quote: "Paint me red all over and send me to a four-alarm fire, sirens blazin'!" Something you may not know about Bernard: His siblings' names are Bettina, Beulah, Benjamin, Boris, and Bosco.

Album 8

Beyond Expectations

"Stuff Me with Feathers and Call Me a Pillow!": The Introduction of Bernard Walton

The episode "By Any Other Name" introduced everyone's favorite window washer: Bernard Walton. Actor Dave Madden's portrayal of Bernard was heavily influenced by the Reuben Kincaid character he played on the television show *The Partridge Family* . . . and by Dave's own personality. Many of Bernard's lines (such as "I'd have to get better to die") were actual Dave Madden quotes.

We originally imagined the Bernard character as an Eeyore-type who always mumbled under-the-breath lines. Through Dave's vocal performance, Bernard became one of our most endearing characters and soon revealed that there was real heart beneath all his complaining.

The first episode that showed a quirky side of Bernard was "Suspicious Minds." He got some rather malicious enjoyment out of Eugene and Connie's silliness as they tried to catch the "criminal." Dave Madden ad-libbed Bernard's continual chuckle through the last scene. It broadened the character of Bernard even further. When told that he made the script even better because of his performance, Dave Madden replied, "Well, that's the job of a good actor. If all we do is read what's on the page, you could get anybody!"

Episode Information

106: By Any Other Name
Original Air Date: 3/3/90
Writer: Paul McCusker
Sound Designer: Bob Luttrell
Scripture: Proverbs 11:3
Theme: Calling things what they are
Summary: Curt Stevens runs for student council and makes Lucy Cunningham his campaign manager. The trouble starts when he makes all sorts of impossible promises in order to get the votes.

107: Bad Luck
Original Air Date: 3/10/90
Writer: Paul McCusker
Sound Designer: Dave Arnold
Scripture: Exodus 20:3
Theme: Superstitions
Summary: Robyn Jacobs thinks she's got bad luck after she throws away a chain letter.

110: A . . . Is for Attitude
Original Air Date: 4/14/90
Writer: Phil Lollar
Sound Designer: Bob Luttrell
Scripture: Proverbs 3:5-6
Themes: Positive thinking, trusting God
Summary: Connie starts to think that simply having a positive attitude can solve all of life's problems.

111: First Love
Original Air Date: 4/21/90
Writer: Paul McCusker
Sound Designer: Dave Arnold
Scripture: 2 Corinthians 6:14
Theme: Being unequally yoked
Summary: Connie falls in love for the first time with a guy named Jeff Lewis, who turns out to be a non-Christian.
PARENTAL WARNING:
This is a story about whether it's right or wrong to date a non-Christian. Although handled delicately, the subject matter may be too mature for younger listeners.

112: Curious, Isn't It?
Original Air Date: 4/28/90
Writer: Phil Lollar
Sound Designer: Bob Luttrell
Scripture: 1 Thessalonians 4:11
Theme: Minding our own business
Summary: Friends Ben and Esther overhear a conversation and come to believe that Mr. Whittaker is getting married.

113: Suspicious Minds
Original Air Date: 5/5/90
Writer: Paul McCusker
Sound Designer: Dave Arnold
Scripture: Isaiah 30:15
Themes: Trusting each other, not jumping to conclusions
Summary: Money mysteriously disappears from the cash register at Whit's End, and Connie and Eugene are determined to find the perpetrator.

115: An Act of Mercy
Original Air Date: 6/16/90
Writer: Paul McCusker
Sound Designer: Dave Arnold
Scripture: Matthew 18:21-35
Theme: The parable of the unmerciful servant
Summary: Tom Riley forgives Rodney Rathbone for trying to steal his apples, but when given a chance to forgive someone else, Rodney doesn't pass on the act of mercy.

120: Pranks for the Memories

Original Air Date: 7/21/90
Writer: Phil Lollar
Sound Designer: Dave Arnold
Scripture: Philippians 2:3-4
Theme: Pranks
Summary: Curt Stevens pulls a series of practical jokes, each more elaborate than the last.

121: Missing Person

Original Air Date: 7/28/90
Writer: Paul McCusker
Sound Designer: Dave Arnold
Scripture: Luke 15:11-32
Theme: You can't run away from your problems.
Summary: Rodney Rathbone is missing, and the crew at Whit's End tries to find him. Is it a case of kidnapping, or is he a runaway?

122 and 123: Castles and Cauldrons, I and II

Original Air Date: 8/4/90 & 8/11/90
Writer: Paul McCusker
Sound Designers: Bob Luttrell & Dave Arnold
Scripture: Deuteronomy 18:10-13
Themes: The dangers of fantasy role-playing games, Satan worship, the occult
Summary: Jimmy Barclay's cousin Len comes for a visit, and brings along a very mysterious—and dangerous—game.
PARENTAL WARNING:
This is a story about fantasy role-playing games and how they can lure their participants into satanic activity. It is very intense in spots and not meant for listeners under 10 years of age. Parents should listen along with their older children.

124: The Winning Edge

Original Air Date: 8/18/90
Writer: Phil Lollar
Sound Designer: Dave Arnold
Scripture: Romans 15:2
Theme: Competitiveness
Summary: When Bart Rathbone starts coaching a girls' softball team, some of the players take the game a little too seriously.

125: All's Well with Boswell

Original Air Date: 8/25/90
Writer: Phil Lollar
Sound Designer: Bob Luttrell
Scripture: Luke 16:10-12
Theme: Responsibility
Summary: Robyn gets her first real baby-sitting job, but it turns out to be a cat named Boswell.

138: The Adventure of the Adventure

Original Air Date: 12/29/90
Writer: Paul McCusker
Sound Designer: Bob Luttrell
Theme: The story of *Adventures in Odyssey*
Summary: A history of the characters of *Adventures in Odyssey*

Eugene in "Suspicious Minds"

Behind the Scenes: Bad Luck

The first time that we heard from Bernard's wife, Maude, was in this episode. Maude was played by *Odyssey*'s announcer Chris Anthony. We didn't hear from Maude again until years later in "Silent Night" (album 45) and "Prequels of Love" (album 48).

BTS: A . . . Is for Attitude

This episode features an appearance by Cheryl McCormick, Connie's friend who we last heard in "Go Ye Therefore" (album 4). We thought it would be good for Connie to maintain some friends her own age since it seemed like she only hung around the children and older characters. However, none of the friends we introduced for her seemed to stick.

Sound Bites

The music for "First Love" was a complete departure from the normal *Adventures in Odyssey* style. Composer John Campbell built a specific theme and then created underscores and bridges from that theme. It was inspired, in part, by the music of composer and jazz artist Dave Grusin (b. 1934). Previously, many cues could be easily interchanged between shows (and often were). From this point on, the bar had been raised and most of the shows were approached with the same concept.

My Take: Paul McCusker

Though at first glance "First Love" would seem to deal with a teen issue, I wasn't really writing it for them. I was thinking of the 8- to 12-year olds. The idea that Christians shouldn't date nonbelievers had been instilled in me long before I thought much about

Bernard

dating, which made a big difference in my dating life. I remember thinking—and still believe—that it's important for *Adventures in Odyssey* to introduce our listeners to a biblical perspective on life issues *before* the kids are in a position to make choices. Or, as one pastor once said to me: "The time to decide whether or not you're going to cheat on a test *isn't* when you're in the middle of a test you haven't studied for. You must decide cheating isn't an option long before the test comes along."

BTS: Curious, Isn't It?

"Curious, Isn't It?" was inspired by an episode of *The Andy Griffith Show* ("The Rumor") where Barney sees Andy giving a ring to a girl and immediately thinks Andy is getting married.

Goof Alert!

In "An Act of Mercy," Officer O'Ryan tells Bart Rathbone, "Thanks for your cooperation, Bill." Oops! Isn't his name *Bart*? Also, contrary to what Whit and Connie say while playing checkers, you actually can't force a win if you play the best three out of four, four out of five, and so on. In even numbered games, a tie is possible. To force a win, one player must have won a simple majority of wins in an odd number of games. They should have said, "three out of five, four out of seven . . ."

The Officer Harley Remakes

Problem 1: We had decided not to re-air the Officer Harley shows any more (see "The Trouble with Harley," album 1), but the shows were still good stories.

Problem 2: Odyssey writers Phil Lollar and Paul McCusker had a very busy year between writing *Odyssey* novels, launching a video series, and much more.

Solution: Take the Harley shows and rewrite them with new characters filling the Harley role. (See chart below.)

So You Want to Know the Punch Line of Officer O'Ryan's Joke?

Officer O'Ryan tells a joke at the beginning of "Pranks for the Memories." He begins: "There's these two hunters, see, and one of them had a bird dog. Well, they were out there by the lake and they spotted some ducks, so the owner of the dog fired, dropped a duck into the lake, and ordered the hound to go get it. The dog ran over to the edge of the water, sniffed, and then walked across the top of the lake and retrieved the duck! The owner was amazed! He brought down another duck and, again, the dog walked across the top of the water to get it. Well, the owner turned to his friend, beaming with pride, and says, 'Notice anything special about my dog?' The friend turns back and says—"

Harley's Undoing

Original Harley episode	New non-Harley episode	Character who replaced Harley	Changes from the original
The Quality of Mercy	An Act of Mercy	Officer O'Ryan	Officer Patrick O'Ryan enabled us to introduce a less goofy (but still fun) policeman, also played by Will Ryan.
Doing Unto Others	Isaac the Benevolent	Eugene Meltsner	Isaac (rather than Johnny Bickle) learns about the Golden Rule.
Bobby's Valentine	The Trouble with Girls	Eugene Meltsner	Eugene's bike was covered in valentines instead of Harley's squad car.
The Case of the Missing Train Car	What Happened to the Silver Streak?	Curt Stevens	The remake of this show enabled us to explore another side of Curt's character.
Missed It by That Much	Better Late than Never	No one	Officer Harley originally showed up to comment on a few scenes (such as the girls gathering at Whit's End), but his commentary wasn't needed for the remake.
Gotcha!	Pranks for the Memories *and later* It Began with a Rabbit's Foot . . .	Officer O'Ryan	Only the first scene of "Pranks for the Memories" is a remake of "Gotcha!" The rest of the episode follows a new plot. "It Began with a Rabbit's Foot . . ." isn't a remake of the show, but contains several flashbacks to "Gotcha!"
Harley Takes the Case	Missing Person	Isaac Morton	The original episode was in two parts and featured more mystery-solving scenes. It also featured a wild dog attack.
The Return of Harley	The Boy Who Cried "Destructo!"	Harlow Doyle	This was the only episode where Harley's replacement—Harlow—actually replaced Harley in a show.

At this point in the joke, O'Ryan is interrupted and never finishes. At the end of the episode, Chris encouraged listeners to send in their own punch lines to the joke. We've received many creative punch lines over the years (usually mentioning something about the lake being frozen). But the original punch line is this: "The friend turns back and says, 'Yeah! Your dog can't swim!'"

BTS: Castles and Cauldrons

This episode was carefully reviewed by Dr. Dobson and the entire team throughout the production process because of the supernatural nature of the subject matter. It is the only episode (so far) with a personal caution from Dr. Dobson.

BTS: The Winning Edge

Though Bart appeared in several earlier episodes, "The Winning Edge" set the tone and style for what Bart Rathbone's character would become—a shyster/swindler who would do anything for a quick buck . . . or in this case, he'd do anything to win.

Sound Bites with Bob Luttrell

I actually dumped a complete bag of cat food all over my kitchen floor just to get the right sound effect for "All's Well with Boswell." I also stayed locked up in my home studio for hours with a neighborhood cat, trying to get just the right meows for Boswell. By the way, I don't recommend this to anyone.

Actor Dave Madden, voice of Bernard Walton

This Sidebar Is Absolutely Free . . . with a $10 Purchase: The Creation of Bart Rathbone

The character of Bart Rathbone came almost by accident. We had written a scene for Rodney's father in "An Act of Mercy," but had planned to get one of our Focus staff members to do the voice. Walker Edmiston was already at the session performing as Tom Riley and volunteered to try Bart's voice. His performance was so fascinating that we made immediate plans for him to become a regular character.

Walker Edmiston remembers, "I based him on a friend of mine from New York. He was literally an Archie Bunker kind of guy, with attitudes and thoughts similar to that [cantankerous] character from the old TV series *All in the Family*" [1971–1979].

Actor Walker Edmiston, voice of Bart Rathbone

Character:
Jimmy Barclay
Birthplace: Odyssey
Something you may not know about Jimmy:
His earlobes turn red when he gets mad.

Album 9

Just in Time

The Bickering Barclays

In "Wishful Thinking," Donna wishes that Jimmy never existed and then seems to get her wish—she sees how her life would be different without Jimmy. The plot of this episode was inspired by George Bailey's wish that he had never been born in the film *It's a Wonderful Life* (1946). (See "Introducing the Barclays" in album 2 for more on how this movie influenced the creation of the Barclays.)

Jimmy and Donna's antics and arguments provided fodder for many episodes. Their alternate versions of how the TV caught on fire in "Two Sides to Every Story" came from the classic Japanese movie *Rashomon* (1950). In that movie, four people involved in a crime tell varying accounts of what happened and each account reflects the person's point of view.

The two siblings didn't always fight, however. Their mutual concern for their parents' marriage drove the drama in "The Vow." Just like real brothers and sisters, their love for their family superseded any petty squabbles.

Episode Information

109: Two Sides to Every Story
Original Air Date: 3/24/90
Writer: Paul McCusker
Sound Designer: Dave Arnold
Scripture: Proverbs 20:23
Theme: Considering another person's point of view
Summary: Jimmy and Donna Barclay tell their parents two different versions of how their TV caught fire.

114: The Big Broadcast
Original Air Date: 6/9/90
Writer: Paul McCusker
Sound Designer: Bob Luttrell
Scripture: Luke 10:25-37
Themes: The parable of the good Samaritan, creativity
Summary: Whit and Tom reopen the Kids' Radio studio with the Good Samaritan story.

118: What Happened to the Silver Streak?
Original Air Date: 7/7/90
Writer: Phil Lollar
Sound Designer: Bob Luttrell
Scripture: Matthew 18:21-35; 1 Corinthians 13:7
Themes: Forgiveness, unconditional love
Summary: Young Traci Needlemeyer's model train car mysteriously disappears, and Curt Stevens points a suspicious finger at Michelle Terry, a girl with a reputation for taking things that don't belong to her.

119: Better Late than Never
Original Air Date: 7/14/90
Writer: Paul McCusker
Sound Designer: Bob Luttrell
Scripture: Matthew 25:1-13
Theme: Lateness
Summary: Robyn Jacobs has developed a habit for being fashionably late, but gets a taste of what life would be like if her tardiness turned into an epidemic.

126: Wishful Thinking
Original Air Date: 9/1/90
Writer: Paul McCusker
Sound Designer: Dave Arnold
Scripture: Genesis 4; 37:18-35; 1 John 2:10-11
Theme: Dealing with a pesky sibling
Summary: Donna Barclay gets a surprise when she wishes her brother, Jimmy, had never been born—and it seems to come true!

127: Have You No Selpurcs?
Original Air Date: 9/8/90
Writer: Phil Lollar
Sound Designer: Bob Luttrell
Scripture: Proverbs 14:8-9, 15-16
Theme: Scruples
Summary: Whit concocts an unusual game to teach Curt Stevens and Lucy Cunningham-Schultz about scruples.

129: Not One of Us
Original Air Date: 9/22/90
Writer: Paul McCusker
Sound Designer: Dave Arnold
Scripture: Acts 17:26; Romans 3:29; 1 Corinthians 12:13
Theme: Bigotry
Summary: For an article on bigotry, Lucy and Connie go to the country town of Sloughburg, where everyone seems to be bigoted against *them*!

130 and 131: Bernard and Joseph, I and II
Original Air Dates: 10/27/90 & 10/30/90
Writer: Phil Lollar
Sound Designers: Dave Arnold & Bob Luttrell
Scripture: Genesis 37; 39-46:7
Themes: The biblical story of Joseph, God's sovereignty
Summary: Bernard Walton tells Artie Powell, a boy with many siblings, the exciting life story of Joseph and his 11 brothers.

133: **Cousin Albert**
Original Air Date: 11/24/90
Writer: Phil Lollar
Sound Designer: Bob Luttrell
Scripture: Proverbs 23:12
Theme: Illiteracy
Summary: Lucy discovers that her cousin Albert Schultz, a high school basketball star, has a problem that could destroy his future.

140: **The Vow**
Original Air Date: 1/12/91
Writer: Phil Lollar
Sound Designer: Dave Arnold
Scripture: Matthew 19:5-6
Theme: The sanctity of marriage
Summary: When Donna and Jimmy become convinced that their parents' marriage is falling apart, they take drastic action to save it.

141: **Over the Airwaves**
Original Air Date: 1/19/91
Writer: Paul McCusker
Sound Designer: Dave Arnold
Scripture: Matthew 21:28-46
Theme: Parables about the kingdom of heaven
Summary: Kids' Radio tells several parables including one about the wicked tenants in a skit called "Young Guns Bonanza!"

502: **Live at the 25**
Original Air Date: 11/30/02
Writers: Paul McCusker, Marshal Younger
Sound Designer: Jonathan Crowe
Theme: Celebration
Summary: Connie and the crew at Whit's End celebrate what they *think* is the 25th anniversary of Whit's End!

JUST IN TIME

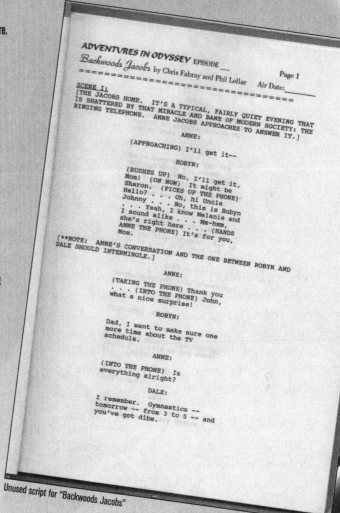

Unused script for "Backwoods Jacobs"

Robyn Jacobs in "Better Late than Never"

My Take: Paul McCusker

After "Two Sides to Every Story" aired, we received mail from firefighters who said we must inform our listeners to never put out an electrical fire with water (as Jimmy did in the story). We rerecorded Chris warning kids about this in her wrap-up.

Lucy Who?! Part One

Lucy's last name is one of the biggest goofs in the *Adventures in Odyssey* canon. In two episodes in album 5, "Our Best Vacation Ever" and "The Battle," Lucy's last name is given as "Cunningham." But then, in "The Big Broadcast," Lucy says that her last name is Schultz. For episodes after this, Lucy is alternately referred to as "Lucy Schultz" or "Lucy Cunningham-Schultz." See "The Truth About Zachary" (album 23) to discover how we fixed this goof.

Behind the Scenes: Better Late than Never

The name "The Twilife Zone" originally appeared in "Missed It by That Much" and then in its remake "Better Late than Never." It later appeared as a recurring Kids' Radio feature (and the title of an episode in album 21). The name came from a dramatic sketch written years before by Paul McCusker.

Focus on Social Issues

Several episodes in this collection were written in response to a request by Dr. Dobson. He asked all the divisions at Focus on the Family to touch on the social issues of the day and present a godly response to them. The *Odyssey* staff agreed and produced episodes on morality ("Have You No Selpurcs?"), racism ("Not One of Us"), illiteracy ("Cousin Albert"), and even abortion ("Pamela Has a Problem," *The Lost Episodes*).

BTS: *Not One of Us*

For the character of Mr. Slough, actor Walker Edmiston used a Henry Fonda voice (Mr. Fonda was a famous movie actor who performed from 1935 to 1982). Walker had done voice matching for Mr. Fonda on many motion pictures. Also, Paul McCusker named the character Slough after an English town that often suffers from unflattering jokes about its lack of sophistication.

Sound Bites

If you listen carefully to the newscaster in "Not One of Us," you'll notice that he says Philip Glossman is leaving Odyssey to take a position with the Webster Development Company. From previous episodes, we know that Webster Development is actually owned by Dr. Blackgaard. This was also a way of saying good-bye to the character because Paul McCusker was moving to England and hoped never to play Glossman again. (He didn't get his wish.)

BTS: *Bernard and Joseph*

In this episode, window washer Bernard Walton emerged as a storyteller with his own style (loosely based on the 1987 feature film *The Princess Bride*). Some on the team weren't convinced that simply retelling a Bible story without a kid character interacting with the Bible characters—as in "The Imagination Station" (album 5) or "Elijah" (album 6)—would be entertaining. However, the success of this show led us to retell many Bible stories through Bernard.

Sound Bites

The Christian comedy duo of Custer and Hoose provided several of the vocal characterizations for "Bernard and Joseph." Jim Custer, who often played young Whit in episodes like "Rescue from Manatugo Point" (album 6) and "The Triangle" (album 36), was cast as Joseph. Bob Hoose played Simeon and, years later, became a producer and writer for the show.

Backwoods Jacobs

Around the time that the episodes in this album were written, we recorded another episode called "Backwoods Jacobs." The show featured the Jacobs family visiting some relatives who were too hick for Robyn and Melanie's tastes. As it turned out, the idea looked better on paper than it did in the finished product. After editing just the voice tracks, we reviewed the material and decided that it wasn't working at all. So we neither finished producing nor aired the episode.

My Take: *Paul McCusker*

Chuck Bolte had requested that we do an episode from his favorite genre—the Western. I wrote "Over the Airwaves" while I was ill with the flu. I finished the first draft and handed it off to the *Odyssey* team. I was sure that they would throw it out because I had written it in a delirious state of mind. Instead, it became a very popular episode. Maybe I should write while feverish more often.

Staff members Dave Arnold, Paul McCusker, Marshal Younger, Nathan Hoobler, and Chuck Bolte revise the script the night before performance.

From Left: Actor Townsend Coleman, writer John Fornof, and actor Aria Curzon

Actors signing photos for *Odyssey* fans

Sound designer Rob Jorgensen performing live Foley and sound effects

Live at the 25!

To celebrate the 25th anniversary of Focus on the Family, we recorded two performances of this episode in front of a live audience on July 26–27, 2002. The second recording also featured a half-hour, live question-and-answer segment, of which about seven minutes were used in the episode "Inside the Studio" (*The Lost Episodes* album).

This show includes a live version of the "Young Guns Bonanza" sketch, originally heard in "Over the Airwaves." Several changes and cuts were made to accommodate the live audience and the cast. The character of Wes Chester was changed to Emma Darling, now played by Chris Anthony.

The "Sam Maritan" sketch from "The Big Broadcast" was also preformed live, but cut from the final episode because we ran out of time. It featured Jason Whittaker as the character Sam, Mandy Straussberg as the character Lucy Cutie, Bart Rathbone playing the part of the religious leader, Whit as the Levite, and announcer Chris playing the innkeeper.

For the ending of the episode, Chris performed her wrap-up for the live audience and even asked them to participate in reading the address.

Five hundred tapes on the ceiling represent the first 500 episodes.

Album 10

Other Times, Other Places

Jimmy Barclay Meets Pirates, Angels, and the Grim Reaper

One of our most popular and enduring episodes, "Someone to Watch Over Me," was based on a script that Phil Lollar pitched to *The Twilight Zone* television series.

The episode was demanding for all involved. Actor David Griffin (who played Jimmy) remembers, "That episode was a great challenge to perform because it was very dramatic. But getting to see Hal Smith's amazing vocal range in person always fascinated me." Hal played many variations on the character of Grim, including the dread pirate Grimbeard. (See the pirate with the *G* on his hat at left.)

Dave Arnold also had a very challenging task with the sound design. The space sequence was especially difficult. Dave says, "For the computer voice, I recorded my wife and me saying the lines together and then ran them through a processor to get the digitalized sound."

The popularity of the episode caused it to be transformed into an *Odyssey* video of the same name. The animated version features Dylan Taylor instead of Jimmy Barclay, with a few variations. Most notably, the sea battle with pirates is cut entirely.

And one more thing . . . Did you notice that if you rearrange the letters of Jimmy's protector's name (Nagle), you get another form of protector?

Episode Information

135, 136, and 137: Back to Bethlehem, I, II, and III
Original Air Dates: 12/8/90, 12/15/90 & 12/22/90
Writer: Paul McCusker
Sound Designers: Dave Arnold & Bob Luttrell
Scripture: Matthew 1:18–2:1; Luke 2:1-20
Theme: The birth of Jesus Christ
Summary: Connie and Eugene discover that the first Nativity wasn't how they imagined it at all.

139: Melanie's Diary
Original Air Date: 1/5/91
Writer: Paul McCusker
Sound Designer: Bob Luttrell
Scripture: Deuteronomy 32:35
Themes: Empathy, the folly of revenge
Summary: Robyn Jacobs blabs details about her little sister's diary, so Melanie comes up with a way to get revenge.

144: Someone to Watch Over Me
Original Air Date: 2/9/91
Writer: Phil Lollar
Sound Designer: Dave Arnold
Scripture: Psalm 91:11-12; Matthew 18:10
Themes: God's protection, guardian angels
Summary: Jimmy Barclay goes on his most incredible adventure ever when he meets a gentleman named Mr. Nagle on a World War II bomber.

145: The Second Coming
Original Air Date: 3/2/91
Writer: Paul McCusker
Sound Designer: Dave Arnold
Scripture: Matthew 24:36-42
Theme: The return of Jesus
Summary: Melanie Jacobs becomes convinced that she knows the exact day and time of the return of Jesus.

146: Emotional Baggage
Original Air Date: 3/9/91
Writer: Phil Lollar
Sound Designer: Bob Luttrell
Scripture: 1 Corinthians 13:5, 7
Theme: Holding grudges
Summary: Connie starts behaving strangely when she learns her aunt is coming for a visit. When Whit asks why, Connie reveals that she's harboring resentment against her aunt.

148: Isaac the Procrastinator
Original Air Date: 4/6/91
Writer: Phil Lollar
Sound Designer: Bob Luttrell
Scripture: Proverbs 10:4
Themes: Procrastination, laziness
Summary: Isaac Morton keeps putting off doing his work, so Whit comes up with a solution to help him finish his projects.

155 and 156: Waylaid in the Windy City, I and II
Original Air Dates: 6/22/91 & 6/29/91
Writers: Paul McCusker & Phil Lollar
Sound Designers: Dave Arnold & Bob Luttrell
Scripture: Proverbs 29:25
Themes: God is in control, the folly of revenge
Summary: On a trip to Chicago, Whit and Connie get caught up in a dangerous mystery involving a portable computer, the Department of Defense, and some familiar—but not very friendly—faces.

Other Times, Other Places

157: Last in a Long Line

Original Air Date: 7/6/91
Writer: Phil Lollar
Sound Designer: Dave Arnold
Scripture: Proverbs 17:6
Theme: The importance of family heritage
Summary: Eugene makes an amazing discovery while walking through an old cemetery—the tombstone of his long-lost father.

159: The Homecoming

Original Air Date: 7/20/91
Writer: Paul McCusker
Sound Designer: Dave Arnold
Scripture: Matthew 6:12
Theme: Forgiveness
Summary: Odyssey is in an uproar when Richard Maxwell returns to town to apologize for everything he did while working with Dr. Regis Blackgaard.

The Odyssey Times

THE ONLY ONE WE'VE GOT

ALWAYS Free

Whittaker Unveils New Invention

The Imagination Station 'brings the Bible to life.'
By Dale Jacobs
Times City Editor

John Avery Whittaker, owner of Odyssey's popular ice cream and discovery emporium called Whit's End, unveiled a new invention at his shop last night that he claims "will help kids use their imaginations to bring Bible stories and history to life."

With grand flourish, Whittaker—or "Whit," as he is best known around Odyssey—then introduced the Imagination Station to more than 100 spectators gathered for the occasion in the Bible Room, one of the many special-subject rooms at Whit's End.

Closely resembling the cockpit of a small helicopter, the Imagination Station is computerized and pre-programmed to send anyone who uses it "to distant lands and times, from the fall of Jericho to the signing of the Declaration of Independence," according to Whit.

"I won't bore you with the details," Whit smiled, "all you have to do is get in and push the button."

The Imagination Station is tested and approved by city building inspectors, Whit assured the crowd. Ralph Myers, one of Odyssey's inspectors, concurred and added that he tried one of the time adventures himself. "I helped Moses get the Israelites across the Red Sea," he beamed. "It was unlike anything I've ever experienced."

The creation of the Imagination Station is part of Whit's ongoing desire to turn Whit's End into a place "where

the entire family can come, have fun and learn," Whit explained.

Longtime Odyssey residents may remember that Whit's End was originally the site of the derelict Fillmore Recreation Center, until 1984, when it became the source of an intense city-wide debate. Jenny Whittaker, Whit's wife, spearheaded a restoration campaign to thwart efforts by outside developers from turning the site into a shopping mall. Mrs. Whittaker died suddenly before the issue was resolved.

At a last-minute city council vote, Whit himself purchased the building and converted it into what is now Whit's End. "It was partly out of a sense of civic duty and partly out of respect for my wife's last wishes," Whit recalled.

"I think she would be pleased with how it's turned out."

Current attractions at Whit's End include an ice-cream parlor, the county's largest electric train set, games, an extensive lending library, a theatre for film or live performances, craft workshops and, in the Bible Room, a number of interactive displays to "enhance biblical understanding."

"Most of all," Whit added, "it's a place where kids—of *all* ages—can just be kids."

The Imagination Station is located in the Bible Room at Whit's End (open Monday through Saturday from 9 a.m. to 9 p.m., except for holidays). As is true with every attraction in the shop, admission is free.

John Avery Whittaker unveiling his Imagination Station.

"Odyssey" Takes to the Airwaves

By Campbell Freed
Times Staff Writer

It began as an experiment. Dr. James Dobson of Focus on the Family, an international ministry based in California, decided to produce a family drama series for the radio. Early announcements from the ministry indicated the program would take place in a small town where characters could explore the events, concerns and issues facing today's families.

After a nationwide search for the "right town," our own Odyssey was chosen as the model for the show. In 1983, a 13-week test series was aired on the "Focus on the Family" broadcast. It was called "Family Portraits" and chronicled the lives and times of Odyssey residents—including John Whittaker, his family and Whit's End. Apart from a few geographical mistakes, Mr. Whittaker thought the representation of Odyssey was "commendable" and "a worthwhile effort."

Audience response was so favorable (no surprise to the folks here in Odyssey), Focus on the Family went one step further to create "Adventures in Odyssey." Not only did Whit and the gang at Whit's End encounter new and exciting situations, but some of the best

continued on page 4

WEATHER:
Temperatures today will set record-breaking highs while settling to more moderate ranges by this evening. Tomorrow: pleasant. The Connellsville Weather Service is expecting rain—but nobody else is.

On This Day in History
By Dr. Petronius Lawler, Historian, Campbell College

On this day in history in 1834, the town of Odyssey was born. But, like most births, it took a long time to happen. I wonder how many of our citizens know the story behind our beloved town? Recent excavations and document research have enlightened us about our history.

In the late 1700s and early 1800s, the land where Odyssey now rests was inhabited by a small, obscure tribe of Indians. They were so obscure, in fact, that we know little about them, their origins or their language. What we do

know is thanks to the diaries and letters of French missionaries who preached to the tribe during the time. (See related article about the LeMonde treasures.)

One remnant of the French missionaries can be found in Whit's End. It was originally part of a church steeple, preserved then annexed to the Fillmore Recreation Center early in this century. As everyone knows, the Fillmore Recreation Center later became Whit's End.

The Indians called this area "Wey-Aka-Tal-Ah-Nee-Tee," which means

"Land That Stinks Like Swamp." Since there isn't a swamp within hundreds of miles, we assume the Indians migrated from the swamplands of the south and remembered the aroma of that area when they arrived. Odyssey became "swamp-would come, causing Trickle Lake to overflow and flood the plains. With nowhere else to drain, the water became stagnant and, after a few weeks, would become quite ... well, gamey.

The Indian tribe moved on to sweeter-smelling pastures and an East-

Coast lad named Horace McCalister arrived with his wife in the early 1850s to tame the land. Others followed and the settlement became a town.

Though many believe the name "Odyssey" came from the classic work by the Greek writer Homer, it was actually Horace who named the growing city. "It's a beautiful valley," he said at the decisive town meeting, "and a place everyone *oughtta* see."

The townspeople couldn't disagree—and Odyssey was born.

The first edition of *The Odyssey Times*

Behind the Scenes: Back to Bethlehem

Our first three-part adventure was based on *Step into Bethlehem,* a play by Paul McCusker. Katie Leigh (Connie) often mentions these episodes among her favorites, and they're some of our most requested CDs. Due to their popularity, the programs were edited into an hour-long episode for radio stations to air as a Christmas special.

Goof Alert!

In "Melanie's Diary," Eugene states that he doesn't keep a diary because he simply memorizes everything. However, in "It Ended with a Handshake" (album 20), Eugene makes it clear that he keeps his journal/diary on his computer. In "The Time Has Come" (album 25), he inputs the diary of his entire life in Odyssey into the Imagination Station. During his adventure, he sees parts of his life that occurred shortly before and after "Melanie's Diary." So maybe he was keeping a journal after all.

BTS: Melanie's Diary

"Melanie's Diary" was Paul McCusker's first show written from his new home in England. He sent *Odyssey* scripts and ideas to the staff in California via the Internet, which was then considered new technology.

Sound Bites

Erin Bolte, voice of Melanie Jacobs, recalls: "Most of the fights Melanie had with Robyn weren't acting at all. Paul McCusker wrote my character into "Melanie's Diary," and he based the arguments between Melanie and Robyn on arguments that he overheard between my

Actors Erin (*left*) and Sage Bolte in the studio

sister, Sage (who plays Robyn), and me. Sage and I would simply get into the studio and reenact our latest argument!"

My Take: Paul McCusker

I wrote "The Second Coming" to respond to yet another round of predictions of Christ's return we heard about in the news. I wanted kids to understand from the Bible what we can know—and *not* know—about that event.

BTS: Emotional Baggage

In this episode we learned more about Connie's family, including how her father originally left and about her Aunt Helen.

These characters would figure prominently in later episodes such as "Father's Day" (album 14) and "A Touch of Healing" (album 24).

After doing a story about Connie's family, it seemed appropriate to explore Eugene's back story in "Last in a Long Line." Eugene's family had barely been mentioned before this show, and this episode became a touchstone for defining his past and, in particular, his childhood. This was also the episode where Bernard found that he was related to Eugene, a source of consternation for Odyssey's window washer for years to come.

One line from the show —"I was always told that my parents were lost on an anthropological mission in the rainforests of Zaire in Africa. I was only seven"—eventually set off an entire miniseries of episodes concerning the search for Eugene's missing father and the explanation for his lengthy absence (see "Prisoners of Fear," album 45).

My Take: Phil Lollar

Isaac's predicaments in "Isaac the Procrastinator" and his reasons for not completing his work come directly from my own life experience. Not that I put things off. On the contrary, I always do my best to finish everything I sta

Sound Bites

Listen closely when Richard is taking a bus at the end of "The Homecoming." The PA announcer says that the bus is headed to "Colorado Springs, Colorado," which is also where Focus on the Family was moving to when this episode was produced.

Jimmy Barclay parachuting in "Someone to Watch Over Me"

The Writing of "Waylaid in the Windy City"

by Paul McCusker

Shortly after I moved to England, I read an article in the newspaper about a military attaché who was driving across London with a laptop computer sitting on the front seat next to him. It was filled with all kinds of top secret government information. He stopped to use the bathroom and when he came back to his car, the laptop was gone. The police were convinced that the thief had no idea what he had stolen. Out of that came the idea of Whit's luggage mix-up and the story that followed.

My original outline was set in London, not Chicago. I had all kinds of jokes about Americans overseas such as Connie complaining that there were only four television channels and things like that. Originally, the investigating officer was Agent James Duffield, the son of Reginald Duffield from "Operation: Dig-Out" [album 6]. Ultimately, we decided not to set it in London due to the difficulty of finding actors with authentic accents.

When I started writing, I wasn't sure who the bad guy was going to be. I got to the point in the outline when Connie was kidnapped and the elevator doors opened to reveal the mastermind behind the plot. I realized that no one could really be standing behind those doors except Dr. Blackgaard. And, of course, once Dr. Blackgaard appeared, Richard Maxwell couldn't be too far behind.

Album 11

It's Another Fine Day

Actor David Griffin's "Coming of Age"

The *Odyssey* policy had been to drop child characters from the show when the actors' voices began to change. Actor David Griffin, voice of Jimmy Barclay, remembers the situation the day in the studio he thought would be his last.

> I had noticed my voice changing, so whenever I went into the studio, I tried to keep my voice in the high register so it didn't crack.
>
> This one day, it felt as if 90 people were in the studio. My line in the scene was "Donna!" When I yelled, my voice cracked! I'd never heard silence like that. Nobody looked at me, and I felt this queasy, oily feeling in my stomach.
>
> In the studio, soundproof glass separates the engineers and the director from the actors. Actors can't hear people in the other room. I could see people whispering back and forth, and it felt like it dragged on endlessly. Finally, Phil Lollar came on the talkback and said, "Oh Dave." He stopped and then said, "Oh, Dave, Dave, Dave, Dave . . ."
>
> "No, wait! I can do it again!" I said. I tried it three more times, but my voice just kept cracking. I was positive that was the end of my job.

After this incident in the studio, we decided to address David's voice change through the character of Jimmy Barclay. Phil Lollar wrote the episode "Coming of Age," which described the many changes happening to Jimmy. A secondary purpose to the show was to say good-bye to Jimmy and family since the Barclay kids were getting older. After the show aired, however, many fans wrote in urging us to keep the Barclays (and Jimmy specifically) on the show. As a result, we continued writing Barclay episodes for years to come.

Episode Information

143: Muckraker
Original Air Date: 2/2/91
Writer: Paul McCusker
Sound Designer: Bob Luttrell
Scripture: Proverbs 6:16, 19
Theme: Handling the power of media responsibly
Summary: Lucy Cunningham-Schultz decides to write an investigative journalism article about the shampoo from the Calvin Bloom Company.

147: Where There's a Will . . .
Original Air Date: 3/30/91
Writer: Paul McCusker
Sound Designer: Dave Arnold
Scripture: Ephesians 5:17
Theme: Knowing God's will
Summary: George Barclay considers a job change that would move the family away from Odyssey.

149: By Dawn's Early Light
Original Air Date: 4/13/91
Writer: Phil Lollar
Sound Designer: Dave Arnold
Scripture: Psalm 33:12-22
Themes: American War of 1812, respect for the flag
Summary: Curt Stevens and Lucy travel back in the Imagination Station to see the American War of 1812.

150: Home Is Where the Hurt Is
Original Air Date: 4/20/91
Writer: Paul McCusker
Sound Designer: Bob Luttrell
Scripture: Proverbs 20:1; Ephesians 5:18
Theme: Dealing with an alcoholic parent
Summary: A crazy scheme to get out of math homework causes Curt to reveal more about his home life than he wanted anyone to know.

151: . . . The Last Shall Be First
Original Air Date: 4/27/91
Writer: Phil Lollar
Sound Designer: Dave Arnold
Scripture: Matthew 18:12-13; 20:1-16
Themes: The parable of the workers, salvation
Summary: Connie tries to get her stubborn uncle, Joe Finneman, to go to church with her.

152: The Meaning of Sacrifice
Original Air Date: 5/4/91
Writer: Paul McCusker
Sound Designer: Bob Luttrell
Scripture: 1 Samuel 15:19, 22
Theme: Sacrifice
Summary: The Barclay family decides to try sacrificing their television viewing for a month.

153: Mayor for a Day
Original Air Date: 5/11/91
Writer: Paul McCusker
Sound Designer: Dave Arnold
Scripture: Romans 13:1-7
Themes: Responsibility, leadership
Summary: Curt wins a contest to become the city's most powerful official for 24 hours.

154: Coming of Age
Original Air Date: 5/18/91
Writer: Phil Lollar
Sound Designer: Bob Luttrell
Scripture: Deuteronomy 31:6; Matthew 10:30; 1 Timothy 4:12
Themes: Adolescence, growing up
Summary: Jimmy Barclay journals about the many changes going on in his life, from shaving to first crushes.
PARENTAL WARNING:
This episode deals with Jimmy Barclay's entry into adolescence and all the embarrassment, anguish, and awkwardness that go along with it. Although tastefully handled, it may be too mature for younger listeners.

It's Another Fine Day...

158: A Day in the Life
Original Air Date: 7/13/91
Writer: Paul McCusker
Sound Designer: Bob Luttrell
Scripture: John 8:32
Theme: Distinguishing truth from falsehood
Summary: A Hollywood film company comes to Odyssey to make a movie about the town.

160: A Rathbone of Contention
Original Air Date: 7/27/91
Writer: Phil Lollar
Sound Designer: Bob Luttrell
Scripture: Proverbs 21:5; 26:27
Theme: The folly of taking shortcuts
Summary: Bart Rathbone is constructing a new electronics warehouse in Odyssey, and he takes nothing but shortcuts to finish it for the inspector.

165 and 166: Bernard and Esther, I and II
Original Air Date: 8/31/91 & 9/7/91
Writer: Phil Lollar
Sound Designers: Bob Luttrell and Dave Arnold
Scripture: The book of Esther
Theme: The biblical story of Esther, courage, God's protection and providence
Summary: Bernard Walton tells Robyn Jacobs and her sister, Melanie, the biblical story of Esther.

Lucy Cunningham-Schultz in "Muckraker"

Behind the Scenes: Where There's a Will...

Focus on the Family was preparing to move to Colorado Springs when this episode was written. The Barclays and Focus employees were facing similar uncertainties and dilemmas associated with moving. We employees could empathize with the Barclays.

Donna and Jimmy Barclay in "Where There's a Will"

Goof Alert!

After recording "By Dawn's Early Light," we dicovered that the name "Cockburn" should actually be pronounced as "Coburn." Then again, characters pronounce Dr. Blackgaard's name alternately as "Bla-*guard*" and "Black-ard." Both Blackgaard brothers pronounce it "Bla-*guard*," and you would think they would know.

BTS: By Dawn's Early Light

This story was written to address the issue of flag burning. In 1991 when the script was written, there were several prominent flag-burning cases in the news; at least two of those made it to the Supreme Court.

Sound Bites

"Home Is Where the Hurt Is" was recorded with Chris doing her cheerful wrap-up as usual. However, upon hearing the final episode, the team decided that the ending really needed a more serious tone since the show dealt with such a troubling issue—alcoholism. To get that somber note, we recorded executive producer Chuck Bolte doing the wrap-up instead. His voice and style were well suited to the subject. Chuck also did the wrap-up on one other serious episode—"The Mortal Coil."

My Take: Phil Lollar

"...The Last Shall Be First" was inspired by a touching story Shirley Dobson (wife of Dr. James Dobson) told at a Focus on the Family chapel service about her unsaved father. He'd had a debilitating stroke and was on his deathbed, unable to speak. Shirley went to him and told him the parable of the workers,

Jimmy Barclay

Actor David Griffin, age 10

Actor David Griffin, voice of Jimmy Barclay, now

making the same point Connie makes in this episode: It's never too late to come to Jesus. But because Shirley's father couldn't speak, she won't know if the message got through to him . . . until she's in heaven. We later used a similar idea in "A Question About Tasha" [album 27].

BTS: *Mayor for a Day*

This episode was inspired by two movies, the Marx Brothers' *Duck Soup* (1933) and Jimmy Stewart's *Mr. Smith Goes to Washington* (1939).

BTS: *A Day in the Life*

"A Day in the Life" was our good-natured tip of the hat to the *Adventures in Odyssey* videos. To make the transition from audio to animation, the videos portrayed Whit as a goofy eccentric who moved from place to place in a vehicle with oars and helium balloons. Eugene seemed to always be eating and Connie was eliminated completely until much later in

Art by Bethany P., "Bernard" modeled after actor Dave Madden

BTS: *A Rathbone of Contention*

In "Waylaid in the Windy City" (album 10), Dr. Blackgaard said that he'd be opening a chain of stores (including one in Odyssey) with "every conceivable electronic device for every conceivable need." In "A Rathbone of Contention," Bart Rathbone uses the same phrase to describe the Electric Palace and says that it's owned by the Webster Development Company, which careful listeners know is Dr. Blackgaard's company. All of these subtle hints enabled us to set up small connections that would become significant much later in the *Darkness Before Dawn* miniseries. Despite this ominous hint, the Palace was the source of more hilarity than real menace in future stories.

the series. We wanted to spoof, or poke fun at, these changes and "A Day in the Life" was our way of doing it. (See the artwork on this album's opening page.)

Sound Bites

If you listen closely to the background movie playing in the final scene of "A Day in the Life," you'll notice that it's the dialogue from the *Odyssey* episode "That's Not Fair" (album 6) with audience laughter added.

Parley Baer: From Roy Stoner to Uncle Joe

Connie's Uncle Joe (played by Parley Baer) was introduced in ". . . The Last Shall Be First." Parley filled a number of other characters for us, including Mr. Burgelmeister in "Eugene's Dilemma" (album 5), Hezekiah in "Back to Bethlehem" (album 10), and Whit's old friend Reginald Duffield. Like Hal Smith, Parley was an alumnus on *The Andy Griffith Show*. He played Mayor Roy Stoner on that series.

Actor Parley Baer, voice of Uncle Joe

Album 12

At Home and Abroad

Eugene Goes Indiana Jones

We envisioned "The Cross of Cortes" to be the beginning of an exciting episode series where our characters would visit foreign lands and exotic locations, sort of like the Indiana Jones movies from the 1980s. However, this effort uncovered several production difficulties including creating exotic sound effects and finding actors with proper foreign accents. After this program we waited 184 episodes until "The Search for Whit" (album 27) to let our characters venture overseas again.

Additionally, the sound effects for the bull scene (see left), were difficult to create. Dave Arnold recalls: "We couldn't find any decent bull snorts in any of our sound effect libraries. The bull snorts you hear on these shows are purely human. Bob Luttrell and I took turns acting the role in front of a microphone. Of course, we did make our voices sound deeper, but otherwise very little else was added to the performance. We each laughed as we watched while the other snorted and bellowed."

Episode Information

163: A Model Child
Original Air Date: 8/17/91
Writer: Paul McCusker
Sound Designer: Dave Arnold
Scripture: 1 Samuel 16:7
Themes: Vanity, the source of real beauty
Summary: When Bart Rathbone sponsors a Young Miss Odyssey modeling competition, Melanie Jacobs is keen to join in.

168: The Curse
Original Air Date: 9/21/91
Writer: Phil Lollar
Sound Designer: Bob Luttrell
Scripture: Ephesians 6:12; 1 John 4:4
Theme: The folly of believing in curses
Summary: An "Indian Medicine Man" puts an ancient curse on Whit—and it seems to come true!

169: Hold Up!
Original Air Date: 10/26/91
Writer: Paul McCusker
Sound Designer: Bob Luttrell
Scripture: Ecclesiastes 7:20; Jeremiah 17:9; Romans 3:23
Themes: Humankind's basic nature, God's protection
Summary: A criminal named Hank Murray takes Connie and Eugene hostage while he tries to rob Whit's End.
PARENTAL WARNING:
This episode is about a holdup at Whit's End. Though it is comical and no one gets hurt, several gunshots are fired during the program.

170: A Test for Robyn
Original Air Date: 11/2/91
Writer: Paul McCusker
Sound Designer: Bob Luttrell
Scripture: Psalm 51:17
Themes: Procrastination, cheating
Summary: Robyn Jacobs puts off studying for a test at school and then tries to cram at the last minute.

171 and 172: The Cross of Cortes, I and II
Original Air Dates: 11/9/91 & 11/16/91
Writer: Phil Lollar
Sound Designer: Bob Luttrell & Dave Arnold
Scripture: Deuteronomy 6:13-15; Luke 4:8
Themes: Greed, God's sovereignty, the object of our faith
Summary: Whit and Eugene journey to Mexico in search of a valuable and mysterious historical artifact.

173: A Thanksgiving Carol
Original Air Date: 11/23/91
Writer: Phil Lollar
Sound Designer: Dave Arnold
Scripture: 1 Thessalonians 5:18
Themes: Thanksgiving, being thankful
Summary: Whit and the gang use Kids' Radio to tell Charles Dickens's *A Christmas Carol* with an unusual twist.

174: Where's Your Daddy?
Original Air Date: 11/30/91
Writer: Paul McCusker
Sound Designer: Dave Arnold
Scripture: Matthew 25:31-46
Theme: Having a parent in prison
Summary: The Myers family come to Odyssey with a secret: Father and husband Ernie Myers is in jail.

175: **East Winds, Raining**
Original Air Date: 12/7/91
Writer: Paul McCusker
Sound Designer: Bob Luttrell
Scripture: Psalm 33:11-13, 16; Galatians 3:26-28
Themes: Don't judge others, trust in God
Summary: Connie's uncle, Joe Finneman, remembers the December 7, 1941, attack on Pearl Harbor and a hero who tried to stop it.

176 and 177: **The Star, I and II**
Original Air Dates: 12/14/91 & 12/21/91
Writers: Phil Lollar & Paul McCusker
Sound Designers: Bob Luttrell & Dave Arnold
Scripture: Matthew 2:1-15
Theme: The Christmas story about the visit from the Magi
Summary: Connie and Eugene take another Christmas trip in the Imagination Station to meet King Herod, three wise men, and the baby Jesus.

178: **Room Mates**
Original Air Date: 12/28/91
Writer: Paul McCusker
Sound Designer: Bob Luttrell
Scripture: Leviticus 19:18; Mark 12:28-31
Themes: Family relationships, getting along with others
Summary: Eugene moves in with an unlikely roommate—window washer Bernard Walton!

Eugene and two wise men in "The Star"

Sound designers Bob Luttrell (*left*) and Dave Arnold working on "The Cross of Cortes"

Goof Alert!

In "Recollections" (album 1), Whit states that he will buy the "Fillmore Recreation Center and its adjoining land." However, later in "The Curse," Whit misspeaks by telling Connie and Eugene, "You both know that I don't own the land around Whit's End, just the building." This later becomes a huge plot point in two Blackgaard saga episodes in album 25: "Moving Targets," and "The Return."

Behind the Scenes: The Curse

The portrayal of Native Americans in this episode drew some audience criticism because it featured a "medicine man" speaking haltingly and pronouncing curses on Whit. However, upon hearing the complete episode, listeners might realize that the complaints were unfounded since the so-called medicine man was not a Native American at all, and he intentionally played up the stereotype for reasons revealed in the plot.

BTS: Hold Up!

We gave a tip of the hat to Hal Smith's other acting roles in this episode. Robber Hank Murray looks through the objects in Whit's safe. "What's this?" he says. "An autographed picture of Andy Griffith?" Connie responds that Whit is "a big fan." Hal played Otis Campbell, the town drunk, on *The Andy Griffith Show.*

Goof Alert!

In "Hold Up!" Connie complains that no one told her about the safe at Whit's End. However, in an earlier episode titled "Suspicious Minds" (album 8), Whit told her that he was going to put money "in the safe."

BTS: Where's Your Daddy?

This episode was written in conjunction with Angel Tree, a division of Chuck Colson's Prison Fellowship ministry. Angel Tree sent copies of the program to thousands of inmates and their families to encourage them during the holiday season. This program was also the last one recorded in the Pomona, California, Focus studios. In 1991 the ministry moved to Colorado Springs, Colorado, and all subsequent episodes have been recorded in rented studios in Southern California.

Sound Bites

Actor Joe Dammann, the voice of Eric Myers, also played Nicholas Martin, the main character in the McGee and Me! video series. Actor Amber Arnold, daughter of production engineer Dave Arnold, played Brooke Myers.

Sound Bites with Bob Luttrell

Before working in postproduction, I spent four years in the Navy as a radioman. One of my jobs was a Morse code operator. In "East Winds, Raining," you can hear international Morse code in the background of one scene, and I thought it would be fun to have the Morse code saying, "This is Bob Luttrell sending code." Not very creative, huh?

BTS: East Winds, Raining

This story was originally imagined as a Kids' Radio episode produced in the style of Orson Wells's famous 1938 "War of the Worlds" radio drama. We thought that we would interrupt the normal Kids' Radio programming with news reports about the bombing of Pearl Harbor. However, the team felt a more personal approach with storyteller Joe Finneman would work better. The "War of the Worlds" concept was used later in "Terror from the Skies" (album 18).

My Take: Paul McCusker

In late 1990, I moved to Sunninghill, England, to write freelance and experience life in my wife's homeland. I was still in England when I started on "East Winds, Raining," and I quickly discovered that information about Pearl Harbor wasn't in abundance since the bombing is not a significant event in Britain as it is in the United States (and this was before information on the Internet was readily available.) After scouring libraries for tidbits of information, I went to a bookstore one day and found a big coffee-table book with the details of Pearl Harbor. It was expensive—and I was cheap—so I used a scrap of paper to write down all the information I could. Much of the episode's details about the attack, including the title "East Winds, Raining" came from that book.

Goof Alert!

In "The Star," the character Proclus says that the temple is nothing compared to the Colosseum in Rome. The story takes place around 1 B.C., but the Colosseum wasn't ordered to be built until the reign of Vespasian, some 70 years later.

Actor Corey Burton, voice of young Uncle Joe in "East Winds, Raining"

Sound Bites with Corey Burton

"East Winds, Raining" was my first *Odyssey* episode, and I was playing the character of the young Uncle Joe. Parley Baer was playing the older Uncle Joe. Parley had his own unique accent from some very specific county in Appalachia somewhere, and I was worried that I wouldn't be able to match that regional sound convincingly. Parley had a much stronger handle on country-style accents, having roots in Oklahoma and Texas as well. I solved the dilemma by cheating it with a very light twang. Since regional accents come and go as people age and move around the country, I aimed to present the young character's accent as it might have sounded before his life journey altered his original voice.

Cut Scenes

Paul McCusker's original script for "Room Mates" had to be heavily edited to keep the show down to proper time. As a result, many humorous scenes were lost. And we do mean

lost. In those predigital days, the show was edited on tape with a razor blade. Unused sections were cut out and thrown away. All that remains of those lost lines can be found only in the original script.

Why was the script long in the first place? Because of the nature of radio drama, it can be difficult to tell how many pages a script should be to get it to the proper length for a 25-minute program. Actors read at different speeds, and some scenes read at slower or quicker paces. Oftentimes very good scenes ended up on the cutting room floor—literally!

Episode Swapping

Album 12 was released during the summer of 1992. But there was a small problem. If we followed our broadcast chronology, the collection in that album included Thanksgiving and Christmas episodes, which we didn't want to release in June. So, we swapped the order and released *It All Started When . . .* that summer instead, making *At Home and Abroad* come out later in the year. For the Gold Audio Series, however, we restored the proper chronology.

Original covers for *At Home and Abroad* and *It All Started When*

Sound designer Dave Arnold creates the sound of walking on leaves.

Character: Connie
Birthplace: Los Angeles, California
Something you may not know about Connie:
She once saved money to buy a "brand-new"
1967 Ford.

Album 13

It All Started When . . .

An Album of Virtues

In late 1991, Focus on the Family moved lock, stock, and barrel from Pomona, California, to Colorado Springs, Colorado. No small feat for all concerned. Several team members decided to stay in California, including Phil Lollar and Bob Luttrell, who continued to work on the show from there. Meanwhile, Paul McCusker returned from England to become Odyssey's producer. With all this upheaval, the team felt that the next collection should center on a common goal. Remembering the success we had with our series of 12 Christian basics in *FUNdamentals* (album 4), we decided to create 12 shows based on Christian virtues. For the fun of it, the script of each episode began with the phrase "It all started . . ."

Episode Information

167: **Dobson Comes to Town**
Original Air Date: 9/14/91
Writer: Phil Lollar
Sound Designer: Dave Arnold
Theme: Video/daily *Odyssey* promotion.
Summary: Whit's End welcomes a very special visitor—Dr. James Dobson!

179: **You Gotta Be Wise**
Original Air Date: 1/4/92
Writer: Paul McCusker
Sound Designer: Dave Arnold
Scripture: Proverbs 22:6
Themes: Wisdom, discernment
Summary: Robyn Jacobs and her father, Dale, have a clash of wills over music from a band called the Bones of Rath.

180: **Isaac the Pure**
Original Air Date: 1/11/92
Writer: Paul McCusker
Sound Designer: Bob Luttrell
Scripture: Matthew 5:8
Theme: Purity
Summary: Isaac Morton sets out on a quest to keep himself pure from all worldly things.

181: **It Takes Integrity**
Original Air Date: 1/18/92
Writer: Phil Lollar
Sound Designer: Bob Luttrell
Scripture: Proverbs 10:29
Theme: Integrity
Summary: Curt Stevens and Lucy Cunningham-Schultz compete to be elected student body president, but Curt's campaign turns underhanded.

182: **The Scales of Justice**
Original Air Date: 2/15/92
Writer: Phil Lollar
Sound Designer: Bob Luttrell
Scripture: Psalm 89:14
Theme: Justice
Summary: Isaac Morton finds a bag filled with money and wants to keep it, but it's up to Judge Eugene Meltsner to determine what will happen to the loot.

183: **Tales of Moderation**
Original Air Date: 2/22/92
Writer: Phil Lollar
Sound Designer: Bob Luttrell
Scripture: Matthew 6:19-21; Luke 18:18-25
Theme: Moderation
Summary: Connie reads three stories from Whit about moderation, which include a talking toaster, two farmers, and a young prince.

184: **Isaac the Chivalrous**
Original Air Date: 2/29/92
Writer: Phil Lollar
Sound Designer: Dave Arnold
Scripture: Job 13:15
Theme: Chivalry
Summary: After a journey in the Imagination Station, a brave knight follows Isaac into modern times.

185: **A Question of Loyalty**
Original Air Date: 3/7/92
Writer: Paul McCusker
Sound Designer: Dave Arnold
Scripture: Micah 7:5
Theme: Loyalty
Summary: Lucy befriends Emily, a shy, would-be writer from her school, who starts writing for *The Odyssey Owl*.

186: The Conscientious Cross-Guard
Original Air Date: 3/14/92
Writer: Phil Lollar
Sound Designer: Bob Luttrell
Scripture: Proverbs 20:6
Themes: Conscientiousness, perseverance
Summary: A young Bernard Walton faces a difficult task as a school crossing guard.

187: An Act of Nobility
Original Air Date: 3/21/92
Writer: Phil Lollar
Sound Designer: Dave Arnold
Scripture: Luke 22:24-26
Theme: Nobility
Summary: Whit tells the story of a young adult named James Armor who puts his life on the line in a foreign country to save an irresponsible prince.

188: The Courage to Stand
Original Air Date: 3/28/92
Writer: Paul McCusker
Sound Designer: Bob Luttrell
Scripture: 2 Chronicles 32:7-8
Theme: Courage
Summary: Robyn must make a choice when she's asked to go to an unchaperoned party with the most popular girl in school.

189: No, Honestly!
Original Air Date: 4/4/92
Writer: Phil Lollar
Sound Designer: Bob Luttrell
Scripture: Proverbs 12:22
Theme: Honesty
Summary: No one believes Rodney Rathbone when he claims he's discovered a con artist in Odyssey.

192: Modesty Is the Best Policy
Original Air Date: 4/25/92
Writer: Paul McCusker
Sound Designer: Dave Arnold
Scripture: 1 Timothy 2:9
Theme: Modesty
Summary: Donna Barclay wants to wear an outfit to a school banquet that her father thinks is immodest.

Bart Rathbone confronts Connie in "The Scales of Justice"

My Take: Dr. Dobson

This program takes me back to 1956 during my sophomore year of college. I was an actor in the stage production *12 Angry Men*. That was my last effort in acting before "Dobson Comes to Town." This episode pushed me into unfamiliar circumstances. After hearing my performance . . . well, let's put it this way: Acting is not my great gift!

Cut Scenes

"You Gotta Be Wise" was created to support another Focus on the Family ministry called Learn to Discern. This group, led by Bob DeMoss, helped parents deal with their kids' media choices. It later evolved into the extremely popular ministry and magazine named *Plugged In*.

"You Gotta Be Wise" featured several scenes of Dale Jacobs and Whit discussing the type of music that the Bones created. Some of the song titles included "I Don't Like You" and "Beasts of Hades." The two men noted that the type of music didn't make it bad . . . it was just the lyrics. We decided to remove these lines so as not to offend those in the audience who believe that various types of music, apart from lyrics, can be evil.

Actor Jerry Houser, voice of Mr. Morton

Behind the Scenes: Isaac the Pure

Actor Jerry Houser made his first appearance in this episode playing Isaac Morton's father. Jerry later appeared as the *Darkness Before Dawn* (25) villain named Jellyfish and as Ben Shepard, Aubrey's father (see album 33).

Q & A with the Fans

Q: Fans have wondered for years about the Professor Sherlock feature that appears in "The Scales of Justice." Why was it there?

A: Phil Lollar's love of science led him to create several variations on the Super Sleuth idea—short segments that would teach kids interesting science stuff. This particular one notes facts about human skin. The idea of the science facts never quite caught on; however, we later used a similar idea called "Did You Know?" in B-TV episodes starting in album 23.

Q: Does the final twist of "An Act of Nobility" mean that James Armor was actually the young John Avery Whittaker?

A: Whit could have heard the story from another source. Character James Armor is played by Corey Burton, while young Whit is played by actor Jim Custer. However, it is interesting to note that the initials of James Armor are the same as John Avery. Hmmm.

Sound Bites with Dave Arnold

"Isaac the Chivalrous" is one of only two episodes where we scrapped the complete musical score and began totally from scratch. Our regular composer, John Campbell, was too busy to write the music for this show. At the time we really didn't have a backup composer. I asked John if he could recommend someone, and he suggested a fine gentleman and mentor who had a long list of credentials. This fellow agreed to the work and turned the job around quickly. When the score came in, however, it was far from our typical *Odyssey* sound. I knew it wasn't a matter of tweaks; it was a matter of style and personal approach. We would never be able to fix the music of the new composer. So I said thank you to the man and paid him—then in a panic, I called John. Being the great guy he is, John took on the job and somehow fit it into his schedule. The result was one of the most creative and innovative scores he had ever done. (See photo on the next page.)

BTS: *The Conscientious Cross-Guard*

This exciting episode was a tribute to the 1952 Gary Cooper classic *High Noon*. It turned out to be a nostalgic show because it featured many of our former child actors. Young Bernard was played by David Griffin (the voice of Jimmy Barclay), bully Tanyer Hyde was played by Donald Long (the voice of Jack Davis), and Bernard's friend Nick was played by Chad Reisser (the voice of Digger Digwillow and Monty Whittaker-Dowd). It also featured the voices of nearly all of our crewmembers, including Dave Arnold, Chuck Bolte, Phil Lollar, Bob Luttrell, and Paul McCusker.

Sound Bites with Dave Arnold

On the morning of recording "The Conscientious Cross-Guard," we were all at a café talking about the cast lineup

for the day's session. Our faces went pale when we realized that we had somehow forgotten to cast the part of Nick. In a panic,

Actors Chad Reisser (Digger Digwillow) and Donald Long (Jack Davis)

Paul McCusker ran to the phone and called Chad Reisser. Chad's mom agreed to help out and rushed to get him out of school and to the studio. He arrived just in time to do the part.

BTS: *An Act of Nobility*

This episode was originally titled "Return to Zenda" because it was inspired by Anthony Hope's classic 1894 novel *The Prisoner of Zenda*. Muldavia is an allusion to an ancient country that is now Romania.

BTS: No, Honestly

To keep our characters fresh and interesting, we often find new situations to put them in, situations that are outside their normal experiences. For example, we let Rodney Rathbone have the one-time experience of narrating a story in this episode. It was also one of the few times where Rodney turned out to be reasonably innocent. True to his character, however, he still didn't learn his lesson.

John Campbell composing music at his computer

Dr. Dobson and actor Hal Smith, the voice of Whit

Dr. Dobson Comes to Odyssey

"Dobson Comes to Town" was written and produced to promote the new *Odyssey* video series and was the only episode in which anyone real visited Odyssey as himself. This episode aired (in slightly different versions) on the *Focus on the Family* daily broadcast and the *Adventures in Odyssey* time slot. The *Focus on the Family* version began with Dr. Dobson and his cohost discussing a "strange incident" that happened in the studio. The *Odyssey* version begins with Whit journaling about a "very special visitor" who arrived in Odyssey.

When Dr. Dobson gets into the Imagination Station at the end of the program, the Station accidentally drops him at Chuck Swindoll's program before taking him back to the Focus on the Family studio.

In the wrap-up of the program, our host, Chris, notes that this is the 200th *Adventures in Odyssey* episode. Though it is actually the 167th *new* episode, it aired on the 200th weekend of the program.

Left to right: Actors Walker Edmiston, Will Ryan, Dr. Dobson, Katie Leigh, and Hal Smith

Album

14

Meanwhile, in Another Part of Town

A License to Thrill

Actors Katie Leigh (Connie) and Will Ryan (Eugene) both mention "A License to Drive" as among their favorites episodes. And no wonder! It's full of excitement both on the show and behind the scenes. The title was a twist on a popular James Bond film. Announcer Chris Anthony played the pregnant woman in this show, not realizing at the time of recording that she was expecting a child in real life.

The production was almost as intense as the scene depicted on the album cover (see left). Bob Luttrell recalls:

> Recording sound effects for "A License to Drive" was the second time I almost ruined my car [see "A Mission for Jimmy" album 6]. My wife was with me with a portable recorder to capture all of the car sounds. I thought it would be great if I could listen to the scene while she held the microphone. It actually became pretty funny. As I was listening to the voice tracks on headphones, Connie was telling Eugene what to do, like, "Turn right here." Since I wanted to have the sound work perfectly with the voice tracks, I would turn right at the exact same time that Connie said it, even though there was no street to turn right on! I ended up doing crazy things like suddenly turning into someone's driveway or stopping in the middle of the street. My wife—who was scared to death—said, "If you don't get a ticket, you'll kill us both!" She was right. It's dangerous to record live car sound effects while driving in the city. What was I thinking?

Episode Information

162: **Peacemaker**
Original Air Date: 8/10/91
Writer: Paul McCusker
Sound Designer: Bob Luttrell
Scripture: Matthew 5:9
Theme: Being a peacemaker
Summary: Connie tries to calm a dispute between Donna Barclay and her friend Jessie Morales.

164: **Sixties-Something**
Original Air Date: 8/24/91
Writer: Paul McCusker
Sound Designer: Bob Luttrell
Scripture: Hebrews 13:8; Revelation 22:13
Themes: God's unchanging nature, the consequences of drug use, the true source of peace
Summary: Bart Rathbone urges Odyssey to celebrate the 1960s, but Whit has reasons not to celebrate.

190 and 191: **Moses: The Passover, I and II**
Original Air Dates: 4/11/92 & 4/18/92
Writers: Phil Lollar & Paul McCusker
Sound Designers: Dave Arnold & Bob Luttrell
Scripture: The book of Exodus
Theme: The biblical story of Moses and the Exodus
Summary: George Barclay follows his son, Jimmy, into the Imagination Station. They "travel" to ancient Egypt's land of Goshen.

193: **A Tongue of Fire**
Original Air Date: 5/2/92
Writer: Phil Lollar
Sound Designer: Bob Luttrell
Scripture: James 3:1-12
Theme: Watching your words
Summary: Jimmy Barclay records an embarrassing secret about Eugene . . . and airs it on his Kids' Radio show.

194: **A License to Drive**
Original Air Date: 5/9/92
Writer: Phil Lollar
Sound Designer: Bob Luttrell
Scripture: Proverbs 10:4
Theme: Diligence
Summary: When Eugene needs help getting his driver's license, he turns to Connie for help.

195: **Father's Day**
Original Air Date: 6/20/92
Writer: Phil Lollar
Sound Designer: Bob Luttrell
Scripture: Malachi 2:14-16
Theme: Dealing with parents' divorce
Summary: Connie's father surprises her by visiting Odyssey . . . and brings even more surprising news.

196: **Harlow Doyle, Private Eye**
Original Air Date: 6/27/92
Writer: Paul McCusker
Sound Designer: Dave Arnold
Scripture: Luke 17:5-6; 2 Timothy 2:15; Hebrews 10:25
Theme: Faith
Summary: Harlow Doyle, Private Eye, opens an office in Odyssey, and his first big case is to help Jessie find her lost faith.

197: **The Midnight Ride**
Original Air Date: 7/4/92
Writer: Phil Lollar
Sound Designer: Bob Luttrell
Scripture: Psalm 33:12
Theme: The American Revolution, Paul Revere, duty, patriotism
Summary: Whit tells the story of Paul Revere, his famous ride, and the "shot heard 'round the world."

198: Treasure Hunt

Original Air Date: 7/11/92
Writer: Paul McCusker
Sound Designer: Dave Arnold
Scripture: Proverbs 10:29
Theme: God's protection
Summary: Isaac Morton and Eugene join a war games contest that includes some water pistols that look like real weapons.

200: Feud for Thought

Original Air Date: 7/25/92
Writer: Phil Lollar
Sound Designer: Bob Luttrell
Scripture: Ephesians 4:31-32
Theme: Forgiveness
Summary: Eugene joins Bernard Walton for a family reunion—and uncovers a dark secret about his grandfather Meltsner's past.

202: Timmy's Cabin

Original Air Date: 8/22/92
Writer: Phil Lollar
Sound Designer: Dave Arnold
Scripture: Psalm 33:18
Themes: The importance of family memories, God's protection
Summary: Philip Glossman arrives in Odyssey, hoping to build a highway through Tom Riley's land.

Behind the Scenes: Peacemaker

This episode was originally written with the character Lucy Cunningham-Schultz as the peacemaker. We changed that role to Connie to demonstrate her budding maturity. Jessie Morales and Donna Barclay both mention that Connie is starting to sound like Mr. Whittaker.

Secret Message

In 1992, we held a Secret Message call-in contest on *Odyssey*. Listeners had to identify seven secret words from several episodes. More than 6,500 entries were submitted into a drawing. Angela R. of San Antonio, Texas, won first prize: a trip to Colorado Springs and a ride in a hot-air balloon. What was the secret message that won the prize? "Welcome to our side of the radio."

Sound Bites

If you listen closely to the Kids' Radio broadcasts in the background of "A Tongue of Fire," you'll hear our announcer Chris Anthony doing an *Adventures in Odyssey* commercial.

My Take: Corey Burton

The character of Cryin' Bryan Dern was originally intended to sound pretty much like a famous, rude radio personality. But I never was able to do a good impression of that person, and didn't think that voice would have been dynamic enough to make the role particularly entertaining. Instead I based Cryin' Bryan's voice on another brash radio personality, who had a much more exciting range of tone and expression to play with. It's a big, loud, bold voice, it projects attitude and sarcasm through exaggerated debate-style theatrics, delivered in fits and starts between long, dramatic pauses—much like legendary broadcaster Paul Harvey or the great Jack Benny. I also wanted to impart a certain humanity to the character and make him a little more childish rather than sinister. After all, his apparent outrage is much more about putting on a compelling show to keep listeners tuned in than anything else.

From *Clubhouse* magazine, May 1992

From *Broadcast News*, September 1992

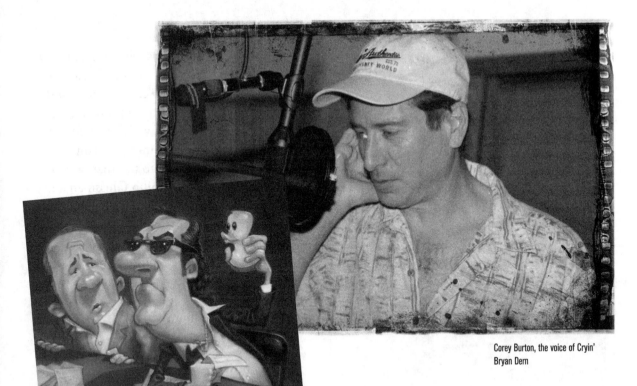

Corey Burton, the voice of Cryin' Bryan Dern

Walter Shakespeare (*left*) and Bryan Dern

BTS: *Father's Day*

Bill Kendall's first wife's name was June. In "Father's Day," we find he married a woman named April. Years later, in "Something Blue" (album 41) he has a girlfriend named May.

Sound Bites

Though Harlow refers to Miss Turner in many later episodes, "Harlow Doyle, Private Eye" was the only episode in which she appeared. Astute listeners will recognize that the voice of Miss Turner would later show up as Katrina Shanks. The same actor would also play Doris Rathbone.

Goof Alert!

"The Midnight Ride" purports to correct mistakes in the famous 1860 poem by Longfellow; however, the show itself contains several inaccuracies. After the "shot heard 'round the world," Major John Pitcairn is heard ordering his men to fire. However, we know historically that Major Pitcairn rode among his men ordering them not to fire and they disobeyed his orders. Also, Whit insists that the lights were hung in North Church, not Christ Church. However, both are names for the same place.

Sound Bites with Dave Arnold

"Treasure Hunt" contains one of the longest scenes in *Odyssey* history (with no musical interludes): 10 minutes, 30 seconds. The perspective begins with Bryan Dern and Bart

Art by fan Thea M.

BTS: *Timmy's Cabin*

In an episode of the 1960s television comedy *Gilligan's Island*, the show began with a handful of generals trying to decide where to test an atomic bomb. One general pointed to a deserted island on a map, which turned out to be Gilligan's Island. "Timmy's Cabin" was the first Odyssey episode to use that same sort of prologue. Character Philip Glossman and a crony talk about building a major highway that cuts through a small farm, which inevitably turns out to be Tom Riley's. We called it the "*Gilligan's Island* beginning" and used it in later shows like "For the Fun of It" (album 40), "Odyssey Sings!" (album 45), and "The Highest Stakes" (album 49).

Rathbone, cuts through the radio to Whit and Tom, cuts back through the radio to Bryan, stays with Eugene and Isaac, moves back to Bryan, and finally cuts through the radio to stay with Tom and Whit. It was a bit of an homage to a 1922 Robert Altman film, in which the opening tracking shot is 8 minutes.

BTS: *Feud for Thought*

This episode brought back character Ralph Reams, first heard in "Last in a Long Line" (album 10). In that episode, sound designer Bob Luttrell voiced the character. In "Feud," Ralph is played by actor Tom Williams.

Jumping Jars of Marmalade!

The Creation of Harlow Doyle

We missed the wacky humor that Officer Harley brought to the show and had often brain-stormed ways to bring it back. We decided to introduce Harlow Doyle, Private Eye, believing that since he wasn't an authority figure, it was perfectly all right to have a little fun with him. Will Ryan used a version of his Harley voice for the part. The new character's name is a reworked version of Harley's name (Harlow) and a twist on Hoyle playing cards (Doyle).

Photo courtesy of Will Ryan Music Company.

Actor Will Ryan

Harlow Doyle

Album **15**

A Place of Wonder

Look Out, Destructo! Lawrence Hodges Is on the Scene!

The Barclay kids were growing up quickly, and they were already out of the 8- to 12-year-old age range we write for. We didn't want to lose the family entirely, so we discussed ways to introduce some younger voices with our established characters. We debated adding a Barclay baby, but it would be years before the child could become the kind of character we needed. So we discussed the possibilities of the Barclays adopting a younger child or having a younger cousin come to stay with them.

Ultimately, our brainstorming turned toward Jimmy mentoring a younger friend who could fill the role of the young, energetic "every kid." This led to the creation of the imagination-charged Lawrence Hodges, played by actor Gabriel Encarnacion. Lawrence's imagination often got out of control (as in the picture at left); the character was inspired, in part, by a similarly imaginative young boy in a Warner Bros. cartoon. Lawrence's mother was played by Janet Waldo, who later became the character Joanne Allen.

Episode Information

199: The "No" Factor
Original Air Date: 7/18/92
Writer: Phil Lollar
Sound Designer: Bob Luttrell
Scripture: Ecclesiastes 3:2-8, 11
Themes: Being wise with your time, the danger of overcommitment
Summary: Connie takes on more projects than she can handle.

201: Fair-Weather Fans
Original Air Date: 8/15/92
Writer: Charlie Richards
Sound Designer: Bob Luttrell
Scripture: Proverbs 18:24
Themes: Friendship, discernment
Summary: Isaac Morton makes a new friend and starts selling cooling fans door to door.

203: Double Trouble
Original Air Date: 8/29/92
Writer: Paul McCusker
Sound Designer: Dave Arnold
Scripture: 1 Samuel 16:7
Theme: Judging a book by its cover
Summary: Lucy Cunningham-Schultz goes to interview the new owner of the Harlequin Theatre . . . only to discover that it's R. E. Blackgaard! Is it the same man who traumatized Odyssey several years ago?

204: Wonderworld
Original Air Date: 9/5/92
Writer: Phil Lollar
Sound Designer: Bob Luttrell
Scripture: Psalm 104
Themes: The proper use of imagination, creativity
Summary: Jimmy Barclay thinks he's too old for Whit's End, but he learns otherwise while baby-sitting an imaginative boy named Lawrence.

205: Flash Flood
Original Air Date: 9/26/92
Writers: Rich Peterson & Paul McCusker
Sound Designer: Dave Arnold
Scripture: Proverbs 17:17
Theme: Friendship
Summary: Whit, Tom Riley, Bernard Walton, and Eugene go camping and find themselves facing dangerous weather.

206: Pen Pal
Original Air Date: 10/3/92
Writers: Vann Trapp & Paul McCusker
Sound Designer: Bob Luttrell
Scripture: Psalm 146
Themes: Friendship, compassion for the handicapped
Summary: Melanie Jacobs gets a big surprise when her pen pal, Jenny Roberts, suddenly arrives in Odyssey for a visit.

207: The Case of the Candid Camera
Original Air Date: 10/10/92
Writer: Phil Lollar
Sound Designer: Bob Luttrell
Scripture: Numbers 32:23
Themes: Honesty, the consequences of sin
Summary: Harlow Doyle takes a case involving a missing camera, a Bible Bowl, and Rodney Rathbone.

208: Pipe Dreams
Original Air Date: 10/17/92
Writer: Chris Fabry
Sound Designer: Dave Arnold
Scripture: Luke 19:11-26
Theme: Making the most of a bad situation
Summary: "Chunky" Charles Thompson signs up for the sheriff's department on career day and is assigned to water management instead.

210: On Solid Ground
Original Air Date: 10/31/92
Writer: Phil Lollar
Sound Designer: Dave Arnold
Scripture: Genesis 13:1-14:24; 18:1-19:29
Theme: The biblical story of Abraham and Lot
Summary: On Kids' Radio, the O. T. Action News team gives up-to-the-minute reports about Abraham, Lot, and a city called Sodom.

215: Caroling, Caroling
Original Air Date: 12/19/92
Writer: Paul McCusker
Sound Designer: Dave Arnold
Music Mix: Tim Jaquette
Scripture: Luke 2:1-20
Themes: Celebrating Christmas, the birth of Jesus
Summary: Whit, Connie, and the kids from Whit's End take a sleigh ride through Odyssey and sing Christmas carols.

217: Rights, Wrongs, and Reasons
Original Air Date: 1/2/93
Writer: Phil Lollar
Sound Designer: Bob Luttrell
Scripture: Romans 6:1
Theme: Doing the right thing for the right reason
Summary: Whit, Connie, and Jenny Roberts play a unique game involving ethical dilemmas and the reasons people do the things they do.

218: A Class Act
Original Air Date: 1/9/93
Writer: Paul McCusker
Sound Designer: Bob Luttrell
Scripture: James 2:1-4
Themes: Honesty, relying on God, favoritism
Summary: Edwin Blackgaard agrees to teach an acting class in Odyssey after he receives an anonymous donation.

223: Real Time
Original Air Date: 3/13/93
Writer: Phil Lollar
Sound Designer: Dave Arnold
Scripture: Luke 12:16-21
Themes: God's protection, making the most of each moment
Summary: Whit and Cryin' Bryan Dern's plan to have an on-air debate about the existence of God. But their plans get put on hold when they find themselves trapped in an elevator during a bomb threat.

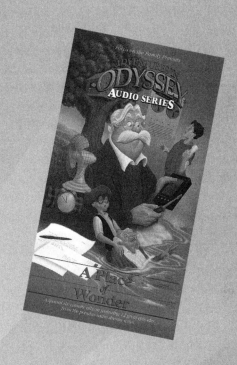

Behind the Scenes: The "No" Factor

The play that Jack Davis is directing is the script from *Odyssey*'s "The Boy Who Didn't Go to Church" (album 4).

Goof Alert!

At the end of "Double Trouble," Whit said, "I got something in my mail last night . . ." We later find out it contained information about events that happened on that very day. The delay time for mail would make that impossible.

Sound Bites with Dave Arnold

The lengthy flash flood sequence at the end of "Flash Flood" was one of the most difficult to create since the series began. It revealed several problems with action sequences of this sort (notably having to describe the action through dialog) and kept us from doing any more water action scenes for a very long time.

BTS: Pen Pal

This episode introduced the blind girl named Jenny Roberts. She was the first recurring character on the show with a handicap. People often wrote in to ask if the actress who played Jenny is blind in real life. The answer is no; however, we did a lot of research on blind children's experiences, which led to more realistic and relatable episodes.

BTS: Wonderworld

In this episode, Whit says, "I feel like Christopher Robin just left Pooh Corner." Hal Smith, who played Whit, was well-known as the voice of the title character on *The Many Adventures of Winnie the Pooh* (1977).

Also, when Jimmy is baby-sitting Lawrence, the television in the background is playing *Stalag 5*, a reference to the movie *Stalag 17* (1953). Lawrence says he is agent NCC-1701, which refers to the serial number of the USS *Enterprise* from the original *Star Trek* television series (1966–1969). But we're not influenced by movies or television shows, really!

Cut Scenes

A lengthy dream scene in "Pipe Dreams" was cut for time. Character Charles Thompson imagined a day at the sheriff's office where he rescued the Tumweiler twins, played by Janet Waldo and Katie Leigh. He also caught the kidnapper, played by Will Ryan, when the ransom note was signed with his real name— Big Harry Swindler.

BTS: On Solid Ground

Inspired by the gripping stories of embedded reporters in the 1990–1991 Persian Gulf War, "On Solid Ground" introduced a new format to Kids' Radio: the historical news report. The show was originally called "O. T. Action News," but the title was changed to honor a request from executive producer Chuck Bolte to have titles capture the episodes' themes. Future episodes, like "Rights, Wrongs, and Reasons" and "Treasures of the Heart" (album 16) also reflected this request.

Sound Bites with Dave Arnold

To create the sound of Lot's wife turning into a pillar of salt in "On Solid Ground," I combined several sound effects, including an Easter basket that I twisted. Then I used several processing ideas to get that crystallizing sound in her voice as she solidified.

Sound Bites

"Caroling, Caroling" was originally produced as a sing-along retail product, then later as an hour-long Christmas radio special. For broadcasts, it was cut down to 25 minutes, which removed scenes with Eugene, Bernard Walton, and George Barclay, and songs, including Eugene's "Seasonal Felicitations" and Whit singing the famous song "White Christmas." Actor Hal Smith's solo on "White Christmas" was a spontaneous idea we had while recording the kids' choir at another studio. Hal agreed to it, so Dave Arnold drove across Los Angeles to another studio to get the solo while recording with the choir continued.

Cut Scenes

"A Class Act" ended up being several minutes too long, so a few hilarious scenes had to be cut out. These included Edwin Blackgaard horribly butchering lines from a Shakespearean play and a scene of his students butchering acting in general. One of the cut scenes involved Eugene and Edwin debating inanimate objects. The dialog included this exchange:

EDWIN: Since you're so interested in trees, Eugene, why don't you become one?

EUGENE: A tree? Er, precisely what kind of tree were you thinking: deciduous, coniferous, perhaps a . . .

EDWIN: Be a tree, Eugene. A tree blowing gently in the wind.

EUGENE: Of course. But what is my motivation? Is the tree blowing gently because it is old and beaten by decades of weather or is it—

EDWIN: Forget the wind. You're standing perfectly still.

EUGENE: But why would—

EDWIN: With your bark tightly covering your mouth.

EUGENE: (*through tight lips*) Yes, sir.

Later, when Edwin talked to the class about their performances as inanimate objects, the following dialog occurred:

EDWIN: Jack, your imitation of a house with a two-car garage having a pizza delivered was most . . . imaginative. Connie, I appreciated your attempt at being a broken milkshake dispenser. Charles, your large dirt clod was unforgettable. Shannon, your appearance as a rose petal was without compare.

SHANNON: Thank you. You know, I played an entire rose bush in my first-grade prod—

EDWIN: Yes, thank you.

EUGENE: (*clears throat*) And what about me, sir?

EDWIN: Eugene. Yes. Your tree. The words escape me.

BTS: Double Trouble

The genuinely British Elizabeth McCusker (wife of writer Paul McCusker) plays Edwin Blackgaard's assistant, Miss Minion. She returns later in the album during "A Class Act."

My Take: Phil Lollar

"Real Time" was inspired by an episode of *M*A*S*H* (1979) that took place in real time. Since then, it's become a popular dramatic vehicle for television shows to use.

Sound Bites with Dave Arnold

To accomplish the real time feel, we read through the script to get a rough estimate of the timing. We couldn't know the actual timing until we edited the show and added the music and commercial breaks. So, we recorded four or five phrases for each mention of the minutes ("We've only got 12 . . . 11 . . . 10 . . . 9 minutes!"). Then we used the appropriate version after the voice tracks were edited.

Walter Shakespeare

Actor Earl Boen, voices of Edwin and Regis Blackgaard

Edwin Blackgaard

Fair Citizens of Odyssey, Welcome Edwin Blackgaard!

"Double Trouble" features the first appearance of Edwin Blackgaard and his faithful servant, Walter Shakespeare, played by Earl Boen and Corey Burton respectively.

The creation of Edwin Blackgaard was the result of a single desire—to keep working with actor Earl Boen. We loved his performances as Regis Blackgaard, but we knew that character would eventually come to justice and go away. So, how could we give Earl a role that would demonstrate his versatility as an actor, without repeating what he'd already done with Regis? A twin brother was the answer: a hammy and harmless thespian named Edwin, who was the complete antithesis to the villainous Regis.

Edwin and his sidekick, Shakespeare, were loosely based on Edmund Blackadder and his servant, Baldrick, from the long-running British situation comedies know as Black Adder (1983–2000). Paul McCusker remembers suggesting to Earl Boen that "Edwin thinks he's the world's greatest actor, but he's probably the world's worst."

Earl remembers, "My wont is to overact anyway, so it's very easy to tap into that." Earl based his Edwin performance on a one-man show he had seen where the actor *horribly* overacted.

Corey Burton worked hard to find a voice for Shakespeare. He began by mimicking the voice of Academy-Award-winning actor James Mason (1909–1984), then blended that with the voices of British actors Michael York (b. 1942) and Roddy McDowall (1928–1998). Incredibly versatile, Corey has played more *Odyssey* characters than any other actor.

Walter Shakespeare

Character: Whit
Quote: "Most folks around here call me Whit."
Something you may not know about Whit:
He was very good at hide-and-seek.

Album 16

Whit's Brush with Mortality

"The Mortal Coil" is one of the popular *Adventures in Odyssey* episodes, but it was also one of the more controversial. Even before the show aired, we knew that it would trigger a lot of listener responses because of its cliff-hanger ending, so we put into place some unusual efforts to help offset the intensity of the fans' reactions. We asked the local stations to have their on-air announcers warn parents about the show, suggesting that they listen before allowing their children to hear it.

We also had executive producer Chuck Bolte replace Chris Anthony for the wrap-up at the end of part I, hinting at the happy ending to come when he said that "Whit's adventure would continue" the following week. What we didn't fully realize was the effect the show would have by airing the Saturday *before* Thanksgiving—which meant that a lot of families wouldn't be at home for the conclusion the next Saturday. The letters and phone calls came. Kids begged us, saying, "Please don't kill Mr. Whittaker," while a few parents were annoyed that we would put their children through a week of suspense. Despite all this, the episodes proved powerful, and many listeners wrote in to thank us for producing them.

Episode Information

209: Columbus: The Grand Voyage
Original Air Date: 10/24/92
Writer: Phil Lollar
Sound Designer: Bob Luttrell
Scripture: Psalm 22:27-28
Themes: Christopher Columbus, courage.
Summary: Lawrence Hodges joins Christopher Columbus for an incredible trip across the seas by way of the Imagination Station.

211 and 212: The Mortal Coil, I and II
Original Air Dates: 11/21/92 & 11/28/92
Writer: Paul McCusker
Sound Designer: Dave Arnold
Scripture: 1 Corinthians 2:9; 2 Corinthians 4:18–5:2;
1 Thessalonians 4:13-15; Revelation 7:17; 21:4
Themes: Death, heaven
Summary: Whit programs the Imagination Station to show what life after death might be like. Against the advice of Tom Riley, he tries the program on himself . . . with dangerous results.
PARENTAL WARNING:
This episode about life after death may prove to be too intense for listeners under the age of 10.

213: Best Intentions
Original Air Date: 12/5/92
Writer: Paul McCusker
Sound Designer: Dave Arnold
Scripture: Matthew 25:36
Theme: Compassion
Summary: Connie and Eugene try to ensure that Whit gets his rest while recovering from being in the hospital.

214: The Living Nativity
Original Air Date: 12/12/92
Writer: Marshal Younger
Sound Designer: Bob Luttrell
Scripture: Romans 13:1-7
Theme: Freedom of religion
Summary: A nativity display at Odyssey's city hall sparks a controversy over the "separation of church and state."

216: Like Father, Like Son
Original Air Date: 12/26/92
Writers: April Dammann & Paul McCusker
Sound Designer: Bob Luttrell
Scripture: Matthew 7:1-2
Theme: Judging others
Summary: Teenager Eric Myers is accused of stealing from the soccer team's cash box.

219: Treasures of the Heart
Original Air Date: 1/16/93
Writers: Paul McCusker & Geoff Kohler
Sound Designer: Dave Arnold
Scripture: Matthew 6:19
Theme: Setting proper priorities
Summary: The Barclay family holds a yard sale to tidy up their cluttered attic.

220: This Is Chad Pearson?
Original Air Date: 2/20/93
Writer: Marshal Younger
Sound Designer: Bob Luttrell
Scripture: Philippians 2:3-11
Theme: The folly of hero worship
Summary: Bart Rathbone holds a big contest and the winner gets a date with television star Chad Pearson. It's a prize every girl in Odyssey wants . . . except the winner!

221: **It Is Well**

Original Air Date: 2/27/93
Writer: Phil Lollar
Sound Designer: Dave Arnold
Scripture: Philippians 4:12-13
Themes: Trusting God through all life's circumstances, the power of faith.
Summary: Whit tells Lucy the moving story behind the writing of the old hymn "It Is Well."
PARENTAL WARNING:
Though this is an inspirational and moving story, it does contain a realistic shipwreck as well as several deaths. While handled tastefully, these scenes may frighten younger listeners.

226 and 227: **An Adventure in Bethany, I and II**

Original Air Dates: 4/3/93 & 4/10/93
Writer: Paul McCusker
Sound Designers: Bob Luttrell & Dave Arnold
Scripture: John 11:1-12:11
Themes: The biblical story of Lazarus, the power of Jesus
Summary: Lucy takes an Imagination Station trip to first-century Bethany where she meets Marta, Miriam, and Eleazar preparing a feast for a special guest—Jesus!

228: **A Game of Compassion**

Original Air Date: 4/17/93
Writer: Jeff White
Sound Designer: Dave Arnold & Mark Drury
Scripture: James 2:14-26
Themes: Helping others, sacrifice
Summary: Eric Myers makes a secret promise to help a despondent widow, but the promise will keep him from the season's most important soccer game.

Flights of Imagination cover art

Sound Bites

Actor Brian Cummings, a voice-over legend, made his first *Odyssey* appearance as the title character in "Columbus: The Grand Voyage." He later played a variety of characters including Jesus in "An Adventure in Bethany" and Wooton's boss in "Welcoming Wooton" (album 36). "Columbus" also featured the first appearance of actor Carol Bilger. We liked her voice so much that she became the "new" Mary Barclay, the last in a long line.

Behind The Scenes: The Living Nativity

Marshal Younger, a freelance writer who would later join the *Odyssey* staff at Focus, wrote this episode for his first show. The controversial nature of this story launched an hour-long debate among our actors in the studio about the first amendment and the true meaning of "separation of church and state."

Sound Bites

"The Mortal Coil" was actor Walker Edmiston's favorite episode. Walker remembers a moment when his character Tom Riley had a lengthy scene at Whit's bedside: "The feelings between Hal and me at the moment, being close friends, brought something to that show that you don't normally feel in acting unless the true emotions get in there. When I read this speech—this monologue— I thought, *I can get through that.* I said, 'Let's not rehearse. Let's just turn the machine on.' That's the way we recorded it—without any practice at all. We got that raw emotion.'"

Memo to radio stations about "The Mortal Coil"

My Take: Paul McCusker

We wrote the first part of "The Mortal Coil" to be put away in case Hal Smith died. The plan was to record part I, and then put it away until we needed it. But we liked the story so much that we decided to finish it. Sadly, Hal's wife, Louise, died weeks before the recording, so we were worried about how Hal might react to the content. Being the professional he was, Hal insisted that the show must go on. We dedicated the shows to Louise.

BTS: The Mortal Coil

When Whit is in the Imagination Station thinking back through his life, we hear the line, "I'd like you to meet Jenny. I think

The Whittaker family during recording of "The Mortal Coil."

you've seen her at the Pasadena Library." Years later, when "The Triangle" (album 36) told that full story, we made sure that character Jack Allen said this exact phrase. This way, it sounded like Whit's Imagination Station adventure was flashing back to a scene from "The Triangle." Sound designer Jonathan Crowe delivered this line in "The Mortal Coil," but *Odyssey* producer Marshal Younger played young Jack in "The Triangle."

Sound Bites

In "Best Intentions," much of character Tom Riley's fumbling with the Old English in *The Pilgrim's Progress* was genuine. We didn't show the script to actor Walker Edmiston ahead of time and recorded his first pass at trying to figure out the obscure words and phrases. Much of his ad-libbing was so funny that we left it in the final show.

Sound Bites

At the last minute, actor Steve Burns (who plays Rodney Rathbone) was unavailable to record "Like Father, Like Son." Actor Matt Hurwitz stepped in and did an admirable impression of Rodney. In fact, we've never received a single letter from anyone asking why we had a fill-in voice. Dave Arnold's son, Landon, played Rodney's cousin Scrub. He later went on to play Cody Carper.

Sound Bites

In "An Adventure in Bethany," Martha was played by Lucille Bliss, who is well-known as the voice of *Crusader Rabbit* (1949–1951) and Smurfette on *The Smurfs* (1981–1989).

Sound Bites with Dave Arnold

Midway through production on "A Game of Compassion," I had a sports accident (appropriate for a show about soccer!) that took me away from work for a week. Since we were so close to the broadcast date, Mark Drury stepped in to finish the show, even though he'd never done a full production for *Odyssey* before. This was a proving ground for Mark, and he went on to become one of the most talented sound designers for the program, producing more than 50 episodes.

Actors Landon Arnold and Hal Smith share a comic moment.

Where Odyssey Is Not

Listeners always want to know where Odyssey is located. It might be easier to figure out where Odyssey is *not* located, based on lines from Odyssey characters. Thanks to OdysseyScoop.com for this information.

State:	Episode:	Line:	Speaker
Alaska	The Black Veil	"I'm in Alaska."	Jason Whittaker
Arizona	It Happened at Four Corners	"We're right outside Four Corners, Arizona."	Bernard Walton
Arkansas	Our Daily Bread	"The company is closing the Odyssey plant and moving it to a place called Hope, Arkansas."	George Barclay
California	Stormy Weather	"I don't want to go home. I want to go to California."	Connie Kendall
Colorado	Third Degree	"Precisely where in Colorado are we?"	Eugene Meltsner (after having traveled through several other states)
Connecticut	Blessings in Disguise	"My pen pal, Thor Douglass. He lives in Connecticut."	Brenda Perry
Florida	Family Vacation	"We're going to Florida to Uncle Burt and Aunt Ruby's."	Jimmy Barclay
Hawaii	Aloha, Oy!	"You, Jimmy Barclay, and four guests will fly first class on an all-expenses-paid trip to . . . Hawaii!"	Bart Rathbone
Idaho	Fifteen Minutes	"It was a local commercial. . . . Kuna, Idaho. Didn't run very long."	Greg O'Neil
Iowa	Second Thoughts	"We're in the middle of Iowa."	Bernard Walton
Kansas	Welcoming Wooton	"I'll betcha it's from Mrs. Randolph's granddaughter in Kansas."	Wooton Bassett
Maine	Green Eyes and Yellow Tulips	"I moved here last week from Maine."	Robert Mitchell
Maryland	By Dawn's Early Light	"Odyssey? Is that here in Maryland?"	Dr. Banes (Curt replies, "No, it's in another state.")
Montana	Around the Block	"Barring the time in Montana when I was a child and my head was wedged between two fence rails."	Eugene Meltsner
Nebraska	Clara	"I came here and took [Whit] back home with me . . . Nebraska."	Jack Allen
New Jersey	Double Trouble	"There was that time in New Jersey, sir."	Walter Shakespeare
New York	Where There's Smoke	"I won [my boxing ring] back in New York."	Nick Mulligan
North Carolina	Thank You, God	"When I was about Rodney's age, we moved to Raleigh, North Carolina."	John Whittaker
Oregon	Breaking Point	"I've got family in Oregon!"	Barry Muntz
Pennsylvania	Top This!	"Pennsylvania, near Philadelphia."	Hannah, explaining where's she's from
South Dakota	Chains	"I'm from South Dakota."	Mary Hopkins
Utah	A Day in the Life	"You give the man a wrench in Utah, he thinks he owns the world."	Clark Gilbert
Virginia	The Benefit of the Doubt	"You're moving to Virginia?"	Connie Kendall
Washington, D.C.	Where There's a Will . . .	"Our head office in Washington wants me to work for them . . . and that's why we might have to move."	George Barclay

My Take: Marshal Younger

"This Is Chad Pearson?" was one of many episodes included in the Chick-fil-A Kids' Meals. It triggered controversy thanks to the comedic line that "27 Middle-Eastern terrorists" were holding someone hostage. A handful of people decided to protest against Chick-fil-A. Unfortunately for them, they held their protest on a Sunday—when Chick-fil-A is closed.

I never realized I was such a controversial person until my first two *Odyssey* shows (this one, and "The Living Nativity") both caused such a stir. I was fortunate the *Odyssey* crew didn't give up on me.

Chick-fil-A cassette sleeve package of "This Is Chad Pearson?"

Character: Eugene
Birthplace: Chicago, Illinois
Something you may not know about Eugene:
He once developed radish-flavored ice cream
for Whit's End.

Album 17

On Earth as It Is in Heaven

The R.O.C. of Whit's End

Phil Lollar recalls: " 'Into Temptation' introduced the Room of Consequence (R.O.C.). I had proposed an entirely separate series about a Ring of Consequence created by a crazy inventor to teach young people that their actions do have consequences. When it was initially proposed, some thought that it was too similar to the Imagination Station. As we discussed the idea, we decided that the difference was that the Imagination Station sent kids *back* to experience the past and the R.O.C. sent them *forward* to a possible outcome. In this same round of discussion, we also talked about an invention that would enable you to step into other people's shoes and experience life as they felt it. Many years later, that idea came to fruition when Whit invented the Transmuter in 'Another Man's Shoes' [album 33]."

Unlike the Imagination Station, the R.O.C. works a little differently each time.

Episode	R.O.C. enabled the user to . . .
Into Temptation	See the outcome of buying a toy
For Thine Is the Kingdom	Understand the lifelong outcome of bitterness
Why Don't You Grow Up?	See what it's like to be 22 years old
Soaplessly Devoted	Enter a soap opera
A Victim of Circumstance	Experience the outcome of a lack of responsibility
Gloobers	Enter a video game
The Eternal Birthday	Live the same day over and over
What Do You Think?	Hear what other people were thinking
No Boundaries	Live without rules
Hindsight	Experience life backward

Episode Information

230: Our Father
Original Air Date: 5/15/93
Writer: Phil Lollar
Sound Designer: Dave Arnold
Scripture: Psalm 68:5
Theme: The importance of fathers
Summary: Lawrence Hodges gets tangled up with the Bones of Rath. His need to find a father figure results in several hilarious flights of imagination.

231: Hallowed Be Thy Name
Original Air Date: 5/22/93
Writer: Phil Lollar
Sound Designer: Bob Luttrell
Scripture: Mark 14:55-62; Luke 1:26-38; John 18
Themes: God's name, the holiness of God
Summary: Through Whit's new invention, BEAVRS, Connie learns some of the names of God.

232: Thy Kingdom Come
Original Air Date: 5/29/93
Writer: Paul McCusker
Sound Designer: Dave Arnold
Scripture: 2 Corinthians 4:18
Theme: The kingdom of God
Summary: Whit attempts to explain the kingdom of heaven to Eugene.

233: Thy Will Be Done
Original Air Date: 6/5/93
Writer: Paul McCusker
Sound Designer: Bob Luttrell
Scripture: Matthew 6:10
Theme: Knowing God's will
Summary: Lucy Cunningham-Schultz struggles over a job offer from a liberal school newspaper, and Connie pushes Eugene to make a decision about faith.

234: Our Daily Bread
Original Air Date: 6/12/93
Writer: Phil Lollar
Sound Designer: Bob Luttrell
Scripture: Matthew 6:31-33
Themes: Seeking God first, trusting in His protection and provision
Summary: The Barclay family is thrown into turmoil when George gets laid off from his job.

235: Forgive Us as We Forgive
Original Air Date: 6/19/93
Writer: Phil Lollar
Sound Designer: Dave Arnold
Scripture: Luke 6:37-38
Theme: Forgiveness
Summary: When his father returns from prison, Eric Myers comes face to face with his own lack of forgiveness.

236: Into Temptation
Original Air Date: 6/26/93
Writer: Phil Lollar
Sound Designer: Bob Luttrell
Scripture: 1 Corinthians 10:13
Theme: The folly of giving in to temptation
Summary: Whit's new invention—the Room of Consequence—lets Jimmy Barclay see what could happen if he buys a portable computer game against his parents' wishes.

237: Deliver Us from Evil
Original Air Date: 7/3/93
Writer: Phil Lollar
Sound Designer: Dave Arnold
Scripture: Daniel 1–3
Theme: God's protection
Summary: Bernard Walton and Eugene tell the story of Shadrach, Meshach, Abednego, and the fiery furnace.

238: For Thine Is the Kingdom
Original Air Date: 7/10/93
Writer: Paul McCusker
Sound Designer: Dave Arnold
Scripture: Romans 8:28
Theme: God's lordship in our lives
Summary: Courtney Vincent hopes to become a world-class ballerina, but a car accident abruptly ruins her dreams.

239: The Power
Original Air Date: 7/17/93
Writers: Marshal Younger & Paul McCusker
Sound Designer: Bob Luttrell
Scripture: Matthew 6:13 (KJV)
Theme: The abuse of power
Summary: Isaac Morton finds himself at the mercy of a techno-bully who has the ability to change grades and alter school records.

240: And the Glory
Original Air Date: 7/24/93
Writers: Marshal Younger & Paul McCusker
Sound Designer: Bob Luttrell
Scripture: Galatians 1:5
Theme: Giving glory to God
Summary: Lawrence Hodges and Jimmy banter as announcers on Kids' Radio and can't agree on who makes the better Odyssey Coyotes sportscaster.

241: Forever . . . Amen
Original Air Date: 7/31/93
Writer: Phil Lollar
Sound Designer: Bob Luttrell
Scripture: Matthew 19:13-14
Themes: God's love for us, dealing with loss
Summary: Youngster Danny Schmidt wonders about death and eternity when his mother's unborn baby dies as a result of miscarriage.

The Barclay family in "Our Daily Bread"

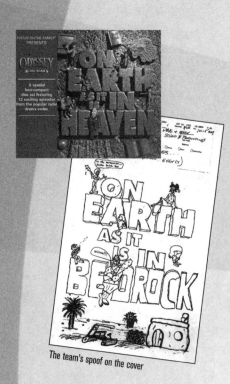

The team's spoof on the cover

A Rocky Cover

A few members of the team thought the original cover treatment for this package looked a bit "prehistoric," so they came up with their own version, pictured here.

Pastor Barclay

George lost his job in "Our Daily Bread." This launched a storyline that culminated in George attending seminary and, eventually, moving the Barclay family from Odyssey. The following episodes chronicled that story:

Our Daily Bread	Pet Peeves	Unto Us a Child Is Born
A Prayer for George Barclay	George Under Pressure	Preacher's Kid
Making the Grade	A Call for Reverend Jimmy	Pokenberry Falls, R.F.D., I and II

This episode introduced the first of several changes in the Barclay family. We had decided that their lives were running too smoothly and needed a good shaking up. George promptly lost his job. There's also a joke you may have missed: George's company closed its Odyssey plant and moved it to a place called Hope, Arkansas—the hometown of then President Bill Clinton.

Sound Bites with Dave Arnold:

In "Our Father," Lawrence's journey inside the human body is a tribute to the movies *Fantastic Voyage* (1966) and *Innerspace* (1987). This particular scene required composing more than 50 separate audio tracks, each with multiple layers of sound effects. However, at the time, I was recording to and mixing from a tape machine that had only eight tracks. So I had to mix these sound-effects layers separately, hoping that once they were all put together they would sound congruent to one another. I had to start over several times to get it just right. "Our Father" ultimately became one of my favorite shows. I loved the parodies that Phil Lollar wrote into the script. Very creative stuff.

Behind the Scenes: Hallowed Be Thy Name

"Hallowed Be Thy Name" introduced BEAVRS, the Bible Education Audio/Video Research System, another invention from Whit to help kids learn about the Bible.

Cut Scenes

In the first draft of "Forgive Us as We Forgive," Tom (not Whit) taught Eric Myers a lesson about forgiveness—strangely enough using hacksaw blades. Also, in that draft, Eric was so angry at his father for embarrassing him that he purposefully dumped his cafeteria tray on the floor for his father (then the school janitor) to clean up. So Eric wouldn't appear to be such a brat, we changed this to Eric accidentally dropping his tray. The *Adventures in Odyssey* team continues to search for ways to balance the need to provide good role models while also dealing realistically with kids' emotions and struggles.

Executive Producer Chuck Bolte laughing at the script

My Take: Marshal Younger

When I first handed off the script for "And the Glory," Paul McCusker called me and said, "Chuck laughed at this script—and he never laughs out loud." I later found out that Chuck laughs at nearly everything and *very much* out loud. Paul was probably trying to boost my self-esteem by letting me think my script was really funny. But at the time, I thought Chuck's reaction was pretty cool.

Character:

Edwin Blackgaard

Quote: "Can't you see I'm having an over-dramatic fit?!"

Something you may not know about Edwin:
He takes mud baths for skin elasticity.

Album 18

A Time of Discovery

Music to Bart Rathbone's Ears

Dave Arnold recalls: "Edwin was really the star of 'My Fair Bernard,' but my favorite part of the show was a little surprise we put in. When I was producing the show, I thought of creating a jingle or musical theme around the commercial for Rathbone's Electric Palace. The slug line that came to me was, 'Rathbone's cleans you out,' but I didn't have a tune in mind. The only thing I told composer John Campbell was that I wanted the music to be cheesy to match Bart's taste. He agreed. I also wondered if John knew of anyone that could sing the jingle. He coyly said that he did. When the music came in, I listened to the jingle and laughed out loud. Not only was it exactly what I was looking for, but John sang the lead and harmony. It was perfect."

BART: Hi, friends and neighbors! This is Bart Rathbone of Rathbone's Clean-Up Service! Are you tired of janitorial services that call a streaky window "clean"?

SINGERS: Rathbone's!

BART: Have you had it with finding trashcans that are supposed to be empty, but are still half full?

SINGERS: Rathbone's!

BART: Do you get all choked up at the dust that's still on your furniture after your janitor leaves?

SINGERS: Rathbone's!

BART: Well, if your answer is "yes," then you need Rathbone's Clean-Up Service! We do all of the above—and more—for less! In fact, you have my personal guarantee that if we don't do a better job for less money, your windows will still be dirty! So call Rathbone's Clean-Up Service at 555-9424! We clean up where the competition leaves off!

SINGERS: Rathbone's cleans you out!

Episode Information

222: The Jesus Cloth
Original Air Date: 3/6/93
Writer: Phil Lollar
Sound Designer: Bob Luttrell
Scripture: 2 Timothy 1:12
Theme: The object of our faith
Summary: The appearance of a piece of cloth supposedly from Jesus' robe creates great hubbub in Odyssey.

224: Greater Love
Original Air Date: 3/20/93
Writer: Phil Lollar
Sound Designer: Dave Arnold
Scripture: John 15:12-13
Theme: Jesus' love for us
Summary: Whit hears the story of how Tom Riley's son died . . . from the man who claims to be responsible.

225: Count It All Joy
Original Air Date: 3/27/93
Writer: Phil Lollar
Sound Designer: Bob Luttrell
Scripture: Nehemiah 8:10; James 1:2-4
Theme: Joy
Summary: Middle-schooler Erica Clark tries to find joy in every situation but nearly has an emotional breakdown in the process.

229: The Marriage Feast
Original Air Date: 4/24/93
Writer: Phil Lollar
Sound Designer: Bob Luttrell
Scripture: Matthew 22:1-14; Romans 6:23
Theme: The parable of the marriage feast
Summary: Kids' Radio tells the story of a king's generous invitation to his son's wedding and the subjects who rudely reject it.

242: Hymn Writers
Original Air Date: 9/4/93
Writer: Phil Lollar
Sound Designer: Bob Luttrell
Scripture: Psalm 96:1-2
Themes: Christian composers, the importance of singing hymns
Summary: Kids' Radio tells the inspiring stories behind popular hymns written by Christian greats Martin Luther (1483–1586), Philip Bliss (1838–1876), and Fanny Crosby (1820–1915).

243: Family Values
Original Air Date: 9/11/93
Writer: Phil Lollar
Sound Designer: Dave Arnold
Scripture: 1 Timothy 5:8
Theme: The importance of strong families
Summary: To win a contest, the Rathbones go on a frantic quest to become a perfect family.

244 and 245: The Mysterious Stranger, I and II
Original Air Dates: 9/18/93 & 9/25/93
Writer: Paul McCusker
Sound Designers: Dave Arnold & Bob Luttrell
Scripture: Exodus 20:17
Theme: Greed
Summary: Whit is pulled into a perplexing mystery when a strange man arrives at Whit's End and claims to have lived there as a small boy.
PARENTAL WARNING:
This is a mystery crafted in the traditional style of mysteries, which means there are a few scary spots. While older children should be able to handle the suspense, this story is not intended for younger listeners.

246: My Fair Bernard
Original Air Date: 10/2/93
Writer: Phil Lollar
Sound Designer: Dave Arnold
Scripture: 2 Chronicles 15:7
Themes: Doing your best, the value of hard work
Summary: Bernard Walton tries to improve his image by being in a play about his life, which is being produced by Edwin Blackgaard.

247: Why Don't You Grow Up?
Original Air Date: 10/9/93
Writers: Charlie Richards & Paul McCusker
Sound Designer: Bob Luttrell
Scripture: Philippians 4:6-7, 11
Themes: Being content, maturity, acting your age
Summary: Erica Clark gets in the Room of Consequence to see what it's like to be 22 years old.

248: Terror from the Skies
Original Air Date: 10/30/93
Writer: Paul McCusker
Sound Designer: Bob Luttrell
Scripture: 1 Thessalonians 5:21
Theme: Don't believe everything you hear
Summary: Edwin Blackgaard produces a live broadcast about monsters from outer space, but the broadcast is a little too real for some listeners.

249: The Case of the Delinquent Disciples
Original Air Date: 11/6/93
Writer: Paul McCusker
Sound Designer: Dave Arnold
Scripture: 2 Timothy 2:15
Themes: The importance of Bible study, commitment
Summary: Harlow Doyle investigates an attendance decline at Connie's Tuesday night Bible study.

Behind The Scenes: *Greater Love*

Several of our successful albums had featured a uniting series of themes, such as the basics of Christianity in *FUNdamentals* (album 4), and Christian virtues in *It All Started When . . .* (album 13). In *A Time of Discovery* we decided to dramatize the nine fruits of the Spirit. We began the series with "Greater Love" and "Count It All Joy," but an episode on peace proved problematic since we'd recently done "Peacemaker" (album 14). We ultimately moved from the series concept and on to other projects. The fruits-of-the-Spirit collection remains unfinished.

My Take: *Phil Lollar*

"The Jesus Cloth" was written around the time that the Dead Sea Scrolls were being released to the public. Some people conjectured that the scrolls would contain material contradictory to Scripture. This led us to ask, "Upon what are we basing our faith?"

BTS: *The Jesus Cloth*

Character Alfred Brownlee, mentioned briefly in this episode as a "real-life Indiana Jones," would later play a major role in "The Search for Whit" (album 27).

Sound Bites

Hal Smith's performance as the Duke of Terra in "The Marriage Feast" was inspired by actor Thomas Mitchell's performance as Gerald O'Hara in the 1939 movie *Gone with the Wind*. Hal gives a dynamic line adapted from the movie: "Land is the only thing worth livin' for, worth fightin' for, worth dyin' for!"

Bernard Walton in the Kids' Radio studio

Sound Bites

If you listen closely to the radio in the background of "Terror from the Skies," you can hear some interesting dialog, including a commercial for a product called Oxymoron. The announcer says:

> Listen, friends . . . Are you sick and tired of those annoying red spots, pimples, and blackheads? Then maybe it's time you tried the clear, tingling feeling of Oxymoron! That's right, Oxymoron is the only acne medicine containing carbonite-benzedrine-peroxide—the patented formula designed to get rid of pimples and keep them away! So the next time you look in the mirror at those ugly red things, just say to yourself "Oxymoron." Available at all fine drug stores and Rathbone's Electric Palace where you can buy one and get the second for the same price! Batteries not included. Void where prohibited. Some assembly required.

Broadcasting from Whit's End! A List of Kids' Radio Episodes

Episode	Program or Format	Episode	Program or Format
Kids' Radio	Variety show	The Devil Made Me Do It	Three sketches
The Big Broadcast	Old-time radio show	Two Roads	"The Twilife Zone"
Over the Airwaves	Variety show	The Great Wishy Woz	"Playhouse of the Airwaves"
A Thanksgiving Carol	"Playhouse of the Airwaves"	Opportunity Knocks	"Candid Conversations with Connie"
A Tongue of Fire	"The Jimmy Barclay Show"	Red Herring	"Candid Conversations with Connie"
On Solid Ground	"O. T. Action News"	O. T. Action News: Battle at the Kishon	"Good Housekeeping Throughout History"
The Marriage Feast	"Adventures in the Bible"	O. T. Action News: Battle at the Kishon	"O. T. Action News"
And the Glory	Sports play-by-play	Secrets	"Candid Conversations with Connie"
Hymn Writers	"A Moment in Time"	Plan B: Resistance	"Candid Conversations with Connie"
Pilgrim's Progress Revisited, I and II	"Playhouse of the Airwaves"	Under the Influence	"Candid Conversations with Connie"
The Twilife Zone	"The Twilife Zone"	Live at the 25	"Candid Conversations with Connie"
Siege at Jericho	"O. T. Action News"	It's All About Me	"Ask Dr. Wise"
Unto Us a Child Is Born	Live Christmas show	It's All About Me	"Ask Dr. Wise and Professor Brilliant"
Share and Share Alike	Live share-a-thon	The Defining Moment	Sports play-by-play
Hidden in My Heart	Three sketches	My Girl Hallie	"The Twilife Zone"
Saint Paul: Voyage to Rome	"Adventures in the Bible"	Fairy Tal-e-vision	Variety show
Saint Paul: An Appointment with Caesar	"Adventures in the Bible"	The Last "I Do"	"Playhouse of the Airwaves"
The Time of Our Lives	"The Twilife Zone"	The Power of One	Variety show
The Decision	"Candid Conversations with Connie"	Blood, Sweat, and Fears	News broadcast
It's a Wrap!	Documentary	Mum's the Word	"Candid Conversations with Connie"
New Year's Eve Live!	Live variety show	The Triangled Web	"Candid Conversations with Connie"
O. T. Action News: Jephthah's Vow	"O. T. Action News"	Rights, Wrongs, and Winners	"Candid Conversations with Connie"

Sound Bites

In "The Case of the Delinquent Disciples," Giselle was played by Myeisha Phillips and was one of the first kids on *Odyssey* who sounded ethnic. We had intended to build a family around this character. Our auditions never yielded the right talent, and unfortunately, the family was never created. Myeisha later played twins in some of the Mulligan family episodes.

BTS: The Mysterious Stranger

It had been awhile since we'd produced a mystery along the lines of "The Case of the Secret Room" (album 2)—in which we not only had suspense, but learned a little more about the history of Odyssey. "The Mysterious Stranger" solved this, creating a mystery and giving us more about the background of Whit's End. However, we worried about the intensity of these episodes, so we put a parental warning at the beginning *and* in the middle of the shows.

The *Odyssey* crew investigates in "The Mysterious Stranger."

"Who Wants Pork Rinds?" The Rathbones Arrive in Odyssey

The Rathbone family values provide a contrast to Whit and his friends' values. Actor Walker Edmiston comments: "I think one of the great things about the show 'Family Values' is that Bart Rathbone is just a scam artist who runs the Electric Palace, but then the writers bring in a family! Now you get to know a little bit more about the guy and you find that he's not all one-dimensional and shallow. He's got this kid he's gotta raise!"

The Rathbones also provide a lot of laughs. "Family Values" was the first appearance of Doris Rathbone. She finally filled out the Rathbone family and was the source of much hilarity to come. Unfortunately, the hilarity and fun of "Family Values" went on too long for the broadcast time. The show was nearly five minutes overtime. But several of the scenes were so hilarious that we couldn't bear cutting them permanently. Instead, we included them in the retail version. That way even though the people listening to the broadcast wouldn't hear the scenes, those who purchased the packages would get the bonus minutes. Since then, we've done the same on many other programs.

Doris Rathbone

Character:
Katrina Shanks
Quote: "Eugene! We missed our own wedding!"
Something you may not know about Katrina:
She once had her tooth broken by Hans
Holstein.

Album 19

Passport to Adventure

"I'm Katrina Shanks, by the Way"

"Truth, Trivia, and 'Trina" introduced Katrina Shanks, a bright and charming young woman. But she triggered a controversy on the team and with fans. In the show, Katrina clearly won over Eugene, which bothered those fans who believed that Connie and Eugene belonged together. A couple of team members couldn't imagine how her character would develop, since she seemed like a clone of Eugene. Paul McCusker, who championed continuing the character, believed that she would bring a balance to Eugene, understanding his intellectual quirks while bringing even more heart to his life. And he believed that she would allow us to put Eugene into new and potentially comedic situations.

As it turns out, the chemistry between the actors playing Eugene and Katrina eventually clicked so well that it became difficult to imagine the show without her.

Episode Information

250 and 251: Pilgrim's Progress Revisited, I and II
Original Air Dates: 11/13/93 & 11/20/93
Writer: Phil Lollar
Sound Designers: Bob Luttrell & Dave Arnold
Theme: The Christian life
Summary: Kids' Radio retells John Bunyan's classic book *The Pilgrim's Progress* (1678) with many familiar Odyssey characters taking roles.

252: The Bad Hair Day
Original Air Date: 12/11/93
Writer: Phil Lollar
Sound Designer: Bob Luttrell
Scripture: Proverbs 22:24-25
Themes: False accusations, taking the law into your own hands
Summary: When it's apparent that a petty thief is on the loose in Odyssey, Rodney Rathbone convinces 10-year-old Henry Thomas to take the law into his own hands.

253: A Time for Christmas
Original Air Date: 12/18/93
Writer: Paul McCusker
Sound Designer: Dave Arnold
Scripture: Luke 2
Theme: The history of the Christmas holiday
Summary: Whit takes middle-schooler Courtney Vincent on an Imagination Station tour of Christmases past.

254: Truth, Trivia, and 'Trina
Original Air Date: 1/8/94
Writer: Paul McCusker
Sound Designer: Dave Arnold
Scripture: Proverbs 13:3
Themes: Competition, pride, relationships
Summary: Bart Rathbone's TV trivia contest pits Eugene and Connie against a college student named Katrina Shanks, who seems to have captured Eugene's heart.

255: The Boy Who Cried "Destructo!"
Original Air Date: 1/15/94
Writer: Phil Lollar
Sound Designer: Bob Luttrell
Scripture: Proverbs 14:7
Theme: Controlling your imagination
Summary: Lawrence Hodges claims that agents from Destructo have kidnapped Harlow Doyle near a mysterious cave.

256, 257, and 258: Aloha, Oy!, I, II, and III
Original Air Dates: 1/22/94, 1/29/94, & 2/5/94
Writer: Phil Lollar
Sound Designers: Dave Arnold, Bob Luttrell, & Mark Drury
Scripture: Psalm 68:6
Theme: Family togetherness
Summary: The Barclays win a contest for an all-expenses paid vacation to Hawaii, but the Rathbones are coming along!

259: The Potential in Elliot
Original Air Date: 2/12/94
Writer: Marshal Younger
Sound Designer: Bob Luttrell
Scripture: Romans 12:10, 15
Theme: Encouragement
Summary: Middle-schooler Sam Johnson tells his friend Elliot Richie to stop his weird science experiments, but then Sam takes an Imagination Station trip where he meets another young man who tinkers with inventions.

260: Naturally, I Assumed . . .
Original Air Date: 2/19/94
Writer: Paul McCusker
Sound Designer: Dave Arnold
Scripture: Philippians 4:8
Theme: Don't make assumptions
Summary: Eugene comes to Connie for advice to win the heart of Katrina Shanks, who seems to be interested in another man.

262: A Prayer for George Barclay
Original Air Date: 4/2/94
Writer: Paul McCusker
Sound Designer: Dave Arnold
Scripture: 1 Corinthians 9:14, 16
Themes: God's call to the ministry, dealing with change
Summary: The Barclay children pray that their father will finally find a job.

Sound Bites with Dave Arnold

Hal Smith could do a wonderful gravelly voice and was perfect for the character Apollyon in "Pilgrim's Progress Revisited." To aid the transformation to a dragon, I pitched his voice down and added an assortment of animal noises. To create the giant's footsteps, I used sonic booms and earthquake effects.

In one particularly memorable moment at the studio, we were recording the background voices for the demons-in-hell scene. Will Ryan humorously suggested that we should do a take playing the demons as a takeoff of the Disney character Goofy. It didn't make it to the final mix, of course, but we do have a version of that scene with a bunch of Goofy-sounding demons.

Katrina Shanks

Behind the Scenes: The Bad Hair Day

Bones of Rath band member Brian "Butch" Evans is first mentioned in this episode. However, we don't hear from the character until 18 months later in "The Good, the Bad, and Butch" (album 23). Originally titled "The Incident," this show was inspired by the 1940s Walter Van Tilburg Clark book and movie *The Ox-Bow Incident*.

BTS: Truth, Trivia, and 'Trina

The original ending featured Connie and Katrina ganging up on Eugene for his continued overabundance of information. However, in the studio, the actors suggested to change it to a debate on the construction date of the famous Taj Mahal, a building completed in India around 1648. Dave Arnold's major contribution to the script was adding a line describing Eugene's eyes as "periwinkle blue."

BTS: The Boy Who Cried "Destructo"

During the summer of 1991, we had rewritten the script and rerecorded most of the Officer Harley stories as brand-new episodes with new characters. However, we had neglected "The Return of Harley." We decided to remake it as a single episode— "The Boy Who Cried 'Destructo!'" It was the only Officer Harley remake in which Harley's replacement (Harlow Doyle) actually replaced Harley.

BTS: Aloha, Oy!

This episode was intended as a spoof of television sitcoms, such as *The Brady Bunch* (1969–1974) and *Happy Days* (1974–1984), that inevitably had episodes take place in unusual or exotic locations. "Aloha, Oy!" brought the Rathbone family to life as never before. Several of the actors, including Steve Burns (Rodney) and Gabriel Encarnacion (Lawrence) list these shows as their all-time favorites. The part of Don Iowa was written specifically for musician and actor Randy Crenshaw's dead-on impersonation of Hawaiian singer Don Ho (1930–2007). Our character Captain Quid was Phil Lollar's tribute to the late actor Robert Shaw (1927–1978) and his role in the movie *Jaws* (1975).

Part of the title is actually a mistake. Phil Lollar, who was a freelance writer at the time, had written the title as "Aloha, Oi!"

Katrina + Eugene are Engaged!

Art by Megan U. and Jane H.

Paul McCusker, who was on staff, thought the spelling was potentially confusing and "corrected" it to the phonetic "Oy," thinking Phil was playing on the phrase "Aloha, Hoy!" Paul had completely missed Phil's allusion to "Oi" as a Yiddish exclamation of exasperation. Oi!

Sound Bites

When Jimmy and Lawrence are on the plane in "Aloha, Oy!" Jimmy starts to pretend he's a 747 captain. Then Lawrence jumps in and yells "Mayday! Mayday! This is Flight 714— We're going down!" This is a reference to the Tintin graphic novel *Flight 714* (late 1960s), in which Tintin, Captain Haddock, and others are in a jet, which is eventually forced to crash-land on a tropical island.

Sound Bites with Dave Arnold

The scripts for "Aloha, Oy!" were the normal length for an *Odyssey* show (around 30 pages). However, the pace for the shows was so fast that all three parts ended up being *very* short. When we finished editing the voice tracks, we briefly considered cutting a few scenes and turning the story into two parts instead of three. Since we didn't want to cut too much of the comedy, we decided instead to lengthen the shows by adding more music and more clips of previous episodes, and giving the shows a more leisurely, laid-back pace than our typical *Odyssey* shows. In the end, they were still short.

My Take: Steve Burns

There was a lot of physical action in "Aloha, Oy!" and I loved being able to do things that I never got to do before, like surf and parasail. I love being Rodney. The Barclays and the Rathbones should go on vacation at least once a year!

"I'm Beside Myself!" Actors Talking to Themselves

The following scenes depict actors talking to themselves as different characters:

Episode	Character
Aloha, Oy!	Doris Rathbone and the plane stewardess
Tom for Mayor	Walker Edmiston as Tom Riley and Bart Rathbone
Marriage Feast	Kenny Mars as the king and the rude subject
The Return	Earl Boen as the Blackgaard brothers
Broken Window	Steve Burns as Rodney Rathbone and Robert Mitchell

My Take: Paul McCusker

We heard the playback of "A Prayer for George Barclay" shortly after Hal Smith passed away. Hearing him talk about answered prayer was one of those magical moments. The line "The best is yet to come" seemed especially poignant and almost prophetic in a way. In fact, we decided to use that very line as the climax of the episode "Gone . . ." when the character of Whit leaves town.

BTS: A Prayer for George Barclay

After deciding that George Barclay should lose his job, the writers then had to figure out what was next for the Barclay family. As we discussed their future, we decided that it wasn't dramatically compelling for George to find another job. We wanted him to pursue a calling of God—something that would take the family in new directions spiritually. So, we decided to have George go to seminary to become a pastor.

This was also a good idea because Focus on the Family has an entire ministry dedicated to helping pastors and their families. This new storyline for the Barclays allowed us to get ideas from that ministry so we could, in turn, present stories that might be helpful to them.

The Progress of "Pilgrim's Progress Revisited"

The first draft of "Pilgrim's Progress Revisited" was an Imagination Station adventure titled "Lawrence's Progress." Whit described it as a "narrated game" in which Lawrence would become a takeoff character based on John Bunyan's classic book, *The Pilgrim's Progress*. It ended with Lawrence accepting Jesus, much in the same way that Digger Digwillow did in the original "Imagination Station" (album 5) adventure. However, the team felt the story would be more engaging with characters we knew. This made Kids' Radio a better vehicle to tell the story than the Imagination Station. Mrs. Busywork doesn't appear in Bunyan's novel. We created that character to give actress Katie Leigh another role.

Album

20

A Journey of Choices

We Interrupt This Program

On Friday, January 28, 1994, Terry Smith, the son of Hal Smith, found his father sitting in a very relaxed repose in his favorite armchair, "looking as if he were sleeping." Hal passed away while listening to his favorite old-time radio dramas on a Los Angeles radio station. He was 77 years old.

The Odyssey team was shocked and grief stricken with the news. We had lost a talented actor and a close friend, a man who had shaped so much of what *Odyssey* became.

Prior to the news, the team had been planning our most ambitious recording session ever. We hoped to record eight full episodes rather than our usual four or five. All eight episodes featured Whit, but Hal passed away one week before the recording. We immediately adjusted several of the scripts (including "When Bad Isn't So Good" and "Pet Peeves") to remove Whit. (See chart later in this chapter.) Thankfully, we also had several episodes already recorded with Hal as Whit. We interspersed these with the new shows that didn't feature Whit to buy us some time to plan for the future.

Episode Information

261: Afraid, Not!
Original Air Date: 2/26/94
Writer: Paul McCusker
Sound Designer: Bob Luttrell
Scripture: Isaiah 41:10
Theme: Conquering fear
Summary: A bully makes young Danny Schmidt afraid of walking to school.

263: When Bad Isn't So Good
Original Air Date: 4/9/94
Writer: Phil Lollar
Sound Designer: Bob Luttrell
Scripture: Psalm 1:1-5
Theme: Goodness is its own reward
Summary: Edwin Blackgaard and Sam Johnson come to the conclusion they need to be "bad" once in a while to get noticed.

264: Making the Grade
Original Air Date: 4/16/94
Writer: Paul McCusker
Sound Designer: Mark Drury
Scripture: Proverbs 12:1
Themes: Personal discipline, the importance of education
Summary: Jimmy Barclay discovers that all that "worthless stuff" he neglected to learn in school was more important than he thought.

265: War of the Words
Original Air Date: 4/23/94
Writer: Marshal Younger
Sound Designer: Bob Luttrell
Scripture: Proverbs 21:23
Themes: Swearing, using bad language
Summary: A carelessly uttered word from Eugene creates havoc as it becomes the fashionable insult for the kids in Odyssey.

266: It Began with a Rabbit's Foot . . .
Original Air Date: 4/30/94
Writer: Paul McCusker
Sound Designer: Dave Arnold
Scripture: Romans 3:10, 23; 5:8; 10:8-10
Themes: Redemption, salvation
Summary: Whit tells Lucy Cunningham-Schultz about the creation of the Bible Room, and the discussion leads Katrina Shanks to a very important decision.

267: It Ended with a Handshake
Original Air Date: 5/7/94
Writer: Paul McCusker
Sound Designer: Dave Arnold
Scripture: 1 Corinthians 13:5, 7
Themes: Communication, love
Summary: Eugene's relationship with Katrina takes an unexpected turn when his computer disk filled with unsent love letters goes missing.

268: Pet Peeves
Original Air Date: 5/14/94
Writers: Paul McCusker & Chris Fabry
Sound Designer: Bob Luttrell
Scripture: Hebrews 13:8
Themes: Responsibility, dealing with change
Summary: Donna Barclay tries to cope with all the change going on in her life by adopting a stray dog.

269: Fences
Original Air Date: 5/21/94
Writer: Marshal Younger
Sound Designer: Mark Drury
Scripture: Ecclesiastes 4:9-12
Themes: Communication, dealing with disappointment
Summary: Upset that her father has canceled his visit to Odyssey, Connie unleashes her anger on men in general.

270: The War Hero

Original Air Date: 5/28/94
Writer: Phil Lollar
Sound Designer: Mark Drury
Scripture: Romans 12:1
Theme: Heroism
Summary: Connie's uncle, Joe Finneman, is reluctant to reveal the true story of what he did in a remote village in the South Pacific during the waning days of World War II.

271: The Secret Keys of Discipline

Original Air Date: 6/4/94
Writer: Phil Lollar
Sound Designer: Dave Arnold
Scripture: Proverbs 13:8
Theme: Self-discipline
Summary: Danny can't seem to force himself to practice the piano for the talent show at Whit's End.

272 and 273: Two Brothers . . . and Bernard, I and II

Original Air Dates: 6/11/94 & 6/18/94
Writer: Phil Lollar
Sound Designer: Dave Arnold & Bob Luttrell
Scripture: Genesis 25:20-34; 27:1–33:20
Themes: The biblical story of Esau and Jacob, brotherly love
Summary: Bernard tells the story of Jacob and Esau—and the cunning deceit that nearly destroyed the brothers.

Actor Hal Smith drawn by *Odyssey* fan Hannah H.

Where's Whit?

The following episodes were written before Hal Smith passed away and were adjusted after his death.

Episode	Characters who replaced Whit
When Bad Isn't So Good	Eugene and Bernard Walton
Making the Grade	George Barclay and Mrs. Hodges
It Ended with a Handshake	Bernard and Connie
Pet Peeves	Connie
The War Hero	Uncle Joe Finneman
The Fundamentals	Dale Jacobs
A Book by Its Cover	Jack Allen

Cut Scenes

In "When Bad Isn't So Good," we recorded Edwin reading a postcard that he'd received from Regis, but had to cut it for time. The postcard read:

> Dear Edwin
>
> Just a quick note to let you know that I am doing very well. I have received several six-figure grants from philanthropic concerns here in Europe. How is your little theatre venture going? I'm sure the citizens of Odyssey are standing in line to partake of the culture you offer. I often think fondly of the time I spend there—perhaps one day I shall return to renew my old acquaintances.
>
> Your loving brother, Regis

Goof Alert!

In "War of the Words," Eugene says, "Just last week, I recalibrated my barometer to study what the effect would be if the Earth's atmosphere were made up of 3 percent nitrogen instead of 4." The Earth's atmosphere is 78 percent nitrogen, not 4 percent. Surely Eugene should know that!

My Take: Marshal Younger

"War of the Words" was an episode that showed the dangers of using profanity. But, of course, we couldn't use actual bad words. So the "profanity" had to be a mangled form of some word that Eugene used that Connie wouldn't understand. And it needed to sound like an insult. So Eugene saying "maladroit" turned into "milajoit." You would be amazed how difficult it was to come up with just the right word!

Behind the Scenes: It Began with a Rabbit's Foot . . .

The Bible Room, an important place at Whit's End, was introduced in the episode "Gotcha!" However, "Gotcha!" featured the now-banned Officer Harley, and it hadn't been aired since 1988. To retell the story of the creation of the Bible Room, we used flashbacks to non-Harley scenes of "Gotcha!"

in "It Began with a Rabbit's Foot . . ." This new episode also featured Katrina Shanks making a commitment to Christ, which led to *many* more stories and complexities in her relationship with Eugene.

BTS: It Ended with a Handshake

Hal Smith passed away between the recordings of "It Began with a Rabbit's Foot . . ." and "It Ended with a Handshake," so we had Whit off running errands in the second episode. This show also introduced the language-skewering character of Fred Holstein, played with aplomb by Kenneth Mars. This show was also the source of one of the team's favorite actor ad-libs. Katrina said, "Eugene, your eye is twitching." Eugene quickly responded, "Calcium deficiency."

BTS: Pet Peeves

"Pet Peeves" was originally an episode where Whit counseled Donna Barclay about the changes in her life and her desire to "adopt" a mangy-looking dog (see album cover art). When Connie replaced Whit in the last draft, we intended to start Connie's growing-up process. However, we didn't have her graduate from high school for another four years. *Odyssey* time is a time all its own.

Sound designer Mark Drury with actor Amber Arnold

Sound Bites with Bob Luttrell

I've been saddled with several episodes that prominently feature animals; first "All's Well with Boswell" (album 8) and then "Pet Peeves," which featured several long recording sessions with my own dogs. My poor dogs won't bark on cue, but they sure will bark when I don't want them to.

My Take: Marshal Younger

When I look back on the show "Fences," I consider it one of the worst shows I've ever done because I portrayed Connie so poorly. And Katie Leigh wasn't happy with it either. When I attended the following recording session, she confronted me about my poor writing: "When you mess with Connie, you mess with me." That moment made me realize just how seriously the actors took their characters. I was impressed by that. And also petrified. It took me awhile before I had the nerve to write dialogue for Connie again.

Sound Bites

Actor Amber Arnold (Brooke Myers) actually composed and played the piano piece that Danny Schmidt plays in "The Secret Keys of Discipline."

BTS: *The War Hero*

Actors Hal Smith (Whit) and Parley Baer (Uncle Joe) both served in the armed forces in World War II. Both of the characters they played were also veterans who told stories about the war.

Historical Episodes

The following episodes dramatize true events or take place in historical settings.

Event	Year	Episode
The creation of the Julian calendar	46 B.C.	New Year's Eve Live!
Saint Valentine	circa 270	The Last "I Do"
Saint Nicholas	circa 300	B-TV: Redeeming the Season
Telemachus	404	Telemachus, I and II
Saint Patrick	circa 450	Saint Patrick: A Heart Afire, I and II
Saint Augustine makes Christmas a holiday.	circa 600	B-TV: Redeeming the Season
The early history of Christmas	Various	A Time for Christmas
The voyage of Christopher Columbus	1492	Columbus: The Grand Voyage
The writing of "A Mighty Fortress Is Our God"	circa 1528	Hymn Writers
An interview with John Bunyan	1678	BTV: Grace
The martyrdom of William Tyndale	1536	When in Doubt . . . Pray!
Paul Revere's ride	1775	The Midnight Ride
The battle at Lexington and Bunker Hill	1775	The American Revelation, I and II
The signing of the Declaration of Independence	1776	The Day Independence Came

Event	Year	Episode
The War of 1812	1812	By Dawn's Early Light
The writing of "Amazing Grace"	1750–1772	Amazing Grace
The Underground Railroad	1850	The Underground Railroad, I, II, and III
Thomas Edison's childhood	1857	The Potential in Elliot
Anna Bartlett Warner	1860	Something Significant
Abraham Lincoln	1865	Lincoln, I and II
Reverend George Müller	1845	When in Doubt . . . Pray!
The writing of "It is Well"	1873	It Is Well
The writing of "My Redeemer"	1876	Hymn Writers
Charles Finney's prayer	1876	When in Doubt . . . Pray!
Fanny Crosby	1900	Hymn Writers
Circuit riders	1905	Arizona Sunrise
Amy Carmichael	1913	Something Significant
Pearl Harbor	1941	East Winds, Raining
The Battle of Guadalcanal	1942	Rescue from Manatugo Point *and* Operation: Dig-Out
The story of *PT-109*	1943	Something Significant
The battle for New Guinea	1945	The War Hero
The Vietnam War	1971	Memories of Jerry

Where's Gary?

Illustrator Gary Locke draws all of the amazing images for *Adventures in Odyssey*. He occasionally paints himself into a piece of art. In the picture below he is the second man from the right with the moustache and beard. Can you spot him in any more illustrations?

Album 21

Wish You Were Here

Wish Who Were Here?

While the album title *Wish You Were Here* seemed to allude to Eugene and Bernard's travels—even down to the postcard motif in the original album art at left—it also expressed the team's sense of loss over the death of Hal Smith. So we really "wished Hal were here."

Rather than call the six road-trip episodes by a name followed by the part number, we decided to give each episode an individual name in numerical order. Our hope was that our audience would listen to them in the proper sequence. We began with "*First*-Hand Experience," followed by "*Second* Thoughts," and so on. Paul McCusker recalls, "I thought of the perfect title for the final episode of the road trip—'Six on the Richter Scale'—about a month after it was broadcast. Too late!"

233

Episode Information

274: First-Hand Experience
Original Air Date: 7/23/94
Writer: Paul McCusker
Sound Designer: Bob Luttrell
Scripture: Colossians 3:17
Themes: Friendship, doing good things for God's glory
Summary: Eugene decides to go to California, and his journey unexpectedly intersects with Bernard's trip to San Diego.

275: Second Thoughts
Original Air Date: 7/30/94
Writer: Marshal Younger
Sound Designer: Mark Drury
Scripture: John 15:17
Theme: Family relationships
Summary: Eugene and Bernard's cross-country journey gets waylaid in the middle of Iowa. There Bernard and Eugene meet Graham, a kid who desperately wants to leave his small-town life.

276: Third Degree
Original Air Date: 8/6/94
Writer: Marshal Younger
Sound Designer: Dave Arnold
Scripture: Proverbs 27:17
Themes: Friendship, making proper choices
Summary: In Colorado, Eugene meets a group of people who are just like him. Bernard is not so fortunate; he fights a traffic ticket in court.

277: It Happened at Four Corners
Original Air Date: 8/13/94
Writer: Phil Lollar
Sound Designer: Bob Luttrell
Scripture: Proverbs 1:19
Theme: Greed
Summary: An old prospector, a torn map, and a legendary gold mine interrupt Eugene and Bernard's journey to California and infect them with gold fever.

278 and 279: The Fifth House on the Left, I and II
Original Air Dates: 8/20/94 & 8/27/94
Writer: Paul McCusker
Sound Designers: Bob Luttrell & Mark Drury
Scripture: Matthew 6:19-21
Themes: Trusting God in all situations, salvation
Summary: In Hollywood, Bernard and Eugene meet the Smith-Hammer family. Bernard tells a little girl about Jesus, and Eugene is cast to star in a movie.

280: Gone . . .
Original Air Date: 9/3/94
Writer: Paul McCusker
Sound Designer: Dave Arnold
Scripture: 1 Corinthians 15:51-52
Theme: Dealing with loss
Summary: Bernard and Eugene finally return to Odyssey to find a huge surprise waiting for them—Whit has left town!
PARENTAL WARNING:
When this episode was released, it proved to be a highly emotional episode because the most-loved character of Whit departs. This episode may be used as an opportunity to talk with your child about the difficulty of responding to God's call, losing those we love, or even the subject of death.

281: But Not Forgotten
Original Air Date: 9/10/94
Writer: Phil Lollar
Sound Designer: Dave Arnold
Scripture: Deuteronomy 31:8
Themes: Dealing with loss, change
Summary: Tom Riley, Connie, and Eugene find that running Whit's End takes more time than they thought it would. Tom asks an old friend of Whit's, Jack Allen, to help out.

282: The Fundamentals

Original Air Date: 9/17/94
Writer: Marshal Younger
Sound Designer: Mark Drury
Scripture: Proverbs 1:5
Theme: The importance of learning and wisdom
Summary: Jimmy Barclay attends basketball camp with Phil McFarland, a teen who thinks he knows everything there is to know about the game.

283: A Book by Its Cover

Original Air Date: 9/24/94
Writer: Paul McCusker
Sound Designer: Bob Luttrell
Scripture: Matthew 7:1-2
Theme: Judging others
Summary: Connie and Eugene try to see Jack's secret painting, and Katrina Shanks tutors a difficult student.

284: The Election Deception

Original Air Date: 10/1/94
Writer: Marshal Younger
Sound Designer: Bob Luttrell
Scripture: 3 John 11
Themes: Honesty, integrity
Summary: When Courtney Vincent's diary disappears from her locker, events conspire against her hopes of being elected president of the student council.

288: The Twilife Zone

Original Air Date: 10/22/94
Writer: Phil Lollar
Sound Designer: Bob Luttrell
Scripture: 1 Corinthians 6:12-13
Themes: Addiction, self-control
Summary: Kids' Radio tells the story of a talking toy chicken that enslaves its owner in a web of strange demands.
PARENTAL WARNING:
This episode is about the dangers of addiction. Although presented in a comical and nonthreatening way, we suggest you listen with your children and use the episode as a springboard to discuss the subject of drug abuse.

What Now?

The *Odyssey* team met in February 1994 to discuss the future of the show without Hal Smith. Essentially, we saw four options:

1. Discontinue *Odyssey* completely
2. Continue *Odyssey* by replacing Whit's voice immediately
3. Discontinue *Odyssey* and create a spin-off series
4. Continue *Odyssey* without Whit . . . at least for a period of time

We quickly ruled out option 1 because we felt that there were many more stories to tell. For option 2, we did a wide-ranging search for Hal Smith sound-alikes. We even auditioned his son, Terry, as well as actor Herbert Lahr, son of Bert Lahr, the cowardly lion from *The Wizard of Oz* (1939). We didn't find anyone whose voice was close enough to Hal's to make it work.

Option 3 held some promise. We discussed a number of concepts, including a series featuring Connie as the main character and another where we would permanently switch to a Kids' Radio format. But we weren't sure if our audience would accept such a radical change in format.

So that left us with option 4. We should continue *Odyssey* without Whit.

But should Whit die on the show? Though we debated it, we finally decided that Whit was an icon, a central character, not only in the radio show, but in the entire *Adventures in Odyssey* franchise. We couldn't "kill" Whit—he had to leave.

That decision left us with a dilemma. How could we explain Whit's departure from Odyssey in a way that would make sense to our fans? Our solution was to follow the lead of the popular TV show *M*A*S*H*, which lost one of its main actors between seasons. To explain his disappearance, the producers had lead character Hawkeye Pierce return from a weekend leave to find that his best friend, Trapper, had been abruptly shipped home.

In a similar manner, we sent Eugene and Bernard out of town for the whole summer, allowing our listeners to go with them. This gave sufficient time for Whit to make his off-air decision to leave and gave us a dramatically compelling means to continue the show while we searched for an actor to play Whit.

Actor Hal Smith

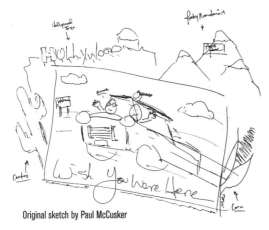

Original sketch by Paul McCusker

Though it was a difficult time for us, we believe it created a very rich year of episodes for *Adventures in Odyssey*.

My Take: Marshal Younger

"Third Degree" started with this idea: "What would happen if Eugene stumbled upon a town of Eugenes?" Since it took place in Colorado where Focus on the Family's headquarters is located, I thought that it would be a perfect place for an inside joke. In my first draft, Bernard was pulled over by none other than Dr. James Dobson rather than a regular police officer. Not only did Dr. Dobson give Bernard a ticket, he also gave him some life advice. In the end, however, this idea started to take the episode in another direction, so we gave up on it.

Cut Scenes

For "It Happened at Four Corners," we recorded a scene where Eugene attempted to tell the story of *The Three Little Pigs*, beginning with "Once upon a time, there was a trio of swine, who sought to construct protective domiciles . . ." It had to be cut for time from this episode, but we later used it in "I Want My B-TV" (album 23).

Behind the Scenes: It Happened at Four Corners

We always intended the fourth episode in the road trip to be a desert adventure. Originally titled "Going Forth," our first idea was to do a crossover episode with Focus on the Family's video series *The Last Chance Detectives*. The crossover show didn't end up working out here, but we did 12 *Last Chance* crossover episodes with Jason Whittaker in 2004.

My Take: Phil Lollar

"It Happened at Four Corners" is a tribute to two of my favorite movies: Stanley Kramer's *It's a Mad, Mad, Mad, Mad World* (1963) and Erich von Stroheim's silent film *Greed* (1924). In the *Odyssey* episode, Pete Renaday did a spot-on impression of the Smiler from *It's a Mad, Mad, Mad, Mad World*.

The team had several questions about plausibility in my first draft of the script. Why would the Smiler be in such a huge rush to get to the claims office when no one knew about his find? Why did one character bring handcuffs into the cave instead of a weapon? Where did another character get sleeping powder? Since this was a story within a story, I put all of those questions in Eugene's mouth. It gave us a way to poke fun at the story within the episode itself.

What Then?

After we decided to move Whit away from Odyssey, we considered the future of the series. Since Whit was our central character, we had to find someone to fill that void. Who? Our initial discussions dealt with one of our existing characters—such as Tom Riley or Connie Kendall—taking over Whit's End. The more we talked about it, however, the more we realized we still needed a central character who could carry on the Whit tradition.

Our discussion turned to Whit's second son, Jason. After all, Jason had even hinted that he might move to Odyssey in "The Mortal Coil" (album 16). Perhaps Jason could fill the void left by Whit. We toyed with having a comical episode showing the gang dealing with the practicalities of running Whit's End without Whit (maybe including scenes of Tom trying to figure out the gadgets, et cetera) before Jason arrived to save the day.

The more we brainstormed the Jason character, however, the more we realized we had a potential problem: We were in danger of making Jason too much like Whit. During our creative meetings, he was sounding like a Whit clone with all of the same characteristics.

We liked the idea of bringing Jason to Whit's End, but he couldn't replace Whit alone. So we decided to split Whit's personality into two characters. Jason could show Whit's mysterious, adventurous, and inventive side. But we needed another character to show Whit's grandfatherly, wise, and discerning side. Enter Jack Allen.

Jack Allen

My Take: Katie Leigh

I was very sad when Hal died. It was hard to work on the show and play Connie. Out of respect for Hal's memory, the guys always left his microphone empty, which was right across from mine. I hated having an empty microphone to look at when I was working because it always reminded me that he wasn't with us anymore. It didn't feel right. I was so happy when they started letting people use that mike again.

BTS: But Not Forgotten

Due to scheduling conflicts, "But Not Forgotten" was actually recorded before "Gone . . ." which made for an unusual session. We were nervous about our first

Actor Alan Young, voice of Jack Allen

post-Whit session. One of the first scenes we recorded was the one where Jack and Tom try to put a curlicue on an ice-cream cone. Actors Walker Edmiston and Alan Young had worked together for years on other productions, and Walker thought we should record the read-through without a rehearsal. Their recording chemistry,

Actor Landon Arnold as Scrub, recording a happier scene

which was immediately obvious, gave us hope that maybe—just maybe—this new arrangement would work.

Sound Bites with Dave Arnold

The scene in "But Not Forgotten" where Scrub is crying might sound a little too real. My son, Landon, is an adult now, but at the time, he played the role of Scrub. We were in the studio recording his lines, but he wasn't getting into the emotion of the scene very well. We kept giving him direction, and after a while it got to be too much for the little guy, and the tears started to flow. Instead of stopping to console him, we realized that we should get the lines while he was feeling the emotions of the part. The result was a powerful scene and a lot of razzing from my friends that I was a heartless father. (By the way, Landon was fine afterward, and we have a great relationship to this day. Phew!)

Additionally, "But Not Forgotten" is the second of only two episodes that required a complete music rewrite. When I listened to John Campbells's first pass, I noticed that the cues were negative emotionally, likely because of his personal feelings about a new character taking the place of Whit. I didn't want the music to impart those feelings to our listeners, so I asked John to revise the score. He went back to the drawing board and came up with a completely different approach, one that moved the show into a new season in a powerful and positive way.

My Take: Phil Lollar

We saw how Eugene reacted to Whit's departure in "Gone . . . ," but we thought that we would rob the audience if we didn't show how Connie felt in "But Not Forgotten." That's what this show tried to do. In many ways, the scene between Connie and Scrub wasn't so much about Whit going away as it was about Hal Smith dying. We wanted to assure Connie (and, in turn, the audience) that Jack wasn't going to *replace* Whit.

Sound Bites with Dave Arnold

"Gone . . ." was probably the most difficult show I had ever produced; it was physically and emotionally draining. But I wanted to do it as a labor of love to Hal Smith. We wanted

Actor Hal Smith

to hear from Whit in the show, but we obviously couldn't record new lines. Paul McCusker and I discussed how to find the Whit lines from existing tracks. Paul wrote a draft with ideas of what the lines needed to be, and I culled through hundreds of old episodes and session recordings to find just the right lines, sighs, and vocal sounds to make those few Whit scenes work.

To help soothe our emotions, we also wanted Whit to say some sort of good-bye to the town (and our listeners), but we never had Hal record anything like that for *Odyssey*. We had to go to an unusual source. When Hal's wife, Louise, had passed away a year-and-a-half before, Hal recorded a message thanking the Focus staff members for praying for him and sending sympathy cards. I carefully edited this message to create Whit's good-bye to the town.

We had originally considered doing several episodes with Whit using lines from older episodes. However, after discovering how much time it took, we abandoned the idea. Apart from "Gone..." we used old Whit lines on two other occasions: our release of "Christmas Around the World" (*Joy to the World* package) and as a phone message for Eugene in "The Time Has Come" (album 25).

Also of note: "Gone . . ." was the first show we produced on a digital audio workstation. This truly was a new beginning for us in more ways than one.

What Should We Tell?

Apart from the traumatic impact it had on everyone, Hal Smith's death created a unique public relations problem. How should we communicate something so significant to our audience? Should we announce it somehow on the *Adventures in Odyssey* program itself? Should we mention it on the *Focus on the Family* broadcast?

This question laid heavy on our minds. We felt we should do something, since he was such a huge part of the program. However, we also knew that the vast majority of our listeners didn't know that Hal Smith was the voice of Whit, and any announcement might be misconstrued as an announcement that Whit himself was dead. In spite of our desire to honor Hal, we decided to hold off acknowledging his

Focus on the Family magazine May 1995

death until the episodes introducing Jack Allen had aired, which we hoped would assure our audience that the show would continue.

Finally, after enough time had gone by, we put an item in the *Focus on the Family* magazine about Hal's passing. A few months later, *Clubhouse* magazine mentioned his death as well.

BTS: The Fundamentals

This episode was written in part to help promote Focus on the Family's basketball camps. It also features the appearance of an adult character named Alex Jefferson. In "The Eternal Birthday" (album 33), we introduced a kid character named Alex Jefferson because we forgot that we'd already used that name for a basketball player.

My Take: Marshal Younger

I've always loved sports, and I love writing sports episodes. "The Fundamentals" was similar to an experience my ninth-grade basketball team had. Our best player always made every shot he took, but he had a strange technique—so the coach told him to change it. I wanted to say, "Leave him alone! He's doing great!" But the kid did what the coach said, and his skills improved.

Goof Alert!

In "The Election Deception," the last name of Odyssey Middle School's principal is McSpadden. But in "Pipe Dreams" (album 15), he was Principal McFadden. Perhaps the name changed because he got married.

My Take: Phil Lollar

For "The Twilife Zone," I had originally written a much darker script where Courtney Vincent became addicted to a talking toy doll named, of all things, Mary Jane. But after reviewing the script, we came to the conclusion that it might scare kids away from playing with their dolls and action figures. What to do?

One of the [voice impressions] I could always get a laugh with around the office—especially from Chuck Bolte—was the voice of one of my favorite Jay Ward [cartoon characters]—Super Chicken. Chuck suggested that the way to make the story lighter and funnier—but still get the message across—was to change the doll to a talking toy chicken. So I used that voice for Henny.

Welcome, Jack Allen

While auditioning new actors, we met Alan Young. Alan remembers: "They told me that they weren't replacing Hal, because you couldn't replace him. But they were looking for someone who might have the same feel that Hal had, and they thought I might have that feel." We were so charmed by Alan that we decided to create a character for him—one that would reflect his own personality, just as Whit had reflected Hal's.

But who would this character be?

We wanted him to be like Whit in many ways, but to have distinct differences. Originally, we planned on naming him John *Lewis* Allen, with his middle name being a reference to another one of our favorite authors. But, since Whit was "John," we knew we had to make this character "Jack," a reference to C. S. Lewis's preferred nickname. (Lewis wrote the beloved Chronicles of Narnia books in the 1950s.)

We worked out Jack's biography, just as we had with Whit. We decided that Jack had been Whit's closest friend and a significant influence as they grew up. We all agreed that Jack should share some of Whit's best attributes: kindness, wisdom, gentleness, understanding, and discernment.

Character:

Jason Whittaker

Quote: "The name is Bond. James Bond."
Something you may not know about Jason:
He was valedictorian of his high school
graduating class.

Album **22**

Who Is Jason Whittaker?

To create the character of Jason Whittaker, we started with what we knew about him from previous episodes, which wasn't much. We knew that he was Whit's younger son and that, like his father, he had a love of discovery. Connie even compared Jason to his father in "The Mortal Coil" (album 16).

Beyond that, we were free to invent. We had been anxious to explore Whit's mysterious dealings with the government but had been wary of going into too many spy adventures, which would change the tone of the show and the character of Whit. Jason's character finally gave us the chance to explore those stories. We thought of him as a code breaker for the National Security Agency (NSA) and conjectured he may have worked for other government agencies as well.

We concluded that Jason was not married, though we liked the idea of him having a love interest, a woman who was an adventurer like him, coming in and out of his life. This turned into the character of Tasha Forbes.

We also wanted Jason to be a little more reckless than his father, acting more impulsively. This would lead him to make errors in judgment. His advice could be faulty, and he would often act before thinking things through. This would make him an excellent contrast to Jack Allen.

Who should play this new character? Katie Leigh suggested her friend Townsend Coleman. We auditioned Townsend using an appropriate spy scene from "The Last Great Adventure of the Summer" (album 2). As soon as he read the first few lines, we knew Townsend was a perfect fit.

The character was really coming together. Now, we just needed to introduce him to Odyssey . . . and our audience!

Episode Information

285: George Under Pressure
Original Air Date: 10/8/94
Writer: Paul McCusker
Sound Designer: Dave Arnold
Scripture: Colossians 1:9-13
Themes: Family togetherness, dealing with stress
Summary: Because George Barclay's demanding schedule is exhausting him, Jimmy and Donna are determined to make sure he takes a day off.

286 & 287: Tom for Mayor, I and II
Original Air Dates: 10/29/94 & 11/5/94
Writer: Paul McCusker
Sound Designers: Dave Arnold & Bob Luttrell
Scripture: John 17:11
Theme: God's guidance in times of trouble
Summary: Philip Glossman returns to look for toxic chemicals on Tom Riley's farm. Meanwhile, Odyssey's mayor resigns, so Tom and Bart Rathbone compete for the office.

289: A Call for Reverend Jimmy
Original Air Date: 11/19/94
Writer: Marshal Younger
Sound Designer: Mark Drury
Scripture: Isaiah 30:21
Theme: God's calling
Summary: Donna Barclay is annoyed to find herself a source for sermon illustrations, and her brother, Jimmy, wonders if God may be calling him to the ministry.

290: A Name, Not a Number, I and II
Original Air Dates: 11/26/94 & 12/3/94
Writer: Phil Lollar
Sound Designers: Dave Arnold & Bob Luttrell
Scripture: Psalm 27:5-6
Theme: God's protection
Summary: Jason Whittaker, Whit's son, gets sidetracked from his move to Odyssey when he's called to Europe on a mission. He has to find a missing friend who has been kidnapped by the terrorist organization Red Scorpion.
PARENTAL WARNING:
These episodes are about international political intrigue and the threat of biological terrorism. While presented in a way that most will find enjoyable, these episodes may be too intense for younger listeners.

292: Siege at Jericho
Original Air Date: 12/10/94
Writer: Phil Lollar
Sound Designer: Mark Drury
Scripture: Joshua 1:10–6:27
Themes: The biblical story of Rahab and Joshua and the walls of Jericho.
Summary: The O. T. Action News team breaks the story of Joshua, Rahab, and a standoff at the walls of Jericho.

293: A Code of Honor

Original Air Date: 12/17/94
Writer: Paul McCusker
Sound Designer: Dave Arnold
Scripture: Ephesians 2:10
Theme: Doing good works
Summary: Jack Allen and Jason Whittaker find a mysterious codebook in Whit's workroom that leads them to a secret gang called the Israelites.

294: Unto Us a Child Is Born

Original Air Date: 12/24/94
Writer: Paul McCusker
Sound Designer: Mark Drury
Scripture: Luke 2
Theme: The Christmas story
Summary: On Christmas eve, Jimmy produces a live Kids' Radio presentation of the birth of Jesus—which includes an unexpected *real* birth.

295: Soaplessly Devoted

Original Air Date: 12/31/94
Writer: Marshal Younger
Sound Designer: Dave Arnold
Scripture: Proverbs 17:24
Theme: Discernment
Summary: Jason programs the Room of Consequence so that Erica Clark can actually live in *Medical Center of Love*, her favorite soap opera.

296: Red Wagons and Pink Flamingos

Original Air Date: 1/7/95
Writer: Marshal Younger
Sound Designer: Bob Luttrell
Scripture: Matthew 5:23-24
Themes: Friendship, forgiveness, resolving conflicts
Summary: Erica and her best friend, Kim Peterson, have an argument that may end their friendship. Meanwhile, Jason and Jack disagree about putting video games in Whit's End.

297: Blackbeard's Treasure

Original Air Date: 1/14/95
Writer: Phil Lollar
Sound Designer: Bob Luttrell
Scripture: Proverbs 21:25-26
Theme: Greed
Summary: Two young boys, John Whittaker and Jack Allen, venture into a secret cave and fight off pirates in their quest to find Blackbeard's buried treasure.

Cut Scenes

In "George Under Pressure," we sought to balance the pressures of becoming a pastor with the joy of following God's call. Poor George Barclay was having a difficult time because he seemed besieged and stressed by his work. Even down to the day of recording, we struggled with scripting the tension right. The original script for the show ended with George getting a phone call about an urgent need and leaving his family to take care of it. But in the studio, Chuck Bolte suggested a different ending. Chuck's idea was to have George ask the caller if the need could wait until tomorrow so he could stay with his family. We used this ending instead, believing that it demonstrated how a pastor must learn when to say no to someone's request for the sake of his family.

Behind the Scenes: Tom for Mayor

This episode reintroduced the Edgebiter Chemical scandal (introduced in "One Bad Apple," album 7) and Philip Glossman (last heard in "Timmy's Cabin," album 14). It set the stage for future episodes, most notably album 25, *Darkness Before Dawn.* Our plan was to have a series of shows after Jack's and Jason's arrivals in Odyssey that would lead up to Dr. Blackgaard's return. We wanted a dramatic showdown where we would tie up all plot and story elements. What few people knew was that some of the team thought it really was time to bring Odyssey to an end and create a spin-off or an entirely new series. Would we end the series after we tied up all the plots? We would wait to decide then.

Actor Walker Edmiston, voices of Tom Riley and Bart Rathbone

Sound Bites with Dave Arnold

Tom Riley and Bart Rathbone have a lengthy debate in "Tom for Mayor," and Walker Edmiston plays both characters. We offered to record these parts separately to make recording the scene easier for Walker. We thought it might be difficult for him to switch from voice to voice. He refused: "Nah, let's just do them at the same time. It'll be easier that way." It was so much fun to watch because when he changed parts, he also changed his facial expressions. We sat in the control room half the time mesmerized, the other half laughing hysterically. The arrangement worked so well that Bart and Tom met up in a number of future episodes including "A Christmas Conundrum" (album 45) and "A Cheater Cheated" (album 46).

Drawing Jack and Jason

We drew Jack Allen to look like Alan Young except without white hair. We hoped the illustration would look something like Alan did when he played Wilbur on *Mister Ed*.

Jason Whittaker was a variation on the lead in Disney's 1992 *Aladdin* but slightly older since Jason was in his 30s. We also wanted Jason to look somewhat like Whit but with dark hair.

Jack Allen   Jason Whittaker

My Take: Marshal Younger

Paul McCusker and I were in his cubicle at Focus trying to figure out how to end "A Call for Reverend Jimmy." We didn't know if we should reveal the gender of the

Actor Townsend Coleman, voice of Jason Whittaker

Barclay baby, and so we worked it out that the noise of an airplane covers up the answer—which is similar to the way the movie *Patriot Games* (1992) ended. We were laughing so hard about this idea that it disturbed people in the cubicles around us. An additional benefit to that ending was that we had more time to decide whether the Barclay baby should be a boy or a girl.

Jason Whittaker: Agent 1131 The Writing and Recording of "A Name, Not a Number"

Originally titled "Codebreaker," "A Name, Not a Number" was designed to introduce Jason Whittaker, reintroduce Dr. Blackgaard, and set the stage for a final, dramatic showdown of all our storylines. We decided that as soon as Whit left Odyssey, Dr. Blackgaard would continue his evil plans . . . whatever those might be.

Phil Lollar wrote the two-part show from outline to final draft in just over a week, which is fast for the creation of an *Odyssey* episode, let alone a two-part plot as complicated as this. The biggest difference in the early draft dealt with the climax of part II. In that version, Tasha Forbes showed up in Odyssey with her 12-year-old assistant, Molly. She was kidnapped by the terrorist named Mustafa when she was visiting the Wonderworld tree

house. Mustafa threatened to drown Molly at the Odyssey Water Works near Trickle Lake. Jason and Tasha managed to rescue Molly but not before Mustafa made off with the formula for making the dangerous substance called TA-418. In the final scene of the episode, Dr. Blackgaard confronted Mustafa and took the formula for TA-418, which is what he wanted all along. (One version of the show even revealed that Jack Allen was an NSA agent!)

We worried about the scariness factor—and violence level—of a young girl being threatened by a terrorist, so we removed the Molly character from part II. (In the recording script, Donovan tells Jason that they found Molly's body in a river. We edited this line out of the final show because we decided it was too violent.)

The Water Works scene posed another problem. We had major trouble with water scenes in previous episodes (most notably "Flash Flood," album 15), so we changed the climax to something simpler, namely a showdown between Jason and Mustafa in the park.

We cast Alan Young, who was already playing Jack, as Donovan, asking him to use the same accent he had used for the character of Filby in the 1960 film version of *The Time Machine*. As an inside joke, we used the name Filby for the British turncoat agent played by Walker Edmiston in our episode, not knowing that Filby was also the name of a true-life turncoat agent.

We cast actress Michelle Hannah, who had previously played Melissa in "A Book by Its Cover" (album 21), as Tasha. However, in the studio, we realized that Michelle's voice sounded too young to be Jason's love interest. We desperately searched around for another actress, but no one could come on such short notice. Just as we were beginning to panic, the owner of the studio where we recorded suggested an actor named Connie Zimet. She was recording at that same studio that day and was happy to give Tasha a try. It worked wonderfully, so she spent the day running between her project in one studio and ours in the other. By the way, Michelle Hannah ended up playing Molly.

BTS: A Name, Not a Number

In the original outline for this episode, the terrorists hailed from a specific real-world country. Rather than offend listeners, we decided to create our own country of "Rakistan." We used this fictional country in later episodes, including "Room Enough for Two" (album 40).

Additionally, this episode turned out to be popular but somewhat controversial due to the intensity of a handful of scenes. Because so many of our fans listen to *Odyssey* while going to bed, we pulled it from our regular broadcast rotation so it wouldn't produce nightmares. We didn't air the show again until 2004.

BTS: Siege at Jericho

Originally an Imagination Station episode about Rahab, "Siege at Jericho" contains a reference to The Three Stooges—a character named Hassan Ben Soba appeared in both our episode and in a 1949 short film titled *The Three Stooges: Malice in the Palace*. Many of our staff members are fans of Moe, Larry, and Curly.

Goof Alert!

In "A Prayer for George Barclay" (album 19), Whit states that George painted Emma Douglas's garage. However, in "A Code of Honor," Emma says that Billy MacPherson was the last person to paint her garage. Billy had painted it long before George could have.

BTS: A Code of Honor

This episode brought Jack Allen and Jason Whittaker together for the first time. It also hinted at their personality differences, which would lead to conflicts later on. Additionally, the episode introduced an unusual aspect to Jack's character: the power of his dreams.

The show revisits several plot elements from the *Odyssey* novel *The Secret Cave of Robinwood*. It includes a "good gang" called the Israelites, which was led by Billy MacPherson, and the elderly character of Emma Douglas. In another reference to the novels, Jason found an early version of the Imagination Station in the basement, which explained the machine's use in the first novel, *Strange Journey Back*. The idea of a "good gang" was based on a real-life group that secretly helped people around Paul McCusker's hometown, Uniontown, Pennsylvania.

BTS: *Unto Us a Child Is Born*

"Unto Us a Child Is Born" was inspired in part by the 1982 Michael Frayn play, *Noises Off*, which is a farce about a stage play where everything goes wrong. This same concept later inspired "B-TV: Behind the Scenes" (album 40).

Since all of the Barclay family members had been named for characters or actors from *It's a Wonderful Life*, we named the Barclay baby Stewart Reed, after lead actors Jimmy Stewart and Donna Reed.

Sound Bites

Actress Carol Bilger (Mary Barclay) wasn't available the same day that we recorded the other actors for "Unto Us a Child Is Born," and so writer Marshal Younger read her lines in the studio, which led to much chuckling from the actors when he was doing the birthing scene. Carol later recorded her lines, which were edited into the scene. Marshal's performance, though stellar, is forever lost.

My Take: Marshal Younger

We began to explore the conflict between Jack and Jason by having them debate the value of having video games at Whit's End. At the end of the show, they compromised by putting the games in a soundproof room. However, many of our listeners didn't like the idea of video games at Whit's End in any capacity—soundproof room or not. So, after mentioning the games only a few more times in various episodes, we ignored them completely.

BTS: *Blackbeard's Treasure*

"Blackbeard's Treasure" was meant to be a pilot episode for a spin-off series of adventures featuring young Whit. The series didn't materialize . . . but it still could!

The name "Ewell Mosby" is a combination of names from two Civil War generals, Richard Ewell and John S. Mosby. And, any resemblance between the names of Sheriff Randy and Deputy Arney and another sheriff and deputy from a popular 1960s television sitcom about a small Southern town is purely intentional.

Hey, Aren't You . . . ? Kids Who Played More than One Role

Several of our child actors have come back to play different roles after their tenure as kids on the show ended. Can you spot these voices?

Actor	Original Character	Album number	Later Character
Justin Morgan	Isaac Morton	7	Larry Melwood in "With a Little Help from My Friends" (album 27)
Kyle Ellison	Sam Johnson	*The Lost Episodes*	Junior, a gang member in "Chains" (album 36)
Shawn Svoboda	Rusty Gordon	17	Greg O'Neil in "Fifteen Minutes" (album 36)
Sara Buskirk	Courtney Vincent	17	Hallie in "My Girl Hallie" (album 41)
Fabio Stephens	Curt Stevens	7	Tony, a gang member in "Best Laid Plans" (album 35)
Chris Castile	Zachary Sellers	22	Nick Mulligan premiering in "Just Say Yes" (album 29)
Donald Long	Jack Davis	2	Greg Kelly in "Waylaid in the Windy City" (album 10)
Kris Kachurak	Dwayne Oswald	29	Todd in "Under the Influence" (album 38)

Actors Fabio Stephens (*left*) and Donald Long 1989

Character:
Rodney Rathbone
Quote: "Do I look like I'm stupid?"
Something you may not know about Rodney:
He once tried to sell an autographed picture
of Robert "M." Lee.

Album 23

Twists and Turns

The Truth about "The Truth About Zachary"

by Marshal Younger

"The Truth About Zachary" introduced a new character, a young boy in a wheelchair who dealt with bitterness over his condition.

The recording of the show was one of my lowest moments working on *Adventures in Odyssey*. We had a number of new cast members in this episode, including Vaughn Tinder-Taylor as Zachary Seller's mother. (Vaughn also played the mom on the *McGee and Me!* videos.) While that choice was a good fit, we quickly realized that the young boy we cast as Zachary simply couldn't get into the part. We tried working with him for hour after hour, but we didn't get what we needed. A few months later, we completely rerecorded the episode with a new actor in that role, which was something we'd never done before.

The good thing, though, was that on the second time around, we cast Christopher Castile as Zachary. He ended up being terrific in the part and led us to write an entire storyline for Zachary.

Episode Information

298: I Want My B-TV
Original Air Date: 1/21/95
Writer: Phil Lollar
Sound Designer: Bob Luttrell
Scripture: Philippians 4:8
Themes: Foundations, cooperation, the importance of watching and listening to quality programs
Summary: Bernard Walton and the gang at Whit's End create a new television variety show.

299: The Truth About Zachary
Original Air Date: 1/28/95
Writers: Marshal Younger & Paul Malm
Sound Designer: Bob Luttrell
Scripture: Romans 15:1-3
Themes: Friendship, encouragement
Summary: Lucy Cunningham-Schultz tries to write a news article about Zachary Sellers, an angry middle-school boy in a wheelchair.

300: Preacher's Kid
Original Air Date: 2/4/95
Writer: Marshal Younger
Sound Designer: Mark Drury
Scripture: Romans 3:23; Ephesians 5:1
Theme: Being imperfect
Summary: Donna Barclay is tired of everyone expecting her to be the perfect pastor's child, but her rebellion goes too far.

301: The Good, the Bad, and Butch
Original Air Date: 2/11/95
Writer: Marshal Younger
Sound Designer: Bob Luttrell
Scripture: Psalm 1:1-2
Themes: Making proper choices, choosing friends wisely
Summary: Sam Johnson wants to renew his friendship with Butch Evans even though Butch is now a member of the Bones of Rath.

302: Share and Share Alike
Original Air Date: 2/18/95
Writer: Marshal Younger
Sound Designer: Mark Drury
Scripture: Hebrews 13:16
Theme: Sacrifice
Summary: Kids' Radio stages a share-a-thon to benefit a local homeless shelter.

303: All the Difference in the World
Original Air Date: 2/25/95
Writer: Paul McCusker
Sound Designer: Dave Arnold
Scripture: Colossians 1:21-23
Theme: What it means to be a Christian
Summary: Danny Schmidt rebels against his parents because it seems as if other kids get everything they want.

304: Saint Paul: The Man from Tarsus
Original Air Date: 3/4/95
Writer: Phil Lollar
Sound Designer: Bob Luttrell
Scripture: Acts 6:8–8:1; 9:1-31
Theme: The biblical story of the apostle Paul
Summary: In the Imagination Station, Rodney Rathbone and Sam meet the biblical Peter, Barnabas, and a violent man named Saul.

305: Saint Paul: Set Apart by God

Original Air Date: 3/11/95
Writer: Phil Lollar
Sound Designer: Dave Arnold
Scripture: Acts 6:8–8:1; 9:1-31
Theme: The biblical story of the apostle Paul
Summary: Rodney and Sam's Imagination Station adventure continues as Saul has a radical conversion.

306: A Victim of Circumstance

Original Air Date: 3/18/95
Writer: Phil Lollar
Sound Designer: Mark Drury
Scripture: Genesis 3
Theme: Taking responsibility for your actions
Summary: When Rodney steps through a skylight at Whit's End and breaks his leg, the Rathbones take Jason Whittaker to court.

309, 310, and 311: The Perfect Witness, I, II, and III

Original Air Dates: 4/8/95, 4/15/95, & 4/22/95
Writer: Paul McCusker
Sound Designers: Dave Arnold & Mark Drury
Scripture: 1 Samuel 16:7; Mark 7:1-23; 2 Corinthians 5
Theme: God judges people by their hearts, not their physical appearance
Summary: A mystery is triggered when two armed men hold up Holstein's Books and take a hostage—a blind girl named Jenny Roberts.
PARENTAL WARNING:
This three-part mystery includes an armed robbery and kidnapping, which are played and replayed throughout all three parts. Although no one gets hurt in the episodes, they may be too intense for younger listeners.

1994 *Odyssey* team members Phil Lollar, Mark Drury, Dave Arnold, and Paul McCusker

The Creation of B-TV!

Cocreator Phil Lollar originally hoped that the *Adventures in Odyssey* series would be a variety/sketch program in the spirit of the *Rocky and Bullwinkle Show* television cartoons (1959–1973). Even though the idea didn't work out there, it never left him, and Phil introduced it again in a show originally called "I Want My C-TV." In that version, the naturally upbeat Connie seemed like the perfect host.

The first outline for our introductory "C-TV" episode began with TV show personality Kalamity Klown in desperate straights for a guest on his show. Since Eugene was at the TV station and "looked interesting," Kalamity pulled him in. Once onstage, however, Kalamity collapsed! Instead of canceling the show, however, Connie and Eugene ad-libbed the rest of the program. To everyone's surprise, they were a big hit. Since Kalamity would be out sick for some time, the station manager asked Eugene and Connie to do the show on a regular basis. After several weeks on the air, Connie and Eugene got into an argument about who was really the star of the show. A disagreement commenced between the two that played out live on TV with Eugene being rude to Connie and vice versa. Soon, kids in Odyssey were copying Eugene and Connie's on-air antics. Upon seeing this, the pair learned a tough lesson about what it means to be role models.

The *Odyssey* team liked the C-TV concept but didn't like the idea of Eugene and Connie acting so immaturely. So, Phil came up with a new and unique format—a group of characters discussing ideas for the show while actually hearing them played out. Bernard Walton (instead of Connie) was the team's choice for a host; as a result, "I Want My B-TV" was born. Much later, "B-TV: Behind the Scenes" (album 40) would give listeners a comedic glimpse of the happenings in a TV studio.

Behind the Scenes: I Want My B-TV

Eugene started to tell the story of the three little pigs in this episode. Have you ever wondered what nursery rhymes would sound like if Eugene told them? Kim M. from Alstead, New Hampshire, let us know:

A trio of sightless rodents.
A trio of sightless rodents.
Observe how they perambulate.
Observe how they how they perambulate.
They perambulate around the agricultural spouse,
who amputated their posterior extremities with a kitchen utensil,
did ever you observe such a phenomenon in all your existence,
as a trio of sightless rodents?

Bernard Walton in "I Want My B-TV

BTS: *The Truth About Zachary*

"The Truth About Zachary" was the first and only episode in which an elevator was mentioned at Whit's End.

Lucy Who?! Part Two

Lucy's last name was a big goof that we hoped to correct with "The Truth About Zachary." We explained that her father (Hal Cunningham) died in a car accident when she was nine and that her mother then married a man named Schultz. But Lucy also says that Mr. Cunningham worked at *The Odyssey Times*. But wait a minute! George Barclay worked with Lucy's father in "Our Best Vacation Ever" (album 5). So when he lost his job in "Our Daily Bread" (album 17), why did he go to *The Odyssey Times* to try to get a new job? Hmmm . . .

My Take: Marshal Younger

Much of my writing for the Barclay kids comes from my experience as a "preacher's kid" (PK) as well as the experiences of a lot of people I knew who were sons and daughters of pastors. There did seem to be different rules for us; PKs were held to much higher standards than others, and I felt a sense of unfairness about that. This episode was a perfect example of the struggle we always face between making our *Odyssey* kids good role models as well as making them realistic. We received letters from people who felt that Donna was too rebellious and letters from others who felt it was too easy for the Barclay kids.

Goof Alert!

In "The Good, the Bad, and Butch," Sam Johnson says that he doesn't know any dirty jokes, but he had no problem telling Isaac one in "Isaac the Pure" (album 13).

BTS: *The Good, the Bad, and Butch*

This episode introduced Bones of Rath member Butch Evans, who would figure prominently in the album *Darkness Before Dawn*. John Burdick, real-life cousin of Steve Burns (Rodney), played Butch.

Art by fan Sierra H., Woodstock, Georgia

BTS: *Share and Share Alike*

In "Share and Share Alike," Jack Allen mentions that he has 20 mugs that say "World's Greatest Grandpa." So far, we've still never heard anything about his children on the program, let alone his grandchildren. Maybe he's a collector.

Sound Bites

In "Share and Share Alike," Matt Hurwitz's performance as Everett Nielson (who notes that he saw a woman making spaghetti without a strainer) was an impersonation of Ted Baxter (Ted Knight) from *The Mary Tyler Moore Show* (1970–1977).

BTS: All the Difference in the World

In "All the Difference in the World," Jeff Marsden was played by actor Jeff Ellison, real-life brother of actor Kyle Ellison (Sam). Jeff later played character David Straussberg in episodes such as "I Slap Floor" (album 34) and "No Boundaries" (album 34). Character Ron Marsden was played by popular Christian author Bill Myers. Bill later played several other roles for *Odyssey*, most notably Mike Mulligan.

BTS: Saint Paul: The Man from Tarsus

The first Saint Paul stories were outlined as an Imagination Station adventure in which Charles Edward Thompson witnessed Paul's shipwreck. We thought it would make more sense to backtrack and tell the story of Paul's conversion first. A year later in album 26, we told the shipwreck story in "Saint Paul: Voyage to Rome."

BTS: A Victim of Circumstance

In this episode, Jason Whittaker's lawyer is named Fenimore Cooper. James Fenimore Cooper is the name of an American author, best known for writing *The Last of the Mohicans* (1826). Judge Bailey F. Lee is a fairly obvious reference to F. Lee Bailey, a real-life lawyer often seen on television news.

Several lawsuits mentioned in the Room of Consequence sequence (including the thief suing a homeowner over breaking glass) were based on actual cases.

Sound Bites

Harlow Doyle wasn't originally written into "The Perfect Witness." The script included Fred Holstein telling the story of the robbery of his shop to an unnamed person. Actor Will Ryan was in the studio to play Eugene and, on the spur of the moment, ad-libbed Harlow's dialogue with Fred.

The Creation of "The Perfect Witness"

by Paul McCusker

For a long time, I was keen to do a mystery that was specific to radio. For example, "The Case of the Secret Room" (album 2) and "The Mysterious Stranger" (album 18) were mysteries that could easily have been made for film. So I wanted to use sounds as clues as a way to unfold this mystery.

The inspiration for "Perfect Witness" was a 1960s British film with a fascinating premise: A photographer accidentally takes a picture of a murder. He doesn't realize it at first, but as he develops the picture—and blows it up to check details—he realizes what he has stumbled onto. After I saw the film, I wondered, *What would happen if we did this with sound?*

There is a cardinal rule of writing radio drama that we often have to repeat to ourselves: Your audience is blind, but you must never make them feel that way. For "The Perfect Witness," I decided that, if the audience is blind, I should make the victim of the crime a blind person—namely Jenny Roberts. Through her, we could go over the clues of the sounds of the mystery and try to solve it.

Dave Arnold and I sat down to talk about what kinds of sounds would be different and compelling, like specific car sounds, railway crossings, footsteps, patterns of speech, and so on. Then I pieced the mystery together from there.

One element of the story that I wanted to explore was Jenny's feeling of self-worth. When I first researched blindness and how it affects kids' lives, I spoke to one of the teachers at a school for the blind in Colorado Springs. One thing that emerged in the conversation was how blind kids get tired of people handling them with kid gloves. Those who are blind want to be treated with respect. They don't want to be a burden; even more, they hope to contribute to society. That's why I called the show "The Perfect Witness." At the beginning, the criminals think Jenny will be the perfect hostage because she can't see. They underestimated her. At first, Jenny also underestimates herself, but then she learns something about her own potential and limitations, too. More important, she learns that everyone has value—everyone has a place in God's world, even if it isn't always obvious.

Album 24

The Creation of "The Underground Railroad"

This episode proved to be extremely popular among *Odyssey* fans. But how did it come together?

"I have always been fascinated with the Underground Railroad and how it worked," explains writer Marshal Younger. "My passion is in writing fiction, and I don't really enjoy dramatizing actual events because there is less room to invent. Doing the story of Harriet Tubman intrigued me, but I didn't want to do her actual story. If I had, that would have limited the story to the historical events, and I couldn't really change the plot or the characters."

Instead, Marshal took the historical background of the Underground Railroad and wrote a fictional story *inspired* by actual events. "Almost everything in the story has some basis in fact," says Marshal. "Families being torn apart and taken to different states, getting across the Ohio River, and even the story of the slave being transported in a box—they all actually happened. Only the characters are fictional."

After the show aired, there were a few negative responses. Some listeners accused us of rehashing the myths that the South was a horrible place to live and all white Southerners were evil. They contended that many slave owners were actually very civil to their slaves.

Producer Paul McCusker admits having difficulty with some of the letters: "In the end, it didn't matter to me that some of the slave owners treated their slaves civilly—I suppose I should be glad about that—but the point is that an entire race of human beings were still *slaves*."

"Most of the comments, though, have been very favorable," Marshal adds. "I've had a few people who said that the gospel was made more relevant to them through this episode, and that's the kind of comment that I like best."

Episode Information

307: Poetry in Slow Motion
Original Air Date: 3/25/95
Writer: Marshal Younger
Sound Designer: Bob Luttrell
Scripture: Proverbs 15:22
Themes: Asking for help, humility
Summary: Charles Edward Thompson has a terrible time writing poetry in middle school, but he refuses to ask anyone for help.

308: Subject Yourself
Original Air Date: 4/1/95
Writer: Paul McCusker
Sound Designer: Bob Luttrell
Scripture: Romans 13:1
Theme: Obeying those in authority
Summary: Lawrence Hodges battles his doctor over getting braces while his mother battles the school board over a new curriculum.

312: Rewards in Full
Original Air Date: 4/29/95
Writer: Phil Lollar
Sound Designer: Mark Drury
Scripture: Matthew 6:1
Theme: Having pure motives
Summary: Jack Allen and Erica Clark both come up with ideas that help the community; however, neither of them gets credit for it.

313: Top This!
Original Air Date: 5/6/95
Writer: Marshal Younger
Sound Designer: Bob Luttrell
Scripture: Jeremiah 9:23-24
Themes: Unhealthy competition, putting God first.
Summary: Courtney Vincent gets into an intense rivalry with her cousin Hannah, and radio shock jock Cryin' Bryan Dern tries to outdo a competing radio station.

314, 315, and 316: The Underground Railroad, I, II, and III
Original Air Dates: 5/13/95, 5/20/95, & 5/27/95
Writer: Marshal Younger
Sound Designers: Bob Luttrell, Dave Arnold, & Mark Drury
Scripture: Psalm 82:3
Themes: God in history, the sanctity of life
Summary: A stranger tells Jack the story of the Ross family and their courageous run for freedom to escape slavery.

Album 24: *Risks and Rewards*

264

317: **B-TV: Envy**

Original Air Date: 6/3/95
Writer: Phil Lollar
Sound Designer: Bob Luttrell
Scripture: Genesis 4:1-16; 2 Samuel 11:1–12:23; 1 Kings 21
Theme: The dangers of envy
Summary: B-TV tells several Bible stories about envy, including Cain and Abel, David and Bathsheba, and Ahab and Jezebel.

318, 319: **A Touch of Healing, I and II**

Original Air Dates: 6/10/95 & 6/17/95
Writer: Paul McCusker
Sound Designers: Mark Drury & Dave Arnold
Scripture: 1 John 5:14
Theme: Accepting things beyond our control
Summary: Jason Whittaker's new Imagination Station program seems to heal people with disabilities. Meanwhile, Connie's elderly grandmother arrives in Odyssey and her health takes a turn for the worse.
PARENTAL WARNING:
This story contains material about dashed hopes for healing and the death of a loved one. It may be too sensitive for younger listeners.

320: **Where Is Thy Sting?**

Original Air Date: 6/24/95
Writer: Paul McCusker
Sound Designer: Dave Arnold
Scripture: 1 Corinthians 15:54-57; 1 Thessalonians 4:13; 1 Timothy 6:17-19
Theme: Dealing with the death of a loved one
Summary: The death of Connie's grandmother causes her family to ponder what death means for a Christian. Connie's father ponders what death means for a non-Christian.

322: **The Turning Point**

Original Air Date: 7/8/95
Writer: Paul McCusker
Sound Designer: Dave Arnold
Scripture: 2 Corinthians 6:14
Theme: God's plans for individuals
Summary: Eugene and Katrina's relationship takes a surprising turn after Eugene meets Katrina's father, Armitage Shanks.

Goof Alert!

In "Poetry in Slow Motion," Charles Thompson calls Rusty by the last name of Gordon. But in "Our Father" (album 17), his name is Rusty Malone.

I Like Pants

I put on pants every day
To go to school or to play
I like pants
Sometimes I wear pants of blue
Or brown to go with my shoe
I like pants
Sometimes I feel sorry for ants
Because they can't wear pants
I like pants
Pants cover my legs so that I can go
Without them I would be cold, I know
I like pants
I like them so.

—Charles Edward Thompson from "Poetry in Slow Motion"

Behind the Scenes: Rewards in Full

The Electric Palace's address is 1313 Mockingbird Road. The address was inspired by the television series *The Munsters* (1964–1966). Harry Wainwright was named after two characters in *It's a Wonderful Life*: Sam Wainwright and Harry Bailey.

BTS: Top This

The original idea for this episode was that Cryin' Bryan Dern's radio station switches from a rock format to an all-Christian music format. Because he finds Christian music unbearable, Dern locks himself in the studio until the music is changed back. For the final version, we decided on a switch to all-polka format, which is just more fun, don't you think?

Q & A with the Fans!

Q: So what *is* being said in the clip that Bryan Dern plays in "Top This"?

A: Dern plays a clip of a hard-to-understand rock star. To accomplish this, we asked musician John Campbell to ad-lib lyrics. Characters call in to suggest that the singer is saying: "The monkey man has no place in the circle of confusion" and "The meter maid has no peace in the cycle of conviction." So, what is the singer *really* saying? The world may never know.

Sound Bites

In the background of Dern's radio show in "Top This!" we hear a commercial for Jumbo Fork. Here is what the announcer is saying:

```
How many times has this
happened to you? You're
happily eating spaghetti,
twirling your fork into
a nice ball of pasta and
suddenly, you run out of
fork! You've got another
three yards of spaghetti to
twirl, and you have no fork
to put it on. What can you
do? Introducing Jumbo Fork—
the biggest fork you'll ever
see in your life! Get Jumbo
Fork and get it all in your
mouth! Available at Pete's
Gas 'n' Chow, your beef
jerky co-op.
```

BTS: A Touch of Healing

As a team we discussed and pondered the potential of the Imagination Station. We wondered what would happen if a handicapped person got into the invention. If that person imagined that he could walk or see again, could he? This question was a driving inspiration behind "A Touch of Healing." Originally, we thought we would have Jason create a take-home version of the Imagination Station. This would allow Zachary and Jenny to be "healed," even when at home. But we dismissed that idea because of the addictive nature of the machine. What person wouldn't want to be "healed" all the time, if only in his imagination? We opted to take the story in a different direction.

Cut Scenes

"Where Is Thy Sting?" is one of the longest *Adventures in Odyssey* programs ever produced. Over 12 minutes of dialog were cut for the broadcast version, and 6 minutes were cut for the album version. One of the lost scenes dealt with various perspectives on death, including dialogue with Eugene relating his point of view as a result of his Imagination Station experience in "The Mortal Coil" (album 16).

BTS: The Turning Point

Eugene has a discussion with Jack about Samson and Delilah in "The Turning Point." This came from an idea for an entirely different episode—an Imagination Station adventure where Eugene would actually meet Samson and then Katrina would meet Delilah. In the course of the episode, they would learn about how Samson betrayed himself by marrying an unbeliever. We decided that the story of Samson and Delilah would be better told as its own story, which we later did in "The Power of One" (album 44).

BTS: The Turning Point

The name of Armitage Shanks in "The Turning Point" comes from a porcelain/plumbing company in England. In other words, Armitage Shanks is to England what American Standard is to the United States. When it came time to name Katrina's great grandmother in "Wrapped Around Your Finger" (album 31), we wanted an appropriate name. We balked at naming her "Commodius," but then the perfect name dawned on us. What could be more fitting than "Porcelain" Shanks?

BTS: Risks and Rewards

The cover illustration for this album depicting "The Underground Railroad" episode was also used for a *Clubhouse* magazine story in October 2007. The plot of the *Clubhouse* story had nothing to do with the Underground Railroad, but with a few adjustments, the art fit the story perfectly.

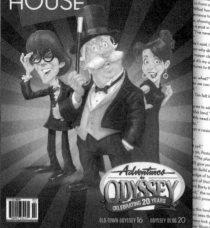

Clubhouse magazine, October 2007

Getting On Top of the Underground Railroad

Up to this point, we hadn't worked with many African-American adults. So we held auditions, bringing in as many African-American actors as we could find. Since most of these actors hadn't worked together before, the team wasn't sure that the actors would gel as a family.

Marshal recalls, "We went into the studio, and we got everyone into the back room and read through the entire script—which is something we don't normally do. We usually just go right into the studio and record. But the actors started right in on scene 1, and I was literally shaking in my shoes. They sounded like they had worked together for years! It was incredible. I looked up at Dave Arnold and Paul McCusker, and they nodded and smiled at me. This was going to work. It was truly God doing His thing. The actor did such a good job on the scene where the son says good-bye to his mother's grave. It had me crying like a baby."

Marshal remembers another special moment: "One of my all-time favorite scenes is the one between the plantation woman, who is a closet abolitionist, and the slave William. I loved how the actors played it from complete distrust of each other, to questionable trust, to trust. There was so much subtext in that scene, so much emotion, but none of it could be displayed openly. The acting of Mimi Monaco and Angelo Sales was tremendous, and so was the music."

After recording, the show was handed off to the sound designers. "The Underground Railroad" was not the first show to use snow effects, but it was the first one to use them extensively. Sound designer Mark Drury remembers: "I needed the sound of Henry and Caroline trudging through the snow, falling down, and going to Reverend Andrew's cabin. I got a shovel and two pans from our cafeteria and started bringing snow into my studio. I set up the mikes and put the pans on the floor side by side with the snow in them. I then walked in one pan with my left foot, the other with my right. Every 15 minutes, I had to go out and empty the quickly melting snow and bring in more. I got the sounds I needed for the scene, leaving a 10-foot wet spot on my carpet! The custodial folks were not thrilled with me."

Fellow sound designer Dave Arnold dealt with some interesting sound effects in part II. "I had to create the sound of people walking on ice and then crashing through. The walking-on-ice sounds came from broken shards of fluorescent tube glass plus some corn flakes. The crash through the ice was a combination of dry ice cracking as it warmed, planks of wood snapping, glass breaking, and many other sounds combined together."

269

Album 25

Darkness Before Dawn

Armageddon in Odyssey

The *Darkness Before Dawn* miniseries was designed to bring *Adventures in Odyssey* to a natural stopping point. The plan was to wrap up the many story-lines involving Dr. Blackgaard (see image at left), Eugene and Katrina, the conflict between Jack and Jason, the Israelites, and more, so a new program could be launched. We would have called it *Adventures in Odyssey Presents* or *Odyssey Theater*.

This epic miniseries went through many changes, especially since we planned to use these episodes to end *Adventures in Odyssey*. The story started as a six-part series, then expanded to eight parts, then nine, and finally eleven. At several points in our outlining, it was 12 episodes, and we thought of cutting "A Little Credit, Please," since its content didn't have much to do with the theme of the album. But further brainstorming and outlining led to significant changes.

As often happens with *Adventures in Odyssey*, every answer we attempt to give actually raises more questions. So, rather than bring a conclusion to the series, *Darkness Before Dawn* forced a new beginning. It brought up questions like these: What would happen to Eugene and Katrina now that Eugene was a Christian? What would become of Edwin Blackgaard?

We decided that we couldn't shut down the series, especially not now. Instead of wrapping this up, we'd opened a whole new set of adventures, as we'll see in the next album. However, we didn't stop our plans for a spin-off series. *Odyssey Theater* later turned into *Radio Theatre*, an ongoing collection of book adaptations and original stories recorded primarily in England. *Radio Theatre* continues today as a separate series. For more information visit radiotheatre.org.

Episode Information

323: A Little Credit, Please
Original Air Date: 7/15/95
Writer: Paul McCusker
Sound Designer: Mark Drury
Scripture: Luke 16:10-12
Theme: Stewardship
Summary: Connie gets a dose of financial reality after she gets her first credit card, and Bernard Walton gets a new assistant.

324: Small Fires, Little Pools
Original Air Date: 7/22/95
Writer: Phil Lollar
Sound Designer: Bob Luttrell
Theme: Spiritual warfare
Summary: When an outbreak of vandalism hits Odyssey, the gang at Whit's End tries to find out who's responsible.

325: Angels Unaware
Original Air Date: 7/29/95
Writer: Phil Lollar
Sound Designer: Bob Luttrell
Theme: Spiritual warfare
Summary: A mysterious "clean-up" crew suddenly counters the vandalism around Odyssey. Connie has her suspicions about who is responsible for these new acts of goodness.

326: Gathering Thunder
Original Air Date: 8/5/95
Writer: Marshal Younger
Sound Designer: Mark Drury
Theme: Spiritual warfare
Summary: To help the gang called the Israelites, Butch spies on the Bones of Rath until his loyalty comes into question.

327: Moving Targets
Original Air Date: 8/12/95
Writer: Paul McCusker
Sound Designer: Dave Arnold
Theme: Spiritual warfare
Summary: Jason and Jack clash about how to handle the growing crisis around Odyssey, leading to Jack's resignation from Whit's End. Meanwhile, Philip Glossman and Professor Bovril show up to investigate the tunnel under Whit's End.

328: Hard Losses
Original Air Date: 8/19/95
Writer: Phil Lollar
Sound Designer: Bob Luttrell
Theme: Spiritual warfare
Summary: A new scandal erupts when Tom Riley is accused of unethical campaign practices.

329: The Return
Original Air Date: 8/26/95
Writer: Phil Lollar
Sound Designer: Dave Arnold
Theme: Spiritual warfare
Summary: Dr. Blackgaard returns to Odyssey to challenge Tom Riley's position as mayor.

330: The Time Has Come
Original Air Date: 9/2/95
Writer: Paul McCusker
Sound Designer: Dave Arnold
Scripture: Ephesians 2:8-9
Theme: Salvation
Summary: Despondent over his helplessness to influence the ominous events in Odyssey, Eugene creates a search program for the Imagination Station that lets him replay key moments of his life.

331: Checkmate
Original Air Date: 9/16/95
Writer: Phil Lollar & Paul McCusker
Sound Designer: Mark Drury
Theme: Spiritual warfare
Summary: The Israelites clean up the Bones of Rath hideout, Lucy Cunningham-Schultz is kidnapped and pressed for information by Jellyfish, and Glossman finally succeeds in shutting down Whit's End.

332: Another Chance
Original Air Date: 9/23/95
Writer: Phil Lollar
Sound Designer: Bob Luttrell
Theme: Spiritual warfare
Summary: Rodney Rathbone tells Richard Maxwell about a laptop computer that may contain valuable information about Blackgaard's plans for Odyssey.

333: The Last Resort
Original Air Date: 9/30/95
Writers: Phil Lollar & Paul McCusker
Sound Designer: Mark Drury
Theme: Spiritual warfare
Summary: Bernard goes on a covert mission to get information from Jellyfish's laptop computer, and the police arrest Jason Whittaker.

334: The Final Conflict
Original Air Date: 10/7/95
Writer: Phil Lollar & Paul McCusker
Sound Designer: Bob Luttrell
Theme: Spiritual warfare
Summary: The battle between Blackgaard and the crew at Whit's End draws to an explosive close.

FOCUS ON THE FAMILY PRESENTS

Adventures in ODYSSEY AUDIO SERIES

Darkest before Dawn

A extraordinary 12-part mini-series portraying the clash between good and evil.

Early drawings of the cover for *Darkness Before Dawn*

273

Sound Bites

In "A Little Credit, Please," Simon Birtles was supposed to be from Australia and so a boy from Australia was cast in the part. Unfortunately, he'd lost his accent after living in America for years, which made him sound fake to some of our Australian listeners. The name "Simon Birtles" is taken from names of the Little River Band members, an Australian pop group popular in the mid-1970s.

Behind the Scenes: Gathering Thunder

The name "Jellyfish" came from a San Francisco-based rock band of the same name. Professor Bovril is named after a British beverage made from beef.

My Take: Marshal Younger

As it turned out, I only wrote one of the 12 adventures in *Darkness Before Dawn* because these sorts of episodes weren't really my strength at this point in my writing career. I did write a second episode called "Betrayed," in which the Israelites lost the focus of what they were doing and actually dismantled the Bones' hideout. But the show was cut completely because we didn't have room for it.

Sound Bites

A favorite moment in "Gathering Thunder" can only be heard by those listening carefully! If you listen closely to the movie theater scene, you can hear the following dialogue in the background:

ROCK: I gotta go the distance and prove that I can still fight!

MANAGER: You're crazy!

ROCK: I gotta do it for my kids!

MANAGER: For crying out loud, Champ, they're married and have their own kids! They can fend for themselves. You've proved yourself to them, now you gotta move on.

ROCK: To what, Mick?! I can't do nothin' but box! I don't know nothin' else! I know what it is. Yeah, I know! You're gonna put me in a nursing home, aren't you?

MANAGER: Oh, Rock!

ROCK: You don't want me back in that ring 'cause it'll prove I can take care of myself!

MANAGER: I'm not doubting that you can take care of yourself!

ROCK: Oh, yes, you are! And I'm gonna prove it to you.

MANAGER: You don't have to, Rock!

ROCK: I'm gonna do 50 sit-ups, right here in front of you.

MANAGER: Oh, Rock, you don't have to do that.

ROCK: No, you don't believe me. *(Rock gets on the floor.)*

ROCK: Hold my feet.

MANAGER: Okay, if it'll make you feel better. *(After a long while and much struggling . . .)*

MANAGER: One.

Goof Alert!

In "The Return," Blackgaard says, "Your father deprived Europe and the United States of information that would have benefited both nations immeasurably." Europe is not a nation; it's a continent.

Actor Earl Boen, voice of Dr. Blackgaard

Sound Bites with Dave Arnold

One of the most challenging scenes I ever produced was the Imagination Station scene from "The Time Has Come." That single scene alone took me at least two weeks of work. To create it, I canvassed every script we'd ever recorded searching for ideas that would be instrumental in Eugene's salvation journey. I highlighted all the ones that seemed appropriate, which amounted to around 40 minutes of audio. Then I had to condense that into the most relevant and compelling eight minutes possible, assemble them so that the pace built with Eugene's emotion, add engaging sound effects, and process the clips individually so that they all worked together as one cohesive, powerful scene.

Then I sent it off to John Campbell to compose the score, which turned out to be magical. I'll never forget mixing the show frantically, trying to make our airdate. At the very end of the Imagination Station scene, I included a clip of Whit, to add an emotional exclamation point, since Whit was away in the Middle East. Somehow during the mix, that clip got erased. I felt heartsick. I didn't have time to reinsert it. So I mixed the scene without it. I've always regretted losing that clip because I felt that it was the perfect ending. But I also wondered why it got erased and trusted that God knew what was best for the show.

As a fun side note: If you listen to the very first moments of the show, you'll hear Eugene whistle the distinctive seven notes of the *Odyssey* theme. That's me whistling.

BTS: The Final Conflict

As we reached the finale of the Blackgaard shows and the intensity heated up, we faced the dilemma of making the conclusion appropriately dramatic and exciting without going too far with its potential violence. Richard's confrontation with Jellyfish and his capture at the hands of Dr. Blackgaard were two examples. In our early drafts, Richard used a stun gun to subdue Jellyfish. We changed it to an electrical stunner in later versions.

More problematic was Richard's capture by Dr. Blackgaard. In our first outlines, Billy MacPherson and Sam Johnson found Richard beat up under a pile of leaves after Dr. Blackgaard and Jellyfish had finished with him. However, we realized that it made Dr. Blackgaard look sloppy because he didn't "finish the job." But we couldn't take the violence any further. How to fix the dilemma? Sound designer Mark Drury came up with the solution: Jellyfish and Bovril would take Richard off to some horrible fate, and on the way, Richard would jump out of the car in a public place where he would not likely be recaptured.

BTS: Another Chance

We later learn in "Blackgaard's Revenge" (album 33) that during the course of the drama Blackgaard planted a virus in the Imagination Station's computer.

Everything Changes! Original Ideas for Darkness Before Dawn

Here are a few ideas we considered for this album, but did NOT use:

- George Barclay leads a group of parents who protested the goings-on at Whit's End. They demand an explanation for the unsafe materials found there.
- Richard Maxwell takes pictures of the Bones of Rath's attack on Whit's End, proving that they were indeed responsible. Richard follows Blackgaard's gang to their hideout at the Harlequin Theatre. He is hurt in a fall from the rafters while taking pictures of Dr. Blackgaard and cronies. He gives a cryptic message to the good guys about "looking in the rafters." The good gang later finds his pictures there and uses them against the Bones.
- When Eugene is using his Imagination Station search program, Katrina shows up in the Underground Railroad tunnel with Reverend Andrew. Eugene proposes to Katrina, and Reverend Andrew offers to perform their wedding ceremony.
- Edwin Blackgaard returns from far-off lands to try to stop his brother with a swordfight.
- Richard Maxwell dies in the hospital.
- Tasha Forbes returns to Odyssey to stop Blackgaard. She ends up trapped underground with Jason after Dr. Blackgaard's bomb goes off in the tunnel.

- When Jellyfish is trying to escape from Whit's End, he attempts to jump out of a window but bounces off! The window—an invention of Whit's—isn't actually a window but a hologram. In this way, Whit actually helps to stop the trouble in Odyssey even though he isn't there.

- Eugene and Bernard chase Professor Bovril's escape van and run it off the road!

- After Jack's offer of salvation in the tunnel, Blackgaard hears the sounds of the "minions of hell" coming for his soul. He accepts Jack's offer and asks to receive Christ. After the bomb goes off, both Jack and Blackgaard are hanging from a ladder in the basement of Whit's End. Blackgaard realizes that the only way Jack can live would be for him to let go. So he lets go of the ladder, giving his life to save Jack.

- The series ends with Whit's End burned to the ground.

- Or, the series ends with a tip of the hat to the series finale of the 1982–1993 television sitcom *Cheers:* Whit's End closes but is opened again the next day.

- After the end of Dr. Blackgaard, Jellyfish goes on trial with Richard Maxwell as the key witness against him. Richard deals with his need to forgive Jellyfish.

The Odyssey Times, volume V

Sound Bites

In order to get Jason arrested in "The Last Resort," Dr. Blackgaard gave to the police an edited tape of his conversation with Jason. We created two versions of this tape—one where it was obviously edited together and a second where the conversation was very smooth. We used the former in the episode (so it was obvious to the listener that it was pasted together), but in hindsight, some wished we had used the other version. The current version makes the authorities sound a little silly for believing the obviously edited version of the tape.

Character:
George Barclay

Quote: "Lost? Me? George Rand McNally Barclay?"

Something you may not know about George: He had a dog named Sparky when he was a kid.

Album 26

Back on the Air

Saint Paul: The Man of Many Stories

The evolution of the Saint Paul episodes ultimately took the team through all of its storytelling styles. First we intended them to be narrated by Bernard Walton, but some new ideas for the Imagination Station caught our attention, and we told the story of Paul's conversion in the Station. For the later parts of Paul's life, telling the stories with the Station proved problematic because the narrative jumps quickly through several years, which is cumbersome in the Imagination Station. So we went back to the idea of narrating them and wrote the episodes with Jack Allen telling the story to Charles Edward Thompson. Then the show changed *again* to a Kids' Radio episode. We're either incredibly creative—or indecisive!

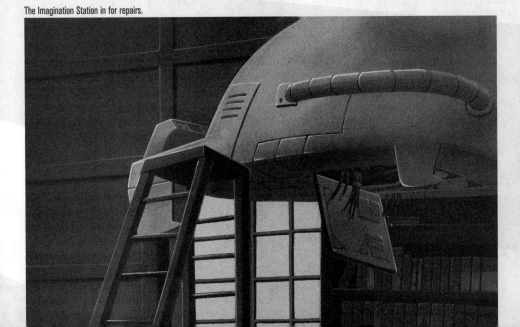

The Imagination Station in for repairs.

Episode Information

321: Hidden in My Heart
Original Air Date: 7/1/95
Writer: Marshal Younger
Sound Designer: Bob Luttrell
Scripture: Psalm 119:11
Theme: Memorizing Bible verses
Summary: To teach about Bible memorization, Kids' Radio spoofs three popular television programs. Kids' Radio renames them "Star Trip," "Rescue 119," and "Laffie the Wonder Dog."

335, 336: Love Is in the Air, I and II
Original Air Dates: 10/28/95 & 11/4/95
Writer: Paul McCusker
Sound Designers: Dave Arnold & Mark Drury
Scripture: 1 John 4:7-12
Themes: Love, romance, God's will for our lives
Summary: Katrina Shanks and Tasha Forbes arrive back in town, causing all sorts of romantic high jinks with Eugene, Jason, and even Connie.

337: W-O-R-R-Y
Original Air Date: 11/11/95
Writer: Marshal Younger
Sound Designer: Bob Luttrell
Scripture: Matthew 6:25-34
Theme: Worry
Summary: Erica Clark tries to look her best for school pictures; Sam Johnson worries about the upcoming Academic Olympics.

338: Easy Money
Original Air Date: 11/18/95
Writer: Marshal Younger
Sound Designer: Dave Arnold
Scripture: 1 Timothy 6:10
Themes: Gambling, responsibility
Summary: To buy new hockey equipment, Sam Johnson and Butch need money. Sam gets a job and nearly works himself to death while Butch resorts to gambling.

339: Do, for a Change
Original Air Date: 12/2/95
Writer: Marshal Younger
Sound Designer: Mark Drury
Scripture: Luke 18:9-14
Themes: Pride, humility, patience
Summary: Zachary Sellers and Eugene face their first difficulties as new Christians.

340, 341: Pokenberry Falls, R.F.D., I and II
Original Air Dates: 1/6/96 & 1/13/96
Writer: Paul McCusker
Sound Designers: Mark Drury & Dave Arnold
Scripture: Romans 8:28; Philippians 1:6
Theme: God's providence
Summary: The Barclays are presented with a difficult choice when a small church in New England asks George to be its pastor.

342: Welcome Home, Mr. Blackgaard
Original Air Date: 1/20/96
Writer: Phil Lollar
Sound Designer: Dave Arnold
Scripture: Matthew 6:14-15; 18:21-22
Theme: Forgiveness
Summary: Edwin Blackgaard returns to Odyssey to take over the Electric Palace and reopen the Harlequin Theatre.

Original back cover art of album 26

343: The Pretty Good Samaritan
Original Air Date: 1/27/96
Writer: Marshal Younger
Sound Designer: Mark Drury
Scripture: Luke 10:30-37
Theme: Treating others with kindness
Summary: Charles Edward Thompson's attempt to act like a Good Samaritan is challenged when he meets an annoying boy named Glenn.

346: Saint Paul: Voyage to Rome
Original Air Date: 3/2/96
Writer: Phil Lollar
Sound Designer: Todd Busteed
Scripture: Acts 24–28
Theme: The biblical story of the life and ministry of the apostle Paul
Summary: A young Antonius sets off on a sea journey with his father and a prisoner—the apostle Paul.

347: Saint Paul: An Appointment with Caesar
Original Air Date: 3/9/96
Writer: Phil Lollar
Sound Designer: Mark Drury
Scripture: Acts 24–28
Theme: The biblical story of the life and ministry of the apostle Paul
Summary: The apostle Paul arrives in Rome for his appointment with the emperor.

Sound Bites

On the day before recording "Hidden in My Heart," sound designer Bob Luttrell figured out how many entrances and exits the skit called "Star Trip" contained. Then he came up with the idea of having the captain run into all the doors.

My Take: Marshal Younger

When I was writing "Hidden in My Heart," I was having so much fun that I said to myself, "I can't believe they're paying me to do this." Also, I don't think I've laughed harder at any point in my *Odyssey* career than in the studio directing that show. The performances and impersonations were so dead-on. Actor Steve Bridges's take on Sulu in the *Star Trek* parody had me on the floor for about five minutes.

Behind the Scenes: Love Is in the Air

We had always imagined Tasha Forbes as a woman who often came in and out of Jason Whittaker's life. With *Darkness Before Dawn* behind us, we brought Tasha back for "Love Is in the Air" in hopes of doing several light-hearted, romantic comedy stories. This show also enabled us to explore the postsalvation relationship of Eugene and Katrina and add a rival for Eugene—Brandon Tuller, the seemingly perfect Christian.

The show originally ended with Tasha getting kidnapped by unknown forces. We decided to cut this plot point as we had just finished the intense *Darkness* miniseries and thought we should stick with more normal episodes for a while.

Sound Bites

Steve Bridges is an impressionist/comedian who did many voices for *Adventures in Odyssey* over the years, most notably Howard J. Weasel in "A Victim of Circumstance" (album 23). In "Easy Money," he played six roles: the mechanic, Pete Johnson, Keith Jackson, Marv Albert, John Madden, and an employee. In 2000 Steve became famous for his impression of President George W. Bush on *The Tonight Show*.

My Take: Marshal Younger

"Do, for a Change" and "Pretty Good Samaritan" were the only installments in a series of shows based on Jesus' parables. "The Pretty Good Samaritan" had the theme of

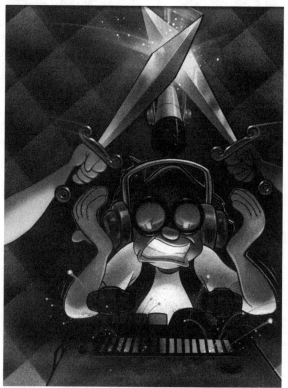

Eugene's productions for Kids' Radio get a little too realistic at times.

using Scripture as a basis for living our lives, and "Do, for a Change" was a dramatization of the prideful pharisee and the humble sinner in Luke 18. But the series was abandoned quickly when we discovered that we had already done so many parable themes.

My Take: Marshal Younger

I never really considered gambling a kids' issue until I noticed two of our child actors in the recording studio hallway playing a game where they won each others' Pokémon coins. In essence, they were gambling. I saw this to be a new trend, and so "Easy Money" came about.

Sound Bites

Actor Howard Morris (1919–2005) played Ellis Birch in "Pokenberry Falls, R.F.D." Howard was best known as the character of Ernest T. Bass on *The Andy Griffith Show*, Gopher on various Winnie the Pooh animated movies, and an assortment of guest characters on the animated television shows *The Flintstones* (1960–1966), *The Jetsons,* and *DuckTales* (1987–1990).

Howard was surprisingly nervous when he came into the studio to record. The *Odyssey* team was shocked by his timidity. Here was a man who had made a huge mark in the entertainment industry going all the way back to Sid Caesar's *Your Show of Shows* (1950–1954). His credits included comedian, actor, writer, director, and well-known voice-over artist. *He was nervous to come and work for us!* After a while, however, Howard got in the groove, settled in, and felt comfortable—and he made a terrific Ellis Birch in the process.

Sound Bites

In "Pokenberry Falls, R.F.D.," during George Barclay's graduation, several other graduates' names are called. They include William Bailey (an American painter), Ralph Emerson (a prominent writer in the 1800s), Philip Glassborow (playwright and producer of *Focus on the Family Radio Theatre*), Clive Lewis (aka Christian author C. S. Lewis), and J. B. Phillips (a Bible translator, writer, and clergyman). George's class was quite talented!

BTS: Pokenberry Falls, R.F.D.

The original name of the town where the Barclays moved was going to be "Dry Point." Then it was changed to "Bedford Falls" in keeping with their connection to *It's a Wonderful Life*. In a writers' meeting, executive producer Chuck Bolte couldn't remember the name of the town and blurted out, "Pokenberry Falls, or whatever it's called!" The name stuck.

Goof Alert!

Emperor Nero assigns a horse a seat in the senate in the episode "Saint Paul: An Appointment with Caesar." However, Nero didn't do this. Emperor Caligula did before Nero became emperor.

Whit's Inventions

Over the years, Whit's inventing bug has led to many interesting gizmos that both teach and entertain.

Invention	Episode
A pizza oven from a copy machine	Whit's Flop
Whit's Boredom Buster	Family Vacation
Instant Freezer	The Case of the Secret Room
Environment Enhancer	The Shepherd and the Giant
A prayer vending machine	And When You Pray . . .
Imagination Station	The Imagination Station
BEAVRS	Hallowed Be Thy Name
Room of Consequence	Into Temptation
Transmuter	Another Man's Shoes
A flying machine made out of a boat with oars and big helium balloons	I Slap Floor
A system that can turn any telephone into a motion-sensor microphone	Sounds Like a Mystery
Mix-O-Matic	Broken-Armed and Dangerous
Edu-Link	The Impossible
The Gallery	A Capsule Comes to Town

Strateflyer

Whit's Boredom Buster

Room of Consequence

The Barclays Say Good-bye

The decision to allow the Barclays to leave Odyssey in "Pokenberry Falls, R.F.D." was based on the realization that Jimmy and Donna had to grow up. And if they grew up and acted like real teens, the stories would be too mature for our target audience of 8- to 12-year-olds. So the Barclays had to leave town.

An early draft of "Pokenberry Falls, R.F.D." took place partially in Odyssey and involved Simon Birtles adjusting to Jimmy's school. Also in that early draft, Donna was so against moving to Pokenberry Falls that she threatened to stay behind in Connellsville with her uncle. At the time we wrote those unproduced drafts, we had hoped to create several individual episodes or even a whole spin-off series featuring the Barclays in Pokenberry Falls. Aside from "It's a Pokenberry Christmas" (album 31), however, we never followed through with this idea.

The Barclay family actors (*from left*): David Griffin, Azure Janosky, Chuck Bolte, Carol Bilger

Character: Whit
Quote: "Let's see if this thing works."
Something you may not know about Whit:
He taught junior high school English for
15 years.

Album 27

The Search for Whit

Another "Whit Sighting"

After Hal Smith passed away in 1994, dozens of talented voice-over artists auditioned for the voice of John Avery Whittaker. We also had many "Whit sightings," calls from people telling us of actors who they thought would be perfect to fill the part. (In one case, a couple brought in a man who physically resembled Whit but didn't sound like him at all!) But no one captured the warmth and magic of Whit's character, so we gave up looking.

Then, in the fall of 1995, a Seattle-area radio-station manager called Chuck Bolte. He said he'd heard a few radio ads voiced by a man who sounded very much like Hal Smith. The manager had gone to the trouble of finding the actor's name, Paul Herlinger, and passed it on to Chuck.

Paul McCusker, the producer at the time, called the number. Paul got Mr. Herlinger's answering machine. "From the first 'hello,' chills went down my spine," Paul remembers. "He sounded so much like Hal."

Chuck Bolte flew to Seattle where he auditioned Paul Herlinger reading lines from the scripts "Flash Flood" (album 15) and "The Prodigal, Jimmy" (album 4). When the team heard the audition tapes, they all agreed that Paul was very close to Hal—not an exact match, but close.

There's more to a character than just a voice, however. We needed to know how Paul would portray Whit's character, and if he would fit in with the rest of the *Odyssey* cast. We decided to find out by doing a test run, so we taped an episode using Paul in the role of Whit. That's how "The Search for Whit" came to life.

Episode Information

344: Letting Go
Original Air Date: 2/3/96
Writer: Marshal Younger
Sound Designer: Mark Drury
Scripture: Psalm 147:3
Theme: Dealing with loss
Summary: Zachary Sellers has a hard time adjusting when his mother starts dating again.

345: B-TV: Compassion
Original Air Date: 2/10/96
Writer: Phil Lollar
Sound Designer: Dave Arnold
Scripture: Galatians 5:14
Theme: Compassion
Summary: Bernard Walton, Eugene, and the B-TV crew talk about compassion with the help of Marty the shoemaker.

348: With a Little Help from My Friends
Original Air Date: 3/16/96
Writer: Phil Lollar
Sound Designer: Dave Arnold
Scripture: Romans 12:2
Theme: Peer pressure
Summary: Sam Johnson, Connie, and her mother, June Kendall, compare stories about giving in to peer pressure.

349: Blessings in Disguise
Original Air Date: 3/23/96
Writers: April Dammann & Marshal Younger
Sound Designer: Mark Drury
Scripture: Proverbs 12:19
Themes: Trust, honesty, friendship
Summary: Brenda Perry's pen pal, Thor Douglas, comes to visit, and Brenda is panicked because she has to live up to all the exaggerations she's written.

350: The Time of Our Lives
Original Air Date: 4/13/96
Writer: Marshal Younger
Sound Designer: Mark Drury
Scripture: Ephesians 5:15-17
Theme: Making the most of your time
Summary: Kids' Radio tells a Twilife Zone sketch of Kathy and Jeremy, two kids who have a propensity for wasting time.

351: What Are You Gonna Do with Your Life?
Original Air Date: 4/20/96
Writer: Paul McCusker
Sound Designer: Dave Arnold
Scripture: Isaiah 42:16
Themes: God's plans for our lives, career plans
Summary: As Connie tries to decide on a career, she experiments with several new jobs.

352: Memories of Jerry
Original Air Date: 4/27/96
Writer: Phil Lollar
Sound Designer: Mark Drury
Scripture: Psalm 73:23-26
Themes: Doing what's right, courage
Summary: An old postcard triggers Jason Whittaker's memories about the last weekend he spent with his older brother, Jerry.

353: A Question About Tasha
Original Air Date: 5/4/96
Writer: Campbell Freed
Sound Designer: Dave Arnold
Scripture: 2 Corinthians 6:14-18
Theme: The importance of Christian marriage
Summary: Jason Whittaker and Tasha Forbes announce that they're getting married . . . tomorrow!
PARENTAL WARNING:
This is an emotional story about the importance of Christian marriage. It is sensitively told, but may be too mature for younger listeners.

354: Blind Justice

Original Air Date: 5/11/96
Writer: Marshal Younger
Sound Designer: Todd Busteed
Scripture: Isaiah 59; Micah 6:8
Themes: Justice, peer pressure
Summary: Eugene and Bernard wind up on the same jury and must decide the fate of a young boy accused of burglary.

355, 356, 357: The Search for Whit, I, II, and III

Original Air Dates: 5/18/96, 5/25/96, & 6/1/96
Writer: Paul McCusker
Sound Designers: Dave Arnold & Mark Drury
Scripture: James 1:16-18
Themes: Knowing what you believe, the joy of reunion
Summary: Jason and Eugene get a cryptic message from Whit in the Middle East, which leads them on a wild investigation that could change Christian history as we know it.

Whit discovers Eugene and Jason in "The Search for Whit."

Cut Scenes

We recorded an extra skit for "B-TV: Compassion" that was narrated by Eugene. In the sketch, a young couple named Brad and Muffy force Muffy's father to eat at the far end of the table. They later learn that their young daughter is planning on treating them the same way when they are old. We cut the sketch because the show was too long and we have never found a place to reuse it.

Behind the Scenes: B-TV: Compassion

The story of Marty the shoemaker is an adaptation of a classic story by the nineteenth-century Russian author Leo Tolstoy. He based his story on the words of Jesus from Matthew 25.

A faithful adaptation of the story has been produced by *Radio Theatre*. It is included in the holiday package "Traveling Home for Christmas" (2005).

Sound Bites

One of the rules for the writers of *Adventures in Odyssey* is to avoid what we call "verbal bell-bottoms"—meaning that we try to avoid writing details into the script that will date them to a specific time period. For example, in "B-TV: Compassion," we cut Bernard's funny line, "Paint me purple and call me Barney," in the belief that the popular children's dinosaur might not always be recognizable.

BTS: With a Little Help from My Friends

This episode is loosely based on the *Family Portraits* episode "A Different Kind of Peer Pressure."

BTS: Blessings in Disguise

April Dammann wrote the early drafts of "Blessings in Disguise." April is the mother of Joe Dammann, who played the character of Eric Myers on *Adventures in Odyssey* and Nicholas in the McGee and Me! series.

My Take: Marshal Younger

I loved the "Blessings in Disguise" character of Glenn Adams. He was the annoying doomsayer who tried to get everyone to consider the impending threat of killer bees, volcanoes, and number 2 pencils. I wrote a line for him, which he said to someone wearing a lot of makeup, "Did you fall into a vat of blush?" The word "vat" is funny; it's one of my favorites.

BTS: What Are You Gonna Do with Your Life?

One of the time schisms in the *Adventures in Odyssey* world allowed Connie to stay a teenager (around age 16) year after year while the other young characters around her grew up normally. Eventually we conceded that Connie couldn't stay in high school forever, and we began to think about her future. "What Are You Gonna Do with Your Life?" kicked off that new thinking. Over the next several years, we saw her graduate from high school in "The Graduate" (album 31) and look at career plans in "Malachi's Message" (album 32).

Actor T. J. Lowther with the *Odyssey* team

Goof Alert!

In "Memories of Jerry," young brothers Jason and Jerry Whittaker are talking about the cabin on Lake Michigan. Jason asks Jerry if they can go across the lake into Canada. Later, a character actually does cross the lake into Canada. Unfortunately for us, Lake Michigan doesn't border Canada.

BTS: Memories of Jerry

Dave Lipson played the coach in "Memories of Jerry." Dave played Coach Zachary in several early *Odyssey* episodes.

Sound Bites

T. J. Lowther plays young Jason. T. J. had starred in the two movies *A Perfect World* (1993) with Kevin Costner and Clint Eastwood and *Mad Love* (1995) with Drew Barrymore and Chris O'Donnell. He additionally appeared in the television movie *One Christmas* (1994) with Katherine Hepburn. T. J. was a huge *Adventures in Odyssey* fan and was very excited at the chance to appear on the program.

My Take: Phil Lollar

We had never done a story about Whit's older son before "Memories of Jerry." We had seen him in "The Mortal Coil" (album 16) but never really explored his story. There is a lot of me embodied in Jason: I was nicknamed "The Judge" when I was small because I didn't smile until I was two years old. My older brother was the first one to make me laugh. The whole high-jump bar incident actually happened to me. Also, I've never really liked camping outside if there [was] a cabin readily available. My uncle was a languages specialist, just like Jerry. I was also Jason's age when the [war in] Vietnam was raging, got caught up in a riot on a university campus, and knew a few fellows who lost their lives in Southeast Asia. Perhaps more than any other *Odyssey* episode I've written, this one truly followed the old adage, "Write what you know."

BTS: A Question About Tasha

Like the episode ". . . The Last Shall Be First" (album 11), "A Question About Tasha" was inspired by a story that Shirley Dobson told about her father during a Focus on the Family chapel. When we wrote "Love Is in the Air," we thought Tasha Forbes and Jason Whittaker might get married. But we quickly realized that Jason and Tasha couldn't get married because Tasha wasn't a Christian. So, to send a consistent message about the wisdom of not being "unequally yoked," we decided to have them break up . . . but we knew it wouldn't be easy.

On a lighter note, this episode featured the introduction of Connie's wedding planning service Dreams by Constance, which orchestrated many weddings in Odyssey including Jack and Joanne Allen's in "For Whom the Wedding Bells Toll" (album 29) and Eugene and Katrina Meltsner's in "For Better or for Worse" (album 44).

BTS: Blind Justice

This episode was originally titled "Two Angry Men" in reference to the classic juror movie *12 Angry Men* (1957). Writer Marshal Younger remembers: "I had fun figuring out how the

robbery would work. I called a safe manufacturer and asked him how to rob a safe. He said, 'I'm not telling you how to rob a safe!'"

Cut Scenes

In the recording script for "The Search for Whit," Jason notices that Eugene is wearing *Dumbo's Circus* pajamas, a reference to a 1985 television series on which Hal Smith, Katie Leigh, Will Ryan, and Walker Edmiston had all worked. The line was cut from the final show.

Actor Paul Herlinger, voice of Whit

The Production Team's Search for Whit

"The Search for Whit" was originally titled "The Mentiri Files" and contained the reappearance of character Alfred Brownlee who was introduced (though not heard) in "The Jesus Cloth" (album 18).

"The Search for Whit" contained an intentional tease for *Odyssey* fans hearing it for the first time. Since Hal Smith's death, we had dropped in Whit's lines from older shows in various episodes such as "Gone . . ." (album 21) and "The Time Has Come" (album 25). Some fans realized what we had done and prided themselves on identifying in which episodes the original lines had appeared. So, in part I of "The Search for Whit," we purposefully put Whit's voice on the telephone message so that fans would try to figure out where the lines had come from. Only in part II did we introduce the new Whit live and in person.

We also had to employ another voice disguise later in the episode when we hear the villain talking. We didn't want to give away his identity, so we made use of a new voice-masking technology that had appeared in several action-adventure movies.

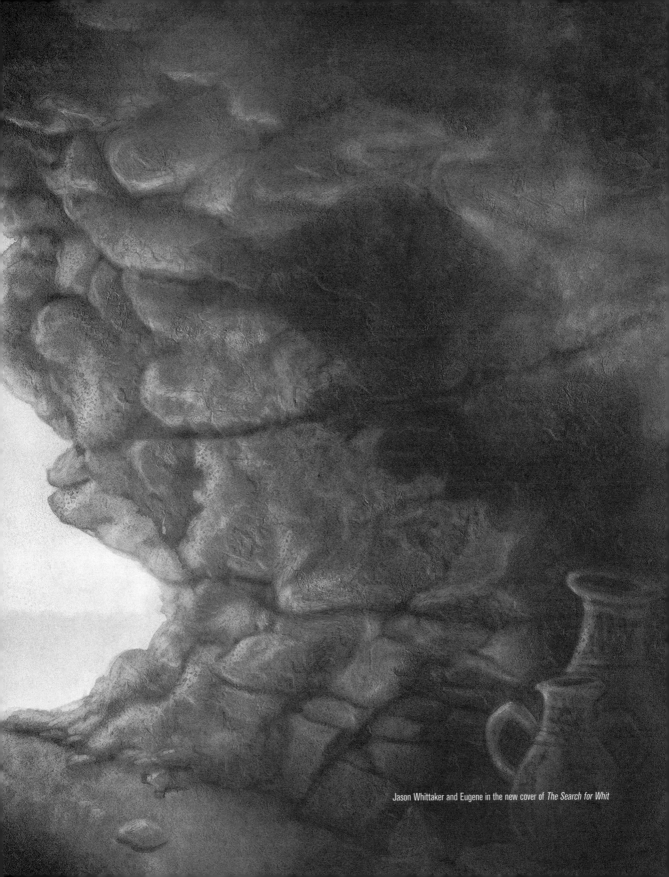

Jason Whittaker and Eugene in the new cover of *The Search for Whit*

Character: Jack Allen
Quote: "What have I gotten myself into?"
Something you may not know about Jack:
He didn't like geometry in school.

Album **28**

Welcome Home!

Should Whit Return to Odyssey?

With actor Paul Herlinger on board as the voice of Whit, our main character could finally return to *Adventures in Odyssey*, but we weren't sure that he should return to the *town* itself. For a while, we considered making his character more adventurous. Maybe we could send him off on missionary trips to exotic foreign countries with Connie or Eugene. "The Right Choice" was the beginning of that idea when the Universal Missions Board offered to send him to several churches around the world.

However, we wondered if "losing" Whit to missions work might put missionaries in a bad light. Would listeners be upset that Whit left Odyssey (again) to do missions? On the other hand, having Whit become a missionary could also highlight their value.

Another problem was Paul Herlinger's chemistry with the other actors in the studio. It wasn't bad—just the opposite! His chemistry with the main characters brought a wonderful feeling to the shows. Why would we want to lose that chemistry so soon after bringing him in?

Our final problem was that we had decided to take a break from recording to think about the future of the show (from December 1996 to September 1997). We worried that sending Whit away from Odyssey again might give a message that we were ending the show itself, which we weren't.

So we decided to bring the show back to where it began with Whit behind the soda fountain at Whit's End, and all being right with the world.

Episode Information

358: The Secret Weapon
Original Air Date: 9/21/96
Writer: Phil Lollar
Sound Designer: Todd Busteed
Scripture: John 8:32
Themes: Leadership, believing in the right thing
Summary: Connie becomes coach of the Odyssey Coyotes baseball team and has a plan for boosting Sam Johnson's confidence.

359: The Merchant of Odyssey
Original Air Date: 9/28/96
Writer: Phil Lollar
Sound Designer: Ramsey Drexler
Scripture: James 2:13
Theme: Mercy
Summary: Edwin Blackgaard has to borrow money from Bart Rathbone to pay his taxes.

360, 361: Three Funerals and a Wedding, I and II
Original Air Date: 10/5/96 & 10/12/96
Writer: Phil Lollar
Sound Designers: Mark Drury & Todd Busteed
Scripture: The book of Ruth
Themes: The biblical story of Ruth, loyalty
Summary: Connie tells the romantic story of Ruth, who risks all to stay committed to her family.

362, 363: The Right Choice, I and II
Original Air Date: 10/19/96 & 10/26/96
Writer: Paul McCusker
Sound Designers: Mark Drury & Todd Busteed
Scripture: Psalm 27
Themes: God's plans for our lives, waiting on the Lord
Summary: Stopping in Chicago on the way home from the Middle East, Eugene learns that Katrina Shanks may be marrying someone else!

364: Home, Sweet Home
Original Air Date: 11/2/96
Writer: Phil Lollar
Sound Designer: Mark Drury
Scripture: Psalm 84:3
Themes: The joy of reunion, the importance of home
Summary: Whit finally returns to Odyssey—but Connie can't seem to meet up with him.

A scene from "Home, Sweet Home"

298

365: **Clara**
Original Air Date: 11/9/96
Writer: Phil Lollar
Sound Designer: Dave Arnold
Scripture: Proverbs 17:17
Themes: Forgiveness, friendship
Summary: Jack Allen tells Eugene about a shocking incident from his past: Whit gets angry and says that he never wants to see Jack again.
PARENTAL WARNING:
This is an emotional show about love, loss, and adoption. It may be too mature for younger listeners.

366: **Solitary Refinement**
Original Air Date: 11/16/96
Writer: Paul McCusker
Sound Designer: Mark Drury
Scripture: Philippians 4:6-7
Theme: The importance of solitude
Summary: Eugene considers joining a monastery to get over the pain of losing Katrina.

367: **The Decision**
Original Air Date: 11/23/96
Writer: Phil Lollar
Sound Designer: Dave Arnold
Scripture: Proverbs 3:5-6
Theme: Seeking God's will for our lives
Summary: Whit must decide whether or not to accept an offer to return to the mission field, and so Connie sets out to prove that he is needed in Odyssey.

368: **The Other Woman**
Original Air Date: 11/30/96
Writer: Paul McCusker
Sound Designer: Todd Busteed
Scripture: Proverbs 16:28; 1 Peter 3:12
Themes: The danger of spreading rumors, dealing with the mentally ill
Summary: The Rathbones sniff out a scandal when they catch Tom Riley visiting a mysterious woman at Hillingdale Haven.

369: **It's a Wrap!**
Original Air Date: 12/7/96
Writer: Paul McCusker
Sound Designer: Todd Busteed
Scripture: Psalm 118:24, Proverbs 27:1
Theme: God's role in everyday life
Summary: Lucy Cunningham-Schultz and the Kids' Radio team take an in-depth look at Whit's End and the return of John Avery Whittaker.

Clubhouse magazines, April and May 1993

Behind the Scenes: The Secret Weapon

"The Secret Weapon" originally appeared in story form in the April and May 1993 issues of *Clubhouse* magazine. In the *Clubhouse* story, it was Sam's pitching that needed help instead of his batting. Mr. Whittaker gave him a special baseball. The "grand slam" finale was a tribute to the 1984 Robert Redford film, *The Natural*.

BTS: Three Funerals and a Wedding

A few listeners wrote in questioning why we chose to base an episode name on the R-rated 1994 film *Four Weddings and a Funeral*. The episode, however, does not reference the movie, only the title, and we thought the name was too perfect to pass up.

BTS: The Right Choice

It was time to decide what to do with the relationship between Eugene and Katrina. Our first thought was that Katrina should accept a marriage proposal from Eugene in this episode. After we came up with the "wedding crasher" scenario, however, we rethought things and decided to keep them apart while Eugene matured.

But when we actually recorded "The Right Choice," the chemistry between Eugene and Katrina came alive like never before. It made us rethink whether this show would be the end of their relationship or a new beginning. So much for our plans! We took their story a step further in "For Whom the Wedding Bells Toll" (album 29).

Sound Bites with Mark Drury

We recorded the lounge singer in "The Right Choice" with Steve Bridges singing several lines from songs such as "Feelings" [Morris Albert (1975)] and "Silly Love Songs" [Paul McCartney (1976)]. Though hilarious, we cut the scene from the broadcast because the show was too long. We wanted to put the scene back in for the album but discovered that we would have to pay royalties or obtain permissions from the song writers. So instead, we revoiced the scene with Jim Adam (a Focus employee and songwriter), who wrote his own songs.

Actor Paul Herlinger in the studio

BTS: Home, Sweet Home

Connie's race to catch Whit in "Home, Sweet Home" was meant as a bookend to Eugene's chase in "Gone . . ." (album 21).

Sound Bites with Mark Drury

The crowd scenes in "Home, Sweet Home" were especially difficult to produce. I pulled together a group from the Focus on the Family correspondence department along with some visitors who were touring Focus. Those folks especially enjoyed being the whistlers. To get the sound of Connie's tires squealing, I went into the Focus parking lot, set up a microphone on a boom, and spun out in my new van. Unfortunately, a police officer saw me and pulled me over. But after he found out what I was doing, both of us had a good laugh. I was saved from receiving a ticket!

Goof Alert!

In "Clara," Jack Allen says that he originally came to apologize to Whit. However, in "Gone . . ." (album 21), Jack says that Whit wrote him a letter asking him to come to visit Odyssey. Also, Jack says that he hasn't talked to Whit since the Clara incident, but in "The Search for Whit" (album 27), Jack has sent letters to Whit.

Actor Aria Curzon, voice of Clara

Sound Bites

"Clara" features the first performance by actor Aria Curzon as the title character. Aria voices the character of Ducky on *The Land Before Time* television series (2007) and videos, starting with the fifth in the series. On subsequent *Odyssey* albums, Aria plays Mandy Straussberg.

Cut Scenes

"Solitary Refinement" began as an episode called "Eugene's Enlightening" written by Dave Arnold in late 1995. In Dave's draft, Eugene actually joined the monastery. After considering our other developments with Eugene, we decided that he should visit the monastery but not stay. Bernard Walton's daydream about life in a monastery is the only scene left from the original draft.

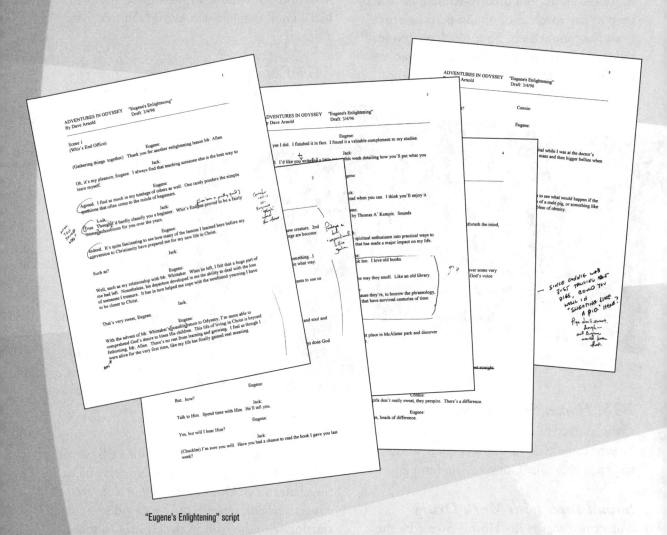

"Eugene's Enlightening" script

Episodes About Whit's Past

Episode	Events
Thank You, God	Whit becomes a Christian as a boy
Blackbeard's Treasure	Whit and his friend Jack in North Carolina
Rescue from Manatugo Point *and* Operation: Dig-Out	Whit in World War II
The Triangle	Whit in college
Prequels of Love	Whit proposes to Jenny, who becomes his wife
Silent Night	Whit's Christmases as a family man
Clara	Whit after Jenny's death
Recollections	Whit opens Whit's End

My Take: Paul McCusker

Eugene's experience at the monastery was partially based on my own experience at a silent prayer retreat. I honestly couldn't believe how difficult it was to quiet my mind enough to pray for any substantial length of time.

Sound Bites

"The Decision" was the first show to feature the Kids' Radio talk show, "Candid Conversations with Connie." It appeared in many later episodes, usually when we needed to reveal something in a dramatic fashion.

BTS: The Other Woman

"The Other Woman" was created to answer a long-standing question: What became of Tom's wife, Agnes? She had appeared in "Thank You, God" (album 3) and then seemed to disappear without a trace. Considering the tragedies endured by both Tom and Agnes, we thought the best explanation was that she suffered from a form of manic-depression. This also gave us the opportunity to finish the story about Horatio Spafford that began in "It Is Well" (album 16).

John Avery Whittaker

Sound Bites

We approached the recording of "It's a Wrap" in a new way. Generally each actor speaks into his own microphone. But, for this recording, we used only one microphone and had the actors walk on and off, jostling it and making "mistakes."

BTS: *It's a Wrap*

"It's a Wrap" was the last episode in which Lucy Cunningham-Schultz and Sam Johnson appeared. Hal's Diner was a tribute to Hal Smith. On recording days, the team often had breakfast with him in small diners near the studio.

It's a Wrap . . . for Now

"It's a Wrap" and several other episodes in *Welcome Home* were designed to wrap up the current storylines of *Odyssey* and allow the team to take a break to plan for the future. We didn't air any new episodes between December 7, 1996, and September 6, 1997. During this period, we cultivated new writers and sound designers as well as the future of the show.

Jack Allen and Connie in "Home, Sweet Home"

Welcome to Odyssey, Joanne!

"The Decision" introduces the character of Joanne Woodston. We had tried for years to find a substantial ongoing role for Janet Waldo (who previously played Lawrence Hodges's mom, among others) and finally decided that a love interest for Jack Allen would be the perfect match. Actors Alan Young and Janet Waldo had worked together for decades on other programs and their chemistry in the studio was perfect.

Actor Janet Waldo, voice of Joanne Allen

Joanne Allen

Album **29**

Signed, Sealed, and Committed

The Creation of Jared DeWhite

All of the kid characaters in the first generation left *Odyssey* during the hiatus because the actors playing them were getting into their late teens. The *Odyssey* team wanted to create a new group of characters who had the same camaraderie of that early team.

Jared DeWhite was one of the new kid characters created. Jared was voiced by actor Brandon Gilberstadt. Dwayne Oswald, voiced by Kris Kachurak, soon followed as Jared's bumbling sidekick.

Two girl characters (Julie and Heather) were also created. For some reason, the girls never caught on like Jared and Dwayne, who went on to become two of our listeners' favorite characters.

Episode Information

372, 373, 374: **For Whom the Wedding Bells Toll, I, II, & III**
Original Air Dates: 9/6/97, 9/13/97, & 9/20/97
Writer: Paul McCusker
Sound Designers: Todd Busteed, Dave Arnold, & Mark Drury
Scripture: Ephesians 5:17
Theme: Discerning God's will about marriage
Summary: Someone is getting married in Odyssey . . . but who? Is it John Whittaker and Margaret Faye, Eugene Meltsner and Katrina Shanks, or Jack Allen and Joanne Woodston?

375: **The Pushover**
Original Air Date: 9/27/97
Writer: Marshal Younger
Sound Designer: Duane Harms
Scripture: Psalm 139:13-14
Themes: Relationships, self-esteem
Summary: Cody Carper is a pushover, and Jared DeWhite is bossy. Whit comes up with a way to help them work together.

376: **Chores No More**
Original Air Date: 10/4/97
Writer: Marshal Younger
Sound Designer: John Tony
Scripture: Ephesians 6:1-3
Theme: Responsibilities
Summary: The kids in Odyssey think they have too much work to do at home, so they organize the first chores strike.

377: Just Say Yes
Original Air Date: 10/11/97
Writer: Bill Myers
Sound Designer: Todd Busteed
Scripture: Romans 12:10
Themes: Foster parenting, sibling rivalry
Summary: The Mulligan family takes in a teenager with an attitude—a relative named Nick.

378: The Painting
Original Air Date: 10/18/97
Writer: Phil Lollar
Sound Designer: Mark Drury
Scripture: Matthew 18:21-35; 1 Corinthians 13:7
Themes: Forgiveness, reconciliation
Summary: Jack and Joanne Allen open J & J Antiques and are immediately caught up in a mystery involving a millionaire and a long-lost painting.

379: Best Face Forward
Original Air Date: 10/25/97
Writer: Marshal Younger
Sound Designer: Duane Harms
Scripture: 1 Peter 2:11
Theme: Consistency in witness
Summary: When Connie hears that a famous writer named Mark Herring is going to stop by Whit's End, she decides to make sure everyone is on his or her best behavior.

380, 382: The One About Trust, I & II
Original Air Dates: 11/1/97 & 11/8/97
Writer: Phil Lollar
Sound Designer: Todd Busteed
Scripture: Proverbs 3:5
Theme: Trust
Summary: While Connie volunteers to work on Margaret Faye's campaign for mayor of Odyssey, she hears some distressing news about Whit.

382: Viva La Difference
Original Air Date: 11/15/97
Writer: Bill Myers
Sound Designer: Todd Busteed
Scripture: 1 Corinthians 12:12
Theme: Appreciating differences in others
Summary: The Mulligans take in some of the animals when the Connellsville Zoo closes down.

384: Amazing Grace
Original Air Date: 12/6/97
Writer: Doug MacIntosh
Sound Designer: Mark Drury
Scripture: 1 Peter 2:24
Theme: God's mercy
Summary: Whit tells Cody Carper the story of John Newton (1725–1807), a man who experienced God's amazing grace.

From "Best Face Forward"

Actor Alexandra Kenworthy, voice of Mayor Margaret Faye

A New Beginning

After the 1997 hiatus of *Adventures in Odyssey*, several staff changes took place. Chuck Bolte and Paul McCusker left their positions at Focus on the Family; however, Paul continued to work for *Odyssey* on a freelance basis as Marshal Younger had been doing since 1995. Dave Arnold became the producer of the program. Several new freelancers also joined the team of writers, including Doug McIntosh, Bill Myers, and Matt Sommer.

Goof Alert!

In "The One About Trust," Margaret Faye accidentally calls Connie "Katie," a reference to actress Katie Leigh. We didn't fix this slip of the tongue.

Goof Alert!

In part I of "For Whom the Wedding Bells Toll," Bernard Walton says the manager of the Antique Emporium is Mr. Peterson. But when they meet the man in part II, his name is Mr. Gumley.

Behind the Scenes: For Whom the Wedding Bells Toll

During Jack and Joanne's wedding (see album cover art), we find out their middle names. Since Alan Young played Wilbur on *Mister Ed*, his character became Jack Wilbur Allen. Likewise, Janet Waldo, former

Actors Alan Young (Jack Allen) and Janet Waldo (Joanne Woodston)

From left: Actor Kris Kachurak (Dwayne), writer John Beebee, and actor Brandon Gilberstadt (Jared)

voice of daughter Judy on *The Jetsons*, was revealed to be Joanne Judith Woodston.

My Take: Marshal Younger

My original ending for "Chores No More" featured Julie marching in the 24-hour chores strike by herself. She was outside late at night chanting "no more chores" to no one in particular. Finally, her mom came to the door and told her to take the garbage out. After a long pause, Julie abandoned her chore strike, said, "Yes, ma'am," and went inside. The team changed the script to end with the chore strike becoming a "family day." Because I was a freelance writer at the time, I didn't know the ending was changed until I heard the final show, and I mourned the original ending for days. In fact, I'm still in mourning. That didn't happen very often; when the staff edited one of my shows, most of the time the final product was better than the way I had written it.

BTS: Just Say Yes

"Just Say Yes" introduced the Mulligan family to Odyssey. We wanted to have a central family on the show again since the Barclays had left for Pokenberry Falls. Bill Myers, a famed Christian author and creator of the McGee and Me! videos, created the Mulligans. Bill played Mike Mulligan while his daughter Nicole played Lisa Mulligan. Nick Mulligan was played by Chris Castile, and Vaughn Tinder-Taylor played his mother, Traci. If this group of actors sounds familiar, it's because Vaughn also played Chris's mother when they were Zachary and Eileen Sellers. And in "Letting Go" (album 27), Bill played Eileen's boyfriend.

Sound Bites with Corey Burton

I have a special fondness for the episode "The Painting," mostly because of actor Pete Renaday's restrained yet deeply moving portrayal of a conflicted man [G. Winston Smith] who is haunted by a particular incident from his late father's hidden Nazi past. I also really enjoyed the rare opportunity to play an otherwise amusing character, an elderly Polish-American rabbi named Myer Abbott, with surprisingly poignant grace and dignity. I had used a similarly colorful Yiddish accent for a few other roles on previous *Odyssey* programs, but I never would have thought that kind of character voice would work so well dramatically. I was glad to have been a part of what turned out to be such a memorable and rewarding piece of radio drama.

BTS: *Amazing Grace*

"Amazing Grace" was originally imagined as a *Radio Theatre* drama before being transformed into a simpler *Odyssey* version. Nearly 10 years later the story was retold in a longer version for *Radio Theatre*. It was released as a tie-in for the 2007 feature film *Amazing Grace*.

Actor Pete Renaday, voice of G. Winston Smith

Odyssey's Twisted Geography

Cody Carper lives next to Bernard Walton in "Best Face Forward." In "Chain Reaction" (album 33) we learned that Bernard also lives next to the Straussbergs. The Straussbergs also live across the street from the Washingtons ("Something's Got to Change," album 42) and the Rathbones ("Tornado!" album 30). It must be quite a popular street!

Of course, the Rathbones also live around the corner from the Electric Palace, which is within hearing distance of City Hall in "The Living Nativity" (album 16). In "A Case of Revenge" (album 30), the Straussbergs live across the street from McAlister Park, which is where Whit's End is located. But, now, wait a minute. Whit and Eugene walked from the location that is now the Electric Palace to Whit's End in "The Battle" (album 5), and Eugene commented that it was quite a distance for a man of Whit's "social position." However, judging by the previously listed geography it shouldn't be far at all, unless McAlister Park is extremely large. Trying to draw a map of Odyssey boggles the mind!

Map by fan Wendy H., Holland, Michigan

Character:
Bart Rathbone
Quote: "Absolutely free . . . with a $10 purchase."
Something you may not know about Bart: As a child, he had a bad experience in Sunday school.

Album 30

The Story of Reverend James Klinger

Many listeners have written in to ask if the story of James Klinger in "Arizona Sunrise" is a true one. In the episode, a circuit-riding minister sets out to save the life and the soul of an old Apache warrior. Though the characters in this episode were fictional, the story is based on an actual historical event. Apaches did go out into the wilderness when they thought it was their time to die. In 1905, a Lutheran pastor went searching for an Apache chief who had done just that. He found the chief, brought him back to civilization, and nursed him back to health.

Also, many circuit riders roamed the American frontier. Pastors traveled from town to town much like James Klinger did in this adventure. Francis Asbury was one of the most famous riders (1745–1816). Like an army general, he organized a group of brave pastor-riders to travel across the country; they made a difference everywhere they went.

Episode Information

388: Leap of Faith
Original Air Date: 1/10/98
Writer: Bill Myers
Sound Designer: Todd Busteed
Scripture: John 16:23
Theme: Trust
Summary: The Mulligan family and their animals are threatened when heavy rains wash away a levy upriver from their farm.

389: O. T. Action News: Jephthah's Vow
Original Air Date: 1/17/98
Writer: Phil Lollar
Sound Designer: Todd Busteed
Scripture: Judges 11:33-35
Theme: Biblical story of Jephthah
Summary: The O. T. Action News team tells the biblical story of Jephthah and his hasty vow.

390: No Bones About It
Original Air Date: 1/24/98
Writers: Wayne Valero, Marshal Younger, & Phil Lollar
Sound Designer: Todd Busteed
Scripture: Proverbs 28:25
Theme: Greed
Summary: Dwayne Oswald and Julie find old bones in a cave, and they pique the interest of Bart Rathbone, who is convinced they are the bones of Bigfoot.

391: The Joke's on You
Original Air Date: 1/31/98
Writers: Marshal Younger & Phil Lollar
Sound Designer: Duane Harms
Scripture: Romans 12:10, 15
Theme: Encouragement
Summary: Julie tells Dwayne that he's funny, which makes him want to be a stand-up comedian!

392: When in Doubt . . . Pray!
Original Air Date: 2/7/98
Writer: Doug McIntosh
Sound Designer: Todd Busteed
Scripture: Mark 11:24
Themes: Prayer, faith
Summary: Eugene takes Mandy Straussberg on an Imagination Station adventure to show her how prayer has made a difference throughout history.

396: Poor Loser
Original Air Date: 3/21/98
Writer: Marshal Younger
Sound Designer: Todd Busteed
Scripture: Romans 8:28; Philippians 1:6
Theme: Losing gracefully
Summary: Eugene nearly has a nervous breakdown when Bernard Walton keeps beating him at chess. Meanwhile, Heather tries to get the volleyball team to work harder.

397: Tornado!
Original Air Date: 3/28/98
Writer: John Beebee
Sound Designer: Mark Drury
Scripture: Matthew 5:44
Theme: Generosity
Summary: A tornado hits Odyssey, and the Rathbones lose their home. Mandy wants to do something to help, but the rest of the town is more reluctant.

From "Tornado!"

398: **A Case of Revenge**

Original Air Date: 4/5/98
Writer: Phil Lollar
Sound Designer: Todd Busteed
Scripture: Romans 12:19-21
Theme: Revenge
Summary: After Rodney Rathbone wrecks Jared DeWhite's science fair project, Jared accuses him of all sorts of additional misdoings around town.

399: **Bernard and Job**

Original Air Date: 4/11/98
Writer: Phil Lollar
Sound Designer: Todd Busteed
Scripture: Philippians 4:12-13
Themes: Trust in the midst of suffering, the biblical story of Job
Summary: After her dog is involved in a tragic accident, Lisa Mulligan hears the biblical story of Job from Bernard Walton.

400: **The Spy Who Bugged Me**

Original Air Date: 4/18/98
Writer: John Beebee
Sound Designer: Mark Drury
Scripture: 1 Thessalonians 5:21
Themes: Discernment, jumping to conclusions
Summary: Jared and Dwayne try to find out what's going on in Sarah's Super Secret Sisters Club.

401: **More Like Alicia**

Original Air Date: 4/25/98
Writer: Marshal Younger
Sound Designer: Jonathan Crowe
Scripture: 1 John 3:2-3
Themes: Satisfaction with who you are, choosing good influences
Summary: Heather wishes she were more like Alicia, the most popular girl in school. Then she gets the chance to be Alicia for one day.

402: **Arizona Sunrise**

Original Air Date: 5/2/98
Writers: Doug McIntosh & Phil Lollar
Sound Designer: Todd Busteed
Scripture: Matthew 18:21-35; 1 Corinthians 13:7
Themes: Forgiveness, love
Summary: Jack Allen tells Cody Carper the story of a circuit-riding preacher named Klinger, who goes on a quest to share the gospel with a dying Native American.

From "A Case of Revenge"

Behind the Scenes: Leap of Faith

"Leap of Faith" featured a step in Nick Mulligan's spiritual journey when he witnessed faith and trust in action. Nick never became a Christian on the radio show, but he did in a *Clubhouse* magazine article in March 1999.

Clubhouse magazine
March 1999

BTS: No Bones About It

Many scripts for *Adventures in Odyssey* go through multiple drafts, though "No Bones About It" went through even more than most. Three different writers took a stab at the script before it was finished. The original draft was titled "Reel Fake," and included Robyn and Melanie Jacobs, Connie, and Jason Whittaker, none of whom appears in the final show. The end of the show is, of course, a parody of the theme song for *The Beverly Hillbillies*: "Black gold! Texas tea!"

BTS: When in Doubt . . . Pray!

"When in Doubt . . . Pray!" features three true, historical stories about prayer. In the first draft of the episode, each of the three stories followed the same pattern: a problem, a prayer, and an answer to the prayer. We wondered if this might be too predictable. Once you heard the answer to one prayer, you could guess the rest of the episode. To fix this problem, we revealed the first scene of each story before we presented any of the conclusions. This was the first time we'd done this style of storytelling in the Imagination Station, and we used it again in "Something Significant" (album 49).

Goof Alert!

Near the end of "Tornado!" Mandy Straussberg's mother tells her, "I'm sure Mr. Allen would give you your money back." Mr. Allen didn't take money from Mandy; he gave her money in exchange for her doll.

Q & A with John Beebee!

Q: So how old is Mandy in "Tornado"?

JB: I pictured Mandy to be about six years old. But after this show, she ended up fast-forwarding about five years in seven months. She probably drank some of that stuff that Alice had in Wonderland. Then, a few years later in "True Calling" [album 43], Mandy said she was 14. They say kids grow up fast— and we like to grow 'em even faster here in Odyssey. Somehow, Mandy ended up being the opposite of Connie; instead of being stuck at one age, she skipped several years!

Goof Alert!

In "A Case of Revenge," Jared calls his radio-controlled airplane a "P-51 Mustang Spitfire." The North American P-51 Mustang was a completely different plane from the Spitfire.

BTS: *The Spy Who Bugged Me*

This episode was originally titled "The Spy Who Came Down with a Cold," a play on the 1960s movie and book *The Spy Who Came in from the Cold*. The final title is a play on the 1977 James Bond movie *The Spy Who Loved Me*. The show was inspired by John Beebee's son, seven-year-old Chris, who thought it would be cool if you could hook up a walkie-talkie to a remote control car and use it to spy on somebody.

Sound Bites

Listen closely to the voice of the old woman at the end of "The Spy Who Bugged Me." Don't tell anyone, but she's played by Paul Herlinger, aka Whit!

Sound Bites

For "The Joke's on You," Marshal Younger wrote some dialogue for the DJ that was to be heard in the background at the skating rink. Although quite funny, it proved to be distracting, so we cut it from the episode. Here is the dialogue:

```
    Okay, let's have all the girls
on the floor now. It's an all-
girls skate time. Guys, head on
off the floor, you'll get your
turn . . .
    All right, everybody with
brown hair, it's your turn.
Blonds, redheads . . . take
a load off. It's an all brown-
haired people skate.
    Okay, everyone who knows the
definition of the word "punctili-
ous" roll to the floor right now.
There will be a quiz . . .
    Anyone who orders their salad
dressing "on the side," get out
here and skate. The floor's
yours . . .
    Okay, people who have college
degrees and make less than
$18,000 a year, get on out here.
You deserve this . . .
```

Album 31

Days to Remember

The True Story of Saint Patrick

This album introduces Saint Patrick. Though there are plenty of legends about him, not much is truly known about his life. Some say he used a shamrock to explain how God, Jesus, and the Holy Spirit make up the Trinity. Others say he drove snakes out of Ireland. One thing is true: Saint Patrick was an amazing man of God.

Saint Patrick was the one of the first people to speak out against slavery. Few Christian leaders condemned slavery until centuries later. But Saint Patrick spoke against it in the early 400s. Perhaps he did this because he was once a slave.

Jesus told His disciples to go into all the world with the good news. But for more than 400 years, no Christians preached in places like Ireland, in part because of the deep spiritual darkness that existed there. Saint Patrick believed the Irish were people created in God's image, and, despite being made a slave at their hands, he took the gospel back to them and eventually changed the entire nation.

Episode Information

383: B-TV: Thanks
Original Air Date: 11/22/97
Writer: Phil Lollar
Sound Designer: Duane Harms
Scripture: Ephesians 5:20; Luke 17:11-19
Theme: Thanksgiving
Summary: B-TV explores Thanksgiving with stories about 10 lepers, a king named David, and Harlow the stonecutter.

385, 386: It's a Pokenberry Christmas, I and II
Original Air Dates: 12/13/97 & 12/20/97
Writer: Paul McCusker
Sound Designer: Mark Drury
Scripture: James 1:17
Theme: Appreciating life
Summary: Whit and Eugene travel to Pokenberry Falls to help George Barclay, who has lost faith that he should be a pastor. During the visit, Eugene accidentally falls in the river, and George must jump in to save him . . . which leads to a bizarre series of events (see album cover art).

387: New Year's Eve Live!
Original Air Date: 1/3/98
Writer: Phil Lollar
Sound Designers: Mark Drury & Dave Arnold
Theme: God's providence
Summary: The gang from Whit's End hosts a wacky New Year's eve celebration—in front of a live audience!

393: Wrapped Around Your Finger
Original Air Date: 2/14/98
Writer: Paul McCusker
Sound Designer: Duane Harms
Scripture: John 15:13
Theme: Commitment
Summary: Jack and Joanne Allen throw Eugene Meltsner and Katrina Shanks a Valentine's Day engagement party. Eugene wants to give Katrina a ring, but Katrina's father gives her a family heirloom ring the same day.

The Whit's End team rings in the New Year.

Sound designer Dave Arnold, writer/director Phil Lollar, and actor Walker Edmiston (Tom and Bart) perform.

394, 395: Saint Patrick: A Heart Afire, I and II
Original Air Dates: 3/7/98 & 3/14/98
Writers: Matt Sommer & Paul McCusker
Sound Designer: Jonathan Crowe
Theme: Hero of the faith
Summary: Whit tells Jared DeWhite the story of Patrick, a slave boy who changed the history of an entire nation through his dedication to Jesus.

403: Faster Than a Speeding Ticket
Original Air Date: 5/9/98
Writer: John Beebee
Sound Designer: Jonathan Crowe
Scripture: 2 Timothy 1:7
Theme: Standing up for yourself
Summary: Whit gets a speeding ticket, and Dwayne Oswald gets a D on a history test. Both believe they were the victims of mistakes.

404: Hide and Seek
Original Air Date: 5/16/98
Writer: Paul McCusker
Sound Designer: Duane Harms
Scripture: Revelation 3:20
Theme: God's search for man
Summary: Kevin gets into the Imagination Station and sees examples of God's search for man.

405: The Graduate
Original Air Date: 5/23/98
Writer: Phil Lollar
Sound Designer: Todd Busteed
Scripture: Mark 11:24
Themes: Prayer, belief
Summary: Connie is finally graduating from high school but faces a dilemma when the principal doesn't want her to pray in Jesus' name at the graduation ceremony.

409: Natural Born Leader
Original Air Date: 10/3/98
Writer: Marshal Younger
Sound Designer: Todd Busteed
Scripture: 1 Samuel 16:7
Theme: Misjudging others
Summary: Jared DeWhite unknowingly selects a mentally challenged student for student council candidacy.

412: A Lesson from Mike
Original Air Date: 10/24/98
Writer: Marshal Younger
Sound Designer: Todd Busteed
Scripture: 1 John 4:7-12
Theme: Loving the lonely
Summary: Julie is surprised by her feelings when a student she barely knows dies a tragic death.

From left: Actors Landon Arnold (Cody), Amber Arnold (Brooke), Walker Edmiston (Tom and Bart), Dave Madden (Bernard)

B-TV!

B-TV episodes have occurrred all over *Odyssey*. Here's a complete list.

Episode:	Location
I Want My B-TV!	Whit's End
B-TV: Envy	Studio
B-TV: Compassion	Factory
B-TV: Thanks	Thanksgiving parade
B-TV: Forgiveness	Odyssey city dump
B-TV: Redeeming the Season	Odyssey mall
B-TV: Grace	Odyssey street
B-TV: Obedience	Foufou's Obedience School
B-TV: Behind the Scenes	Studio
B-TV: Temptation	Studio

Sound Bites with Duane Harms

I developed a love/hate relationship with "B-TV: Thanks." I've always liked the B-TV shows, and it was fun to be able to actually produce one (later I did another, "B-TV: Forgiveness"). Usually we try to make the *Odyssey* shows sound very realistic, but with B-TV, I loved the freedom to be able to use some very unusual effects that were more on the cartoon side of things. The reason I ended up hating the show was that it took so long to produce because all of the unusual stuff in it. By the time I finished the show, I was totally sick of it and never wanted to hear it again! (Okay, okay, I've since repented of my ways!)

Sound Bites with Mark Drury

To make the sound of George Barclay running down Main Street, I brought real snow in the studio and just ran in place and slid around and tried to copy the actions of what I remembered George Bailey doing in *It's a Wonderful Life.*

My Take: Chuck Bolte

Perhaps my all-time favorite Barclay family show is "It's a Pokenberry Christmas." Paul McCusker had done an exceptional job in the script of patterning certain scenes and characters after specific scenes and characters from the movie *It's a Wonderful Life*. That, in turn, required me to fashion my verbal inflections and tones to reflect those of Jimmy Stewart

Actor Chuck Bolte

Focus on the Family magazine, October 1997, recognizes *Odyssey's* 10th anniversary

(1908–1997). The result, I believe, was one of the most entertaining shows in the entire *Adventures in Odyssey* series.

Behind the Scenes: It's a Pokenberry Christmas

Three-year-old Craig Miller, son of Focus on the Family Vice President Clark Miller, played Stewart Barclay in this episode. Though he couldn't read yet, he repeated lines such as "I want to build a snowman."

Clubhouse magazine, June 1997, announces the first decade of *Odyssey*

Sound Bites with Jonathan Crowe

Sometimes the smallest sounds are the hardest to get. The sound of the king dropping the goblet in "Saint Patrick: A Heart Afire" gave me fits. A real cup or glass just didn't sound right. I eventually got a piece of metal and dropped it on a wooden doorsill to get the right sound. I added the liquid spill after.

BTS: Faster Than a Speeding Ticket

Officer Cliffe in "Faster Than a Speeding Ticket" was modeled after a goofy policeman from *The Andy Griffith Show*. In fact, the character was originally named "Officer Knotts" in honor of Don Knotts who played Barney Fife on that show.

Sound Bites with Duane Harms

Some of the most challenging effects I ever produced were in the baptism of Jesus scene in "Hide and Seek." Water effects are notoriously difficult to do in the studio, so I had to go to a small river behind my house, set up microphones, wade into the water, and actually "baptize" a large rock in order to get the effect I needed! The biggest problem was that a small airplane kept flying overhead, and I had to keep waiting for it to leave. I don't think there were airplanes in Jesus' day!

Clubhouse magazine, May 1998, features Connie's graduation

Clubhouse magazine, October 1997, celebrates *Odyssey's* 10th anniversary

BTS: The Graduate

Amazingly, after being in high school for more than 10 years on the series, Connie graduated as valedictorian.

BTS: The Graduate

This episode generated letters from some listeners who were upset that Connie didn't say her own prayer at her graduation. They insisted that Connie did, in fact, have the legal right to pray and wanted the episode changed. Our point in the episode was that Connie didn't want to treat prayer like a political football. However, we decided to update Chris's message at the end to point out that Connie had the right to pray.

BTS: Natural Born Leader

"Natural Born Leader" was inspired by the movie *Being There* (1979) with Peter Sellers, which is about a simple man who everyone believes is brilliant.

My Take: Marshal Younger

The original name of "A Lesson from Mike" was "The Significance of the Insignificant." There's a quilt downstairs in the Focus on the Family Welcome Center that is made up of *Odyssey* fan letters. One is from a girl who was inspired by "A Lesson from Mike." She walked up to a friendless girl and introduced herself— forming what became a lasting friendship. It is a very sweet letter. Whenever I need to remember my purpose in doing *Adventures in Odyssey*, I walk down there and read it.

Live! At New Year's Eve Live!

"New Year's Eve Live!" was recorded in November 1997 at Focus on the Family headquarters in Colorado Springs to celebrate *Odyssey*'s 10th anniversary. There were two performances, one for a Focus on the Family chapel that served as a rehearsal

An *Odyssey* quilt in the Focus on the Family Welcome Center.

and a second showing that was recorded for the episode. After the chapel performance, Phil Lollar and Dave Arnold rewrote much of the script late into the night based on which jokes got laughs from the audience and which ones fell flat.

The recorded event wasn't announced or advertised, but more than two thousand people heard about it through word of mouth and showed up. The crowd, packed so tight there was standing room only, really got into the performance and participated in making some of the sound effects. Paul Herlinger had a last-minute change of plans and couldn't be there for the recording, so he greeted the audience by phone.

After the recording, the actors signed autographs and greeted the crowd. However, the postrecording portion of the show hadn't been fully thought out. Some of the actors ducked for cover when more than two thousand fans raced forward to get autographs.

Actor Katie Leigh signs autographs.

Writer Phil Lollar signs a copy of *The Complete Guide to Adventures in Odyssey*

Fans gather to meet the actors.

The actors sign autographs for fans.

Album 32

Hidden Treasures

A Message of Change

In many ways, "Malachi's Message" was the end of an era. Executive producer Dave Arnold and writer Paul McCusker were moving on to other endeavors and intended to use "Malachi" to hand off the show to the new team. That team included Al Janssen, who took over as executive producer, and Phil Lollar, who eventually stepped into the role of producer.

The writing of "Malachi's Message" contained another allusion to one of our favorite authors, C. S. Lewis. In several of his books, Lewis said that there were three possibilities for Christ. He was a horrible liar, a raving lunatic, or the Lord of all. Lewis used this argument to illustrate that you couldn't simply pass off Jesus as a "great teacher." He had to be more than that. Whit uses the same argument for Malachi's being an angel.

Paul McCusker remembers, "After I finished the first draft of the script, I sent it to my good friend Philip Glassborow, the casting director for *Focus on the Family Radio Theatre*. He called me and stated, 'I've never said anything like this before, but I *must* play Malachi in this episode.' I didn't want to argue with him, so Philip played Malachi."

At the end of the episode, Whit got a sudden burst of inspiration. Paul and Dave hoped the transition to a new team would be a burst of inspiration for *Odyssey*. For Whit, it meant that he would create a new invention at Whit's End. This invention, the Transmuter, was introduced in "Another Man's Shoes" (album 33).

Episode Information

406, 407, 408: Malachi's Message, I, II, and III
Original Air Dates: 9/12/98, 9/19/98, & 9/26/98
Writer: Paul McCusker
Sound Designers: Jonathan Crowe & Duane Harms
Scripture: 1 Thessalonians 5:21
Themes: Discernment, faith
Summary: A stranger comes to Odyssey and claims to be an angel with special messages for the folks at Whit's End. After following the man's instructions, Tom finds a necklace from his son who passed away (see cover art).

410: B-TV: Forgiveness
Original Air Date: 10/10/98
Writers: Torry Martin & Phil Lollar
Sound Designer: Duane Harms
Scripture: Matthew 18:21-35; 1 Corinthians 13:7
Theme: Forgiveness
Summary: With help from the Three Little Pigs, Goldilocks, and the Big Bad Wolf, the B-TV gang teaches about forgiveness.

411: In All Things Give Thanks
Original Air Date: 10/17/98
Writer: Bill Myers
Sound Designer: Todd Busteed
Scripture: Philippians 4:12-13
Theme: Thankfulness in suffering
Summary: Hector, the newest member of the Mulligan clan, wonders what it means to be thankful when he's lived a hard life.

413: The Devil Made Me Do It
Original Air Date: 10/31/98
Writers: Marshal Younger & Phil Lollar
Sound Designer: Jonathan Crowe
Scripture: 1 Corinthians 10:13
Theme: Overcoming temptation
Summary: Kids' Radio presents "Guilt Trip Jeopardy," "20/200," and the "Slimy Awards" to expose the lies of Satan and show believers how to have victory over temptation.

414: Buried Sin
Original Air Date: 11/07/98
Writer: John Beebee
Sound Designer: Jonathan Crowe
Scripture: Matthew 18:21-35; 1 Corinthians 13:5
Theme: Forgiveness
Summary: Jared DeWhite, Dwayne Oswald, and Eugene dig up a mystery when they uncover a long-lost box, which contains the story of a forgotten crime.

415: Gloobers
Original Air Date: 11/14/98
Writer: John Beebee
Sound Designer: Todd Busteed
Scripture: Ecclesiastes 3:2-8, 11
Themes: Video game addiction, using time wisely
Summary: Jared and Dwayne take their favorite computer game, Gloobers, to the next level when they get a chance to play the game "for real" in the Room of Consequence.

416: The Tower
Original Air Date: 11/21/98
Writer: Doug McIntosh
Sound Designer: Duane Harms
Scripture: Genesis 11:1-9
Theme: Evilness of humankind
Summary: Nathaniel Graham takes a trip in the Imagination Station with Eugene to see the Tower of Babel.

417: **Not-So-Trivial Pursuits**

Original Air Date: 11/28/98
Writer: Phil Lollar
Sound Designer: Jonathan Crowe
Scripture: Romans 6:23
Theme: Fairness
Summary: Dwayne Oswald faces a tough opponent on a local quiz show. He also faces a tough decision: What should he do when he's given the answers to the quiz-show questions ahead of time?

420, 421: **Telemachus, I and II**

Original Air Date: 4/17/99 & 4/24/99
Writer: Jim Ware
Sound Designer: Jonathan Crowe
Scripture: John 15:13
Theme: Sacrificing for what's right
Summary: Whit tells a story of a young monk on a journey to find out what it means to be Christlike. But when his travels land him in a gladiator arena, his learning turns to action.

Philip Glassborow, voice of Malachi and writer for *Radio Theatre*

Jason Whittaker fishing in "Malachi's Message"

Goof Alert!

At the beginning of "Malachi's Message," Eugene says that he began college when he was 14. However, in both "Eugene's Dilemma" (album 5) and "The Graduate" (album 31), he said he was 13.

My Take: Marshal Younger

In "The Devil Made Me Do It," I was trying to recreate the success of "Hidden in My Heart" (album 26) with three wacky parodies in the same Kids' Radio show. After I heard the episode, I thought I had failed miserably and that the show was a disaster. However, listeners disagreed and voted the show one of the 12 funniest *Odyssey* episodes of all time. After reconsidering, I would put it in the top 200, maybe.

Behind the Scenes: In All Things Give Thanks

This episode introduced Hector, a boy from Bogotá, Colombia, who is adopted by the Mulligan family. This was also the last episode in which we saw the Mulligans as an entire family. Lisa, Nick, and Mike were heard in future episodes, but we never returned to the Mulligan home.

My Take: John Beebee

I'm fascinated by history and I thought it'd be fascinating to unearth a time capsule in "Buried Sin"—except a very different kind of time capsule that contains a murder confession. By the way, people ask all the time if this is the same Dr. Newcastle who appeared in "The Mysterious Stranger" [album 18]. Yes, it is—and yes, that was on purpose.

BTS: Gloobers

At the recording session, Phil Lollar asked John Beebee to direct the Gloobers since John had created an entire language for them. For example, a Gloober attack was "WA-WA WOOGIE!"

Actors Steve Bridges, Pete Renaday, and Will Ryan voicing the Gloobers

Goof Alert!

Apparently Dwayne and Brian need to check the accuracy of their trivia. In "Not So Trivial Pursuits," both of them agree that Robert E. Lee led the raid on Harper's Ferry. However, the raid was actually led by John Brown. Furthermore, Brian says that Robert E. Lee was the great-grandson of Martha

Washington. However, it was Robert E. Lee's *wife* who was her great-granddaughter, and Lee was not a descendant at all.

The True Story of Telemachus

"Telemachus" was based on a true story from *Foxe's Book of Martyrs*. However, not much is known about Telemachus's life. We don't know for sure why he set out on his journey to Rome. Some have guessed that he felt God telling him that he was needed there, while others believe he was trying to figure out the true meaning of living a quiet life. Even the truth about his experience at the Colosseum is filled with uncertainty. Some believe the gladiators killed him; others think the crowd stoned him for getting in the way of their horrible spectacle.

Whatever questions exist, however, we do know that his death in Rome softened the emperor's heart, and afterward, he banned all gladiator contests. It's a powerful example of how one person standing up for what's right can make a big difference, not only in individual lives, but in the life of an entire nation.

Introducing Liz Horton!

"Not-So-Trivial Pursuits" introduced the character of Liz Horton, played by Lauren Schaffel. At first, Liz seemed to be a first-class brat in shows like "You Win Some, You Lose Some" and "Blind Girl's Bluff" (album 33). However, she gradually warmed up, turned likable, and even became Mandy Straussberg's best friend.

The Case of the Missing Master Tapes

by Jonathan Crowe

Attending my first *Adventures in Odyssey* recording session in Burbank, California, was a dream come true. As a new addition to the *Odyssey* team, I wanted to put my best foot forward. At the time, our process was to make two copies of the digital recordings and have different people carry them back to Colorado as a safety measure in case one set got lost.

After this session, however, I somehow ended up with both copies.

The next morning I searched the hotel parking lot for the rental car, found it, and used the key to open the trunk. I put in my luggage.

Later, I returned to the parking spot to find—much to my amazement and horror—that the rental car was gone, along with my luggage and the only copies of the master tapes for the session. I rushed inside to

Actor Lauren Schaffel, voice of Liz Horton

notify hotel security and check with the parking lot attendants. No one remembered any car matching the description I gave leaving the parking lot.

I wondered if I was simply looking in the wrong row. I walked up and down searching for the missing car. Suddenly, I noticed a vehicle parked about ten spots over from where the missing car had been. Almost afraid to look, I found that the license plate matched the number on my key chain. Then I realized the painful truth—my key could open the trunks of two cars! I now stood next to our rental car, but the trunk was empty. The *Odyssey* master tapes had departed in someone else's car.

Dave Arnold, Mark Drury, and I frantically checked with hotel security to see if the luggage had been turned in.

Nothing.

I couldn't wallow in my agony for long because I realized that my flight was departing soon! I made it to the airport with only minutes to spare—and then discovered that I had another problem . . . I had no ticket. It was neatly packed away in my missing luggage. I told the ticket agent the condensed version of my story, but she was not amused and said I would have to purchase another ticket at full fare. I pled with the agent to be creative and check with her manager to see if something could be done. I must have looked like I was about to cry, because she eventually came back and told me to get on the plane, no extra charges required! I barely made it to my seat before the plane took off.

At last I could appreciate the depth of my misery for losing the tapes. That is, until I realized I had yet another problem. In my mad airport rush, I had forgotten that Focus had rented the car from Avis; I had dropped it off at Thrifty!

When I landed in Denver, I called my wife and told her what had happened. She contacted the rental car companies, but they had already realized my mistake and returned the car to its proper place. At least that part ended well.

But the master tapes were still missing. Several times during the weekend I called the Burbank hotel to see if my luggage had been returned. It had not. I began calculating in my mind the cost of paying all the actors, the studio, and the director to record those shows again. Would declaring personal bankruptcy be an option?

On Monday morning, Focus travel representatives started calling rental car companies around the Burbank area. One agent mentioned in passing that there had been something sitting in the back room all weekend. The agent checked—and my missing luggage with the tapes had been found!

All the shows involved in this ordeal were produced as planned and aired on time. So, if you ever hear a three-part *Odyssey* series called "Malachi's Message," you'll know that there's a unique behind-the-scenes story that's almost as interesting as the show itself and that an angel truly was watching out for me!

Boy Imprisoned by Video Game!

by John Beebee

My son Robert—who was addicted to the Chip's Challenge game at the time—woke up one morning from a terrible dream. In his dream, he was actually inside the game—and he couldn't get out! He went from level to level trying to escape but couldn't! Needless to say, he spent less time playing video games after that. And needless to say, I got a great idea for the "Gloobers" show!

The Master Brain represents the gaming industry. While the game makers may not be inherently evil, the entire industry feeds off of kids' time—an enormous amount of time! (I'm not against video games; I just think kids and parents need to work together to make reasonable limits on the time spent playing them.)

Interestingly enough, Robert's dream was adapted into this show, which was adapted into an *Odyssey* video (*Escape from the Forbidden Matrix*), which was made into a book, and, ironically enough, a video game (*The Great Escape*). So, really all that needs to happen is for Robert to play *that* game and have another dream . . . and the cycle will start all over again!

Escape from the Forbidden Matrix, a video

The Great Escape, a video game

Character:
Aubrey Shepard
Quote: "The most important thing is the people in my life. Now, if you'll excuse me, I have to go pound my toad of a little sister." Something you may not know about Aubrey: She had to turn down the lead role in a play because her parents didn't like the content.

Album 33

Virtual Realities

Opening Day for the Shepards

"Opening Day" was the first episode to describe the new Timothy Center, including the chapel, dormitories, cabins, and stable. The Timothy Center, introduced in "Malachi's Message" (album 32), was an idea that we thought would lead to new and different stories for characters Tom Riley and Connie. Unfortunately, we never got to use it as much as we hoped. The episode also introduced the Shepard family—Ben, Ellen, Aubrey, and Bethany. Writer Jim Ware mapped out detailed back stories for all four characters, plus two older Shepard children. Very little of this back story has ever been told.

Fans often ask if Aubrey's middle name, Andromeda, is connected with the company that owns Novacom, Andromeda Enterprises. The answer is that we hadn't even brainstormed the Novacom saga when "Opening Day" was written. We forgot that Andromeda was Aubrey's middle name until someone pointed it out later. So Aubrey's middle name is certainly unusual but unrelated to Novacom.

Episode Information

418: Opening Day
Original Air Date: 3/6/99
Writer: Jim Ware
Sound Designer: Todd Busteed
Scripture: Ephesians 5:17
Theme: God's leading
Summary: The grand opening of the Timothy Center retreat facilities is full of unexpected surprises, especially when the Shepard family arrives and daughter Aubrey immediately runs away.

419: Another Man's Shoes
Original Air Date: 3/27/99
Writer: Phil Lollar
Sound Designer: Todd Busteed
Scripture: Luke 10:30-37
Theme: Understanding others
Summary: Whit's new invention, the Transmuter, allows Jared DeWhite to walk in the shoes of a school bully for a day.

424, 425: Blackgaard's Revenge, I and II
Original Air Dates: 10/2/99 & 10/9/99
Writer: Phil Lollar
Sound Designer: Todd Busteed
Scripture: Proverbs 4:5-9
Theme: Recognizing deception
Summary: A virus implanted in the Imagination Station with Dr. Blackgaard's personality surfaces and must be destroyed before it takes hold over Aubrey (see album cover art).
PARENTAL WARNING:
This show is about the struggle for a young girl's soul. Although presented in an entertaining and fantastic way, it may be too intense for younger listeners.

426: The Buck Starts Here
Original Air Date: 10/16/99
Writer: Marshal Younger
Sound Designer: Jonathan Crowe
Scripture: Matthew 25:14-30
Theme: Using our resources wisely
Summary: Whit gives Jared DeWhite, Ashley, and Nathaniel Graham money to spend wisely, and they all use it in different ways.

427: Something Cliqued Between Us
Original Air Date: 10/23/99
Writer: Marshal Younger
Sound Designer: Rob Jorgensen
Scripture: 1 John 4:7-12
Theme: Including others
Summary: Liz Horton and Julie are furious when they feel excluded by a clique of girls they call the "Calvin Clones."

428a: The Eternal Birthday
Original Air Date: 10/30/99
Writer: Kathy Wierenga
Sound Designer: Rob Jorgensen
Scripture: Job 36:10-11
Theme: Too much of a good thing
Summary: Liz experiences her birthday over and over again.

428b: Bethany's Imaginary Friend
Original Air Date: 10/30/99
Writer: Lissa Halls Johnson
Sound Designer: Rob Jorgensen
Scripture: Matthew 6:28-29
Theme: Healthy imaginations
Summary: Aubrey Shepard is upset at her sister's overactive imagination.

429: The Y.A.K. Problem
Original Air Date: 11/6/99
Writer: Marshal Younger
Sound Designer: Todd Busteed
Scripture: Matthew 6:25-34
Theme: Don't worry about the unknown
Summary: The Odyssey kids believe a new city council member is planning the Year of Anti-Kids.

430: Blind Girl's Bluff
Original Air Date: 11/13/99
Writers: Lissa Halls Johnson & Marshal Younger
Sound Designer: Duane Harms
Scripture: Proverbs 12:22
Theme: Honesty
Summary: Aubrey Shepard and Lisa Mulligan cook up a scam using a two-way radio to make people believe that Lisa can see—with her mind.

431a: Where There's Smoke
Original Air Date: 11/20/99
Writer: Jim Ware
Sound Designer: Rob Jorgensen
Scripture: Matthew 5:21
Theme: Being a positive role model
Summary: Nathaniel looks up to his new friend Nick Mulligan, and even starts to imitate his less-than-healthy smoking habits.

431b: The Virtual Kid
Original Air Date: 11/20/99
Writer: Anonymous
Sound Designer: Rob Jorgensen
Scripture: Proverbs 14:12
Theme: Caution against computer obsession
Summary: Middle-schooler Alex Jefferson creates a Web site about Whit's End and gets interviewed for the news.

432: You Win Some, You Lose Some
Original Air Date: 11/27/99
Writer: Marshal Younger
Sound Designer: Duane Harms
Scripture: Romans 8:28; Philippians 1:6
Theme: God uses you in ways you don't expect
Summary: Two mean-spirited girls make life miserable for Wendy Zannuck and cause a discouraged Connie to quit her job at the Timothy Center.

433a: The Treasure Room
Original Air Date: 12/4/99
Writer: Kathy Wierenga
Sound Designer: Duane Harms
Scripture: Ephesians 4:32
Theme: Valuing people in your life
Summary: Aubrey and Lisa are determined to find out what Whit keeps in a new secret room at Whit's End—the Treasure Room.

433b: Chain Reaction
Original Air Date: 12/4/99
Writer: Marshal Younger
Sound Designer: Duane Harms
Scripture: Matthew 25:23
Theme: Consequences
Summary: David Straussberg puts off mowing Bernard Walton's lawn, but the consequences of his action are greater than he ever imagined.

Clubhouse magazine, October 1998

Sound designer Jonathan Crowe smashing a watermelon

Sound Bites with Jonathan Crowe

To get the sounds of the mud-ball war in "The Buck Starts Here," I bought a bunch of vegetables, set up a microphone in my back patio, and then dropped the vegetables from various heights. I threw tomatoes into a garbage can to simulate the sound of mud hitting cars. The best sound of all was the watermelon, which made a great big splat sound, perfect for a kid falling off his bike into the dirt.

Behind the Scenes: The Buck Starts Here

The original title, "The Parable of the Entrepreneur, the Sock Shooter, and the Ditch-Digger," had to be changed because the long name wouldn't fit on the cassette-tape labels.

BTS: Something Cliqued Between Us

The character of Cassidy (played by Danielle Judovits) in "Something Cliqued Between Us" was named after Mark Drury's daughter. The team liked

Roy in the midst of the mud-ball war in "The Buck Starts Here"

Danielle's performance as Cassidy so much that they gave her the major role of Aubrey Shepard. She replaced another actor who played Aubrey in "Opening Day" and "Blackgaard's Revenge."

BTS: *Virtual Kid*

This episode marked the first appearance of Alex Jefferson. Alex was loosely modeled after an *Odyssey* fan whose Internet alias was Jeff4Jesus.

My Take: Marshal Younger

Virtual Realities was the first album to feature split episodes. These shows had two short miniepisodes in one. Many of them also had a two-minute skit between the short stories. We tried this idea as an experiment, partially to train new writers—the shorter form was easier to write—and partially to appeal to a younger audience. Though we ultimately decided that the splits didn't work well, I'm glad that we tried something new.

BTS: *The Y.A.K. Problem*

"The Y.A.K. Problem" was originally written for Jared DeWhite, who had become one of the most popular characters on *Adventures in Odyssey*. Unfortunately, Brandon Gilberstadt (who played Jared) began working on the television series *100 Deeds for Eddie McDowd*

(1999–2002) and wasn't available to record for a while. He had to be written out of the show, but there is still a mention of him remaining in this episode. After the *Eddie McDowd* show ended, Jared returned to Odyssey, and his sudden disappearance in "The Y.A.K. Problem" was revealed to be his initiation into the Witness Protection Program. See "Strange Boy in a Strange Land" (album 37).

My Take: Marshal Younger

"The Y. A. K. Problem" was written in response to the "year two thousand" or "Y2K" problem and the associated panic that was climaxing around the turn of the century. Instead of being worried about an impending computer crisis, the kids were worried that they wouldn't be able to have fun, so they stockpiled ice cream and toys. I wrote the first draft more quickly than any other I'd ever written—in a day and a half!

The writing team in 1999. *From left*: Phil Lollar, Lissa Halls Johnson, Al Janssen, Kathy Wierenga, Jim Ware, John Beebee, Charlie Richards, and Marshal Younger

BTS: *Bethany's Imaginary Friend*

"Bethany's Imaginary Friend" and "Blind Girl's Bluff" were written by noted Christian author Lissa Halls Johnson. Lissa wrote or cowrote the China Tate Series (1994–1997), the Brio Girls series (2001–2005), and the best-selling teen book *Just Like Ice Cream* (1982).

Sound Bites

When Nick Mulligan is going down the hallway at the hospital in "Where There's Smoke," the loudspeaker calls "Paging Dr. Jorgensen to the mental ward." The name Dr. Jorgensen is a reference to the sound designer of this episode. Later episodes featured an entire hospital of sound designers: Dr. Crowe, Dr. Montjoy, and Dr. Diehl.

Sound Bites with Rob Jorgensen

The irate parent on the phone in "The Virtual Kid" is my friend Stan Pracht. I called him at his office and said, "When I say 'go,' start yelling into the phone." I recorded his ranting and included him in the show. I wonder what his coworkers thought when they heard him yelling?

Goof Alert!

In "Blind Girl's Bluff," Aubrey Shepard asks, "Who's Jared?" This line implies that he moved away before Aubrey could meet him. However, in "The Treasure Room," she says that she got a lock-picking kit from Jared "before he left," which means that she did, in fact, know Jared.

BTS: *Chain Reaction*

In "Chain Reaction," sound designer Mark Drury and producer Dave Arnold play the parts of the two property owners. When a deal falls through, they decide to sell the land to the law firm of Crowe, Jorg, and Beeboff, a name Mark and Dave came up with to represent fellow sound designers Jonathan Crowe, Rob Jorgenson, and writer John Beebee. Also, although Mark and Dave have appeared in roles in other shows, this was the first and only time they performed in the same scene.

Sound designer Mark Drury and producer Dave Arnold having fun

Sound Bites with Duane Harms

I needed the sound effect of a bicycle crashing into the bumper of a car in "Chain Reaction." I set up microphones in my driveway, took a rusty old bike we owned, and then crashed it over and over into the back of an old car. I got the proper sound I needed—all with my neighbors watching and laughing from a distance. I had some explaining to do afterward—to them and my wife!

Sound Bites

Listen for a parody of the television game show *Wheel of Fortune* (1983–present) in the background of "Chain Reaction." The contestants suggest a few answers to solve the puzzle, including "Don't look a gift horse in the house" and "Don't look a gift house in the house."

Revenge of Blackgaard!

"Blackgaard's Revenge" answered a question that listeners often asked—Was Dr. Regis Blackgaard really dead? The answer: Yes, but he could still come back in a nefarious way through a computer virus in the Imagination Station.

While flashing back on history, Aubrey Shepard sees excerpts of several *Adventures in Odyssey* episodes, including "The Day Independence Came" (album 2), "Columbus: The Grand Voyage" (album 16), and "The Imagination Station" (album 5).

During the recording session, a scene where Regis tortured a sleeping Aubrey with electrical jolts was judged to be too scary for *Odyssey*. We cut the scene and replaced it with one where Blackgaard merely threatened to hurt Aubrey.

The episode is not without a goof, however. In "Blackgaard's Revenge," Aubrey and Blackgaard see Julius Caesar in the Colosseum. However, Caesar died in 44 B.C., more than 100 years before the Colosseum was built. Also, while visiting ancient Greece, the pair see Socrates, Plato, and Aristotle in the same room. Aristotle was born years after Socrates died. Of course, since this history was being presented by Dr. Blackgaard, anything can happen.

Original art for *Virtual Realities*. Regis Blackgaard looks down over Whit, Eugene, and Aubrey Shepard.

Character: Liz Horton
Birthplace: Odyssey
Something you may not know about Liz:
She once jumped in a Dumpster while investi-
gating a news story.

Album 34

In Your Wildest Dreams

Life in a Fishbowl

The first draft of "Sunset Bowlawater" was a mystery about how Mandy Straussberg's fish died. The script seemed to need a creative angle, and the team was brainstorming how to fix the show. As a joke, Kathy Wierenga said, "Maybe the fish could narrate it." Producer Phil Lollar immediately said, "Yes! That's exactly it!" Phil suggested that writer John Beebee use the classic film *Sunset Boulevard* (1950) as inspiration. In that movie, a dead man tells the story that led up to his murder.

In production, to create the impression that Crackers the goldfish was speaking under water, Rob Jorgensen added a sound effect of bubbles breaking the water's surface under each syllable of Cracker's dialogue.

Episode Information

422, 423: Passages, I and II
Original Air Dates: 9/18/99 & 9/25/99
Writer: Paul McCusker
Sound Designer: Rob Jorgensen
Scripture: Proverbs 3:5-6
Theme: Trusting God
Summary: A woman named Alice tells an incredible story about how she and Tom Riley's son, Timmy, traveled to another world called Marus.

437a: Sunset Bowlawater
Original Air Date: 3/4/00
Writer: John Beebee
Sound Designer: Rob Jorgensen
Scripture: Luke 16:10-11
Theme: Responsibility
Summary: Mandy Straussberg's goldfish narrates the story of his untimely death.

437b: The Long Way Home
Original Air Date: 3/4/00
Writer: Jim Ware
Sound Designer: Rob Jorgensen
Scripture: Matthew 6:19-20
Theme: Appreciating what you have
Summary: Aubrey Shepard is desperate to get away from the Timothy Center and attempts to earn money to go on a youth group outing.

438a: The Lyin' Tale
Original Air Date: 3/11/00
Writer: Charlie Richards
Sound Designer: Rob Jorgensen
Scripture: Proverbs 16:18
Theme: Lying
Summary: Aubrey's tale of being scared by a cat seems to become more life-threatening with every telling.

442a: Two Roads
Original Air Date: 4/15/00
Writer: Jim Ware
Sound Designer: Rob Jorgensen
Scripture: Proverbs 4:5-9
Theme: Eternity
Summary: Kids' Radio tells the story of two kids who take very different paths in life and yet meet in the same place.

440: I Slap Floor
Original Air Date: 4/1/00
Writer: Marshal Younger
Sound Designer: Rob Jorgensen
Scripture: Proverbs 15:21
Theme: Don't believe everything you hear.
Summary: Bernard Walton tells Mandy Straussberg and her brother, David, about an extremely strange week in Odyssey.

441a: What Do You Think?
Original Air Date: 4/8/00
Writer: John Beebee
Sound Designer: Duane Harms
Scripture: Ephesians 2:10
Theme: Other people's opinions
Summary: The Room of Consequence allows Liz Horton to hear what other people are thinking.

441b: Idol Minds
Original Air Date: 4/8/00
Writer: Charlie Richards
Sound Designer: Duane Harms
Scripture: Exodus 20:3
Theme: The danger of idols
Summary: When Whit leaves town for a while, Eugene creates a Whit robot to keep the kids happy.

443: Changing Rodney
Original Air Date: 4/22/00
Writer: Kathy Wierenga
Sound Designer: Jonathan Crowe
Scripture: Ephesians 4:32
Theme: Trying to change people
Summary: Mandy goes on a mission to turn Rodney Rathbone into a "good" guy, but it's more difficult than she thinks.

444b: The Bad Guy
Original Air Date: 4/29/00
Writer: Marshal Younger
Sound Designer: Rob Jorgensen
Theme: Leading others into sin
Summary: A "tough" friend of Nick Mulligan's arrives in Odyssey. Things turn unfriendly when Nick finds out that his friend has become a Christian.

444c: Bethany's Flood
Original Air Date: none
Writer: Jim Ware
Sound Designer: Jonathan Crowe
Scripture: Genesis 6-8
Theme: Imagination
Summary: Bethany Shepard dreams about a wacky version of Noah and the flood.

445: No Boundaries
Original Air Date: 5/6/00
Writer: John Beebee
Sound Designer: Jonathan Crowe
Scripture: Proverbs 13:1
Theme: The importance of rules
Summary: Through the Room of Consequence, Alex Jefferson experiences what life would be like if he could do whatever he wanted—without any rules.

446a: A Matter of Manners
Original Air Date: 5/13/00
Writer: John Beebee
Sound Designer: Rob Jorgensen
Scripture: James 5:19
Theme: Speaking the truth in love
Summary: David and Alex are banished from Whit's End for their rude behavior.

446b: The Seven Deadly Dwarves
Original Air Date: 5/13/00
Writer: Jim Ware
Sound Designer: Rob Jorgensen
Theme: The seven deadly sins
Summary: Bethany dreams that she's Snow DeWhite and meets up with the Seven Deadly Dwarves.

447: Potlucks and Poetry
Original Air Date: 5/20/00
Writer: Kathy Wierenga
Sound Designer: Jonathan Crowe
Scripture: Exodus 20:12
Theme: Appreciating your parents
Summary: Aubrey is so embarrassed by her parents that she does everything she can to keep them from showing up at a poetry reading—including not telling them about it at all.

448: Mandy's Debut
Original Air Date: 5/20/00
Writers: Kathy Wierenga & Charlie Richards
Sound Designers: Rob Jorgensen & Jonathan Crowe
Scripture: Matthew 25:23
Theme: Responsibility
Summary: Two plays that Mandy has written are performed at the Little Theatre—starring the Whit's End crew as themselves!

Actor Danielle Judovits, voice of Aubrey Shepard

Sound Bites with Rob Jorgensen

While Aubrey is babysitting in "The Long Way Home," the *Odyssey* episode "Real Time" [album 15] is playing on the television in the background. Also, the scene where Aubrey struggles while singing "Waltzing Matilda" was created by editing together outtakes of actor Danielle Judovits actually missing the notes. Her authentic reactions to her mistakes made for a more realistic scene.

Sound Bites with Rob Jorgensen

The sound of the dishes breaking in "Passages" came from an interesting source. Dave Arnold and Mark Drury had borrowed Dr. Dobson's silver for a *Radio Theatre* recording, promising not to break them. Unfortunately, during the Foley session they got knocked over and a few busted. Fortunately, the recorder was running when the disaster occurred, so at least we got some good sound out of it! [For more information on the Passages books, see the chapter near the end titled "Books."]

BTS: No Boundaries

In "No Boundaries," Alex's parents are said to be using *Dare to Let Go*, a book that teaches an opposite viewpoint of Dr. Dobson's book *The New Dare to Discipline* (1992).

Eugene and Connie in love from "I Slap Floor"

Sound Bites

In "The Seven Deadly Dwarves," Snow DeWhite (Bethany) says "Down with the king! Long live the queen! Liberty, equality, fraternity!" The second half of the quote is the French national motto. The dwarves then sing "Hi, ho" to the tune of the French national anthem.

Sound Bites with Rob Jorgensen

The sound effect for walking around the Cottage Cheese House in "The Seven Deadly Dwarves" was one of the most disgusting noises I ever created. I brought in several boxes of instant oatmeal, made a huge batch of it, and filled a large Foley box with the squishy mess. (Since oatmeal is cheap, easy to make, and appropriately "squishy sounding," we often use it for any scene involving food.) I set up my microphones and stepped into the box. I slipped around for a full day creating the Foley for that show. My shoes were ruined, but the sounds were great.

My Take: Kathy Wierenga

In "Potlucks and Poetry," Ellen Shepard's mom puts Post-it Notes on her daughter's windshield. This inspiration came from my mother, who put Post-it Notes on my car after I returned from a trip to the Bahamas. Because they drive on the left side of the road there, my mom put arrows on the notes reminding me to drive on the right side of the road now that I was home again.

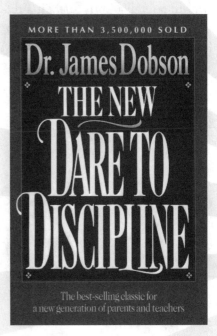

MORE THAN 3,500,000 SOLD

Dr. James Dobson

THE NEW
DARE TO
DISCIPLINE

The best-selling classic for a new generation of parents and teachers

BTS: *Bethany's Flood*

"Bethany's Flood" was originally held back from broadcast because it seemed a little too silly for a Bible story. Upon further review, the team decided to release the show after all. It is the only episode to be put in a retail album *before* it aired on the radio and the only show to air first on the weekday (Monday through Friday) show before airing on the weekend broadcast.

In the cover art, Eugene creates Animatronic Whit.

Actor Dave Madden enjoys teasing people as much as his character, Bernard Walton, does.

Do U Slap Floor?

"I Slap Floor" generated more mail than any other Odyssey episode to date, mainly from people trying to figure out exactly what the phrase "I Slap Floor" meant. We received some unusual guesses. One fan pointed out that if you lined up the words of the title in a certain way, it would spell out the word "ILL."

I
SLAP
FLOOR

The fan incorrectly guessed that Bernard must be ill.

To help listeners figure out what the strange title meant, we added a few hints to the album version of the episode and future airings. We encouraged listeners to rearrange the letters and reminded them that the show first aired "on the first day of the fourth month" of the year. Do you know what it means?

Album 35

Timelines and Radio Waves:
The Idea Behind the Novacom Saga
by Paul McCusker

I had read Michael Crichton's *Timeline* [1999] and noticed that he used big business's research into time travel in the same way that he used their research of dinosaurs in *Jurassic Park* [1990]. I loved the idea of some big conglomerates pouring money into massive top secret projects with an eye to how they might turn a profit later.

I had also been thinking about radio waves and how they send massive amounts of information through the air—and how they control machines, like the signal from a remote control to a television. Then, I wondered what would happen if we could convert brain waves to radio waves so that all we'd have to do is think what we want the TV to do, and it would do it.

Then I took it a step further and thought, *You can be sure some big business is already out there testing these ideas, trying to figure out how to convert radio waves to brain waves and back again.* Of course, there are good and practical benefits to that, but there are also some evil things that could happen if the technology was developed by merciless people. Then I wondered: *What if a dubious company was developing the idea in small pockets around the country, building it in pieces in secret, like the U.S. government did with the atomic bomb in the 1940s? What if Odyssey just happened to be one of the places being used as a test?* That was the starting point of the Novacom saga.

When I returned to be executive producer in 2000, I was working with a team that I didn't really know. It made sense to me that we should all concentrate on that single storyline together, to help bring us together creatively.

Episode Information

449, 450: The Big Deal, I and II
Original Air Date: 9/30/00 & 10/7/00
Writer: John Beebee
Sound Designer: Rob Jorgensen
Scripture: Matthew 14:1-12
Theme: Standing up for what you believe
Summary: Aubrey Shepard takes an Imagination Station adventure to meet the biblical John the Baptist.

451: Life Trials of the Rich and Famous
Original Air Date: 10/14/00
Writer: Marshal Younger
Sound Designer: Bob Luttrell
Scripture: James 2:1-7
Theme: How you treat others
Summary: When Nathaniel Graham's family suddenly becomes very rich, he notices that the kids start to treat him differently.

452: Missionary: Impossible
Original Air Date: 10/21/00
Writer: Kathy Wierenga
Sound Designer: Bob Luttrell
Scripture: Matthew 28:19-20
Theme: Mission work at home and around the world
Summary: Alex Jefferson becomes convinced that he should become a missionary like Jason Whittaker.

453, 454: The Great Wishy Woz, I and II
Original Air Dates: 10/28/00 & 11/4/00
Writer: John Beebee
Sound Designer: Rob Jorgensen
Scripture: John 14:6
Theme: The folly of humanism
Summary: Kids' Radio features a story about a young girl named Dotty who is transported to a strange land.

455: Best Laid Plans
Original Air Date: 11/11/00
Writer: Marshal Younger
Sound Designer: Bob Luttrell
Scripture: Proverbs 16:9
Theme: God's plans sometimes differ from ours.
Summary: When Jason Whittaker is late to speak at the Timothy Center, Connie tries to keep a restless crowd calm.

456: Worst Day Ever
Original Air Date: 11/18/00
Writer: Kathy Wierenga
Sound Designer: Bob Luttrell
Scripture: The book of Job
Theme: Bad days happen
Summary: Mandy Straussberg has one of those days when one thing after another goes wrong. (To get just a sampling of what happens, check out the album cover art.)

457: Opportunity Knocks
Original Air Date: 12/2/00
Writer: Marshal Younger
Sound Designer: Bob Luttrell
Scripture: Psalm 37
Theme: Relying on God even if we don't know the next step
Summary: With the Timothy Center in a financial crisis, it seems like an answered prayer when a company called Novacom offers Tom Riley a lot of money to build a tower on his property.

458: Red Herring
Original Air Date: 12/9/00
Writer: John Beebee
Sound Designer: Rob Jorgensen
Scripture: 1 Thessalonians 4:11
Theme: Curiosity
Summary: Alex Jefferson and his cousin, Cal Jordan, attempt to find out what Eugene is doing at Campbell College.

459: Slumber Party

Original Air Date: 12/16/00
Writer: Kathy Wierenga
Sound Designer: Rob Jorgensen
Scripture: Proverbs 17:17; 27:17
Theme: Friendship
Summary: Mandy has a difficult time keeping control of the girls at her slumber party.

460: Nova Rising

Original Air Date: 2/3/01
Writer: Marshal Younger
Sound Designer: Bob Luttrell
Scripture: Psalm 106:23
Theme: Not compromising your beliefs
Summary: Novacom buys B-TV from Bernard. Meanwhile, Alex and Cal get jobs working for the company.

Arthur Dent points to Tom Riley's property in "Opportunity Knocks."

Cut Scenes

In the early drafts of "The Big Deal," Nick Mulligan and Aubrey Shepard took an Imagination Station adventure together. However, actor Chris Castile (Nick) was unavailable to record, so Aubrey took her adventure alone instead. These earlier drafts also featured a subplot where Nick and Micah dressed in disguises to try to sneak John the Baptist out of prison.

Behind the Scenes: The Big Deal

Kris Kachurak, who originally played Jared DeWhite's sidekick, Dwayne Oswald, plays Micah in this episode. Micah, a follower of John the Baptist, says that he is "son of A-gun."

BTS: Missionary Impossible

The only *Adventures in Odyssey* episode to refer to *Star Wars* underwear is "Missionary: Impossible." The underwear was the source of some controversy. Many listeners thought that mentioning it was inappropriate.

BTS: The Great Wishy Woz

"The Great Wishy Woz" was writer John Beebee's directorial debut and was unique in many ways, including the fact that it's a musical. John remembers, "I had pitched the idea a few

Illustration from "The Great Wishy Woz"

Clubhouse magazine September 2000

times before, but Paul McCusker was the first to really see its true potential. Paul challenged me to come up with metaphors and meaning behind all the zaniness." The first draft of this episode featured "Maharishi" Mountain Lion, instead of "Mystical." He was "played by" Ellis Birch, direct from Pokenberry Falls. The episode became the second most popular one that churches licensed to perform as stage plays. The first is "The Boy Who Didn't Go to Church" (album 4).

Cut Scenes

The Wishy Woz gave the travelers a pop quiz when they returned from their quest: What is the philosophy of Plato? Answer: You shouldn't leave the lid off, or it will dry out.

Sound Bites with Rob Jorgensen

To get the little dog's clicking claws in "The Great Wishy Woz," I attached paper clips to my fingers and "walked" my hand across a hardwood floor. Metal Guy required some unique rattly-clangy sounds as he walked. I bought a piece of sheet metal, cut it into several pieces, drilled holes in each piece, and hung them from my arms, legs, and neck when I did his Foley. To create the sound of Metal Guy getting in the hot tub, Nathan Hoobler and I drove to a local apartment complex where a hot tub was available. While I set up the recording gear, Nathan put on all the sheet metal and some thick, aluminum dryer hoses. In a gallant display of self-sacrifice, Nathan spent the afternoon stepping in and out of the warm, bubbly water.

BTS: *Best Laid Plans*

Marshal Younger wrote this episode two years before it was recorded. It was originally intended to be the introduction to the Timothy Center (in place of "Opening Day," album 33) and featured Whit (instead of Jason) as the person stranded along the road.

Sound Bites with Chad Reisser

I have a great memory of "Best Laid Plans," in which my character, 2-Large, recites a poem. A longtime friend of mine, who is a national slam poetry champion, had recently been working with me on another recording project. When you do an *Odyssey* session, you just walk in, get the script, and start tracking. So, when we got to the poem, I simply recalled the cadence and rhythm and inflections of how my friend does his thing, and it totally worked. The directors thought that I was some sort of acting guru, when in reality I am just a hack with a cool friend.

My Take: *Marshal Younger*

Years after "Best Laid Plans" first aired, one of my coworkers pointed me to a school Web site where a sixth-grade girl had plagiarized the poem that 2-Large reads at the end of the episode. She had used the poem for one of her school assignments. I had never had my work plagiarized before, and in an odd sort of way, it felt like a compliment. I was suddenly a real writer. I decided that I shouldn't just let her get away with it, though, so I contacted the school to let them know what was going on. As it turned out, the poem had actually been turned in years before, and the perpetrator had already graduated from the school. I do wonder whether the girl got an A on my poem. . . .

Executive producer Paul McCusker

BTS: *Opportunity Knocks*

This episode was the beginning of the Novacom saga, the longest story arc in *Adventures in Odyssey* to date. The name Arthur Dent is a tip of the hat to a character in Douglas Adams's radio broadcast, book, television series, and movie *The Hitchhiker's Guide to the Galaxy* (1978–2005). As a foreshadowing of things to come, Arthur Dent says that he "would love to pick" Mr. Whittaker's brain. Novacom later attempted a mind-control scheme.

The business itself went through several name changes. Originally it was "Dark Star

Media," then "Galaxy Broadcasting," and finally "Novacom," after Rob Jorgensen saw the words "nova" and "company" written on a piece of paper.

BTS: Red Herring

"Red Herring" introduced Cal Jordan, played by Adam Pavlakovich, Katie Leigh's son. It also marked the first appearance of the mysterious hacker who went by the code name AREM, voiced as a computer sound by Bob Luttrell. When this show was written, we intended that AREM would later be revealed as Richard Maxwell, and his username represented his initials—R. M. However, actor Nathan Carlson wasn't available, so we later introduced the character of Robert Mitchell (another R. M.) who turned out to be AREM.

BTS: Slumber Party

In this episode, all the girls notice beams of light outside during the slumber party. In the years since this episode first aired, many listeners have asked about the conclusion of the light-beams mystery. "What," they ask, "is the deeper meaning of those light beams? What is their greater significance to the Novacom saga?" The answer is, sadly, *nothing*! We intended the light beams to be the kind of fun, silly thing that happens at real slumber parties. But maybe, just maybe, Novacom was really secretly installing underground transmitters for its brainwave scheme.

Q & A with Adam Pavlakovich (Cal) when he was 13

Q: How did you get involved with *Odyssey*?

AP: They needed an actor for the episode "Sticks and Stones" [an unreleased episode] and they called me up and I did an audition for them over the phone. They liked me, so they gave me my own character, Cal.

Q: What's it like knowing your mom plays Connie?

AP: My mom has been doing Connie since I was born, so I grew up with *Odyssey*. It's still kind of fun though, knowing that there's this huge fan base for my mom.

Q: What was it like to work with Travis Tedford, the voice of Alex Jefferson?

AP: Travis is a very nice and fun person. It's cool because he was Spanky in *The Little Rascals* [1994], and my mom used to call me Spanky. I guess when I was a baby I looked a lot like the original Spanky from the early *Little Rascals* show (1920s–1940s). Spanky is now my nickname.

Uh-Oh! The Near Tragedy of "The Great Wishy Woz"

by Rob Jorgensen

The music for the "Wishy Woz" episode almost didn't happen because of a simple error. As writer John Beebee thought of each song, he hummed the tune into a tape recorder, which he sent to John Campbell. John created "scratch tracks," or simple accompaniment pieces. He sent those to me, and I burned a CD, which we took with us to the recording session in Burbank. In the studio, the actors sang along to that CD. After recording, I prepared the singing tracks while John Campbell finished up orchestrating the music.

When I got the fully orchestrated music back, I excitedly loaded it into my computer and hit play . . . and was shocked by the horrible cacophony that followed. The singers did not match the orchestration at all! They were singing in a completely different key and the tempos were totally different! I immediately called John and we both panicked. We had no idea what had happened.

Finally I realized that it was all my fault. When I made that CD of John's scratch tracks, I set my computer at a faster speed. That caused the CD to be slightly faster and slightly higher in pitch. As a result, the actors sang every song at the wrong tempo and in the wrong key! There was no way we could reassemble the cast, and John's computer equipment couldn't change the pitch or tempo of the orchestration. We were stuck!

In the end, John saved the show. He went back and laboriously fixed each note of every song so that the orchestration matched the singers. "Ding Dong, the Generally Fantastic Composer Saved the Day!"

Dotty and Nono from "The Great Wishy Woz"

Album 36

Danger Signals

Welcoming Wooton! Mr. Bassett Comes to Odyssey

Sometimes the creation of a character comes over a long period of time. Wooton Bassett began as nothing more than a name—it is a small town in England. When Paul McCusker saw the name, he knew he would use it for an *Adventures in Odyssey* character one day.

Meanwhile, the *Odyssey* team had been encouraging Christian author and comedian Torry Martin to develop story ideas for the series. Torry remembers: "One day, I was sitting with Paul when he asked me to create a character based on my own persona. I wasn't sure what my persona was, so I asked him to elaborate. Paul responded, 'You know, create a character like you, someone bumbling, bizarre, gullible, and, naïve.' Well, that was the first time I had ever heard myself described like that, so I was immediately shocked and taken aback. I mean, I was the type of person who hardly ever got even one compliment in life—but four in a row? From the great Paul McCusker? That totally rocked!"

Torry developed the character and wrote an elaborate back story for him, including all his relatives. After reading Torry's material, Paul knew he had found the character for the name he'd been holding on to for years: Wooton Bassett.

When time came to cast the character, actor Katie Leigh suggested that we use her friend Jess Harnell. During the audition, we gave Jess some general direction, but as he read, the character didn't seem to be a match. It sounded as if we'd have to look for another actor. Then Jess suggested trying a different approach to the character, more of a laid-back surfer, based on movie and TV actor Rick Moranis's portrayal as a clueless talk-show host on *SCTV* (1981–1982). When he started reading the lines this way, the character suddenly clicked, and Wooton came to life.

Episode Information

462: The W. E.
Original Air Date: 2/17/01
Writer: Marshal Younger
Sound Designer: Jonathan Crowe
Scripture: Psalm 37:4-7
Theme: Discouragement
Summary: To compete with the new Novacom Kids' Center, Whit experiments with a massive overhaul to Whit's End and its attractions.

463: Green Eyes and Yellow Tulips
Original Air Date: 2/24/01
Writer: Kathy Wierenga
Sound Designer: Bob Luttrell
Scripture: 1 Samuel 16:7
Theme: Judging others
Summary: Connie falls for a Novacom employee named Robert Mitchell. Bart Rathbone protests that Novacom's programming is immoral.

464, 465: The Triangle, I and II
Original Air Dates: 3/3/01 & 3/10/01
Writer: Nathan Hoobler
Sound Designer: Rob Jorgensen
Scripture: Proverbs 17:17
Themes: Friendship, love
Summary: Jack Allen and Whit tell Connie the story of how Whit met his wife in college.

466: Snow Day
Original Air Date: 3/17/01
Writer: John Beebee
Sound Designer: Rob Jorgensen
Scripture: Galatians 6:9
Theme: Determination
Summary: When school is cancelled due to snow, Alex Jefferson accepts a job to deliver cookies to his grandmother. On the way, he must endure many trials and tribulations.

467: Broken Window
Original Air Date: 3/24/01
Writer: Kathy Wierenga
Sound Designer: Rob Jorgensen
Scripture: Proverbs 11:12
Themes: Judging others, justice
Summary: When a window gets broken at Whit's End, Whit puts Rodney, Sarah Prachett, and Alex on trial to see where the responsibility for fixing the window will fall.

468, 469: Chains, I and II
Original Air Dates: 4/28/01 & 5/5/01
Writer: Marshal Younger
Sound Designer: Jonathan Crowe
Scripture: Matthew 25:36
Themes: Compassion, trust
Summary: As construction begins on Whit's End in Connellsville, Whit learns that many people don't want his shop there after all.

470: Break a Leg
Original Air Date: 5/12/01
Writer: Nathan Hoobler
Sound Designer: Rob Jorgensen
Scripture: Numbers 10:29-32
Theme: Appreciating what you have
Summary: In an unfortunate accident, Cal Jordan loses control of his bike. He crashes into Walter Shakespeare, whose leg is broken as a result.

471: Fifteen Minutes
Original Air Date: 5/19/01
Writer: Marshal Younger
Sound Designer: Bob Luttrell
Scripture: Matthew 6; Isaiah 6:9
Theme: The folly of fame
Summary: Alex breaks a miniature-golf record, which rockets him to local fame. Meanwhile, an Odyssey local who made it big in Hollywood returns for a visit.

472: **Welcoming Wooton**

Original Air Date: 5/26/01
Writer: Torry Martin
Sound Designer: Bob Luttrell
Scripture: Philippians 4:1
Theme: Giftedness
Summary: When Wooton Bassett takes time out of his postal route to help at Whit's End, he gets fired for missing too much work.

473: **Breaking Point**

Original Air Date: 6/2/01
Writer: Marshal Younger
Sound Designer: Rob Jorgensen
Scripture: Proverbs 16:9
Theme: Trust
Summary: As construction on the new Whit's End nears completion, Whit finds his time stretched to the limit.

The original cover of *Danger Signals*

Sound Bites

When Nathaniel Graham is looking at the Tower of Babel display in "The W. E.," you can hear faint sound clips from the episode "The Tower" (album 32) playing. In that episode, Nathaniel journeyed back to this very Bible story.

Actor Steve Burns, the voice of Rodney Rathbone and Robert "Mitch" Mitchell

Clubhouse magazine, April 2001, with a feature on the new Whit's End

My Take: Kathy Wierenga

I sometimes feel like Connie's advocate because we are so much alike. I was a little concerned that Connie always hung out with this group of old men—Whit, Bernard, Tom—and never seemed to have any friends her own age. So I pushed for her to get a boyfriend, and suddenly Robert "Mitch" Mitchell was born. My first idea was for a fun, simple love story, but somehow we got a riot (see album cover art) and a whole Novacom plot in Mitch's first episode, "Green Eyes and Yellow Tulips." That's what happens when you write with a bunch of guys. (Just kidding . . . kind of.)

Sound Bites

At the recording of "Green Eyes and Yellow Tulips," we realized that the actor hired to play Mitch wasn't going to work out. Steve Burns was already in the studio to play Rodney Rathbone, and the team tried him as Connie's love interest. It worked, and Steve kept the part.

Behind the Scenes: The Triangle

The flashback scenes of "The Triangle" were recorded in Colorado rather than California. Jim Custer played young Whit, matching the voice he did for the part in "Rescue from Manatugo Point" (album 6). During auditions for the part of young Jenny, writer Marshal Younger filled in the lines of young Jack. Paul McCusker noticed that Marshal's voice had a vocal quality similar to Alan Young's, and so Marshal was quickly cast as young Jack

Allen. Marshal remembers, "The toughest scene for me to do was when young Jack hears the phone ring, and without words he has to convey the feeling of 'I will answer that. . . . No, wait. It might be Jenny, and that would be too difficult to deal with. . . . Of course, I shouldn't be rude to her. . . . No, it's probably not her anyway.' We had to do that scene about 10 times."

Actor Jim Custer, voice of young Whit

My Take: Nathan Hoobler

During my summer internship of 2000, Paul McCusker suggested that I write an episode explaining the line in "For Whom the Wedding Bells Toll" (album 29), where Jack mentions that Jenny was originally his girlfriend. I love knowing the minutiae and the tiny details of the characters, so I started my writing by rereading many of the stories about Whit's history. By the way, characters Nolan and Landon are named after two of my brothers. My sister's name is Emily, the same as Jack's pen pal and future wife. But

this coincidence was not planned because the character of Emily had been named long before I came on the scene.

BTS: Snow Day

Writer John Beebee remembers the inspiration for the wild sledding scene: "Where I grew up north of Pittsburgh, there was a big hill with a creek at the bottom. On snowy days, it was a favorite for death-defying sled rides, complete with an icy creek at the bottom. One day, I took my plastic red saucer for a ride, which was completely useless for steering. I ended up rocketing down the hill backward. I tried to brake by digging my boots in the snow and ended up losing both my boots, plus my gloves. I left a smear of clothing sprawled all over the hillside. This is exactly what happened to characters Alex and Cal in the episode, except they used a garbage-can lid instead of a sled."

But how to create the sound of that scene for the show? That was the challenge for Rob Jorgensen. How did he do it? "Well, by sitting on a garbage-can lid and sliding down a snowy hill," says Rob. "I wasn't pleased with the sounds I was getting in the studio, so I went to Home Depot, bought a metal garbage can and drove into the mountains. My goal was to find a deserted hill away from traffic noise, so I wandered around some backcountry dirt roads until I found the perfect spot. Gathering

The broken window in . . . well . . . "Broken Window"

my digital audio recorder, headphones, microphone, and garbage-can lid, I slowly trudged through the deep snow and made my way to the top of the hill. I sat down on the lid, put the headphones on, put the recorder on my chest, and held the microphone above me. I hit 'record' and shoved off! It was a great ride to the bottom, and I got some incredible sounds along the way. (I have to admit I slid down that hill a few more times than were necessary.)"

Sound Bites with Rob Jorgensen

In "Broken Window," each witness sits in a creaky chair that conjures up images of a courtroom from a *Perry Mason* episode [1957–1966]. Mark Drury brought in a chair from his dining room at home but didn't tell the rest of the sound designers that it was a valuable antique. You hear that chair in a lot of *Odyssey* episodes, and it was, shall we say, *enthusiastically* used. Sorry, Mark!

BTS: Chains

This episode brought back the character of Tony, a gang member from Oswald Heights, first seen in "Best Laid Plans" (album 35). It also introduced his sister, Brianna. For the final scene, rather than bring the actors in for just two lines, Traci and Mike Mulligan's lines were extracted from "Viva La Difference" (album 29).

Actor Jess Harnell, voice of Wooton Bassett

My Take: Marshal Younger

When I was in high school, I wrote and directed a movie with my friends called *Saki*, which was a spoof of the *Rocky* movies [1976–2006]. In one scene of "Fifteen Minutes," Saki prepares for a trivia contest in the same way Rocky did in the movies—with a manager who was pushing him with a stopwatch while Saki speed-read encyclopedias. In the miniature golf scene, Bart Rathbone rigorously coaches Alex Jefferson with ridiculous methods to make him better at miniature golf. I even had composer John Campbell do a spoof of the *Rocky* musical theme.

BTS: Breaking Point

Actor Jess Harnell did the sinister voice at the end of "Breaking Point" as a fill-in. We originally intended on replacing him. However, his performance was so strong, we kept his voice, and, in addition, we created the villainous character Mr. Charles from the voice. Mr. Charles appeared in many later Novacom shows. Before the character's name was revealed, fans and writers referred to him as Mr. X, after a similarly shadowy character on *The X-Files* (1993–2002).

Drawing Wooton

Wooton was such a unique character that we couldn't figure out how to draw him. It seemed as if everyone had a completely different picture for how he should look. So we took a cue from the Wilson character on TV's *Home Improvement* (1991–1999), who was always shown behind a fence, book, or other prop. All illustrations of Wooton (so far) have concealed most of his features.

Wooton in a mailbox, *Clubhouse* magazine, September 2001

Wooton in an igloo, *Clubhouse* magazine, December 2002

Wooton as a giant nose in album 40, *Out of Control*

Comedian and writer Torry Martin at Whit's End with Wooton

Q & A with Torry Martin

Q: How did you get started writing?

TM: My mother thought I had a tendency to talk too much when I was a kid and as a solution she suggested that I write my thoughts down and give her ears a break.

Q: What's the best thing about writing for *Odyssey*?

TM: Having the opportunity to learn more about the craft of writing from some of the best writers I know. Marshal Younger and Paul McCusker have both been a wonderful source of encouragement and help to me. I aspire to someday write at their level. The thing that most surprised me, though, was finding out what a collaborative effort the scripts actually are. Everyone offers input at a read through of the first draft, and there are so many great ideas being bounced around that for me it can be a little overwhelming because I want to incorporate them all.

Q: What characteristics do you share with Wooton?

TM: We're both extremely attractive for one, but I guess that's more about appearances than characteristics, so it doesn't really count. We both collect toys and comic books, we're both a little naïve and gullible, and we both march to the beat of a different piccolo. (I was going to say "drum," but we both think that drums are too loud and don't have much sound variance.)

Q: Where do you come up with the ideas for your characters?

TM: I hate to admit this, but I eavesdrop. I know, I know, but it's true. I listen to people, talk to them, observe them, and take notes. I travel everywhere with a miniature tape recorder and record my ideas into it, which can sometimes lead to embarrassing situations.

Torry with his dog.

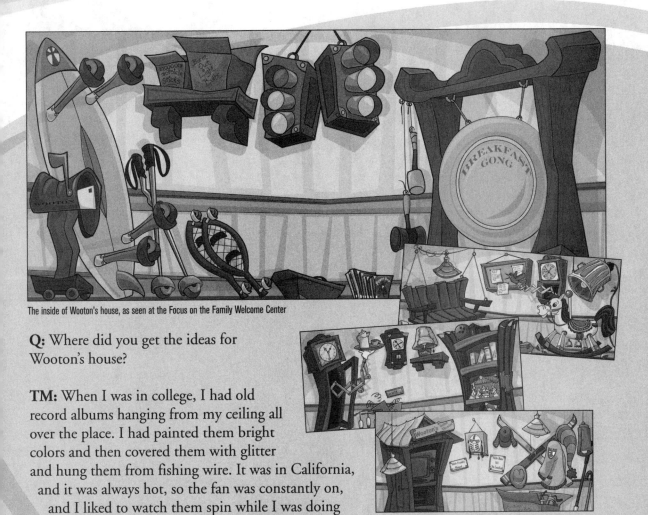

The inside of Wooton's house, as seen at the Focus on the Family Welcome Center

Q: Where did you get the ideas for Wooton's house?

TM: When I was in college, I had old record albums hanging from my ceiling all over the place. I had painted them bright colors and then covered them with glitter and hung them from fishing wire. It was in California, and it was always hot, so the fan was constantly on, and I liked to watch them spin while I was doing homework.

Then a few years later when I was living in my remote cabin in Alaska, I learned to decorate on a budget. I had the backseat of a Volkswagen that I used as a couch, and I started to repurpose things that I found in Dumpsters. For instance, I had one lamp that didn't have a lampshade so I turned a kitchen colander upside down and used that. It looked like a piece of art, but the metal "shade" could get hot to the touch if you left the light on too long. I'd often burn my hand when I turned it off, so I guess you could say that I suffered for my art.

Album 37
Countermoves

We Needed a "Plan B"

The Plan B episodes (along with several others) were scheduled to be recorded the week of September 11, 2001. The directors and sound designers were in California, ready to begin recording. Paul Herlinger was to fly into California on September 11, but his flight was cancelled, and he missed the sessions due to the terrorist attacks in New York, Pennsylvania, and Washington, D.C. Grief-stricken by the attacks, the *Adventures in Odyssey* team members met to discuss whether or not they should continue with the original recording schedule. They decided to press on. Rob Jorgensen remembers: "The mood in the studio that morning was subdued, with everyone's nerves and emotions on edge. The subject matter of our scripts paralleled what we were all feeling." Since Paul was stuck in another state, the *Odyssey* team used the actors who were available and recorded all the scenes that didn't need Whit.

A month later, Paul recorded Whit's scenes from Seattle with special technology that linked his studio to others via phone lines.

The actors who played Eugene and Katrina were unavailable at the time of the recording of "Plan B, I—Missing in Action," so the team meticulously extracted their lines at the wedding from session outtakes, deleted scenes, alternate takes, and other *Odyssey* episodes. The Plan B episodes were partially designed to send Eugene and Katrina out of Odyssey for a while. They were missing from the show for six albums until their triumphant reappearance in album 44, *Eugene Returns!*

Episode Information

474, 475: Shining Armor, I and II
Original Air Dates: 11/10/01 & 11/17/01
Writer: Marshal Younger
Sound Designer: Rob Jorgensen
Scripture: 2 Chronicles 20:15
Theme: Putting our trust in God instead of ourselves
Summary: Jason Whittaker returns to a missions project he set up months before and finds that things have gone terribly wrong.

477: O. T. Action News: Battle at the Kishon
Original Air Date: 12/01/01
Writers: Nathan Hoobler & Paul McCusker
Sound Designer: Bob Luttrell
Scripture: Judges 4; Hebrews 11:32-33
Themes: The biblical story of Deborah and Barak, faith in God during adversity
Summary: O. T. Action News reports on the story of Deborah and Barak and their battle against the Canaanites.

478: Strange Boy in a Strange Land
Original Air Date: 12/8/01
Writer: Marshal Younger
Sound Designer: Rob Jorgensen
Themes: Trust, honesty, loneliness
Summary: Mandy Straussberg and Sarah Prachett go camping far from Odyssey and run into an old friend—Jared DeWhite! But Jared's explanation of his disappearance from Odyssey makes them wonder whether or not to believe him.

479: Happy Smilers
Original Air Date: 12/15/01
Writer: John Beebee
Sound Designer: Bob Luttrell
Theme: The source of true happiness
Summary: A S.M.I.L.E. convention at the Timothy Center falls apart when the S.M.I.L.E. leader has a heart attack in the middle of the festivities.

481, 482: Grand Opening, I and II
Original Air Dates: 1/5/02 & 1/12/02
Writers: John Beebee, Kathy Wierenga, & Marshal Younger
Sound Designer: Bob Luttrell
Theme: Trust
Summary: Whit's End Connellsville opens amidst much fanfare. The celebration is cut short when Whit finds hidden cameras all over the shop (see album cover art).

483: Secrets
Original Air Date: 1/19/02
Writer: Kathy Wierenga
Sound Designer: Jonathan Crowe
Theme: Being yourself
Summary: Connie's relationship with Robert Mitchell is tested when she discovers the picture of another girl in his briefcase.

484: Plan B, I—Missing in Action
Original Air Date: 1/26/02
Writer: Marshal Younger
Sound Designer: Rob Jorgensen
Theme: Dealing with loss
Summary: As tension increases and more pieces of a sinister plot come together, Whit and Connie find that Eugene has eloped with Katrina Shanks and left town.

485: Plan B, II—Collision Course
Original Air Date: 2/2/02
Writers: Marshal Younger & Nathan Hoobler
Sound Designer: Rob Jorgensen
Theme: Trust
Summary: Connie continues to investigate Eugene's disappearance and has to decide if she will trust Mitch. Or is he a spy for Novacom?

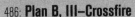

486: **Plan B, III—Crossfire**

Original Air Date: 2/9/02
Writers: Nathan Hoobler & Marshal Younger
Sound Designer: Bob Luttrell
Theme: Dealing with Loss
Summary: Connie mourns the loss of Mitch while Jack Allen and Whit try to retrieve a package with crucial information.

487: **Plan B, IV—Resistance**

Original Air Date: 2/16/02
Writer: Marshal Younger
Sound Designer: Jonathan Crowe
Scripture: 2 Timothy 4:7
Themes: Dealing with loss, the importance of verbalizing your feelings
Summary: Wooton Bassett helps Connie deal with Mitch's departure, while Whit collaborates with FBI Agent Bourland.

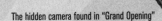

The hidden camera found in "Grand Opening"

Behind the Scenes: Shining Armor

This episode was written as an African adventure. At the time, we had difficulties finding actors with authentic African accents, so the location for the episode was changed to South America. When Marshal Younger wrote "Prisoners of Fear" (album 45) years later, he used several of the African names first intended for this show, including Kwame and Aman.

Sound Bites

Actor Scott Rummell played Victor in "Shining Armor." Before recording the show, he worked on his Spanish accent for several weeks. Once in the studio, however, he realized that his character was actually supposed to be an American. Also of note, actor Keith Silverstein, who played Santo, was later brought back as Agent Peter Bourland in the Plan B episodes.

Sound Bites with Rob Jorgensen

Episodes in exotic locales, like "Shining Armor," are usually difficult to produce. You have to consider sound quality issues such as "What do voices sound like when they're in a hut instead of in a living room or Whit's End?" "What does the background really sound like?" or "How many jungle sounds are too many?"

After I worked on the show for six weeks, my computer crashed and I lost all my work. I was devastated . . . but I started over again. It has happened to every sound designer here at one time or another. We have a motto: Back up, back up, back up.

Cut Scenes

Amazingly enough, in one version of "Battle at the Kishon" character Rodney Rathbone was one of the O. T. Action News correspondents. Those scenes were abandoned because actor Steve Burns wasn't available for recording.

BTS: Battle at the Kishon

This episode caused considerable debate among the team members. We argued over how much of the notorious tent-peg scene should be heard by the audience. The violent moment was heard, but we made it sound very far away.

BTS: Strange Boy in a Strange Land

This was Jared DeWhite's first appearance since his sudden disappearance in "The Y.A.K. Problem" (album 33). Fans often asked why he went missing so quickly, so we explained that he was part of the Witness Protection Program. It seemed appropriate for his character, who was always talking about conspiracy theories, to now be involved in a global conspiracy with the Novacom saga.

Sound Bites with Rob Jorgensen

A particular scene in "Strange Boy in a Strange Land," has Jared falling out of a tree. Unlike other effects like sledding down a hill on a garbage-can lid, this wasn't one I wanted to replicate in real life. Dr. Dobson's studio had some fake decorative trees, so I stealthily snuck one into the Foley room and whacked at it with a backpack full of books. (If you listen carefully, you can hear a branch

Actor Brandon Gilberstadt, voice of Jared DeWhite

crack and break.) Then I threw myself on the ground. I figured falling a couple of feet was better than falling 20.

My Take: John Beebee

I love writing for *Adventures in Odyssey*, but ironically, a show called "Happy Smilers" brought me close to despair. I originally wrote it because I was accused of being happy all the time. In fact, a couple of people were convinced something had to be wrong with me. But the first read through of the script was not a Happy Smiler moment. When Paul McCusker read one of my first drafts, he said it was so saccharine-sweet that he worried people would throw up. And so, at the next read through,

I passed out throw-up bags for everybody. In the end, I think the script turned out all right, although I hope no one gets sick when they hear the Happy Smilers theme song.

Cut Scenes

The first draft of "Grand Opening" featured a scene with Arthur Dent encouraging Robert Mitchell to have a relationship with Connie. But, on the day of recording, actor Christopher Snell wasn't available to voice Arthur, so we changed the scene and had the more sinister Mr. Charles explaining that Arthur had gone. This enabled us to introduce Arthur as a renegade, which came in handy in the later Plan B episodes.

BTS: Secrets

"Secrets" originally contained a separate plot about a show called "Survival" premiering on a Novacom channel. We intended to spoof the reality-show craze sweeping TV at the time. This part of the episode was taken out and saved for the future, but it was never recorded. Also of note, Connie and Nick Mulligan find a script for *Casey's Shadow* in Mitch's briefcase. *Casey's Shadow* was a 1978 TV Western miniseries that featured actor Steve Burns, who now plays Mitch.

BTS: Plan B, I—Missing in Action

This episode featured the long-awaited wedding of Eugene Meltsner and Katrina Shanks. Sadly, actor Bernard Erhard, who originally played Armitage Shanks, passed away before this episode was recorded, so actor Brian Cummings filled in for him.

My Take: Kathy Buchanan

The week that "Plan B, I—Missing in Action" aired, I ordered a cake for the team to celebrate Eugene and Katrina's wedding, and the people at the bakery commented on what a rush it was. Usually wedding cakes are ordered well in advance. So I explained to them how the bride's father was on his deathbed and that the couple decided to get married right in the hospital. The staff was so moved they put a special rush on the cake.

Sound Bites

Jack Allen's crazy taxi driver in "Collision Course" was played by actor David Griffin, aka Jimmy Barclay!

Sound Bites with Rob Jorgensen

To get the sounds of the wild car chase in "Collision Course," Glenn Montjoy and I took his car and our recording equipment out to an unfinished road on the outskirts of town and rode around. Next I sat in the backseat and slammed myself from one side of the car to the other so that it would sound as if Jack were getting tossed around. I remember being very carsick that day.

BTS: Crossfire

This episode finally revealed the full identity of two characters introduced much earlier in the Novacom story arc—Bennett Charles (first heard of in "Chains," album 36) and Monica Stone (first mentioned in "Red Herring," album 35). It also contained the first reference to the mysterious "Chairman" figure, who was apparently behind the whole Novacom plot.

The Dishrag

Connie reads a poem that she wrote about Mitch in "Plan B, IV—Resistance." In the episode, Connie pauses after each line and explains what she means. That's how we know that the dishrag represents Mitch.

The Dishrag
by Connie Kendall
The dishrag sits on the counter,
Catching no one's eye
The polished brass a reflection,
Clear as the cloudless sky.
The dishrag is tossed,
The laundry is its fate.

(Okay, we never said the poem was good.)

Odyssey team, circa 2001. Back row, from left: Jonathan Crowe, Marshal Younger, Rob Jorgensen, Mark Drury, John Beebee; Front row, from left: Kathy Wierenga, Chris McDonald

Album 38

Battle Lines

A Quick Exit

"Exit" holds the record for most scenes in any single show in *Adventures in Odyssey* history: 28. Most episodes average 10 to 14 scenes. Also of note, "Exactly as Planned," another episode in this album, had 23 actors, another *Odyssey* record.

In "Exit," Whit and Tom Riley use the Applesauce computer program to destroy the Imagination Station. Applesauce was introduced in "A Bite of Applesauce" (album 5). In that episode, the program wreaked havoc on the entire system at Whit's End.

During the Imagination Station meltdown sequence that the Applesauce program unleashed, we added clips from many previous adventures, including several with the voice of actor Hal Smith, who originally played Whit. The last minute of the countdown is presented in real time. From the moment when the timer signals "one minute to go" to the moment when Tom pushes the button, exactly 59.5 seconds pass. So Tom had only half a second to spare when he finally pushed the button.

"Exit" became a favorite among fans and team members. Writers Kathy Wierenga, John Beebee, and Nathan Hoobler call "Exit" their favorite Novacom saga episode. Marshal Younger says "Plan B, IV—Resistance" is his favorite. Paul McCusker likes them all, and looks forward to a single collection that will include the entire Novacom story arc, if only to figure out what in the world happened. He says, "It was such a simple idea when we started."

Episode Information

488, 489: Under the Influence, I and II
Original Air Dates: 3/23/02 & 3/30/02
Writer: John Beebee
Sound Designer: Bob Luttrell
Scripture: John 3:16
Theme: Choosing friends wisely
Summary: An old friend pits Aubrey Shepard against her parents and their beliefs.

490, 491: The Black Veil, I and II
Original Air Dates: 04/06/02 & 4/13/02
Writer: Marshal Younger
Sound Designers: Jonathan Crowe & Rob Jorgensen
Scripture: Galatians 6:9
Theme: Spiritual battles
Summary: Jason Whittaker's stop in Alaska reveals strange problems affecting the members of the church. Meanwhile in Odyssey, Whit notices a strange surge of anger and violence.
Parental Warning:
Because of the intensity of a few scenes in this show, we recommend that children under the age of 8 listen with their parents.

492: Twisting Pathway
Original Air Date: 5/18/02
Writer: John Beebee
Sound Designer: Bob Luttrell
Scripture: Proverbs 14:14; 16
Theme: Choosing the right direction
Summary: When Mr. Charles makes demands that Kevin Colburn finds uncomfortable, his daughter, Erica, takes things into her own hands.

493: Sheep's Clothing
Original Air Date: 5/26/02
Writer: Marshal Younger
Sound Designer: Glenn Montjoy
Scripture: Jeremiah 9:6
Theme: Recognizing deception
Summary: Monica Stone tries to steal a disk from Jason, who is in Alaska. Back at Odyssey, Whit and Agent Bourland investigate Novacom.

494: Box of Miracles
Original Air Date: 6/1/02
Writer: Nathan Hoobler
Sound Designer: Rob Jorgensen
Scripture: Psalm 20:7
Theme: Putting our faith in God, not science
Summary: Novacom releases the Novabox, an amazing new technology that seems to heal Tom Riley's wife, Agnes.

495: The Unraveling
Original Air Date: 6/8/02
Writers: Kathy Wierenga & Bob Hoose
Sound Designer: Bob Luttrell
Scripture: 2 Timothy 4:7
Theme: Fighting for what's right
Summary: Connie goes to Maine to talk to Robert "Mitch" Mitchell's sister. Working hard in Odyssey, the kids investigate unusual buying trends connected to the Novabox.

496: Exceptional Circumstances
Original Air Date: 6/15/02
Writers: John Beebee, Kathy Wierenga, & Marshal Younger
Sound Designer: Glenn Montjoy
Scripture: Proverbs 16:25
Theme: Exposing the truth
Summary: Connie passes the kids' Novabox information to Mitch, while Jason discovers that Monica Stone has a personal connection to the Novacom scheme.

497: Expect the Worst

Original Air Date: 6/22/02
Writers: John Beebee, Nathan Hoobler, Kathy Wierenga, & Marshal Younger
Sound Designer: Bob Luttrell
Scripture: 2 Corinthians 1:10-11
Theme: Prayer in times of trouble
Summary: Using Connie's information, Mitch makes a critical connection in proving what Novacom is doing, but the situation changes when the tower on Tom Riley's property blows up.

498: Exactly as Planned

Original Air Date: 6/29/02
Writers: Nathan Hoobler & Marshal Younger
Sound Designer: Bob Luttrell
Scripture: Matthew 5:44; Numbers 32:23
Theme: Hope in troubled times
Summary: Whit and Alex Jefferson work to prove Tom's innocence, and Jason learns that Novacom's final scheme is about to be set in motion.

499: Exit

Original Air Date: 7/6/02
Writers: Marshal Younger & Kathy Wierenga
Sound Designer: Rob Jorgensen
Scripture: Romans 8:28
Theme: The ultimate victory of truth
Summary: Whit, Tom, and Jason race to stop Novacom's launch date, but Mr. Charles has a way to stop them.

Cut Scenes

We wanted Aubrey Shepard's spiritual journey to be an important component of the Novacom saga in the same way that Eugene's salvation was critical to the Blackgaard saga. But how should we bring Aubrey to Christ? A salvation story must ring true to the individual character. The first draft of "Under the Influence" featured Aubrey falling in with bad girl Erica Colburn and following her to a local fair where they vandalized a carnival ride. However, the story was almost totally disconnected from the Novacom plot, so we changed it. We decided that Erica should be the daughter of a Novacom employee and that we would weave her story and Aubrey's into the Novacom story arc.

The Novabox

Behind the Scenes: The Black Veil

This episode was one of the darkest *Odyssey* shows because it showed the seriousness of the Novacom threat. We received letters from a few listeners who questioned the appropriateness of some scenes, so we added a parental warning to future airings. Writer Marshal Younger says, "When I listen to this episode now, I can't believe that I wrote it. I had never written anything so bizarre and intense before."

Sound Bites

If you listen closely to Mr. Charles's scenes with his assistant, Thomas, in "Twisting Pathway," you'll hear fish tanks. Our in-joke was that Charles had tanks of piranhas in his office (as a tip of the hat to another villain's aquatic preferences in "The Last Great Adventure of the Summer," album 2).

Goof Alert!

When Whit and Agent Bourland leave Mr. Charles's office in "Sheep's Clothing," Agent Bourland scoffs that Mr. Charles refers to a "two-week vacation." Unfortunately, this was a reference to a line that was cut, making Bourland's line unnecessary.

BTS: Sheep's Clothing

We knew that Monica Stone would get the disc that Eugene had sent to Jason Whittaker, but we didn't want Jason to look gullible as a result. In an early draft of the script, Jason tells Monica where the safe is. To make Jason's

Melissa Disney, voice of Monica Stone, is not nearly as sinister as she sounds.

character less naive and Monica's more clever, we changed the plot so Monica gives Jason a ring with a tracking device inside.

Sound Bites with Rob Jorgensen
In "The Unraveling," we find out that Robert Mitchell's high school job was at Ken's Burger Den. My first job in high school was flipping burgers in the kitchen of the genuine Ken's Burger Den in Meridian, Idaho.

BTS: Box of Miracles
Agnes Riley mentions having Thanksgiving at Whit's End with Connie and hearing Whit's story about his salvation ("Thank You, God," album 3). Also in

"Box of Miracles," Dr. Jennings, a character from the Passages novels, appears at Hillingdale Haven.

BTS: The Unraveling
This episode explains what became of Justine Baker, a character who was mentioned in "Secrets" (album 37) when Mitch got a "sad look in his eyes." It also contains an appearance by Mr. Jenkins, the grocery store owner, who hadn't appeared on the show since "Cousin Albert" (album 9). The show also featured what some fans considered the biggest twist in the entire Novacom saga—that Mitch was, in fact, still alive and in the Witness Protection Program with Jared.

Sound Bites with Glenn Montjoy

In "Exceptional Circumstances," Tom and Agnes Riley are running in the field near the tower. I inserted the sound of a helicopter passing by to signal the Chairman going on his way to install the upload hardware seen in the later episode "Exit."

The Cover of Battle Lines

Battle Lines was released in September 2002, approximately one year after the September 11 terrorist attacks. Since the album cover featured an exploding tower, we worked extra hard to ensure that the structure didn't resemble the World Trade Center. (See art at the beginning of the chapter.)

BTS: Expect the Worst

The most difficult part of an *Odyssey* writer's job is figuring out how to blend the storyline with a believable lesson for our listeners. Doing so in the Novacom saga was particularly hard since we had so many plotlines running at the same time, with themes interwoven throughout them all. We realized that, in stories of great crisis, the best lesson is sometimes the most obvious. Marshal Younger came up with the idea of interspersing prayers throughout the courtroom drama in "Expect the Worst." In this way, we were able to show prayer in action in a clear and understandable way.

My Take: Marshal Younger

The scene in "Exit" where Mitch rescues Connie could have been melodramatic—with the hero untying the damsel in distress in the nick of time, and the damsel gushing all over the hero—but I decided to make it a Connie moment to get rid of the mushiness. One of the first things out of her mouth is "Did you get your hair cut?" For me, that line makes the show.

Novacom Inspires Fan Fervor

Some fans took the Novacom saga very seriously. In fact, Angelo C. from Mount Prospect, Illinois, wrote his own comic book for a Novacom sequel.

The Novacom Saga

The Novacom saga spans albums 35 to 38 and includes the following episodes:

Opportunity Knocks	Plan B, I–IV
Red Herring	Under the Influence, I and II
Nova Rising	The Black Veil, I and II
The W. E.	Twisting Pathway
Green Eyes and Yellow Tulips	Sheep's Clothing
Chains, I and II	Box of Miracles
Fifteen Minutes	The Unraveling
Breaking Point	Exceptional Circumstances
Strange Boy in a Strange Land	Expect the Worst
Grand Opening, I and II	Exactly as Planned
Secrets	Exit

Later episodes that continue some of the stories started in the Novacom saga include:

Between You and Me	A Most Intriguing Question
The Benefit of the Doubt	A Most Surprising Answer
Here Today, Gone Tomorrow? I–III	A Most Extraordinary Conclusion
Something Blue, I and II	

Actor Townsend Coleman, voice of Jason Whittaker

How Do We End This Thing?

What should be the finale of the Novacom saga? Even from the very early stages of brainstorming, team members debated how it should end. Our initial ideas included Whit announcing on the radio or TV exactly what Novacom had been doing. Another idea involved Arthur Dent being "programmed to kill" Whit, but choosing to kill Mr. Charles instead with Whit leaping in front of the bullet to save Mr. Charles's life.

We ultimately decided that the threat of Novacom should go beyond the town of Odyssey and include the entire world through the towers the company had built. To make the whole thing bigger and more epic, we introduced launch day (the day that Novacom planned to enslave the human race).

We also wanted to explain Novacom's plan without resorting to the classic means of a villain simply explaining it all. So we determined to use Tom Riley's trial as a way for our heroes to reveal publicly what the bad guys were up to. It was loosely based on the movie *Conspiracy* (2001) about the Nazis' master plan during World War II (1941–1945).

Writer Marshal Younger explains that Novacom began as a simple story. What happened?

Character:
Ed Washington
Birthplace: Chicago, Illinois
Something you may not know about Ed:
He once owned his own toy company.

Album 39

Friends, Family, and Countrymen

The Writing of "The American Revelation"

by John Fornof

Did you know that African Americans fought side by side with whites in the American Revolutionary War? I sure didn't. That is, until I met Phil Williams.

When a friend introduced us, I found out that Phil has a passion for history. He doesn't just spout out facts and figures; he makes presentations to schools and colleges, re-enacts historic scenes, makes historic figures come to life, and quotes each one to the letter. So right there in the middle of the Focus cafeteria, Phil brought history to life for me. I was fascinated.

I was also overwhelmed. Over 5,000 African Americans fought in the American Revolutionary War, and it seemed as if there were 5,000 wonderful stories to tell. How could we narrow it down to one episode? Phil and I prayed a lot through this process and God helped us.

The recording session was long but very enjoyable. Paul Herlinger, who plays Whit, told me later he was fascinated by the history that unfolded in the program. "I always enjoy *Odyssey*," he told me, "but today I was enlightened."

At the end of the session, we gathered all the guys in the studio to re-enact the British troops and the American troops battling each other. It was fun directing this part. In the middle of the battle scene, I randomly pointed at one of the guys in the studio as a cue to "die."

The rest is history. Literally! I thank God for how he helped Phil, the team, and me pull this show together. Our hope is that this program will help people rediscover a forgotten piece of history and see that this amazing story of God's providence is for all of us.

Episode Information

461: B-TV: Obedience
Original Air Date: 2/10/01
Writers: John Fornof, Nathan Hoobler, Phil Lollar, Paul McCusker, Jim Ware, Kathy Wierenga
Sound Designer: Bob Luttrell
Scripture: John 14:15, 24; Philippians 2
Theme: Obedience
Summary: B-TV explores the topic of obedience with sketches about the biblical characters Gideon, Naaman, and Moses.

476: Relatively Annoying
Original Air Date: 11/24/01
Writer: Marshal Younger
Sound Designer: Jonathan Crowe
Scripture: 1 Peter 2:17; Leviticus 19:32
Theme: Getting along with people
Summary: Spending a week at his grandparents' house seems like the end of the world to Alex Jefferson.

480: The Popsicle Kid
Original Air Date: 12/22/01
Writer: Torry Martin
Sound Designer: Rob Jorgensen
Theme: Uniqueness
Summary: Rodney Rathbone discourages Austin O'Connor from hanging around Colby Cabrera because he's "weird." Wooton Bassett and the kids try to win a Christmas decorating contest.

503: Between You and Me
Original Air Date: 1/11/03
Writer: Kathy Wierenga
Sound Designer: Bob Luttrell
Scripture: Proverbs 3:5-6
Theme: Putting God first
Summary: Connie wonders if she's spending too much time with Robert Mitchell. Then he gets an offer from the FBI . . . to move to Virginia.

504: Aubrey's Bathrobe
Original Air Date: 1/18/03
Writer: Bob Hoose
Sound Designer: Allen Hurley
Scripture: Colossians 3:17
Theme: Using our ability to serve God
Summary: A super-Christian named Seth Young makes Aubrey Shepard feel inadequate in her new faith.

505: The Toy Man
Original Air Date: 1/25/03
Writer: Marshal Younger
Sound Designer: Allen Hurley
Scripture: Philippians 3:8
Themes: Sacrifice, making tough choices
Summary: Ed Washington thinks about quitting his high-paying job to work at Whit's End. His family considers the sacrifices they'll have to make.

506: For Trying Out Loud
Original Air Date: 2/1/03
Writer: Kathy Wierenga
Sound Designer: Allen Hurley
Scripture: 1 Corinthians 12:11
Theme: Finding your place
Summary: Wooton Bassett wants to help Edwin Blackgaard with an upcoming production. Liz Horton tries to find something—anything—she can do better than others.

507: **The Benefit of the Doubt**

Original Air Date: 2/8/03
Writer: Marshal Younger
Sound Designer: Bob Luttrell
Scripture: Jeremiah 1:17
Theme: Doing what's right
Summary: Robert Mitchell searches for a job in Odyssey, but his work at Novacom scares away potential employers.

508, 509: **The American Revelation, I and II**

Original Air Dates: 2/15/03 & 2/22/03
Writer: John Fornof
Sound Designer: Todd Busteed
Scripture: John 15:13
Theme: American history
Summary: In the new Imagination Station, Marvin Washington hears a rarely told story from the American Revolutionary War.

511, 512: **The Pact, I and II**

Original Air Dates: 3/8/03 & 3/15/03
Writer: Nathan Hoobler
Sound Designer: Bob Luttrell
Scripture: 2 Corinthians 5:20
Theme: Living with an eternal perspective
Summary: Whit, Tom Riley, and Mandy Straussberg attempt to discover what's troubling Agnes Riley.

In "For Trying Out Loud," Edwin Blackgaard ruins yet another Shakespearean performance.

Behind the Scenes: The Popsicle Kid

We originally wrote Whit into this script, but actor Paul Herlinger was unable to fly to the session due to the tragic events of September 11, 2001. Walker Edmiston was already in the studio for the role of Bart Rathbone, so we quickly rewrote Whit's part and gave it to Tom Riley.

BTS: B-TV: Obedience

This episode was written, in part, to include some of the two-minute short skits from the episodes found in *Virtual Realities* (album 33) and *In Your Wildest Dreams* (album 34). They were featured on the broadcasts, but not included in the retail packages. First titled "B-TV: Tough Stuff," the episode was intended to look at difficult passages of Scripture. Then the episode morphed into a show about obedience and featured only one of the shorts—"The Ancient World of Sports: Gideon's Pitch." All of the other sketches had to be cut to make time for the new material. This was also the only B-TV show written by the entire team, with different writers taking different sections of the show. It made the writing of the many B-TV sketches less daunting . . . but the episode credits seemed endless!

Sound Bites

For the unique feel of "Relatively Annoying," composer John Campbell scored "dripping country swamp" music in the style of the movie *O Brother, Where Art Thou?* (2000).

My Take: Marshal Younger

One of our challenges as writers is to make sure that the dialogue isn't too "on the nose," with characters saying exactly how they're feeling. I look for unique ways for characters to say "I love you" without using those exact words. Grandpa's ribbing to his wife of many years in "Relatively Annoying" is one my favorites: "You know

Marvin Washington hides from a British soldier in "American Revelation"

this unselfish act you've been putting on for the last 40 years? You know I'm not buying it, don't you?"

Connie and Mitch: Soul Mates? The Writers Decide Their Fate

When Robert "Mitch" Mitchell returned to Odyssey in "Exactly as Planned" (album 38), we had to decide if we wanted Connie and Mitch to get married. When they first started dating, we thought they might. As time went on, we decided that they shouldn't stay together permanently. Eugene and Katrina had recently married, and we wanted Connie to stay young and single for a little longer. But how should Connie and Mitch break up? In the end, Mitch got an offer from the FBI and his final decision signaled the end of their relationship. (See "Something Blue," album 41).

My Take: Marshal Younger

"The Toy Man" was written to explain what happened to Whit's End Connellsville, which had been created as part of the

Actors Jordan Calloway, voice of Marvin Washington, and Corey Williams, voice of Caesar Bason

Novacom saga. After the storyline ended, we realized we didn't want to abandon the shop completely, so we had our new main family—the Washingtons—take it over.

BTS: For Trying Out Loud

The names of the cheerleaders are twists on several famous actors' names. They are Brenda Frazier (Brendan Fraser), Melanie Gibson (Mel Gibson), Tanya Cruz (Tom Cruise), and Christine O'Donnell (Chris O'Donnell).

Phil Williams, historical consultant for "The American Revelation"

The True History Behind "The American Revelation"

Several characters were combined and a few minor assumptions made in the writing of "The American Revelation." For instance, we don't know for certain that Caesar Bason was at Lexington, but since he lived nearby it's likely he could have been called to the battle.

Otherwise, we remained historically accurate, including the following well-documented facts:

- William Diamond was indeed a 16-year-old drummer at the Battle of Lexington.
- African Americans and whites fought side by side in the Revolutionary War—the most integrated army until modern times. Historical documents show more than 60 African Americans fought at the Battle of Bunker Hill. Among them, Caesar Bason, Peter Salem,

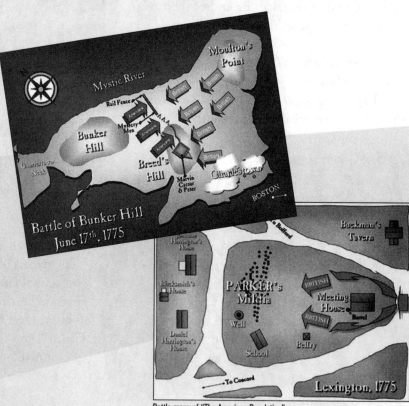

Battle maps of "The American Revelation"

and Salem Poor (referred to as "Mystery Man" in the episode). All told, around 5000 African Americans fought for the American side in the Revolutionary War. About the same number fought for the British, who promised them conditional freedom.

- In the battle, Peter Salem shot British Major John Pitcairn. And Salem Poor shot British Lieutenant Colonel James Abercrombie.

- After stray gunfire disabled Captain Smith's musket, the captain tried to carry his injured soldier to safety. But Caesar was too big for him. Caesar asked the captain to leave him behind. "Give 'em one for Caesar," he said.

Actors Jordan Calloway (Marvin Washington) and Theo Greenley (William Diamond)

It's not clear what happened to Caesar next. Some accounts say he died in the trenches. Others say he was taken prisoner by the British. Either way, it's most probable that he died, since during this era gunshot wounds to the leg were almost always fatal.

Sound Bites

"The American Revelation" was the first *Odyssey* episode that composer Jared DePasquale scored. Jared composed several *Focus on the Family Radio Theatre* dramas released in the early 2000s, including *Les Misérables* and *The Secret Garden*. He recorded an authentic period drum for Marvin Washington's various drum sounds in the show. It was also the first episode where John Beebee started writing under the name John Fornof.

My Take: Nathan Hoobler

After the Novacom arc, we considered creating a story about Agnes Riley's paintings . . . that somehow she was able to communicate through her paintings in a way that she otherwise couldn't, due to her illness.

But what would she be trying to tell people? Days after our brainstorming, I attended my college graduation. During the ceremony, I thought about how long it might be until I saw any of my friends again. I got to thinking how much fun it would be to make a pact that we would meet at a certain place on a certain date years later. I had recently read a short story in O. Henry's book *The Four Million* [1906] about this very thing.

This seemed like the perfect option for Agnes—to greatly desire to meet a friend after many years away but unable to communicate her desire. Then I started to think what a great twist it would be if that person could be one of our existing *Odyssey* characters. Joanne Allen was the perfect choice, and "The Pact" was written.

Welcoming the Washingtons: The Creation of a New Family

The Washington family was cast in an unusual way. Instead of writing the roles first and then finding actors to play them, we found our favorite actors and wrote roles around them. The family was on the show for many years, but like the Barclay family, the Washingtons had one member who often changed actors—Marvin. He has been played by three actors.

Marshal Younger wrote detailed back stories for each of the characters. Marvin's propensity towards drums was included because we had plans to use it in "The American Revelation." We originally wanted the Washingtons to have a rebellious teen with an attitude, but instead we created Ed's recalcitrant nephew, Xavier. The Washingtons' older son, Antoine, is away at college and, to date, has not appeared on the show.

The Washington family in "The Mystery at Tin Flat"

Mark Christopher Lawrence, voice of Ed Washington

Album 40

Out of Control

Jared Has a Brother?

"It's All About Me" featured the return of Jared DeWhite to *Odyssey* after a long absence. It also featured the first appearance of Jared's brother, Trent. Jared had previously mentioned his brother in "The Pushover" (album 29) as a two-year-old who colored outside the lines.

We couldn't keep Jared on the show for very long because the actor's voice had changed, and it seemed odd for a teenager to fixate on adult conspiracies. We hoped his brother, Trent, could carry on the imaginative DeWhite tradition, but in a different way from his brother.

The original story for the episode included a plot involving an ever-escalating "war of pranks" between Rodney Rathbone and Trent, but it was changed at the last minute before recording. The idea showed up later in "The Champ of the Camp" (album 45). The story also featured Mitch telling the kids how to escape from the trunk of a vehicle if they were ever kidnapped (inspired by *The Worst Case Scenario Survival Guide Handbook*). Mitch would later employ this knowledge in the finale of "Here Today, Gone Tomorrow."

Episode Information

510: For the Fun of It
Original Air Date: 3/1/03
Writer: Torry Martin
Sound Designer: Allen Hurley
Scripture: Ecclesiastes 3:1-2
Theme: Having fun
Summary: Talia Bassett decides to get back at her father by spending a week in Odyssey with her uncle—Wooton!

514: Room Enough for Two
Original Air Date: 3/29/03
Writer: April Higgins
Sound Designer: Bob Luttrell
Scripture: Philippians 2:4
Theme: Selfishness
Summary: Liz Horton is excited to see her older brother, Mark, come home, until Mark makes a surprise announcement—he's engaged.

515: B-TV: Behind the Scenes
Original Air Date: 5/3/03
Writers: Nathan Hoobler & John Fornof
Sound Designer: Jonathan Crowe
Scripture: Psalm 133; 1 Corinthians 12
Themes: Unity, working together
Summary: Alex Jefferson turns a microphone on the B-TV crew to see what happens behind the scenes.

516: Bassett Hounds
Original Air Date: 5/10/03
Writer: Torry Martin
Sound Designer: Allen Hurley
Scripture: Deuteronomy 7:7
Theme: Grace
Summary: Bernard Walton accompanies Wooton Bassett to Alaska for an unusual family reunion.

517: It's All About Me
Original Air Date: 5/17/03
Writers: Kathy Wierenga & Marshal Younger
Sound Designer: Bob Luttrell
Scripture: Matthew 6:1
Theme: Credit
Summary: Connie starts a Kids' Radio advice show with Robert Mitchell. At school, Trent DeWhite worries that he's getting credit for something he didn't do.

518: The Case of the Disappearing Hortons
Original Air Date: 5/24/03
Writer: Bob Hoose
Sound Designer: Bob Luttrell
Scripture: Galatians 6:2
Theme: Accepting help from others
Summary: When Liz Horton's entire family abruptly goes missing, it's up to the kids of Odyssey (and a few of their friends) to solve the case.

519: The Defining Moment
Original Air Date: 5/31/03
Writer: Marshal Younger
Sound Designer: Todd Busteed
Scripture: Luke 22:26
Theme: Heroism
Summary: After a disappointment in the last inning of a game, Marvin Washington looks to his cousin, Xavier, to show him how to be a hero.

520: The Mystery at Tin Flat

Original Air Date: 6/7/03
Writer: John Fornof
Sound Designer: Allen Hurley
Scripture: 1 Corinthians 12
Theme: Fitting in
Summary: The Washington family wins an all-expenses-paid vacation to nearby Tin Flat. But when they show up, the town is deserted.

522: All Things to All People

Original Air Date: 6/21/03
Writer: Bob Hoose
Sound Designer: Bob Luttrell
Scripture: Matthew 28:18-20
Theme: Evangelism
Summary: Seth Young counsels Aubrey Shepard on his radical method of evangelism, which causes Aubrey to question her effectiveness as a Christian.

523, 524, 525: Here Today, Gone Tomorrow? I, II, and III

Original Air Dates: 6/28/03, 7/5/03, & 7/12/03
Writer: Kathy Wierenga
Sound Designers: Allen Hurley & Jonathan Crowe
Scripture: Jeremiah 29:11
Theme: Figuring out God's will
Summary: Robert Mitchell has to make a decision about the FBI, but his investigating skills are challenged in a case involving Whit and an old nemesis.

Clubhouse magazine, March 2003, about the episode "Benefit of the Doubt"

Actor Corey Padnos, voice of Trent DeWhite.

Behind the Scenes: For the Fun of It

The morning of recording, the girl we had cast for Talia Bassett was suddenly unavailable. Fortunately, the day before we had auditioned actor Jade Angelica and written down that she would be perfect to play "a girl with an attitude." We called her, and she was able to come in at the last minute and rescue the role.

BTS: Room Enough for Two

April Higgins, a Focus on the Family Visitor Center employee and lifelong *Odyssey* fan, wrote "Room Enough for Two." The episode was written and recorded in the summer and fall of 2002 and scheduled to air on March 29, 2003. We couldn't have known it then, but that turned out to be a mere nine days after the ground war in Iraq began. Suddenly, parts of the show took on meanings we couldn't have foreseen. For example, reference is made to a fictional country called "Rakistan," which had been used years before in "A Name, Not a Number" (album 22). But now the name sounded like a combination of "Iraq" and "Afghanistan." We debated pulling the show out of sensitivity to the war, but decided instead to edit a few lines of dialogue that referred to soldiers dying.

BTS: B-TV: Behind the Scenes

In "B-TV: Behind the Scenes," the music for the Jones Lumberyard commercial with the lyrics "We like wood! Don't like plastic stuff!" was by a group called The Woodchucks. The song is also featured in "And the Glory" (album 17).

Cut Scenes

In the original opening scene of "Bassett Hounds," Wooton talked about his bunny slippers being different colors and able to discern his mood. This had to be cut for time, but we liked the dialogue so much that we used it in a later episode, "Stars in Our Eyes" (album 43).

Sound Bites

"Bassett Hounds" featured identical twins Wooton and Wellington Bassett, played by actors Jess Harnell and Dale Inghram, respectively, while Madison and Marlyse were both played by actor Cari Lyall.

Marvin Washington in "The Defining Moment"

My Take: Marshal Younger

The episode, "The Defining Moment" was inspired by the true story of Donnie Moore, a pitcher for the California Angels. In 1986, the Angels were beating the Boston Red Sox in the ninth inning and were one strike away from going to the World Series. The Angels had never gone to the Series before. Sadly for them, Donnie gave up a two-run homer on the next pitch, paving the way for the Red Sox to go to the World Series instead of the Angels.

Instead of moving on, Donnie Moore had a nervous breakdown and never pitched well again. Tragically, three years later, he committed suicide. I wanted to explore the "right" reaction to making a mistake, so "The Defining Moment" was created.

BTS: The Mystery at Tin Flat

An early version of this episode dealt primarily with the Washingtons on a road trip and their experiences along the way (stopping at the world's largest ball of twine, bugs getting smashed on the window, and the like). We abandoned this idea in favor of creating a parody about reality TV shows, which were the rage at the time.

In the studio, the actor playing Marvin mispronounced *The Tin Flat Gazette* as "Gazett-ee." We left it in because it was such a funny mispronunciation . . . and sounded like something a real kid would say.

My Take: Nathan Hoobler

I had a college class in live TV production where we edited our own TV programs together. Often the things that happened behind the scenes were far more interesting than

The *Odyssey* team (*from left*): Writers John Fornof, Kathy Wierenga, coordinator Chris McDonald, intern Sarah Evans, producer Marshal Younger, writer Nathan Hoobler, intern Lisa Samaniego, sound designers Jonathan Crowe, Nathan Jones, and (*front*) Bob Luttrell

the shows themselves. I thought it might make a fun episode to see what goes on behind the scenes of a big production, like B-TV. People could be running around in costumes, we could see Connie directing, and chaos would reign supreme! (See album cover art.) This was the inspiration for "B-TV: Behind the Scenes."

Sound Bites

The unique nature of "B-TV: Behind the Scenes" led to some innovations in the sound design. Typically, to get the sound of footsteps, the Foley artist walks or runs in place with the microphone positioned near their feet. Since there was so much walking in this show, designer Jonathan Crowe decided to take the mike with him as he walked or ran. He put together a rudimentary mobile mike stand and held it near his feet as he ran around the room acting out the various characters. On the subject of feet, if you listen closely to Wooton's footsteps, you'll find he's wearing "duck feet." They quack every time he walks!

We noticed a bit of unintended poignancy shows up in the final lines of the show. Immediately after we recorded the show, Travis Tedford, the actor who plays Alex Jefferson, moved away to Texas. Appropriately, the episode ends with the line, "The show is over and I'm almost out of tape. This is Alex Jefferson, signing off . . ."

Clubhouse magazine, April 2003, about the episode "B-TV Behind the Scenes"

Scripting Today, Recording Tomorrow

"Here Today, Gone Tomorrow" was planned as a two-part episode with part I called "Here Today" and part II called "Gone Tomorrow." It remained a two-part episode until only a few days before the recording. Upon reading the "final" script, some team members felt that the plot had too much about Connie and Mitch trying to make a decision about their relationship and that the mystery about identity theft wasn't properly developed. So, on the weekend before recording, the script went through several major revisions.

Both versions of the show involved an identity-theft scam orchestrated by Mr. Bennett Charles. His goal was to escape from prison. The first version of the show revealed this fact at the end, just before Mr. Charles was recaptured. However, in the later version, we included scenes that clearly showed Mr. Charles was planning his breakout. This change added an element of suspense: Would the *Odyssey* crew stop Charles from escaping?

Kathy Wierenga remembers, "Once again, the boys changed the episode from my sweet, simple love story to yet another saga of intrigue and mystery involving computers and technical dilemmas. These guys must buy their wives modems for Valentine's Day."

Suddenly our revised two-part episode became three. And just as suddenly, we had a problem because we only had studio time reserved for two episodes. The team scrambled to find a creative way to get all the material recorded. The solution was unprecedented. We recorded the episodes in two studios, with two directors, at the same time. This was the first (and only time so far) we've used a second recording unit for *Adventures in Odyssey*.

Character:

Marvin Washington

Quote: "This is a song I like to call 'The Man
I Used to Be.'"

Something you may not know about Marvin:
He manages a band called *Los Perros Frescos*

Album 41

In Hot Pursuit

All About "Something Blue"

Writer/director Kathy Wierenga, who joined the team in 1999, got married *after* she wrote but *before* she directed the show "Something Blue." As a result the show is written by "Kathy Wierenga" (her maiden name) and directed by "Kathy Buchanan" (her married name). Kathy remembers, "It was really interesting to be in the last couple weeks of planning my wedding while I was writing about Connie calling off hers. I remember Sean—my then fiancé, now husband—coming into the coffee shop where I was writing and finding me in tears because I just felt so bad for her!"

So do the fans. One of the most consistent requests we receive in letters and E-mails is for Robert Mitchell to come back. Kathy responds: "I tell them that it will happen when Ronald McDonald becomes a vegetarian, Starbucks runs out of money, and the Chicago Bulls win the Superbowl (and yes, I know they're a basketball team). Seriously, though, we wouldn't want to put fans through the torture of having Mitch return without him and Connie getting married. And we want Connie to stay single . . . at least for the time being."

Glenn Montjoy remembers "Something Blue" for a different reason: "This episode featured a scene where Agent Bourland's daughter, Michaela, puts on a grass skirt in anticipation of their trip to Hawaii. We didn't have any grass skirts sitting around Focus (they aren't dress code), so I had to improvise. I cut 50 yards of cassette tape into two-foot segments. Then I taped the ends around a strip of masking tape, put it around my waist and, well, danced. Thankfully, there weren't any cameras around that day!"

Episode Information

513: **Do or Diet**
Original Air Date: 3/22/03
Writer: Kathy Wierenga
Sound Designer: Bob Luttrell
Scripture: James 1:4
Themes: Patience, perseverance
Summary: Wooton Bassett, Bernard Walton, and Whit go on a diet to help Connie win a scholarship.

521: **Hindsight**
Original Air Date: 6/14/03
Writer: Marshal Younger
Sound Designer: Bob Luttrell
Scripture: Luke 10:27
Themes: The value of every life, the value of every moment
Summary: In the Room of Consequence, Liz Horton experiences the results of a single choice . . . backward.

526: **Seeing Red**
Original Air Date: 9/27/03
Writer: Marshal Younger
Sound Designer: Glenn Montjoy
Scripture: Matthew 5:23
Theme: Admitting you're wrong
Summary: Mandy Straussberg and Liz nearly destroy their friendship while fighting over Seth Young. Meanwhile Connie argues with Robert Mitchell, an event that prompts her to drive to Washington, D.C., to apologize in person.

Connie chases Mitch in "Something Blue"

527: **Black Clouds**
Original Air Date: 10/4/03
Writer: Bob Hoose
Sound Designer: Allen Hurley
Scripture: Job 31:4; Romans 8:28
Theme: God's presence in tough times
Summary: As Connie and Joanne's road trip to Washington continues, a raging storm forces them to stop at a roadside diner where they meet a runaway young girl and an unusual woman named Ethel.

528: The Taming of the Two
Original Air Date: 10/11/03
Writer: Nathan Hoobler
Sound Designer: Jonathan Crowe
Scripture: Ecclesiastes 4
Theme: Teamwork
Summary: Bart Rathbone wants to make his shop more sophisticated, and Malcolm Lear, a rival of Edwin Blackgaard, has a proposal for him.

529: The Mailman Cometh
Original Air Date: 10/18/03
Writer: Torry Martin
Sound Designer: Bob Luttrell
Scripture: Luke 12:48
Theme: With age and privilege comes responsibility
Summary: The Washington kids, Marvin and Tamika, are determined to show their mom that they should be allowed to do the same things as their older cousin, Xavier.

530: Silver Lining
Original Air Date: 10/25/03
Writer: Nathan Hoobler
Sound Designer: Todd Busteed
Scripture: Romans 12:17-21
Theme: The folly of revenge
Summary: On the way to Washington D.C., Connie and Joanne stop in West Virginia and are pulled into a mystery involving a bank robbery, a brave rescue, and an escaped convict.

531: Teacher's Pest
Original Air Date: 11/1/03
Writer: Torry Martin
Sound Designer: Bob Luttrell
Scripture: Luke 6:27-28
Theme: Loving your enemies
Summary: Max Hampton and Mandy Straussberg, who are complete opposites, must work together on a science project.

532: Pink Is Not My Color
Original Air Date: 11/8/03
Writer: Nathan Hoobler
Sound Designer: Allen Hurley
Scripture: Romans 8:38
Theme: Parental love, relationships
Summary: Connie's arrival in Virginia surprises Mitch—and, while staying with the Bourlands, she intercedes in a father-daughter conflict.

533, 534: Something Blue, I and II
Original Air Dates: 11/15/03 & 11/22/03
Writer: Kathy Wierenga
Sound Designer: Glenn Montjoy
Scripture: Luke 14:25-33
Theme: Counting the cost
Summary: When Connie gets the news that Mitch might leave for Europe in a few days, the two of them decide to get married immediately.

537: My Girl, Hallie
Original Air Date: 2/7/04
Writers: Bob Hoose & Nathan Hoobler
Sound Designer: Glenn Montjoy
Scripture: Habakkuk 2:19
Theme: Relationships with things versus relationships with people
Summary: "The Twilife Zone" skit tells the story of a boy named Joey Patrick who has an unusual friendship . . . with his computer.

My Take: Kathy Wierenga

For years I campaigned to have Whit and Bernard go on a diet! I thought it would be a hilarious show premise. I even put jokes in other scripts about Whit and Bernard gaining weight (which were usually cut before recording). When I finally got to write "Do or Diet," it almost felt like a letdown somehow since I had dreamed about doing it for so long.

Cut Scenes

"Hindsight" is a story told in reverse. We had talked about doing a "backward" episode for several years before figuring out exactly how to do it. An early draft of the show featured Norton Hollingsworth holding Liz Horton at gunpoint and accidentally shooting her. To avoid the intense violence, we instead had Liz slip on the freshly mopped floor.

Goof Alert!

In "Seeing Red," Liz states that Mandy Straussberg has brown hair. But in "Sunset Bowlawater (album 34)," Crackers says Mandy is a blonde. Then again, Crackers is just a goldfish . . . and people do sometimes dye their hair.

Cover art for *The Big Picture* (album 35): A blond hair day for Mandy is only the beginning of her troubles.

My Take: Marshal Younger

After the massive Novacom story arc, we wanted to avoid epic sagas for a while, but we still wanted to explore smaller character-based story arcs. "Seeing Red" introduced three short story arcs: a cross-country journey that would finally resolve Connie and Mitch's relationship; the significance of a valuable compass; and a rift between Mandy and Liz. The Mandy/Liz story arc, which lasted over several episodes, gave us the chance to explore the theme of conflict between friends—and how to properly resolve it.

Behind the Scenes: Seeing Red

In album 21, *Wish You Were Here*, our cross-country trip with Bernard and Eugene featured episode titles that were based on numbers: "First-Hand Experience," "Second Thoughts," etc. For Connie and Joanne's cross-country journey, we used colors in the titles, beginning with "Seeing Red" (though the show was originally called "Red in the Face").

Sound Bites

The sound effect of the lightning strike that hits the diner in "Black Clouds" was recorded by Dave Arnold nearly 10 years before this episode was produced. Dave was at home when a storm rolled in, so he took the opportunity to record the sound of it. To his surprise, lightning struck just across the street. Dave originally used this effect in the 1996 *Radio Theatre* production of *A Christmas Carol*. It has been used in several other *Radio Theatre* productions since then, including a component of the stone table crack in *The Lion, the Witch, and the Wardrobe* (1999).

Sound Bites

"The Taming of the Two" may have been the first *Odyssey* show to be inspired by an audition. While looking for new mothers and fathers for the show, the team came upon actor James Bray who exuded a broad Shakespearean style performance. Producer Marshal Younger was inspired. He wrote down the phrase "Dueling Shakespeares" on the audition sheet, and we soon went to work writing a show about a rival for Edwin Blackgaard.

BTS: The Mailman Cometh

In "The Mailman Cometh," one of the movies that the Washingtons consider seeing is titled *Me and My Honey*. It's a sequel to the *Betsy the Bumblebee* movie that was featured in the episode "Have You No Selpurcs?" (album 9).

Cut Scenes

The story that became the episode "Silver Lining" evolved over several drafts, with many changes and adjustments. An early version featured Connie charmed by a young man who eventually turned out to be a bank robber. Connie was faced with the dilemma of whether or not to turn him in. Another version of the script featured Connie and Joanne Allen in the bank when the actual robbery occurred.

Marvin and Tamika Washington in "The Mailman Cometh"

Sound Bites

To get the sound of the near drowning in "Silver Lining," actress Katie Leigh brought a glass of water into the studio and purposefully coughed and choked on it for several minutes. During postproduction, sound designer Todd Busteed used a special technique to make her voice sound as if it were actually underwater.

Sound Bites

Actor Florence Stanley played Mrs. Sweeny in "Teacher's Pest." Florence was well-known for her roles as an overbearing relative or neighbor in such programs as *Barney Miller* (1975–1977), *My Two Dads* (1987–1990), and *Dinosaurs* (1991–1994). Sadly, this *Adventures in Odyssey* program was her last work, as she passed away shortly after recording the show.

BTS: Pink Is Not My Color

"Pink Is Not My Color" is the only episode to show us Agent Bourland's home life. It was one way for Connie to see what her life would be like as an FBI agent's wife. In "Something Blue," Connie gets another hint of what her life might be like married to Mitch. We thought a dose of reality would help bring their relationship to an appropriate conclusion.

Hallie Unleashed

"My Girl Hallie" was unique in several ways. Our announcer, Chris Anthony, played Joey's mother in the show, while her daughter, Kelsey, played Mary.

On the production side, sound designer Glenn Montjoy remembers the challenge of creating a computer voice: "To get Hallie to sound appropriately electronic, I pieced her lines together word by word using a different take for each word. As Hallie became more human, I used larger and larger pieces of each take, which made her sound more natural."

The ending to the show was also unusual. We recorded two endings (one more sinister and another more positive) and then we let fans vote for their favorite on WhitsEnd.org—the official Web site. After more than five thousand votes, the positive ending won by a very narrow margin—less than one hundred votes. Both endings are included on the album.

Katie Leigh serves ice cream at Whit's End in Colorado Springs.

"My Girl Hallie" voting Web page

Album 42
No Way Out

The Creation of "No Way Out"

"No Way Out" began with two questions: (1) How would we approach an action show featuring the father/son duo of Jason and Whit? And (2) What if we began a show with Jason waking up in a room with no windows or doors?

Producer Marshal Younger remembers, "The whole team wrote the outline together, which is something we don't often do. It fell together so quickly and painlessly, and it was a remarkable example of teamwork." Writer John Fornof says, "Usually outline sessions have periods of head-banging-on-the-wall moments where you're trying to figure out plot points. For this show, the ideas just flowed without stopping."

Our first outline of the show featured Jason trapped in a hidden room with a young boy holding him hostage. As Jason tried to convince the boy to let him out, Whit followed clues to find his son.

As we discussed the idea, we decided that Whit should be the one who was trapped while Jason looked for him. We also decided that it might be too unrealistic for a young boy to hold a sick man hostage, so we made it a sympathetic mentally challenged man instead. The character of Lester was born.

Episode Information

535, 536: **Living in the Gray, I and II**
Original Air Dates: 1/24/04 & 1/31/04
Writer: Marshal Younger
Sound Designer: Allen Hurley
Scripture: Luke 15:23-24
Theme: God's unconditional love
Summary: After the tumultuous events surrounding her near-wedding, Connie stays in Washington, D.C., to meet up with an old friend—Jimmy Barclay!

538: **Stubborn Streaks**
Original Air Date: 2/14/04
Writer: Nathan Hoobler
Sound Designer: Jonathan Crowe
Scripture: Ephesians 4:15
Theme: Admitting you're wrong
Summary: Bernard Walton is shocked when he seems to be losing his customers. At the same time, Liz Horton has to review one of Mandy Straussberg's plays and is worried that her rift with Mandy will taint the article.

539: **Called On in Class**
Original Air Date: 2/21/04
Writer: Bob Hoose
Sound Designer: Todd Busteed
Scripture: John 16:33
Theme: Fear
Summary: Trent DeWhite has to give his oral report in class . . . and he imagines all sorts of disasters that might occur.

540: **The Girl in the Sink**
Original Air Date: 2/28/04
Writer: Bob Hoose
Sound Designer: Bob Luttrell
Theme: Being used by God
Summary: Young Bernard Walton meets a huge man named Ezekiel, who just might be an angel.

541: **Bernard and Saul**
Original Air Date: 3/6/04
Writer: Nathan Hoobler
Sound Designer: Allen Hurley
Scripture: 1 Samuel 9-11, 14-18, 24; Proverbs 14:30
Theme: Jealousy
Summary: Bernard tells the biblical story of Saul and his bitter rivalry with David.

542: **Eggshells**
Original Air Date: 4/24/04
Writer: Marshal Younger
Sound Designer: Bob Luttrell
Scripture: Isaiah 43:4
Themes: Loving others, being sensitive
Summary: Connie returns to Odyssey after her long trip, and the crew at Whit's End isn't sure how to act around her since she's grieving over the end of her relationship with Mitch.

543: **Nothing But the Half Truth**
Original Air Date: 5/1/04
Writer: Torry Martin
Sound Designer: Jonathan Crowe
Scripture: Proverbs 19:9
Theme: Half truths
Summary: Wellington Bassett calls his twin brother, Wooton, for a bizarre favor—he wants Wooton to pretend to be him for a business meeting.

544: **Split Ends**
Original Air Date: 5/8/04
Writer: Kathy Buchanan
Sound Designer: Bob Luttrell
Scripture: Genesis 33
Theme: Holding grudges
Summary: Mandy and Liz are approached by professional agents and find that they will be competing against each other in a modeling contest.

545: Something's Got to Change

Original Air Date: 5/15/04
Writer: Bob Hoose
Sound Designer: Allen Hurley
Scripture: 1 Corinthians 10:24
Theme: Sacrifice
Summary: The Washington family considers moving across town so that Ed can be closer to work.

546: No Way Out

Original Air Date: 5/22/04
Writer: John Fornof
Sound Designer: Allen Hurley
Scripture: 1 John 4:18
Theme: True love casts out fear.
Summary: Whit finds himself trapped in a room with no doors or windows. Meanwhile, "Marvelous" Marvin Washington investigates strange happenings around his house.

547: No Way In

Original Air Date: 5/29/04
Writer: John Fornof
Sound Designer: Glenn Montjoy
Scripture: 1 John 4:18
Theme: True love casts out fear.
Summary: Whit's situation worsens while his son Jason searches for him with Marvin's help.

Clubhouse magazine, February 2004, reveals more about the episode "Eggshells"

Behind the Scenes: Living in the Gray

"Living in the Gray," the last of Connie's road-trip episodes, was the first show with Jimmy Barclay since "It's a Pokenberry Christmas" (album 31) in 1997. The outline of this show was three parts instead of two and featured a subplot where Jimmy almost joined the Army.

My Take: Marshal Younger

"Living in the Gray" generated a lot of mail from listeners asking why Jimmy compromised his beliefs. While it was a surprise to see Jimmy working for a slanderous tabloid, I hoped that we could show what sometimes happens when people lose their way spiritually . . . and how it's never too late to come home and ask forgiveness. The final scene with Jimmy and George was an intentional parallel to "The Prodigal, Jimmy" (album 4) and even featured a few of the same lines. The first scene with Jimmy, George, Connie, and Felicia (Jimmy's less-than-impressive girlfriend) is one of my all-time favorite scenes, brilliantly acted by everyone including Kat Cressida as Felicia.

BTS: Stubborn Streaks

The germ of the idea for "Stubborn Streaks" began with the question, "What's the worst possible thing that could happen to Bernard?" We figured that having to be very polite and smile all the time would fit the bill. This plot-point ended up being a rather

small part of the final episode as we explored the more important theme of knowing when to admit you're wrong.

BTS: Called On in Class

Through Trent DeWhite's wild imagination we were able to explore some of the history of *Odyssey*. Earlier episodes (such as "The Ill-Gotten Deed," album 6) had mentioned the massive floods that hit the town at various times. This show explored what happened to the town during those floods.

My Take: Bob Hoose

The concept behind "Called On in Class" started with the question, "Could we do an entire episode inside someone's head?" I love writing broad character situations, and it was fun to hear Trent's wild imaginings of what terrifying things would happen when he gave an oral report.

David Griffin recording "Living in the Gray"

BTS: The Girl in the Sink

We spent hours as a team trying to figure out the logistics of the climactic scene on the cliff in "The Girl in the Sink." How could we explain the scene to listeners through sound only? We eventually decided to illustrate the scene on the back of the album cover so people who bought the album would have a visual of the scene in case our sound effects didn't quite communicate the full picture.

Cut Scenes

In "Bernard and Saul," a scene in which Saul ordered the killing of the priests of Nob was cut. Though it was biblical, we were concerned about the impact that such a violent action would have on our listeners.

BTS: Bernard and Saul

"Bernard and Saul" features an original song composed by Focus on the Family staffer Carol Eidson and scored by John Doryk. Among the singers were *Odyssey* coordinator Chris McDonald and *Odyssey* brand manager Shari Martin.

The back cover of *No Way Out*

"Saul's Song" (Based on 1 Samuel 18)

> Saul has slain his thousands
> As our mighty king.
> But David slew tens of thousands;
> Glory to him bring!

My Take: Nathan Hoobler

"Bernard and Saul" overlaps the story of Saul and David as told in "Isaac the True Friend" (*The Lost Episodes*) and "The Shepherd and the Giant" (album 3), though those stories were told from David's and Jonathan's perspectives. Many of the same actors played roles they had previously played, including Walker Edmiston as Samuel and Gary Reed as David. I used the exact dialog from "Isaac the True Friend" in one scene—where Saul throws his spear at David.

Sound Bites

Actor Pete Renaday played the Old Testament Saul in "Bernard and Saul." He played the New Testament Saul in "Saint Paul: The Man from Tarsus" (album 23). Pete has played several saints for us, including Saint Paul and Saint Patrick.

BTS: Eggshells

The movie that Connie and June Kendall watch in "Eggshells" is a *subtle parody of the 1942 movie Casablanca.* One character—played by *Odyssey* sound designer Rob Jorgensen—says, "We'll always have Pueblo," a reference to a town south of Colorado Springs.

Sound Bites

In "Eggshells," Connie says that when she was in Washington, D.C., the Lincoln Memorial statue wasn't much for conversation. However, in "A Single Vote" (album 3), host Chris Anthony had no trouble talking to Lincoln.

Cut Scenes

We recorded two versions of the ending of "Nothing But the Half Truth." In the unused version, Wellington did the "Hokey Pokey" instead of "The Chicken Dance."

Sound Bites

The performance of "The Chicken Dance" in "Nothing But the Half Truth" was recorded with a group of Focus on the Family Institute students. The Institute is a college program at Focus that educates students about healthy family values and the Christian worldview. The students were more than willing to do the dance for the microphone.

BTS: Something's Got to Change

When discussing ideas for the Washington family, we decided upon a plot where they would have to move across town and deal with the troubles of living in a new house. Nathan Hoobler wrote an episode where the family made the move. But after reading the script, the team realized we needed an entire episode explaining the family's reasons for moving. The team liked the second story—eventually titled "Something's Got to Change"—better than the first show about the move itself, so the original episode was abandoned.

Sound Bites

Whit's cell phone in "No Way Out" plays "Toccata and Fugue in D Minor" by Johann Sebastian Bach (1685–1750).

My Take: John Fornof

My first draft of "No Way In" featured a scene where Marvin and Tamika Washington followed a trail of Cheese Doodle crumbs with a black light. I was sure that the crumbs would glow under the rays of the glowing, purple light, but I wanted to test to make sure. So my family and I ate a big ol' bag of cheese puffs, and I waved the black light over our fingers and clothes. Our arms glowed, our teeth glowed, our white microwave glowed, but to my astonishment, the cheese puff crumbs didn't glow at all! Bummer. I changed the script to be . . . uh . . . food-accurate.

BTS: No Way In

In the final wrap-up scene of "No Way In," Whit mentions that Jason had to take a last-minute trip to New Mexico. This was a setup for a series of Last Chance Detectives episodes that aired in the *Adventures in Odyssey* time-slot that summer. The first show, "The Day Ambrosia Stood Still," featured Jason.

Jonathan Crowe "Kicks the Bucket"

So often we find that the real thing won't make the sound effect we want. For example, to get the window-washing sounds in "Stubborn Steaks," I looked high and low for a real squeegee. After I finally found one, it simply wouldn't make that perfect "squeak" sound that I wanted. So, I resorted to the old standby—a paper towel and Windex—to get the right sound.

To get the sound of Bart bursting through the door and knocking over Bernard's cleaning supplies, I brought in a metal bucket and gave it a good strong kick. Plastic doesn't have the same *oomph*!

Jonathan Crowe had to "kick the bucket" for "Stubborn Streaks."

Jonathan washing a window to make a sound effect

Album 43

Along for the Ride

The New Switcheroo

"Stars in Our Eyes," "Sunday Morning Scramble," and "Potential Possibilities" were written in an unusual way. Marshal Younger was working on a show about heroes, Nathan Hoobler was working on a show about getting ready for church, and Kathy Buchanan was working on a show about Connie. The writers realized that he or she was more interested in another person's story, so they all switched shows. Marshal started working on the Connie show, Nathan took over on the heroes show, and Kathy finished writing the church show. After each wrote a draft, the stories were switched again. So all three writers created pieces of each episode.

"Sunday Morning Scramble" was Nathan Jones's first production for *Adventures in Odyssey*. (Nathan had previously worked on several *Radio Theatre* series.) Because the actors read faster than expected, the show came in about five minutes too short. Rather than fill the show with commercials, we recorded extra scenes for the closing with Bart Rathbone running amuck in the Washingtons' house. Walker Edmiston took our ideas for the final scenes and ad-libbed dialogue as Bart on a destructive spree. A number of episodes after this one also featured scenes during the closing credits.

Episode Information

548: Sounds Like a Mystery
Original Air Date: 10/2/04
Writer: John Fornof
Sound Designer: Rob Jorgensen
Scripture: Proverbs 12:22
Theme: Deception
Summary: Odyssey is abuzz when a national treasure—a scale model of the Statue of Liberty—comes to town . . . and promptly gets stolen!

549: Think on These Things
Original Air Date: 10/9/04
Writers: Nathan Hoobler & Marshal Younger
Sound Designer: Allen Hurley
Scripture: 2 Corinthians 10:5
Theme: Purity
Summary: Marvin Washington and Trent DeWhite put the Imagination Station to some unexpected uses—to cheat and to get revenge.

550: Fairy Tal-E-Vision
Original Air Date: 10/16/04
Writer: John Fornof
Sound Designer: Bob Luttrell
Scripture: Galatians 6:7-8
Theme: The consequences of sin
Summary: Connie, Jason Whittaker, and Kids' Radio tell about life in Fairy Tale Land.

551: Stars in Our Eyes
Original Air Date: 10/23/04
Writers: Nathan Hoobler, Kathy Buchanan, & Marshal Younger
Sound Designer: Glenn Montjoy
Scripture: 1 Samuel 16:7
Theme: Heroes
Summary: Whit, Connie, Wooton Bassett, and Tom Riley write a TV commercial to tell the benefits of Whit's End.

552: Sunday Morning Scramble
Original Air Date: 10/30/04
Writers: Kathy Buchanan & Marshal Younger
Sound Designer: Nathan Jones
Scripture: Luke 10:38-42
Theme: Worship
Summary: The Washingtons try to get to church on time, which leads to chaos in their home.

553: Potential Possibilities
Original Air Date: 11/04/04
Writers: Marshal Younger, Nathan Hoobler, & Kathy Buchanan
Sound Designer: Glenn Montjoy
Scripture: 1 Timothy 4:14
Theme: Using God's gifts
Summary: When Trent is put in the gifted class at school, he wonders if he'll survive his first week. Meanwhile, Aubrey Shepard learns that she has a real talent with horses.

554: Call Me if You Care
Original Air Date: 11/13/04
Writer: Nathan Hoobler
Sound Designer: Rob Jorgensen
Scripture: Matthew 18:21-22
Theme: Forgiveness
Summary: Connie's cell phone is getting unusual messages from someone named Cindy who is desperate to reach "William."

555: True Calling
Original Air Date: 11/20/04
Writer: Bob Hoose
Sound Designer: Allen Hurley
Scripture: Numbers 14
Theme: Fear of the future
Summary: Liz Horton tries to persuade Irving and Solly, two men from a local nursing home, to come out of retirement to perform a magic act.

556: . . . And That's the Truth

Original Air Date: 12/4/04
Writer: Nathan Hoobler
Sound Designer: Glenn Montjoy
Scripture: Ephesians 4:15
Theme: Speaking the truth in love
Summary: Tamika Washington takes her Sunday school lesson on honesty very seriously. At J & J Antiques, Jack Allen struggles to tell his new employee a difficult truth.

557: A Lamb's Tale

Original Air Date: 12/11/04
Writer: Marshal Younger
Sound Designer: Rob Jorgensen
Theme: Sacrifice
Summary: The Odyssey crew is involved in six interwoven stories about Christmas. It all begins when Tamika gives away her toy lamb for Christmas . . .

558: A Glass Darkly

Original Air Date: 1/5/05
Writers: John Fornof & Nathan Hoobler
Sound Designer: Bob Luttrell
Scripture: Isaiah 57:8; 1 Corinthians 13:12
Theme: God's ways
Summary: Trent finally gets the chance to audition for the Chamber Music Society, but things keep getting in the way, despite his prayers to God.

559: The Coolest Dog

Original Air Date: 1/22/05
Writer: Marshal Younger
Sound Designer: Rob Jorgensen
Scripture: Proverbs 13:10
Theme: Pride
Summary: Wooton shoots a documentary about Marvin's new band, "The Cool Dogs."

My Take: John Fornof

Rob Jorgensen repeatedly said that he wanted to do an episode with just sound effects and no dialogue. (Apparently, Paul McCusker and Dave Arnold had toyed with this idea too.) I knew that we could probably never get away with that, but I thought we could do a *scene* of sound with no dialogue. So the idea for "Sounds Like a Mystery" started from a scene of sound—where Whit's End was robbed—and expanded from there.

Cut Scenes

Many sketches in "Fairy Tal-E-Vision" were cut to save time, including a hospital scene with the Three Blind Mice and a police drama involving Goldilocks.

Behind the Scenes: Fairy Tal-E-Vision

The germ of the idea for "Fairy Tal-E-Vision" was a fun two-minute news feature we'd done about Humpty Dumpty. John Fornof wrote an entire episode called "Fairy Tale Action News," but we thought the news format was too limiting. We broadened the concept to include all sorts of fairy tale TV programs.

BTS: Stars in Our Eyes

"Stars in Our Eyes" is the first episode to feature character Davey Holcomb since episode 1, "Whit's Flop" (album 1), though he is played by a different actor.

BTS: Potential Possibilities

"Potential Possibilities" began as a show about Connie starting college and learning a lesson about responsibility when she allows some of her friends into Whit's End late at night. As we outlined the show, we realized we weren't ready for Connie to go to college quite yet, so we changed the character to Aubrey Shepard. However, once we made the switch, we realized that she had already dealt with a very similar situation in "Twisting Pathway" (album 38). So we brainstormed an entirely different plot where Aubrey learned about living up to her potential. In the end, the show that began as Connie going to college and learning about responsibility contained none of those elements!

My Take: John Fornof

"Potential Possibilities" contains the character Mrs. Nietchew. This character's name came from a traumatic incident at my cubicle when writer Kathy Wierenga deftly crawled beside my chair and swiped one of my shoes. I didn't even notice until I had to take a restroom break. Since Kathy's pranks were well-known around the office, I had a pretty good guess on who the culprit was. I called the operator at Focus on the Family and asked her to do a page over the intercom system throughout the entire campus. Without a second thought, the operator paged: "Kathy Need-shoe, please call extension 1234. Kathy Need-shoe."

BTS: Potential Possibilities

In "Potential Possibilities," Tom Riley tells Aubrey that he was part of a Vaudeville act. Walker Edmiston performed on Vaudeville and actually wrote an entire act for Tom for the ending of the program. Sadly, the act itself was cut for time. Here is how his act would have gone:

> TOM: Okay, now we'd come out on stage, the two of us. He'd start talking and he'd say, "Well, how do you feel this morning?"

And I'd say, "Well, I feel better this morning, but I always feel bad when I feel better because I know I'm gonna feel worse."

And then, you have to have a theme, so we'd talk about hometowns. And he'd say, "Where'd you come from?"

And I'd say, "Well, you see, I come from a poke and a plumb town. When you're driving through, you poke your head out the window, you're plumb outta town!"

And then the town is growing! They put in one of those new freeways. About the only way to get across is to be born on the other side.

With my car, I don't have to wear glasses. I have a prescription windshield.

In our town, there's only two kinds of parking—"illegal" and "no."

I pulled over to the side of the road and a passerby said, "Have a flat?" and I said, "No thanks, I just had one."

BTS: Call Me if You Care

The idea for "Call Me if You Care" came from Paul McCusker, who was getting increasingly urgent messages on his cell phone from someone who clearly had the wrong number. The title was a reference to the movie *Catch Me if You Can* (2002).

My Take: Bob Hoose

The night before our first read through of "True Calling," I was trying to figure out what to do with the climax of the show. My original version had Whit telling Mandy Straussberg not to be afraid, and it seemed *soooo* boring. In the middle of the night, I had the idea for Whit (that creative mastermind) to use the old reverse-psychology bit on Irving and Solly. I was very pleased with the change it made. Whit seemed more cleverly Whit-like and the device tied the two plots together.

Sound Bites

"And That's the Truth" introduced P. J., an apathetic teenager. Every time he showed up around Odyssey, P. J. was working in a different place. In this show, he worked at J & J Antiques. In "A Time for Action" (album 46), he was at a convenience store. In "Buddy Guard" (album 49), he worked at radio station Odyssey 105. P. J. was played by actor Scott Menville.

BTS: A Lamb's Tale

The idea for the incident that set off this episode—Tamika Washington giving away the doll—came from Nathan Hoobler's sister Emily. She gave a favorite doll to a charity after giving it a tearful farewell kiss.

Sound Bites

The script for the food fight scene of "A Glass Darkly" indicated that it should sound like "The Lord of the Rings with Jell-O." Some of the sounds of Jell-O splats and squishes were vegetables originally recorded for the mud ball war in "The Buck Starts Here" (album 33). Later in the episode, Wooton Bassett showed his creative side by inventing a riding vacuum cleaner for Marvin Washington (see album cover art).

Sound Bites

"The Coolest Dog" is one of the few *Odyssey* episodes with all live (not synthesized) music. Sound designer Rob Jorgensen rented a cello from a local music store and borrowed an electric drum set. He asked a couple of fine musicians to come into the studio and play as horribly as they could. Believe it or not, there is a skill to composing bad music! Then Rob added a really terrific saxophonist and a keyboardist, and the band was complete.

Sound Bites

Wooton can play the song "Camptown Races" on any instrument. In "The Coolest Dog," he played it on the saxophone. In "B-TV: Behind the Scenes" (album 40), he played it on the piano. In "For Better or for Worse" (album 44), he played it on the organ. In "Odyssey Sings!" (album 45), he played it on the banjo.

My Take: Marshal Younger

In "The Coolest Dog," the final song sung by Marvin ("I'm the Sorry Man") was inspired by an old Steve Allen [1921–2000] comedy routine where he read the words of a pop song out loud. Disco songs, in particular, sound so ridiculous when they are simply read, with all the *yeah*'s and *baby*'s.

Joy Smoker with actor Katie Leigh, voice of Connie

Adventures in Odyssey Grants Wishes

The *Adventures in Odyssey* team has received several special visitors through the Make-a-Wish Foundation. The foundation grants "wishes" to children with life-threatening medical conditions, and three children have wished to visit *Adventures in Odyssey* headquarters in Colorado Springs.

In September 1998, our first visitor was 10-year-old Jason Townsend. Jason loved listening to *Odyssey* episodes featuring the character of super-spy Jason Whittaker. Interestingly enough, the actor who plays the character is *Townsend* Coleman. Townsend came to meet young Jason, and the two of them recorded a special *Odyssey* scene together.

In 2004, first-grader Anita Litwiller came for a visit with her family. Anita's favorite character, Wooton, made a special phone call to her. Amazingly, both Anita and Wooton loved pepperoni pizza! Sound designer Rob Jorgensen showed Anita how to create sound effects for the shows.

Joy Smoker, a nine-year-old from Pennsylvania, stopped in for a visit in 2005. Joy recorded a special "Candid Conversations" live with Katie Leigh, the actress who plays Connie. Joy was surprised to find that Connie is a little older than she sounds. Afterward, Joy and family visited Dr. Dobson in his office.

Jason Townsend, 1988

Anita Litwiller with Whit at Whit's End

Imagination Station Adventures

The following people have taken a trip in Whit's greatest invention.

Episode	Station Users
The Imagination Station, I and II	Digger Digwillow
A Prisoner for Christ	Nicholas Adamsworth
Elijah, I and II	Jack Davis and Robyn Jacobs
Lincoln, I and II	Jimmy Barclay
Back to Bethlehem, I, II, and III	Eugene and Connie
By Dawn's Early Light	Curt Stevens and Lucy Cunningham-Schultz
Isaac the True Friend	Isaac Morton and Sam Johnson
Dobson Comes to Town	Dr. James Dobson
The Star, I and II	Eugene and Connie
Isaac the Chivalrous	Isaac Morton
Moses: The Passover, I and II	Jimmy Barclay and George Barclay
Columbus: The Grand Voyage	Lawrence Hodges
The Mortal Coil, I and II	John Whittaker, Tom Riley, and Eugene
An Adventure in Bethany, I and II	Lucy Cunningham-Schultz and John Whittaker
A Time for Christmas	Courtney Vincent and John Whittaker
The Potential in Elliot	Sam Johnson
Saint Paul: The Man from Tarsus	Sam Johnson and Rodney Rathbone
Saint Paul: Set Apart by God	Sam Johnson, Rodney Rathbone, Jason Whittaker, and Eugene Meltsner
A Touch of Healing, I and II	Jenny Roberts and Zachary Sellers
The Time Has Come	Eugene
Checkmate	Eugene
The Decision	John Whittaker and Jason Whittaker

Episode	Station Users
Christmas Around the World, I and II	Erica Clark, Sam Johnson, Tom Riley, and Eugene
When in Doubt . . . Pray!	Mandy Straussberg and Eugene
Hide and Seek	Kevin
The Tower	Nathaniel Graham and Eugene
Blackgaard's Revenge, I and II	Aubrey Shepard, Connie, and John Whittaker
A Look Back, I and II	Phil Lollar
The Big Deal, I and II	Aubrey Shepard
Breaking Point	Alex Jefferson
The Black Veil, I and II	John Whittaker
Exit	No one
The American Revelation, I and II	Marvin Washington
Think on These Things	Marvin Washington, Trent DeWhite, and John Whittaker
A Most Intriguing Question	Eugene
A Most Surprising Answer	Eugene
A Most Extraordinary Conclusion	John Whittaker, Connie, Bernard Walton, Katrina Shanks, and Eugene
Bernard and Jeremiah	Marvin Washington and Bernard Walton
Run-of-the-Mill Miracle	Grady McKay
Something Significant	Trent DeWhite
The Imagination Station, Revisited, I and II	Kelly

The Tough Kid: Grady McKay

"A Lamb's Tale" introduced the character of Grady McKay. Grady was based on a boy that Torry Martin knew from church, and his story became an ongoing plot. Producer Marshal Younger imagined Grady as someone who was always getting into fights with kids who were bigger than he was.

During his audition, actor Jordan Orr proved he could perform scenes with genuine anger and was chosen for the part. We thought that the Grady character would have a lot of anger to him. Jordan's real-life sister (Ashley Rose Orr) played Lindy in "Black Clouds" (album 41). The character of Samantha McKay was played by actor Mary Mouser. Mary played the title character on the TV series *Me, Eloise* (2006).

Actor Jordan Orr, voice of Grady McKay

Character: Eugene
Quote: "Greetings and salutations!"
Something you may not know about Eugene:
He invented a solar dishwasher.

Album 44

Eugene Returns!

Eugene Meltsner: How to Bring Him Back?

Just how should Eugene return to Odyssey? After being gone such a long time, we knew the explanation had to be *very* interesting.

Our very first plan featured Eugene returning dramatically at the end of the Novacom saga to participate in Tom Riley's trial. An outline of "Expect the Worst" (album 38) was written with Eugene testifying about Novacom's evil plan, but that didn't work out.

After Novacom ended and still no Eugene, we brainstormed several versions of the show where Connie would encounter Eugene during her travels across the country (album 41). In one scenario, he was hiding at the Barclays' house in Pokenberry Falls, still working on his research. But when Connie returned from her journey (with no Eugene in tow), we decided that Whit should be hiding Eugene in Odyssey instead.

But why hadn't Eugene contacted the folks in Odyssey for so long? Two ideas emerged. In the first, Eugene felt guilty about what had happened with Novacom and didn't want to return. In the second, Eugene had continued his brain-wave study with the National Institutes of Health (NIH) in Washington, D.C., and tried a final experiment on himself, erasing his own memory. The final episodes were a blend of these ideas.

There was one final concern: The reintroduction of the radio-waves concept from the Novacom saga, along with the technological experiments to save Eugene's memory, filled us with some dread. We worried that listeners would roll their eyes and groan, "Not *that* again." So we purposefully centered the episodes on Connie, Tom, and Bernard Walton to help lighten what could have been some very heavy scenes. We counted on the characters' good humor and mutual affection to carry the weight of the plot—and they did!

Episode Information

560: The Present Long Ago
Original Air Date: 1/29/05
Writer: Bob Hoose
Sound Designer: Jonathan Crowe
Scripture: Job 42:2
Theme: Getting advice
Summary: Max Hampton demands that Trent DeWhite give up the key to the science lab . . . or else.

561: Lost by a Nose
Original Air Date: 2/5/05
Writer: John Fornof
Sound Designer: Allen Hurley
Scripture: 1 Samuel 16:7
Theme: True beauty
Summary: Liz Horton wants to expose the Little Miss Odyssey beauty pageant as a sham. One problem: She must enter the contest to bring it down.

562: The Last "I Do"
Original Air Date: 2/12/05
Writer: Leilani Wells
Sound Designer: Bob Luttrell
Scripture: Acts 4:29-30
Themes: Standing up for what's right, the story of Saint Valentine
Summary: Kids' Radio tells the story about a priest who defies a third-century Roman emperor who outlaws marriage.

563: Tuesdays with Wooton
Original Air Date: 2/19/05
Writer: Torry Martin
Sound Designer: Glenn Montjoy
Theme: Relationships
Summary: Every Tuesday, Wooton Bassett meets with a mysterious kid who seems to be hiding something.

564: A Most Intriguing Question
Original Air Date: 4/2/05
Writers: Paul McCusker & Nathan Hoobler
Sound Designer: Glenn Montjoy
Theme: Curiosity
Summary: Whit is doing secret experiments in the Imagination Station. Is that why a government agent is watching Whit's End? Connie, Bernard Walton, and Tom Riley take action to find out what's going on.

565: A Most Surprising Answer
Original Air Date: 4/9/05
Writers: Paul McCusker & Marshal Younger
Sound Designer: Allen Hurley
Theme: Friendship
Summary: Whit has to break the news to Connie, Bernard, and Tom about Eugene's memory loss . . . and his risky plan to fix it.

566: A Most Extraordinary Conclusion
Original Air Date: 4/16/05
Writers: Paul McCusker & Marshal Younger
Sound Designer: Glenn Montjoy
Theme: The power of prayer
Summary: Eugene's closest friends take drastic steps to bring him to a full recovery.

567: Two Friends and a Truck
Original Air Date: 4/23/05
Writer: Nathan Hoobler
Sound Designer: Allen Hurley
Scripture: 1 Peter 3:9
Theme: Mercy
Summary: Eugene panics when he accidentally damages Bernard's prized truck.

568: **The Power of One**

Original Air Date: 4/30/05
Writers: John Fornof & Marshal Younger
Sound Designer: Bob Luttrell
Scripture: Matthew 19:26
Theme: The power of God

Summary: Kids' Radio presents a boxing match between David and Goliath, testimonials from users of an amazing treatment called the Pray Way, and Edwin Blackgaard's rhyming tale of Samson.

569: **The Invisible Dog**

Original Air Date: 5/7/05
Writers: John Fornof & Marshal Younger
Sound Designer: Nathan Jones
Scripture: Matthew 20:34
Theme: Compassion

Summary: Eugene teaches at Odyssey Middle School as a substitute. Meanwhile, Lester shows everyone his new pet—an invisible dog.

570, 571: **For Better or for Worse, I and II**

Original Air Dates: 5/14/05 & 5/21/05
Writer: Kathy Buchanan
Sound Designers: Bob Luttrell, Glenn Montjoy, & Jonathan Crowe
Scripture: Proverbs 16:9
Theme: Competition

Summary: Eugene and Katrina finally plan to have a proper wedding. But the two wedding coordinators (Connie and Millie Shanks) engage in an epic battle of decision making.

Behind the Scenes: The Present Long Ago

After the success of "Called On in Class" (album 42) where we delved into character Trent DeWhite's imaginary past, we thought, *Why not look to his future?* "The Present Long Ago" is the only *Odyssey* program so far to flash forward to the future. Though we've seen *possible* futures in the Room of Consequence, this show featured a glimpse of the *actual* futures of Mandy Straussberg and Trent DeWhite, revealing that they would get married at some point in the future. This knowledge had an impact on their relationship in subsequent shows such as "Mum's the Word" (album 47) and "A Class Reenactment" (album 50).

My Take: Bob Hoose

During the recording of "Here Today, Gone Tomorrow?" [album 40], actor Jess Harnell spontaneously launched into a blur of impressions as a joke. We noted that this guy has talent, and tucked the idea away to do something with his impressions in the future. "The Present Long Ago" seemed like the perfect show for Jess to bring along a few "friends." The parodies of Bill Cosby and Arnold Schwarzenegger were written specifically for Jess.

BTS: Lost by a Nose

This was the last episode to feature Nick Mulligan, though he was occasionally referenced in future shows, usually when we needed someone to watch Whit's End. Nick's character seemed to have run his course, and he wasn't necessary to the plots any longer. This wasn't due to the actor, Chris Castile, who did a brilliant job in the role, but rather the ebbs and flows of many characters in shows. Smaller characters often serve a purpose for a season and then disappear into the background. Then we focus on new characters who offer new ideas and inspiration. The beauty of Whit's End is that it isn't locked into a specific floor plan; neither are *Odyssey's* characters. We can feature some for a while and then discover new ones as we need them.

BTS: The Last "I Do"

For years, the true story behind Valentine's Day was the most requested historical story from our fans. "The Last 'I Do'" was also written around the time that a marriage amendment for the U.S. Constitution was being discussed, and we wanted to do a show that would support marriage in some way. Leilani Wells, an intern for *Adventures in Odyssey*, wrote the script. The original draft of the episode featured Connie telling the Valentine story to Tamika as they worked on paper Valentines.

Cut Scenes

An earlier version of "A Most Surprising Answer" contained Nick Mulligan being recruited by the NIH agent (a woman in that version) to spy on Whit and the gang. Nick even tried to lock himself in Whit's End after it closed. By the time the show was recorded, "Sounds Like a Mystery" had used a similar plot point, so Nick's part of the story was cut. Yet another version of the script featured the whole Odyssey crew thinking that Whit was selling Whit's End to move closer to his grandchildren.

BTS: A Most Surprising Answer

The writing team had several ideas for handling the explanation of Eugene's lengthy disappearance in "A Most Surprising Answer." In an early version, Katrina explained the back story, with several interruptions from Dr. Foster. In another version, Eugene explained the entire back story on videotape in one breath with very, very long sentences. A third version featured Bernard Walton explaining the story to his wife, Maude, over the phone. Both the long-winded Eugene version and the Maude version were recorded. We decided the Eugene version was too confusing (and less funny), so the Maude version ended up in the final show. The Eugene version is available as a bonus track on the CD album.

BTS: Eugene Returns

The actress who had played Katrina in previous episodes was unavailable to continue in the role. Worrying that a change of voice for the popular character might distract listeners from the drama of Eugene's return, we considered recording the *Eugene Returns* shows without Katrina at all—bringing her in later once we'd decided on a replacement. But it seemed inconceivable to bring Eugene back without Katrina, so we did a last-minute round of auditions. The very talented actor Audrey Wasilewski was cast as the "new" voice of Katrina.

Sound Bites with Glenn Montjoy

The various trips in the Imagination Station in "A Most Extraordinary Conclusion" were inspired by a similar sequence in "The Time

Actors Will Ryan, voice of Eugene, and Audrey Wasilewski, voice of Katrina

Has Come" (album 25). (Eugene even says, "The time has come" when he steps into the Imagination Station.)

For some of the *whooshes* in these sequences, I used the sound of a monorail train sped up five times its normal speed. When Eugene tells the computer to "activate downloaded memory files," we hear the voices of each character. This was created by taking all of that character's dialogue from this episode and speeding it up.

Sound Bites

Earl Boen, who plays the Blackgaard brothers, moved to Hawaii shortly before "The Power of One" was recorded. (This explains why

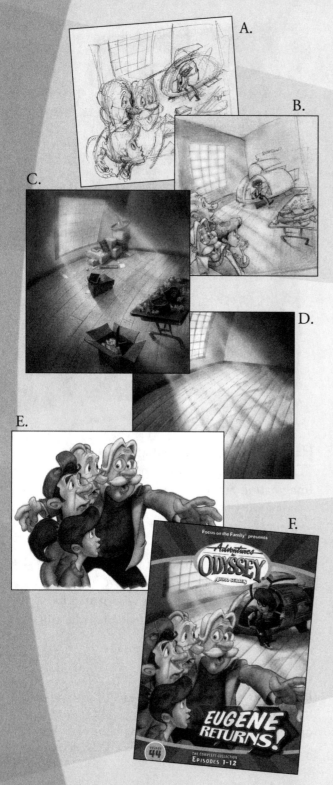

A.

B.

C.

D.

E.

F.

Edwin doesn't appear in many shows after this period.) To make sure that the Samson story (which featured Edwin carrying on a rhyme with Harlow Doyle) worked properly, Earl went to a studio in Hawaii, which was hooked up to our studio in Hollywood through special phone lines. The two actors could hear each other over headphones and got the lines timed perfectly.

The Cover Design of Eugene Returns!

Ever wondered how we design the cover of an *Odyssey* album? It's not as easy as it looks!

A. Once we had decided on the basic concept for the cover (illustrating the end scene of "A Most Intriguing Question"), artist Gary Locke drew this first rough sketch.

B. The script eventually changed so the gang wasn't actually in the Bible Room with Eugene, but we decided to keep the image anyway. Gary did a more detailed sketch before painting.

C. Gary's first painting of the background plate. After seeing this image, we realized that the background was too distracting, so . . .

D. With a bit of dramatic license, we decided on a much simpler background. Gary painted this version and then painted the characters separately.

E. Gary painted the characters and the Imagination Station image on separate "plates" and then our designers incorporated them into a single image.

F. The final cover, the product of dozens of hours of work by artists, designers, and printers!

My Take: John Fornof

Back in 1999 and 2000 when we were writing the split episodes, I had written a half show titled "The Dangerous Haircut," in which Edwin Blackgaard and Harlow Doyle tell the story of Samson partially in rhyme. The episode got shelved when we discontinued the split shows. We brought it back—a full six years later!—for "The Power of One" and paired it with a couple of other skits.

Sound Bites

In "The Invisible Dog," the kid who asks Eugene if "any of this stuff is going to be on the test" is "actor" Ben Williams. Ben was the winner of our *Last Chance Detectives* Collect the Clues contest. The prize included a trip to Colorado Springs and an appearance on *Adventures in Odyssey.*

My Take: Jeff Doucette

Actor Jeff Doucette plays Lester in "The Invisible Dog." Jeff has been doing voice work for cartoons and commercials for over

Sound designer Nate Jones, and actor Jeff Doucette, voice of Lester

Ben Williams performing for "The Invisible Dog"

25 years, appearing in more than 200 TV episodes and 35 films. Here's what he said about the role of Lester:

I experienced great joy and satisfaction playing Lester. I feel a special connection to who he is and how he thinks. I get the connection from having been raised with my dear Aunt Susie. Susie had Down's syndrome. She was only about five years older than me, so we more or less grew up together. There were eight kids in the family, and Susie made nine. She died a few years back, but she has been the inspiration for a number of characters I've played over the years.

My daughter has a form of autism, and I am reminded daily to keep things simple. I refer to my daughter and to my Aunt Susie as angels because they bring out the best in me. Their very presence and approach to life was and is one of pure love and innocence. We could all learn a great deal about life and compassion from these angels.

Sound Bites with Jonathan Crowe

I edited the voice tracks in an unusual way for the bachelor-party scene in "For Better or for Worse." Normally, we try to get a "clean" sound in which there are no mistakes or stumbles. However, to show the raucous nature of this event, I purposefully left in some little stumbles, mistakes, and ad-libs. This gave the scene an off-the-cuff feel.

Sound Bites

In "For Better or For Worse," actor Susan Silo appears as Agnes Riley and actor Julia Kazarian appears as Millie Shanks. Julia played the original Agnes in "Thank You, God" (album 3).

You are cordially invited to celebrate the renewal of the wedding vows of Eugene and Katrina Meltsner

On Saturday afternoon May the 14th at two o'clock at Odyssey Community Church Reception subsequent to the ceremony

All wedding arrangements courtesy of Dreams by Constance

Eugene and Katrina's wedding invitation

Shh! It's a Secret!

Since Eugene's return was such a long time coming, we thought it was important to make it a big event. To have fun with the top secret aspect of the shows, we created a campaign called "Something Big Is Happening in Odyssey." We produced radio spots, installed banners in bookstores, and put up a special section of the Web site with a countdown to April 2, 2005, which was the date "A Most Intriguing Question" first aired. However, we also realized that it's not as easy to keep a secret as it used to be in the days before the Internet. If even one person knew the secret and decided to post it online, hundreds of fans would know about it.

To address this, we created the codeword "Oregon" to refer to Eugene. Oregon is a vague reference to the town of Eugene, Oregon. For a long time, we talked about these episodes as the "Oregon Returns" project. Everyone who worked on the project was sworn to secrecy, and Marshal Younger sent a letter to radio stations, asking them to keep the surprise intact. Though there were a few close calls, the secret was kept until the morning of April 2, when the first show aired.

CONFIDENTIAL

Adventures in ODYSSEY

March 10, 2005

To our friends who kindly air *Adventures in Odyssey* for us:

Thanks so much for your faithfulness and hard work in putting *Adventures in Odyssey* on the air. We have been very pleased with how many people are reached—over 2 million listeners at last count!

As many of you may know, our show has been without one of its most beloved characters for five years now, Eugene Meltsner. We've received boatloads of mail from our constituents wondering where he is and asking when he is going to come back. Well, at long last, on April 2, he returns. Promos featuring Eugene in upcoming shows are in this package. However, we have gone to great lengths, curtailing the efforts of our distributors, websites, etc., in order to keep his return a secret from our listeners. We think it would be great fun for our listeners to know nothing of what's coming, except that it's "something big". Considering how popular Eugene is, our fans will surely love it.

I say all of that to ask you a favor and keep this news under your proverbial hats (as Eugene would say), at least until April 4, a day after the initial broadcast. This is a matter of national security (okay, not really). But, it might be fun for you to hold this over your kids' heads for a couple of weeks.

Again, we thank you for all that you do to help *Adventures in Odyssey* reach people for Christ.

Sincerely,

Marshal Younger

Marshal Younger, Producer
Adventures in Odyssey

Letter to radio stations asking them to keep the secret about Eugene's return

FOCUS ON THE FAMILY
COLORADO SPRINGS, CO 80995
P.O. BOX 9800, STN. TERMINAL, VANCOUVER, B.C. V6B 4G3

Album **45**

Lost and Found

The Search for Leonard Meltsner

We had talked for years about doing a story arc in which Eugene searched for his missing father—and even planned to include it in the Novacom saga. It didn't work out there, but we did use some of the ideas we had plotted.

Our first plan was to adapt the *Adventures in Odyssey* video game (*Treasure of the Incas*) into a radio episode. The villain from the video game (Carlton Freedman) would be the man who held Eugene's parents as hostages. We soon decided, however, that it would be more interesting to create an entirely new villain for the radio show. Working out this villain's plan, his back story with Leonard and Thelma Meltsner, and Eugene's foster-parent situation gave us fodder for many future shows.

The first episode in the Leonard saga was "Prisoners of Fear." The germ of the idea for this show appeared as an article called "The Plane Truth" in *Clubhouse* magazine. (See next page.) We wanted to tell several stories about what happened to Eugene and Katrina while they were missing from Odyssey. We even had Katrina make reference to their time in Africa in "For Better or for Worse" (album 44). With "Prisoners of Fear," we decided to combine their African adventure with the beginning of the Leonard story (see album cover art).

The climax that we first wrote to "Prisoners of Fear" featured Eugene and villager Yosef figuring out how to stop a secret dam from releasing the flood, while Katrina tried to convince the corrupt village leader, Gobir, to reveal the truth. Another idea was to have Katrina practicing her shooting skills early in the show and then put those skills to use by shooting the machine gears to stop the release of water from the dam. In the end, we decided that the scene between Gobir and his son, Kwame, was emotionally dramatic enough without the unnecessary shooting.

Episode Information

572: Odyssey Sings!
Original Air Date: 7/09/05
Writers: Marshal Younger & John Fornof
Sound Designer: Jonathan Crowe
Theme: Fame
Summary: When *America Sings!* comes to Odyssey, many hopeful singers line up to audition.

573: Back to Abnormal
Original Air Date: 10/1/05
Writer: Kathy Buchanan
Sound Designer: Glenn Montjoy
Theme: Dealing with change
Summary: Finding a job becomes Eugene's goal after learning he's not needed at Campbell College. Wooton Bassett tries to help Grady McKay deal with changes at home when his mom starts a new job.

574, 575, 576: Prisoners of Fear, I, II, and III
Original Air Dates: 10/8/05, 10/15/05, & 10/22/05
Writer: Marshal Younger
Sound Designer: Gap Digital
Scripture: Psalm 130:7
Theme: Serving others
Summary: Eugene and Katrina Meltsner take a trip to visit a remote African tribe that believes its village is under a curse.

577: The Business of Busyness
Original Air Date: 10/29/05
Writers: John Fornof & Kathy Buchanan
Sound Designer: Glenn Montjoy
Scripture: Luke 10:38-42
Theme: Being too busy
Summary: The Washingtons can't find time for family devotions, and Eugene's new service organization has him running in circles!

578: All-Star Witness
Original Air Date: 11/05/05
Writer: Nathan Hoobler
Sound Designer: Bob Luttrell
Scripture: Matthew 5:23-24; 18:15
Themes: Communication, forgiveness
Summary: When Coach Tom Riley doesn't choose Ashley Jenkins for the local All-Star softball game, her father, former Mayor Jenkins, files a lawsuit.

579: Always
Original Air Date: 11/19/05
Writers: John Fornof & Marshal Younger
Sound Designer: Allen Hurley
Scripture: Song of Solomon 8:6
Theme: Love of a family
Summary: Aubrey Shepard prepares to leave home for college, but her little sister, Bethany, doesn't want her to go.

580: Tales of a Small-Town Thug
Original Air Date: 12/3/05
Writer: Marshal Younger
Sound Designer: Nathan Jones
Scripture: Proverbs 14:15
Theme: Responding to criticism
Summary: Everyone at Whit's End is in an uproar when a former Bones of Rath gang member writes a scathing book about Odyssey.

581: A Christmas Conundrum
Original Air Date: 12/10/05
Writer: Kathy Buchanan
Sound Designer: Glenn Montjoy
Theme: Giving
Summary: Eugene, Tom, Connie, and Whit get confused over who's giving which Christmas present to whom.

582: Silent Night

Original Air Date: 12/17/05
Writer: John Fornof
Sound Designer: Jonathan Crowe
Scripture: Philippians 2:4
Theme: Selflessness

Summary: At home alone on Christmas Eve, Whit remembers holidays past that were difficult—but still made for treasured family memories.

583: The Champ of the Camp

Original Air Date: 1/28/06
Writers: Kathy Buchanan & Nathan Hoobler
Sound Designer: Bob Luttrell
Theme: Winning isn't everything

Summary: Connie narrates the story of her last year at summer camp and how she got stuck in the midst of the annual prank war at Camp Jumonville.

Clubhouse magazine, May 2005, the article that started Eugene's search for his father.

Behind the Scenes: Odyssey Sings!

The *Odyssey* team was given the task of explaining the musical album *Eugene Sings!* in the context of *Adventures in Odyssey*. Why would Eugene be doing a musical album? To explain the team created a spoof of the popular *American Idol* (2002–present) television program. (For more information about *Eugene Sings!*, see the chapter titled "Music.")

Tamika Washington belts out a tune in "Odyssey Sings!"

Cut Scenes

Our first draft of "Odyssey Sings!" featured Whit hosting the *America Sings!* show with Cryin' Bryan Dern as one of the judges. After being insulted by Bryan, Connie retaliated by telling everyone that he used his grandmother's money to support his gambling addiction. Connie eventually made it up to Bryan, giving us a lesson that "sometimes an apology isn't enough." However, this concept proved a little unwieldy and complicated as we spent too much time on plot twists and not enough on the original purpose of the show. In the end, we simplified the story and focused on the truly fun part of the show—the songs!

Sound Bites with Jonathan Crowe

To give "Odyssey Sings!" a different musical approach, I asked John Campbell to come up with the basic instrumentation for the show. Then I took his tracks and added a number of acoustic instruments, which

Connie with Cryin' Bryan Dern and Shakespeare in "Odyssey Sings!"

were played by four talented musicians here at Focus. They played guitar, acoustic bass, dobro, spoons, and various other instruments such as the mouth harp and accordion.

I'm glad these guys are consummate professionals. They didn't even get too upset with me when I had them come in several times to rerecord their parts. We wanted to be sure to get the best sound possible.

My Take: John Fornof

Marshal asked me to write the songs for "Odyssey Sings!"—which was a lot of fun. I had just bought a new Palm Pilot with a voice recorder in it, and whenever a song would pop into my head, I'd grab the thing and sing into it. Sometimes, I'd be walking down the street, singing "My Ode to Macaroni." I'd get a few stares from passersby who had little appreciation for art.

I'm definitely not a singer, and so it was very nervewracking to come in and play my recordings for the whole team. Marshal told me later that the show rested on those songs. If the songs didn't work, the show would be cancelled. Yikes.

When my funny little ditties rang out in the room, I cringed. But the team was gracious and encouraging. They loved all the songs, and we used each one in the final program!

Have You Ever Been to Odyssey?
lyrics and music by Will Ryan

Have you ever been to Odyssey?
A pretty nice place to be.
Have you ever been to Odyssey? Well,
you'll have to come along with me.
Other places are okay and some are fine.
But as far as hometowns go . . .
well, Odyssey is mine.
Have you ever been to Odyssey? Winter,
spring, or summer, or fall?
Have you ever been to Odyssey?
You'll really have to give a call.
If you think you'd like to meet
a brand-new friend
Simply go and grab a seat right
down at Whit's End.

Oh, it's the place to be.
I'm sure you will agree.
Have you even been to Odyssey?
Where good old Mr. Whittaker's
inventing something new.
While Connie and Eugene (ahem)
are working on it, too.
Bernard and Tom are in a dither,
Joanne and Jack in a canoe.
While Harlow's in a quandary
hoping to find a clue.

—Words and music by Will Ryan.
© 2005 Will Ryan Music. Reprinted courtesy of Snappytoons.com.

My Take: Nathan Hoobler

"All Star Witness" began with the idea of Eugene being Bernard Walton's lawyer for a frivolous lawsuit. Eventually, the idea evolved into a lawsuit against Tom Riley over his coaching techniques. Eugene assisted Tom in his defense. The lawsuit was based on several actual court cases. I noticed that Ashley's last name was Jenkins and that we had a former mayor of Odyssey named Jenkins. I thought it would be fun to tie the two together. However, I now wish we hadn't, since the connection doesn't make sense, all things considered.

BTS: Always

Though many of our *Odyssey* kids simply fade away from the show without explanation or fanfare, we sometimes give them a send-off. "Always" was an example, as we allowed Aubrey Shepard to head off to college, but used the event to explore the emotions of the family she was leaving behind.

BTS: Silent Night

"Silent Night" included a number of appearances by characters who hadn't been heard on the show in a long time. It was the first reappearance of Jana Whittaker-Dowd, Whit's daughter, and the first reappearance of Jenny, Whit's wife, since "The Mortal Coil" (album 16). Jerry Whittaker was last heard in "Memories of Jerry" (album 27), though played by a different actor. Maude Walton, heard in the background on Bernard's phone call, last appeared in "Bad Luck" (album 8). This time, however, Maude wasn't played by host Chris Anthony but by *Odyssey* coordinator Chris McDonald.

A Novel Idea by Connie Kendall

At a writer's meeting in late 2004, we discussed Eugene's return and how it would impact *Odyssey*. We wanted to do several character-based arcs—stories that would give our characters plenty of room to be themselves and wouldn't necessarily involve action-adventure and cliffhangers. The idea for Connie attempting to write a book came out of this meeting and became the center of a few future episodes. Connie's struggles with her book also allowed us the chance to dramatize many of our own difficulties and frustrations as writers.

BTS: Tales of a Small-Town Thug

Mandy Straussberg acted very un-Mandy-like in "Tales of a Small-Town Thug." We later find out the reason in "Now More Than Ever" (album 46).

Cut Scenes

A short subplot about Tom's five-legged dog, Cheddar, was cut from "A Christmas Conundrum." Don't ask.

Sound Bites with Jonathan Crowe

I worked for a long time on "Silent Night" to find the right sound to get into Whit's flashbacks. I tried a variety of *whooshes* and *drones*. In the end, I asked fellow sound designer Nate Jones to play various synthesized sounds on his electric guitar. Then I affected and filtered them as needed.

The episode featured several lengthy scenes where Whit was by himself at home. We wanted to fill these with some vocal effects from Paul Herlinger to indicate what he was doing in each scene. It took a long time to record because we had to think about the exact vocal sounds that would indicate when he was opening the microwave, stoking the fire, or whatever. For days after that, Paul would tell us that he was practicing his vocal Foley.

Actor Dave Madden (voice of Bernard) had moved to Florida by the time this episode was produced. We recorded his voice over the phone. So when he says, "I'm in Florida, Whit," he really is.

My Take: John Fornof

The idea for "Silent Night" came from an *Odyssey* fan. He suggested a show where Whit felt lonely on Christmas. I thought it made perfect sense, since Whit would give and give to everyone else but never take time for himself. As with most shows, I learned a lot by writing "Silent Night." A lot of Whit's thoughts and feelings were taken from my own life reflecting on my boys having grown up.

BTS: The Champ of the Camp

In a flashback in "The Champ of the Camp," teenage Connie mentions that her rival, Goggles, is a geek, and most girls probably tell him to get lost and then throw mud on him. In the episode "The Trouble with Girls" (*The Lost Episodes*) Eugene tells young Jimmy Barclay he received this very same type of treatment.

Sound Bites

In "The Champ of the Camp," camp counselor Mr. Sherman was played by Alfonso Freeman, son of actor Morgan Freeman.

"Eugene Sings!" Art Contest Gallery

In conjunction with the episode "Odyssey Sings!" and the *Eugene Sings!* album release, the official Web site sponsored an art contest. Here are four of the winners.

Danielle O., age 14

Emily J., age 11, Gabriola, British Columbia

Charity M., age 18, Laurel, Maryland

Katherine N., age 14, Apex, North Carolina

Sound Bites

The scripted ending for "The Champ of the Camp" featured Eugene teasing Connie for having a crush on him at camp. In the studio, Will Ryan (Eugene) suggested a different ending in which Eugene runs off to call Whit to tell him the story. The chemistry between actors Katie Leigh and Will Ryan was so good in this alternate take that we used it in the final show.

My Take: Nathan Hoobler

Writer Kathy Buchanan came up with the idea of Eugene and Connie meeting up at camp years ago. Many of the incidents in "The Champ of the Camp" came from our own experiences at camp, though one of our struggles was coming up with fun and original pranks that kids wouldn't try to emulate themselves.

The name of the camp—Jumonville—is taken from the camp I visited during my summers growing up in western Pennsylvania. Interestingly enough, Paul McCusker also grew up in that part of the country and "Connie Goes to Camp" was inspired in part by his visit to the real-life Jumonville.

Get ready for another surprise. Guess what the name of the town down the hill from the real-life Camp Jumonville is? Connellsville.

A Hand Up: The Creation of Eugene's Organization

After Eugene returned to Odyssey with Katrina, we wanted to find something new for him to do. Our first thought was to have him become a teacher at Odyssey Middle School. But we agreed that setting a lot of episodes in a classroom with Eugene wouldn't be enticing for many of our listeners. So we decided that, in light of his inadvertent participation in the Novacom debacle, Eugene would feel motivated to give back to the community—and the idea for his charitable organization was born.

Originally named "General Inquiries," the organization was later called "Stone Soup," named after an old story about a vagabond who unites a town by encouraging the town folk to share. We wrote an entire episode where Eugene subtly re-enacted the ancient fable while building a playground.

The name "Stone Soup" didn't ring true for Eugene, so we went with "Little Things," to emphasize that Eugene would be doing smaller tasks that would help others reach their ministry potential. After even more discussion, we settled on "PLEASE," which stood for Philanthropic Loving Enterprises of Altruistic Services for Everyone—which seemed like a *very* Eugene-like name. Or so we *thought* until we realized that having Eugene trying to be handyman (painting houses, walking dogs, etc.) didn't make sense for his character. It was funny for a single episode, but not more than that. Finally, the organization became *Manus Sursum*, from the Latin phrase meaning "Hand Up." Since most of our listeners weren't fluent in Latin, the organization became simply "hand up." Eugene was inspired to create the organization when he gave Grady and Sam McKay a "hand up" by fixing some appliances around their home.

Actor Mary Mouser, voice of Samantha McKay, with sound designer Nathan Jones

451

Character:
Tamika Washington
Quote: "I've been stuck in Odyssey singing for my brother's garage band. This could mean national exposure!"
Something you may not know about Tamika: She once talked on the phone with actress Sydney Sellica.

Album 46

A Date with Dad (and Other Calamities)

A Baffling "Switch"

The episode "Switch" began as an idea for a very different episode. Writer John Fornof remembers the process of the episode's creation:

> I've always loved the concept of the Wonderworld tree house, and for "Switch" I wanted to write a show where the kids would rediscover Wonderworld. In my first outline, the kids were sick of being kids and they went on an adventure looking for this rumored tree house and discovered . . . Jimmy Barclay! Jimmy was tired of dealing with adult things and wanted to go back to being a kid. He came back to Odyssey and Wonderworld to get back to his roots. Jimmy and the kids switched roles for a day, thus the title.
>
> The problem was that if we were going to bring Jimmy Barclay back, we wanted it to be more of an event, instead of Jimmy going through a bout of depression. So we shelved the Jimmy story (alas!) and turned the show into an episode where the Washington kids switched places with their parents.

The recording of the episode gave actor Paul Herlinger (Whit) a chance to shine in a new way as he played several zany roles, including a German man, an Elmer Fudd soundalike, and a Girl Scout. John leaped at the chance to open up his treasure chest of made-up, funny names and dig out some gems, including Wolfgang Snoffen von Winkenberger.

Episode Information

584: Dead Ends
Original Air Date: 2/4/06
Writer: Marshal Younger
Sound Designer: Glenn Montjoy
Scripture: Philippians 4:19
Theme: God's provision
Summary: Eugene's search for his father continues as he visits his foster parents to find clues.

585: The Poor Rich Guy
Original Air Date: 2/11/06
Writer: Torry Martin
Sound Designer: Jonathan Crowe
Theme: Bible study
Summary: Grady McKay decides that the Bible "makes no sense" after Marvin Washington and his sister, Tamika, conclude that Whit can't go to heaven because he's rich.

586: A Cheater Cheated
Original Air Date: 2/18/06
Writer: Nathan Hoobler
Sound Designer: Jonathan Crowe
Scripture: Matthew 22:39
Theme: The Golden Rule
Summary: Bart Rathbone seeks out Whit's business advice after deciding he wants to make the Electric Palace a "respectable establishment."

587: Bringing Up Dads
Original Air Date: 2/25/06
Writer: Bob Hoose
Sound Designer: Glenn Montjoy
Scripture: Exodus 20:12
Theme: Respecting parents
Summary: Ed Washington struggles to connect with his ever-maturing daughter, Tamika.

588: Broken-Armed and Dangerous
Original Air Date: 3/4/06
Writer: Kathy Buchanan
Sound Designer: Bob Luttrell
Scripture: 1 John 1:9
Theme: Guilt
Summary: When Eugene contributes to an accident that leaves Connie with a broken arm, he tries to make amends by helping her with every task.

589: The Impossible
Original Air Date: 3/11/06
Writer: John Fornof
Sound Designer: Nathan Jones
Scripture: Matthew 19:26
Theme: Nothing is impossible with God.
Summary: In a race against an impossible deadline, Whit and his son Jason join Marvin Washington to try to finish a new invention.

590: Three O'Clock Call
Original Air Date: 4/15/06
Writer: Bob Hoose
Sound Designer: Glenn Montjoy
Scripture: Deuteronomy 1:31
Theme: God as Father
Summary: Mysterious phone calls cause Grady to believe his estranged father is trying to contact him.

591: Switch
Original Air Date: 4/22/06
Writer: John Fornof
Sound Designer: Jonathan Crowe
Scripture: Matthew 25:29
Theme: Managing money
Summary: Because Marvin and Tamika are convinced that being a grown-up is easy, their parents switch places with them for a day.

Tamika Washington refuses to ride in her father's hot-dog car in "Bringing Up Dads"

592: **Now More Than Ever**
Original Air Date: 4/29/06
Writers: John Fornof & Kathy Buchanan
Sound Designer: Glenn Montjoy
Theme: Being there for a friend
Summary: Liz Horton is determined to find out why the usually cheery Mandy Straussberg seems depressed.

593: **Around the Block**
Original Air Date: 5/6/06
Writer: Nathan Hoobler
Sound Designer: Jonathan Crowe
Scripture: Romans 5:3-4
Theme: Persistence
Summary: Eugene tries to help Connie overcome writer's block using a variety of methods.

594, 595: **A Time for Action, I and II**
Original Air Dates: 5/13/06 & 5/20/06
Writer: Nathan Hoobler
Sound Designer: Glenn Montjoy
Scripture: Daniel 4:35
Theme: Taking action
Summary: A scrap of paper leads Eugene to investigate a forgotten relative and information about a tragic accident. He hopes they may lead him to his long-lost father.

Behind the Scenes: Dead Ends

"Dead Ends" introduced us to Eugene's foster parents, the Burnetts. Though Eugene had mentioned having foster parents in previous episodes, we had never seen this part of his life before.

BTS: The Poor Rich Guy

Grady McKay's discovery in "The Poor Rich Guy" marked the first time that anyone outside Wooton's family learned that he writes the *Power Boy* comics. Grady's knowledge would later become important in "The Highest Stakes" (album 49).

Sound Bites

Leonard Meltsner In "Dead Ends," is played by the very talented actor Phil Proctor, who voices characters in many popular animated films, including *Aladdin* (1992), *Treasure Planet* (2002), *Doctor Dolittle 1, 2, and 3* (1998, 2002, 2006), and *Rugrats Go Wild!* (2003).

Sound Bites

"A Cheater Cheated" originally featured Casey, Bryan Dern's boss from "Top This!" (album 24). Sadly, actor Barry Stigler, who played Casey, passed away before recording. We replaced the character of Casey with one named Tanner, played by veteran film and TV actor William Schallert.

BTS: Bringing Up Dads

"Bringing Up Dads" and "Three O'Clock Call" were outlined as one episode with the theme of fatherhood. Both stories were strong enough that we felt they deserved their own shows. The title "Bringing Up Dads" is a play off of Dr. James Dobson's 2003 book, *Bringing Up Boys*.

Sound Bites with Glenn Montjoy

To get the sound of the bubble hat in "Bringing Up Dads," I got a bunch of weird "burp" and "bubble" sound effects and combined them with the sounds of my lips flapping. It made a very bizarre sound effect!

Cut Scenes

"Broken-Armed and Dangerous" was recorded with a subplot of Tamika and Marvin playing hide-and-seek at Whit's End before accidentally breaking Whit's invention. After recording the show, we realized that both Marvin and Tamika's voices were starting to sound older, and they

Actor Phil Proctor, voice of Leonard Meltsner

were too mature to play hide-and-seek. So we carefully edited all references to hide-and-seek out of the show.

BTS: Broken-Armed and Dangerous

"Broken-Armed and Dangerous" featured the second appearance of Edith Sutton, played by actor Mitzi McCall. Paul Herlinger (Whit) often mentioned that he hoped his character would get into a romantic relationship of some kind. We didn't want Whit to get into a serious romance, so we came up with the plot of a friendly woman who had an unrequited crush on Whit. And so Edith Sutton arrived.

BTS: The Impossible

"The Impossible" introduced the Edu-Link, a miniature computer that could be run on solar power or by hand crank. We wanted to get Whit back into inventor mode because it had been some time since we'd seen that side of him. The Edu-Link was loosely inspired by several similar real-life inventions that were being tested for distribution in developing countries. The Edu-Link was important in several future episodes, including "The Undeniable Truth"(album 47) and "The Top Floor" (album 48).

Sound Bites with Nathan Jones

I asked John Campbell to give us the "Indian equivalent of Muzak" for the music when Marvin is on hold with the Indian minister in "The Impossible." The music was so much fun that we also used it in the closing credits.

Sound Bites with Jonathan Crowe

Nathan Jones rightfully earned his radio credit in the production of "Switch." Nathan excels in the role of Foley artist, and he added a bunch of unusual sounds that he created himself, including:

- a short burp after Marvin ate a sundae
- a stomach growl, which he made using his mouth
- a loud *swish* sound for the golf club, which he made using a small tree branch

Actor Robbie Rist, voice of David Straussberg

BTS: Now More Than Ever

Beginning with "Now More Than Ever," actor Robbie Rist took over the role of David Straussberg from actor Jeff Ellison. Robbie previously played Percy in "The Girl in the Sink" (album 42), and on the final season of the 1970s television show *The Brady Bunch, he played Cousin Oliver.*

Actor Robbie Rist pauses during the recording of "Now More than Ever."

BTS: A Time for Action

When Eugene first talked about his missing parents in early episodes like "Last in a Long Line" (album 10), he mentioned that they disappeared in Zaire. He mentioned this country again in "Prisoners of Fear" (album 45). However, in the late 1990s, the country of Zaire changed its name to the Congo. We had Eugene very briefly explain that fact in "A Time for Action." In all episodes after this, we referred to the place as "the Congo."

Goof Alert!

In "A Time for Action," Eugene claims his mother's maiden name is "Mushnik," even though it was established in "Last in a Long Line" (album 10) that her last name was "Kronholm" and his grandmother's maiden name was "Mushnik." Apparently chasing around after his father made Eugene forgetful. Or perhaps Whit's program to restore Eugene's memory in earlier episodes didn't work quite as well as Whit hoped.

My Take: Nathan Hoobler

"Around the Block" may have been the easiest *Odyssey* episode that I've ever written. Since it was about writer's block, something that I often face, I didn't have to do a lot of research. Many of Connie's methods for dealing with writer's block echo things that I have tried in order to break through my own. Like Connie, I often try to write a certain number of paragraphs before rewarding myself with food. The strategies worked better for me than they did for Connie. She quit writing her book while I managed to pour out over 140,000 words for this one.

BTS: A Time for Action

The moment when Eugene finds his own name on a tombstone in "A Time for Action" was meant as a parallel to the moment when he found his father's tombstone in "Last in a Long Line" (album 10). It also gave us a chance to introduce the character of Everett Meltsner, who would become important in future episodes.

The Straussbergs Story

Often, in trying to find the balance between role models and reality, we have touched on broken families—in which kids have spoken of divorced parents—without going into the details of how such things happen to adults and the consequences it has for the children. The team finally decided that the benefits of dramatizing such a story would outweigh the potential problems. But we gave ourselves two stipulations:

1. Each episode in the arc needed a strong take-away lesson.
2. The Straussbergs would not initially divorce, but separate. Their ultimate fate (revealed in "Life, in the Third Person," album 49) would be one that we felt offered the most opportunity for help and healing to those in like situations. We wanted to model how parents could come back from the brink of divorce.

A typical session, recording family style

Character: Connie
Quote: "You are so hopeless, Eugene."
Something you may not know about Connie:
For one day, she was Harlow Doyle's secretary.

Album

47

Into the Light

Out of the Darkness, Into the Light

"Cover of Darkness" introduced the villainous character of Dalton Kearn, played by actor Chuck McCaan. Chuck played multiple characters on *G.I. Joe: The Movie* (1987), *The Fantastic Four* TV series (1994–1996), and the TV series and movie version of *DuckTales* (1987, 1990 respectively).

While Dalton Kearn would eventually be a main character in an action-adventure three-parter (album 48), the Eugene shows in album 47 were more relational. When the writing team was planning the Eugene and Leonard story arc, we imagined it to be mostly intense action. Dave Arnold, executive producer, encouraged us to focus on the "heart stories" between father and son, in addition to the action. So, we decided to explore the spiritual conflict between the two characters. Unlike Eugene, who had started out being some-what sympathetic to Christianity, Leonard was opposed to faith of any kind. This tension played out in "Cover of Darkness" and "The Undeniable Truth," and then later in "The Top Floor" (album 48).

During the recording of one of these relational shows, we saw a perfect example of why we don't want to always rely too heavily on action. In "Cover of Darkness," actor Will Ryan suggested that Eugene would demand seatbelts when he and his father got in the car, even though they weren't going anywhere. It was such a Eugene-like line that we put it in the final show. And it's the kind of moment that wouldn't happen if we focused only on intense action.

Episode Information

596: Cover of Darkness
Original Air Date: 9/23/06
Writer: Marshal Younger
Sound Designer: Jonathan Crowe
Scripture: Psalm 18:2
Theme: Trusting God
Summary: After much searching, Eugene has finally found his father. But secrecy still surrounds Leonard Meltsner, and a ruthless archeologist named Dalton Kearn is seeking him out.

597: Out of Our Hands
Original Air Date: 9/30/06
Writer: Kathy Buchanan
Sound Designer: Glenn Montjoy
Scripture: 1 Peter 5:7
Theme: God is in control.
Summary: Mandy Straussberg is determined to help her separated parents get back together with a play that forces them to see how they're behaving.

598: My Favorite Thing
Original Air Date: 10/7/06
Writer: Mary Fritson
Sound Designer: Glenn Montjoy
Theme: Spending time with family
Summary: The Washingtons get stuck sitting with the Rathbones at a fancy restaurant.

599: Blood, Sweat, and Fears
Original Air Date: 10/14/06
Writer: Kathy Buchanan
Sound Designer: Jonathan Crowe
Scripture: Psalm 56:3
Theme: Facing fear
Summary: Eugene's organization is chosen to coordinate Odyssey's annual blood drive, but Eugene is terrified of needles.

600: The Nudge
Original Air Date: 10/21/06
Writer: John Fornof
Sound Designer: Jonathan Crowe
Scripture: 1 Thessalonians 5:17
Theme: Prayer
Summary: Marvin Washington believes that God may be telling him to give his bike to Grady. Grady, meanwhile, struggles to understand how God can listen to him.

601: Bernard and Jeremiah
Original Air Date: 10/28/06
Writer: Nathan Hoobler
Sound Designer: John Doryk
Scripture: The book of Jeremiah, Hebrews 12:2
Themes: Faith, obedience
Summary: Marvin Washington and Bernard Walton take a trip in the Imagination Station to see the prophet Jeremiah.

602: Mum's the Word
Original Air Date: 11/18/06
Writer: Nathan Hoobler
Sound Designer: Nathan Jones
Scripture: Ephesians 4:25
Theme: Honesty
Summary: True affections and a valentine complicate the relationship between Trent DeWhite and Mandy Straussberg.

603: **The Family Next Door**

Original Air Date: 11/25/06
Writer: Kathy Buchanan
Sound Designer: Gap Digital
Themes: The importance of family, reaching out to others
Summary: With her mom busy and her dad no longer at home, Mandy looks to the Washingtons for emotional support.

604: **Like Father, Like Wooton**

Original Air Date: 12/02/06
Writer: Kathy Buchanan
Sound Designer: Jonathan Crowe
Scripture: James 5:16
Theme: Honesty
Summary: Connie poses undercover as a carnival clown while Grady McKay tells his friends that Wooton Bassett is his father.

605, 606: **The Chosen One, I and II**

Original Air Dates: 12/09/06 & 12/16/06
Writer: Marshal Younger
Sound Designer: Christopher Diehl
Scripture: Matthew 10:42
Theme: Sacrifice
Summary: A runaway girl named Kelly arrives at Whit's End. When her story comes out, the Washingtons are faced with a life-changing decision.

607: **The Undeniable Truth**

Original Air Date: 12/23/06
Writer: Marshal Younger
Sound Designer: Gap Digital
Scripture: Acts 21-22; 2 Corinthians 5:17
Theme: Making a difference as a Christian
Summary: Hand-Up gets in hot water when a local newspaper accuses Eugene of stealing the donation money.

In "Cover of Darkness," Eugene meets his father, Leonard, in unusual circumstances.

Behind the Scenes: My Favorite Thing

"Sunday Morning Scramble" (album 43) took place almost entirely while the Washington family was getting ready for church. After the success of that show, we wanted to put the Washington family in another comedic everyday situation—take a family dinner at a fancy restaurant, add the Rathbones, and you have "My Favorite Thing." (This episode was written by *Odyssey* intern Mary Fritson.)

Sound Bites

Actress Diane Hsu stepped in as the voice of Doris Rathbone in "My Favorite Thing" and future episodes. When doing auditions for this part, the team was amazed at how closely Diane could mimic the original Doris voice.

Sound Bites

For the episode "Blood, Sweat, and Fears," we asked composer John Campbell to create the intro music for Trent DeWhite's Kids' Radio program before we actually recorded the scene with the actors. That allowed Jess Harnell (Wooton) to ad–lib lyrics to it during the session. They included, "It's the Trent show! It's his show and not yours!"

BTS: Bernard and Jeremiah

"Bernard and Jeremiah" was written with Bernard Walton *telling* the Bible story of Jeremiah, much as he had told the story of Joseph, Esther, Job, and others. However, after reading the script, we decided that Jeremiah's story needed a personal touch with *Odyssey* characters actually interacting with the biblical ones. So we turned the show into an Imagination Station adventure. It also gave

The Timeline of Leonard Meltsner:

Eugene learns much of this story in pieces throughout albums 45 to 49. Here is the story in chronological order.

2. In college, Dalton Kearn, a renowned archeologist, trains Leonard. Leonard marries Thelma.

4. Thelma announces her pregnancy. Leonard and Thelma separate.

6. Eugene is born.

1. Leonard is born in England to Hiram Meltsner. His family moves to the United States, near Odyssey.

3. Dalton and Leonard have a strong argument and break their partnership.

5. Thelma visits Joanne Woodston at a pregnancy clinic in Chicago. Joanne convinces Thelma to return to Leonard.

7. Hiram criticizes Leonard's expeditions. Leonard never speaks to him again. (Eugene is two years old.)

us the chance to see what Bernard would be inside that invention. As it turns out, he's a janitor no matter where he goes!

My Take: Marshal Younger

My wife and I had been doing foster care for several years and adopted a young boy named Cory. It was an emotional roller coaster . . . and perfect material for an *Odyssey* episode. The experience led to "The Chosen One." I also liked introducing the character of Kelly because she was in immediate need of grace and salvation. The show ended up being fairly autobiographical because I had been exactly where Ed Washington was in his hesitancy to become a foster parent. But after a lot of prayer, my wife and I decided that this was something we needed to do. And we're so glad we did.

BTS: Like Father, Like Wooton

In the spring of 2006, Josh McDowell spoke at a Focus on the Family chapel service on the importance of fathers. The message inspired us to explore this topic from several angles on *Adventures in Odyssey*. We looked

at "replacement" father figures (with Whit being Eugene's surrogate father in "Dead Ends, " album 46), absent fathers (with Grady's dad in "Three O'Clock Call," album 46, and "Like Father, Like Wooton"), fathers going through a separation (with Mandy's family), and examples of strong fathers (Ed Washington in "Bringing Up Dads," album 46, and Whit in "The Top Floor," album 48).

Sound Bites with Christopher Diehl

"The Chosen One" was my first production for *Odyssey*, and I got to include my three-month-old son, Braydon, as a sound effect. In the scene where Kelly walks over to a homeless woman sleeping on a bench, Braydon is snoring in the background.

BTS: The Chosen One

With the Washington kids getting older—and out of our target age range of 8 to 12—we were looking for new ways to challenge the family without dealing with primarily "teen" issues. Adding Kelly as an extra member of the family brought a new dimension to their family life—and our scripts.

8. Eugene (age 6) conducts a failed experiment on a bathtub.

9. Leonard and Thelma go to South America to find the treasure of the Incas.

10. Leonard and Thelma go to Africa on an anthropological mission. They leave Eugene with Michael Mushnik.

11. The Meltsners live with the Ashanti Tribe. They are given the names Morathi (wise one) and Thandiwe (loving one).

12. Dalton goes to Africa. He forms the Wolof tribe and kidnaps the Meltsners. He forces them to dig for gold.

13. At age seven, Eugene is told that his parents died in Africa. The Burnetts become his foster parents.

14. Hiram creates a grave in Odyssey for Leonard.

15. Dalton bribes Eugene's great uncle Michael to bring him to Africa. The Burnetts won't let Eugene go. Michael dies in train wreck. Dalton tells Leonard that Eugene is dead.

Artist Gary Locke

16. Hiram Meltsner dies in Connellsville.

17. Everett Meltsner is born in captivity.

18. Leonard persuades one of the Wolofs named Aziz to create a video showing their captivity. Aziz keeps the tape in his home.

19. Everett (age 2) is hurt in a fall at the dig site. He's taken to the hospital. His parents are later told that he died, but Dalton raises Everett as his own son.

20. Thelma dies in captivity.

21. Leonard escapes via the secret tunnel. Dalton says he will not rest until he finds Leonard.

22. Leonard returns to Odyssey in hopes of reconciling with Hiram. Believing them all to be dead, he creates graves for Thelma, Eugene, and Everett.

23. Leonard sends a message to Around the World Missions, asking them to help the Ashanti tribe. He then lives his life as a homeless man in Connellsville.

The Art Guy

Want to know more about who draws those amazing *Adventures in Odyssey* illustrations? Gary Locke's over-the-top sketches have graced projects for Quaker Oats, Pepsi, *The Wall Street Journal*, Major League Baseball, Fisher-Price, *Sports Illustrated*, and many others.

Gary draws pictures all day long and sometimes late into the night. Like many great artists, he doesn't keep his work area neat and tidy. Hundreds of pencils and dozens of brushes litter the floor. Pictures of sports figures cover every inch of the walls while a bench press and weight equipment cover half the room. He works surrounded by family (his wife and three children) and select friends: a balding ferret, one dog, and several selfish cats.

24. Eugene and Katrina build a communications tower for the Ashanti tribe. Eugene discovers that his father is still alive.

25. Eugene reunites with his father and learns that Leonard is running from Dalton.

26. Dalton's men destroy the Wolof village in Africa.

27. Leonard, Eugene, and Jason Whittaker track Dalton to New York. They find that Everett (now age 10) is alive and living as Dalton's son.

28. Leonard finds the evidence tape. Dalton is arrested. Everett goes with Leonard, his true father.

29. Leonard and Eugene return to Odyssey. Eugene donates a kidney to Leonard.

30. Leonard becomes a Christian and returns to the Ashanti tribe as a missionary.

Album 48

Moment of Truth

From Top to Bottom on "The Top Floor"

The team wanted "The Top Floor" to tie up all the storylines with Leonard Meltsner and Dalton Kearn. We knew that by the end of the show, Dalton had to be defeated, but we didn't have all the plot-points worked out to bring him to justice. So we outlined the show backward—starting at the end and outlining back to the beginning. The team got the ideas of Whit's sacrificing himself to save Everett Meltsner and Everett betraying his father, and the outlining took off from there—in reverse! By the time it came to scene 1, we had a three-part story outlined.

An exciting element of the storyline was Jason's return to the National Security Agency, albeit temporarily. Seeing Jason in the spy role again, with Whit and Eugene joining him on his mission by donning janitors' garb, was as much fun to picture as it was to write. (See album cover art at left.)

Hoping that Dalton Kearn would be different from our past villains, we gave him a more human dimension. Instead of being obviously evil, we allowed that Dalton had fallen in love with Thelma before Leonard did, and Dalton had raised Leonard's son as his own. In his scenes with Everett, he appeared to be a good father, which gave his character complexity and made him sinister in an unusual way.

The flashback scene in part III where Leonard and Thelma are in captivity was not recorded with the rest of the show because Thelma hadn't been cast yet. Once Salli Saffioti was cast as Thelma, we recorded this scene with the "New Era" flashbacks (see album 49), more than six months *after* the rest of the episode.

And we threw in a fun nostalgic reference. In part III, Whit said, "Let's see if this thing works"—the same words that he said during the opening theme of the early *Odyssey* episodes.

Episode Information

434: B-TV: Redeeming the Season
Original Air Date: 12/11/99
Writer: Jim Ware
Sound Designer: Todd Busteed
Theme: Christmas traditions
Summary: Bernard Walton and the B-TV crew explore the legend of Saint Nicholas and how many Christmas customs first began.

608: Run-of-the-Mill Miracle
Original Air Date: 02/03/07
Writer: Katie Bruhn
Sound Designer: John Doryk
Scripture: Isaiah 55:9
Theme: Miracles
Summary: After his sister is hospitalized, Grady McKay takes an Imagination Station adventure to see biblical examples of miracles.

609: Prequels of Love
Original Air Date: 02/10/07
Writer: Kathy Buchanan
Sound Designer: Jonathan Crowe
Theme: Appreciating those we love
Summary: From chicken costumes to phone scams, we hear the stories of how Bart Rathbone, Whit, and Bernard Walton met, or proposed to, their wives.

610: Hear Me, Hear Me
Original Air Date: 02/17/07
Writer: Kathy Buchanan
Sound Designer: Nathan Jones
Scripture: James 1:19
Theme: The importance of listening
Summary: On the day of the Whit's End science fair, Eugene and Connie stage a contest to see which one is the better listener. Back in the Little Theater, Liz Horton gets frustrated when Trent DeWhite won't listen to her instructions.

611, 612, 613: The Top Floor, I, II, and III
Original Air Dates: 02/24/07, 3/3/07, & 3/10/07
Writer: Nathan Hoobler
Sound Designer: Gap Digital
Scripture: James 2:17
Theme: Behaving as a Christian in every situation
Summary: Jason Whittaker and his father join forces with Eugene and Leonard Meltsner to bring Dalton Kearn to justice once and for all.

614: Best of Enemies
Original Air Date: 4/28/07
Writer: Sherry VanTreuren
Sound Designer: Allen Hurley
Scripture: Romans 12:18
Theme: Loving one another unconditionally
Summary: Both Connie and Tamika Washington have to deal with new—and very challenging—roommates.

615: Only By His Grace
Original Air Date: 5/5/07
Writer: Kathy Buchanan
Sound Designer: Christopher Diehl
Theme: Grace
Summary: Grady wants to go on a rafting trip but can't afford it. Mandy Straussberg's confidence is shaken when her parents, who have separated, consider moving to different cities.

616, 617, 618: The Other Side of the Glass, I, II, and III

Original Air Dates: 5/12/07, 5/19/07, & 5/26/07

Writer: Paul McCusker

Sound Designers: Nathan Jones & Jonathan Crowe

Scripture: 2 Timothy 4:7

Theme: Helping those in need

Summary: The *Power Boy* symbol for "help" appears on windows all over Odyssey. Wooton Bassett is determined to find out who has sent out the urgent signal.

Whit celebrates Christmas in "B-TV: Redeeming the Season"

Cut Scenes

The first draft of "Run-of-the-Mill Miracle" included Samantha McKay falling from the apartment window and being injured on the ground below. In that draft of the story, her injury was actually Grady's fault because he left the apartment before he was supposed to. We thought that version might sound melodramatic, so we changed it to a carbon monoxide scare.

Early sketches of Whit, Eugene, and Jason Whittaker working undercover in "The Top Floor"

Behind the Scenes: Prequels of Love

In "Prequels of Love," we learn Doris Rathbone's maiden name—Vineropoly.

Sound Bites

For "Best of Enemies," the yells and screams of the kids in the water balloon fight are actually the sounds of kids having a *snowball* fight at the Focus on the Family Welcome Center. That's because we recorded the crowd sounds in February—and the water balloons would have been a little too cold.

My Take: Sherry VanTreuren

When I was an intern for *Adventures in Odyssey*, I wrote "Best of Enemies" based on my disagreements with roommates throughout college. I actually had a goldfish named Kerplunk, and I traded the fish for an extension cord with one of my roommates.

My Take: Marshal Younger

In "Best of Enemies," there's a scene where Connie makes Lindsey pancakes with peanuts in them. Lindsey's allergic to them, but eats them anyway just to be nice. This was one of the funniest scenes I've ever directed, but it was met with quite a few negative letters from people saying we were making light of life-threatening allergies—and they're right. We rerecorded Chris's wrap to warn people not to eat anything they're allergic to.

BTS: Only by His Grace

The original title of the Grady/Mandy show was "Fall from Grace"—and the final scene featured Mandy giving up on church because her parents weren't reconciling. However, even after recording and producing the episode with that ending, we wanted a more positive conclusion. We rewrote the final scene and rerecorded it with Aria Curzon a few weeks before the show aired. With the new scenes, the old title didn't make sense anymore, so we changed it to "Only by His Grace."

Sound Bites

In "The Other Side of the Glass," actor June Foray played the store owner, Madge. June is a voice-over legend, having played such characters as Rocky the Squirrel in the *Rocky and Bullwinkle Show* (1959–1961) and Granny in *The Sylvester and Tweety Show* (1976). She also played Mrs. Harcourt in the *Adventures in Odyssey* videos.

Actor Phil Proctor (Leonard Meltsner) played two roles in these episodes: Mr. Corelli and Mr. Montoya.

Sound Bites

The character of Wooton Bassett was named after a town in England. Wooton means "small town by the wood" in Old English. The origin of his name was finally revealed in "The Other Side of the Glass."

Sound designer Nathan Jones records Foley inside a car for "The Other Side of the Glass."

Production assistant Michael Erb records the sound of Nathan's hands sliding across the window.

Adventures Away from Odyssey

Sometimes our characters depart from Odyssey for the majority of an episode. What follows is a list of the shows where our characters took an adventure *away* from Odyssey. (Note: This list does not include biblical or historical episodes.)

Episode:	Location
The Day After Christmas	Foster Creek
Family Vacation	On the way to Florida; Grace and Chester's farm
The Last Great Adventure of the Summer	A train to New York, a plane, and London
Connie, I and II	On the Way to California; Los Angeles
Connie Goes to Camp, I and II	Camp What-A-Nut
The Barclay Family Ski Vacation	A ski resort
Ice Fishing	Summit Lake
The Vow	Washington, D.C.
Train Ride	A train coming from Chicago
Waylaid in the Windy City, I and II	Chicago
The Cross of Cortes, I and II	Mexico
Feud for Thought	Connellsville
Flash Flood	The mountains near Odyssey
Aloha, Oy!, I, II and III	Hawaii
First-Hand Experience	On the road
Second Thoughts	Woodtown, Iowa
Third Degree	Oak Park, Colorado
It Happened at Four Corners	Four Corners, Arizona
The Fifth House on the Left, I and II	Hollywood, California
A Name, Not a Number, I and II	Geneva, Switzerland
Pokenberry Falls, R.F.D, I and II	Pokenberry Falls
Blind Justice	Connellsville
The Search for Whit, I, II, and III	Israel
The Right Choice, I and II	Chicago
It's a Pokenberry Christmas, I and II	Pokenberry Falls

Episode:	Location
Chains, I and II	Connellsville
Breaking Point	Connellsville
Shining Armor	Central America
Relatively Annoying	Alex's grandparents' house
Strange Boy in a Strange Land	The woods near Sarah's uncle's house
Grand Opening, I	Connellsville
Plan B: Parts I–III	Chicago
The Black Veil	Alaska
Sheep's Clothing	Alaska
The Unraveling	Maine
The Toy Man	Connellsville
The Mystery at Tin Flat	Tin Flat
Black Clouds	A diner between Odyssey and Washington, D.C.
Silver Lining	West Virginia
Pink Is Not My Color	Washington, D.C.
Something Blue, I and II	Washington, D.C.
Living in the Gray, I and II	Washington, D.C.
Prisoners of Fear, I, II and III	Congo
Dead Ends	Chicago
A Time for Action, I and II	Chicago and Connellsville
The Top Floor, I, II, and III	Congo and New York City
The Other Side of the Glass, I, II, and III	Greensboro, North Carolina

Whit and Eugene head out of town for another wild adventure.

Oops! I hate it when the finger gets in front of the lens!

A Call for Help

by Paul McCusker

Reconnecting with *Odyssey* after such a long time away was fun—and challenging. I hadn't written an *Odyssey* episode for three years. For my first venture back, we decided that I should pursue some sort of mystery with Bernard Walton, but I wasn't sure which idea to explore. One premise involved Bernard waking up in the hospital after the Timothy Center mysteriously burned down. But that seemed far too dramatic.

We wanted something fun. So I tried to imagine what kind of mystery Bernard might encounter—and realized it should have something to do with windows, of course. But what? I toyed with a variety of ideas—including someone writing the word "help" on windows all over town—but still didn't think it was enough. Then the idea of adding Wooton Bassett came along, and the potential of mixing his personality with Bernard's—combined with the added weirdness of the *Power Boy* help symbol appearing on the windows—sent the script into an entirely different, and more rewarding, direction.

The idea of adding the scam involving illegal workers came about because of some research I'd done about the modern slave trade. Tricking innocent people into working and living in below-standard conditions while intimidating and blackmailing them happens all over the world—including the United States.

Character:

Grady McKay

Quote: "Don't tell me how Power Boy got off the giant lobster planet."

Something you may not know about Grady: Besides the Bassett family, he was the first person to discover that Wooton draws *Power Boy* comics.

Album 49

The Sky's the Limit

An Era of Changes: The Writing of "A New Era"

This album tied up our storylines about Grady McKay, Mandy Straussberg, Connie's book, the grudge between Connie and Kelly, and Eugene's search for his father. To address Eugene's story, we recorded a two-part version of "A New Era." The original recording removed Eugene, Katrina, and Leonard Meltsner from the show. All three decided to permanently leave Odyssey and head for Africa to help the Ashanti tribe (see "Prisoners of Fear," album 45). The title "A New Era" meant *Odyssey* would be different with Eugene gone. In a third episode, "End of an Era," we recorded scenes where the folks in Odyssey say good-bye to the Meltsners.

Why would we want to say good-bye and remove Eugene and Katrina from the show? At the time, actor Will Ryan wasn't able to continue voicing Eugene. In fact, we created the entire Leonard storyline as a way for Eugene to leave Odyssey. If Eugene ever had to leave again, there was no better way than having him head off into the sunset with his long-lost father.

Having decided to write Eugene out of the show, we were pleasantly surprised when Will was able to continue as Eugene after all. We scrambled to change the story, allowing Leonard to go to Africa alone. New scenes were written and flashbacks were incorporated—*finally* the show was where it needed to be.

Or so we thought. After editing the voice recordings, we discovered the shows were 15 minutes too long! Instead of hacking the story to bits, we made the episode three parts again. Before finishing, we recorded portions of the show four times, a new record for us.

So, the episode that began as two parts to say good-bye to three people—Eugene, Katrina, and Leonard—turned out to be a three-part saga to say good-bye to one person, Leonard Meltsner.

Episode Information

619, 620, 621: A New Era, I, II, and III
Original Air Dates: 9/15/07, 9/22/07, & 9/29/07
Writers: Nathan Hoobler & Marshal Younger
Sound Designer: Gap Digital
Scripture: 1 Thessalonians 5:9
Themes: Salvation, the sanctity of life, following God's will, redemption
Summary: Upon returning to Odyssey, Leonard Meltsner faces a medical crisis while Eugene and Katrina get disturbing news from the Ashanti tribe in Africa.

622: B-TV: Temptation
Original Air Date: 10/06/07
Writer: Nathan Hoobler
Sound Designer: Nathan Jones
Scripture: 1 Corinthians 10:13
Theme: Temptation
Summary: B-TV presents the biblical stories of Solomon and Joseph. And Connie tells a fairy tale about a young girl who encounters a very unusual plant. Each character faces temptations and has to make a choice.

623: Buddy Guard
Original Air Date: 10/13/07
Writers: Jymn Magon & Marshal Younger
Sound Designer: Christopher Diehl
Scripture: Deuteronomy 11:17
Theme: Purity of motives
Summary: Grady McKay hires a bodyguard to protect himself from Rodney Rathbone at all times. Meanwhile, at radio station Odyssey 105, Cryin' Bryan Dern convinces his assistant, P. J., to sue people for frivolous actions.

624: Wooing Wooton
Original Air Date: 10/20/07
Writer: Marshal Younger
Sound Designer: Nathan Jones
Theme: Integrity
Summary: Wooton Bassett's father comes to town to get his son's help on a business deal. Meanwhile, Grady must make a decision that could cost his mom her job.

625: Something Significant
Original Air Date: 10/27/07
Writers: Kathy Buchanan & Nathan Hoobler
Sound Designer: Jonathan Crowe
Theme: Obedience to God in all things
Summary: In the Imagination Station, Trent DeWhite journeys to ancient India, the South Pacific, and New York's Constitution Island to see stories of people who were used by God.

626, 627: Life, in the Third Person, I and II
Original Air Dates: 11/03/07, 11/10/07
Writer: Paul McCusker
Sound Designer: Gap Digital
Scripture: Psalm 55:22
Theme: God's comfort in troubled times
Summary: As her parents seem headed for divorce, Mandy Straussberg faces the future with a grim determination. Meanwhile, her father works on making his move to Chicago permanent.

628, 629: The Highest Stakes, I and II
Original Air Dates: 12/01/07, 12/08/07
Writers: Nathan Hoobler & Marshal Younger
Sound Designer: Nathan Jones
Scripture: 2 Corinthians 5:17
Themes: Forgiveness, salvation
Summary: Grady's father, Carson McKay, returns to Odyssey after a long absence. The whole family must decide whether or not to trust him.

630: Chip Off the Shoulder
Original Air Date: 12/15/07
Writer: Marshal Younger
Sound Designer: Jonathan Crowe
Scripture: Ephesians 4:31-32
Themes: Reconciliation, grudges
Summary: Connie must face her bitterness against Kelly. Meanwhile Kelly learns about the importance of rules.

Grady McKay lounges on Wooton's "couch" in "The Highest Stakes."

Gary Locke's sketch of the album cover art for *The Sky's the Limit*

Sound Bites

Actor Melissa Disney plays Victoria Jamison, Wooton's love interest in "Wooing Wooton." Melissa also played Monica, who was Jason Whittaker's love interest in the Novacom saga (album 38).

My Take: Marshal Younger

The sanctity of every human life is one of the cornerstone beliefs at Focus on the Family. We had done several episodes (such as "The Underground Railroad," album 24, and "A Lesson from Mike," album 31) about this topic. But when we addressed the issue of abortion directly in "Pamela Has a Problem" (*The Lost Episodes*) it became a controversial episode. With "A New Era," we hoped to do a show that addressed abortion but wouldn't mention it directly; we chose instead to feature someone who kept her baby. This episode also resolved Eugene's long-running feelings of family rejection that had been mentioned in other episodes.

Goof Alert!

In "A New Era," Joanne Woodston tells the story of seeing a young Eugene through the ultrasound machine. He was rubbing his chin just like his father. This was inspired by a true story from the Option Ultrasound project at Focus on the Family. A woman intent on abortion saw her baby pictured through an ultrasound machine. The baby had his arms behind his head, looking as if he were relaxing. The woman was in the exact same body position. Upon seeing the baby's image, she was overwhelmed with emotion and decided to keep the baby. At the time Eugene was born, ultrasound machines couldn't have produced as detailed an image as was described on the

Actor Jess Harnell, voice of Wooton, and Melissa Disney, voice of Victoria

show. But we decided that it was worth a "goof" to tell a version of this powerful story on *Adventures in Odyssey*.

My Take: Nathan Hoobler

We often introduce bit parts on *Adventures in Odyssey* and resort to various methods of naming them. Since I love climbing mountains, I've named many characters after mountains in Colorado, including: Mr. *Elbert* (a scientist in "Exactly as Planned," album 38), William *Crestone* (the father in "Call Me if You Care," album 43), *Carson* McKay (Grady's dad, "The Highest Stakes"), Mr. *Sherman* and Mrs. *Belford* (counselors in "The Champ of the Camp," album 45), and Evan *Antero* (a missionary in "A New Era").

Sound Bites

"B-TV: Temptation" was originally written for Bart Rathbone to be the evil Heckleberry bush in the "Storytime with Connie" segment. The plant even occasionally broke character with lines like, "You can't chop me down! I'm too strong! Almost as strong as the duct tape they have on sale right now at the Electric Palace." Unfortunately, actor Walker Edmiston, who voices Bart, became ill and couldn't record. Actor Jess Harnell (Wooton) filled in, voicing a character who sounded like Academy-Award-winning actor Joe Pesci (b.1943).

Cut Scenes

The first draft for "Buddy Guard" contained a subplot of Bart Rathbone filing frivolous lawsuits against several people (including Whit for parking too close to Bart's car and Wooton for dropping Bart's mail in the mud). We replaced the Bart storyline with one involving Cryin' Bryan Dern. A scene where P. J. confronted his neighbor about a howling chinchilla was also cut late in production.

Behind the Scenes: Wooing Wooton

"Wooing Wooton" threw a wrench in Grady's journey to salvation. After "Only by His Grace" (album 48), Grady seemed right on the verge of becoming a Christian. We decided that it shouldn't be that easy for him and so we presented a stumbling block—his mother's view of Christians.

My Take: Marshal Younger

The creation of The Pool Boys in "Wooing Wooton" came from an unusual source. When I was in high school, I produced zillions of videos with my dad's video camera. One was called *The Bathtub Show* in which I hosted a talk show from my bathtub, fully clothed but immersed in water. I would interview imaginary famous people who were also in the bathtub (but off camera, of course). I ended every show by singing a song underwater. It was a very absurd idea, and I can't believe I'm using *The Bathtub Show* as part of my career now.

Sound Bites

Shane Baumel plays the young Eugene Meltsner in "A New Era." He also plays Eugene's brother, Everett, in "The Top Floor" (album 48).

Goof Alert!

We finally heard Wooton Bassett's father in "Wooing Wooton." He was played by actor Fred Tatasciore. However, we goofed on his name. In "Wooing Wooton," he's named Winston. But in "Bassett Hounds" (album 40), his name is Winslow.

Actor Fred Tatasciore, voice of Winston Bassett, in "Wooing Wooton"

BTS: Something Significant

Kathy Buchanan wrote "Something Significant" with three storylines about the song "Jesus Loves Me, This I Know." First was the writing of the song by Anna Bartlett Warner; second, a story about a girl who was influenced by the song (Amy Carmichael); third, a story set in a communist country. After concerns were raised that airing the third story might offend people in that country, we altered the script. Four days before the session, we inserted an idea found in the pages of a 2002 *National Geographic* magazine. It was the story of a young John F. Kennedy in World War II.

BTS: *Life, in the Third Person*

"Life, in the Third Person" was another episode that had to be changed after it was recorded. As first written and produced, the episode ended with the Straussberg parents reuniting but deciding to move to Chicago. We intended to say good-bye to the Straussbergs, in part because we understood that actor Aria Curzon (voice of Mandy) was leaving the Los Angeles area and wouldn't be available. However, Aria decided to stay in Southern California, so we recorded a new closing scene with Connie and Mandy, affirming that the parents had reconciled and that the family would remain in Odyssey. Mandy was too good to lose!

Sound designer Jonathan Crowe and assistant Michael Erb recording the slave scene in "Something Significant"

BTS: *The Highest Stakes*

We wanted Grady McKay to become a Christian in "The Highest Stakes," but we hadn't decided what we wanted to do with the character of Carson McKay (Grady's dad). We wrote one ending where he left town again, leaving his family behind. However, after reading the full script, we decided that Grady had been through enough heartache and that his father really should come home for good. Upon hearing the final show, we realized that it wasn't clear that Carson was completely free of his gambling and debt problems. We hoped that future shows with Carson and Grady living safely in Odyssey would help clear up this point.

Ode to an Angel

The Sky's the Limit is dedicated to the memory of Saul "Angel" Cruz-Karaffa. Angel, the foster child of producer Marshal Younger, died on February 18, 2007, at the age of five. Angel "oozed joy" despite his very difficult life. He was an inspiration to everyone he met.

Angel Cruz-Karaffa

Good-bye Eugene!

For "End of an Era," the unused show that said good-bye to Eugene, Bernard wrote a poem expressing his feelings. Whit, Connie, and Tom Riley helped him read it. Here is the text of the recorded, but *unused* poem.

When I first met you, I was scared and perplexed,
'Cause I never knew what would come out of you next.
With orations so long and thoughts so remote,
At times I wanted to shove a cat down your throat.

But things have changed a bit since that day,
You're not nearly as frightening, or offensive, I must say.
But through the years you've changed, we see.
And like a stubborn wart, you've grown on me.

When you first came around, you said farewell and adieu,
Now, you still say farewell, but you say good-bye too.
Your rantings went on, and on and on.
Now your rant ends (after everyone's gone).

Not a soul would listen, whether lonely, dying, or buried,
But I guess you found someone 'cause somehow you're married.
But we found you were more than annoying and smart,
You were a good man, with a really good heart.

I suppose I will miss you, our recovering geek,
It's a bit sad to know I won't see you next week.
We'll miss the gadgets, the gizmos, you trying our patience,
And even your "Greetings and Salutations!"

Though I've laughed at you, scolded you, said things I regret,
You are a good friend that I will not forget.

Album 50

The Best Small Town

An Odyssey Landmark

The Best Small Town was a celebration of many milestones for *Odyssey*. (See cover art at left.) It was the 50th original album, the 20th anniversary of the radio show, and the final album to feature actor Walker Edmiston (voice of Tom Riley and Bart Rathbone). We hoped that the album would be a celebration of the past 20 years of the show, using our classic storytelling approaches to flavor these new stories.

The idea for the main story arc came from Marshal Younger. He and his family ad moved in 1997, and they used the book *The 100 Best Small Towns in America* to determine where they would settle. He wondered, "What if we created a contest and Odyssey competed for the ultimate prize—the *best* small town in the country?" This could lead to all sorts of celebration and excitement. We liked the idea of linking all of the episodes in album 50 with a common storyline, much as we had done in other collections.

Episode Information

631: A Capsule Comes to Town
Original Air Date: 3/1/08
Writer: Paul McCusker
Sound Designer: Jonathan Crowe
Theme: Learning from the past
Summary: Connie narrates a documentary about the people and places in Odyssey against the backdrop of a search for a missing time capsule.

632: Suspicious Finds
Original Air Date: 3/8/08
Writers: Nathan Hoobler & Marshal Younger
Sound Designer: Christopher Diehl
Theme: Living to please God
Summary: An editor from *Home and Country* magazine announces that Odyssey is a contender for Best Small Town in America.

633: License to Deprive
Original Air Date: 3/15/08
Writer: Marshal Younger
Sound Designer: Nathan Jones
Scripture: Deuteronomy 11:17
Theme: Appreciating what you have
Summary: For a historical exhibit, the Washington family must live as people on the frontier did.

634, 635: Accidental Dilemma, I and II
Original Air Dates: 3/22/08 & 3/29/08
Writer: Paul McCusker
Sound Designer: Gap Digital
Scripture: John 16:33
Theme: Good triumphs over evil
Summary: When Jason Whittaker is revealed publicly as an intelligence agent, an old nemesis named The Whisperer tracks him to Odyssey.

636: A Class Reenactment
Original Air Date: 4/5/08
Writer: Nathan Hoobler
Sound Designer: Christopher Diehl
Theme: Doing what's right
Summary: Edwin Blackgaard puts on a "radio reenactment" of the founding of the town of Odyssey. Two of his actors, Mandy Straussberg and Trent DeWhite, are unhappy when they're cast as a young couple in love.

637: The Forgotten Deed
Original Air Date: 4/12/08
Writer: Paul McCusker
Sound Designer: Jonathan Crowe
Theme: Standing up for your faith
Summary: The plan to bury the new time capsule in the basement of Whit's End causes a "separation of church and state" conflict that jeopardizes the future of the shop.

638, 639: The Triangled Web, I and II
Original Air Dates: 4/19/08 & 4/26/08
Writer: Marshal Younger
Sound Designer: Jonathan Crowe
Scripture: 1 Samuel 20:31
Theme: Friendship
Summary: Lucy Cunningham-Schultz becomes the center of attention when Jimmy Barclay, Curt Stevens, and Jack Davis return to Odyssey for a reunion—each young man determined to win her heart at last.

640: Rights, Wrongs, and Winners

Original Air Date: 5/03/08
Writer: Nathan Hoobler
Sound Designer: Christopher Diehl
Scripture: Galatians 6:7-8
Theme: Sacrifice

Summary: The two finalists for "Best Small Town" are in a perfect tie. Each town is given one week to show the heart of the town to win the contest.

641, 642: The Imagination Station, Revisited, I and II

Original Air Dates: 5/10/08 & 5/17/08
Writer: Paul McCusker
Sound Designer: Nathan Jones
Scripture: John 3:16
Theme: Salvation

Summary: Kelly gets in a new version of the Imagination Station and experiences the story of the crucifixion of Jesus.

The celebratory parade continues! Look closely for a rare glimpse of Wooton!

During our brainstorming of *The Best Small Town*, we put each plot point on an index card to organize the complex story. *From left: Odyssey* intern Drew Boone, Marshal Younger, Nathan Hoobler

An Album's Worth of Ideas

Album 50 was an important milestone for the series, so the team wanted it to reflect 20 years of the show, but without the album becoming a review of the series' history. We came up with all sorts of stories for the album, including many that didn't make the final cut. These abandoned stories included:

- In a dark period of Odyssey history from the early 1800s, then-mayor Terrence Blackgaard (Regis's great, great grandfather) wanted to turn Odyssey into a haven for gambling. He tried to take over

the church (where Whit's End now sits) to obtain a mineral that had mysterious healing properties.

- Bart opens a competing business to Whit's End while the real one is closed for renovations. Meanwhile, a couple of the kids try to open their own version of Whit's End and realize that making such a place successful is a lot harder than it looks.
- The Barclays come back to town but have to deal with the changes in Odyssey. Young Stewart Reed doesn't understand why the family loved the place so much until Jimmy shows him Wonderworld.

- To exploit the Best Town contest, Bart Rathbone opens a bed-and-breakfast with a French name (that he found on the Internet). He lures in several families, including the Barclays, and everything that can go wrong does.
- After realizing that Odyssey could lose the Best Small Town award, Connie, Wooton Bassett, and Bernard Walton decide to take a road trip to see what their chief competition is up to. They arrive in a town called Richland and discover what seems to be the perfect little hamlet. Oscar Peterson—former Odyssey kid—is mayor of the town. However, after some investigation, they find that Richland is practically bankrupt. The town has gotten all their money from tourists throwing money into a wishing well that has worn out its "luckiness." The town needs the prize even more than Odyssey does. Connie, Wooton, and Bernard decide that Odyssey needs to lose the contest so Richland can win.
- Tom Riley finds out that his wife, Agnes, has only a few days left to live. He tries to make the most of her final days by planning event after event, but Agnes would rather just spend time with Tom and her friends.
- Chris Anthony joins Dr. Julius Schnitzelbonker to introduce each episode from his lab in Odyssey.

That Sounds Familiar

To celebrate the 50th album and 20th anniversary, we gave each episode a name reminiscent of other *Odyssey* titles.

Title	Original Episode	Album
A Capsule Comes to Town	Connie Comes to Town	1
Suspicious Finds	Suspicious Minds	8
A License to Deprive	A License to Drive	14
Accidental Dilemma	Dental Dilemma	The Lost Episodes
A Class Reenactment	A Class Act	15
The Forgotten Deed	The Ill-Gotten Deed	6
The Triangled Web	The Tangled Web	1
Rights, Wrongs, and Winners	Rights, Wrongs, and Reasons	15
The Imagination Station, Revisited	The Imagination Station	5

Behind the Scenes: A Capsule Comes to Town

This episode featured the documentary that Connie started working on in "Chip Off the Shoulder" (album 49). It was presented as an episode of a fictional series called *At Home in My Town*. We persuaded Focus on the Family commentator Stuart Shepard to play the host. It is the only *Adventures in Odyssey* episode that doesn't feature Chris's voice anywhere in the program.

To make the documentary sound authentic, we enlisted the help of Howard Stableford, a producer and host for various science programs by the British Broadcasting Corporation. He was amused to be involved and said, "*Odyssey* programs are produced with such high quality standards for audio. They wanted a 'newsy' sound to the show, more like what we'd do for a quick production. So, basically, they brought me in to lower their standards!"

One of the changes from a typical show was the style of recording. Normally, each actor speaks into an individual high-quality studio microphone. For this show, we asked actor Katie Leigh (Connie) to hold an inexpensive handheld microphone in front of each actor, as if she was really doing an interview.

Sound Bites

In "A Capsule Comes to Town," Bob Luttrell voiced the construction worker Mr. Pape. He modeled the performance on Ambrose P. Schnook, a character he played in "The Ill-Gotten Deed" (album 6).

BTS: A Capsule Comes to Town

The items that Eugene and Jack find in the Odyssey time capsule (including a ladies' gingham sunbonnet and a Heidelberg Alternating Current Belt) were from a 1901 Sears and Roebuck catalog that Paul McCusker used as a reference. (But sadly, the items were no longer available for purchase.)

Farewell, Walker Edmiston

Actor Robert Easton, voice of Bart Rathbone in *The Best Small Town*

On February 15, 2007, actor Walker Edmiston passed away at the age of 81. He had been a foundational member of the *Odyssey* cast, appearing as early as the original *Family Portraits* series in January 1987. He's best remembered for the much-loved farmer Tom Riley, which he played in over 130 episodes. Later, his voice work as Bart Rathbone brought the audience more than a few laughs.

Walker often said that his favorite thing about *Adventures in Odyssey* was the family feeling he experienced in the studio while recording the show. Dave Arnold remembers it being the other way around, "Walker made you feel like you were part of *his* family."

After Walker's passing, the team carefully considered what we should do with Tom and Bart. Tom's appearance in "A Capsule Comes to Town" was possible using a line from "The Nemesis," (album 5). But in "Suspicious Finds," we were able to add some lines from Walker that had never been heard before. In 2006 Walker had recorded an episode called "The End of an Era" (album 49, see sidebar). In the original scene, Tom helped get Eugene's house ready for sale. In the revised scene for "Suspicious Finds," Tom helps prepare Whit's End for an inspector. Sound designer Chris Diehl blended the lines together perfectly.

Meanwhile, we still needed lines from Bart Rathbone that Walker had never recorded. An exhaustive search for Bart soundalikes led us to actor Robert Easton. He and Walker were close friends and Robert also did roles that Walker turned down, and vice-versa.

"But there's no replacing Walker," Paul McCusker said. "Losing him was like the end of an era, really. Walker represented a generation of actors that are hard to come by: talented, warm, professional, never interested in the spotlight or having their egos stroked. It's hard to imagine going on without him. I was thinking of Walker when I wrote the last few lines of 'The Forgotten Deed.'"

Album 50 is dedicated to Walker, and if you examine the cover image closely, you'll find a hidden tribute to him.

Walker Edmiston's last *Odyssey* recording session, August 2006. *From left:* Paul Herlinger (Whit), Walker (Tom, Bart), Will Ryan (Eugene), Katie Leigh (Connie)

Cut Scenes

In one deleted scene in "Suspicious Finds," Eugene created a computer program that analyzed 47 criteria to determine Odyssey's chances of winning the Best Small Town competition. Eugene believed that the town was doomed for several reasons. The airport had two concourses (previous winners had only one concourse). Odyssey didn't have access to a large amusement park. And Odyssey was headquarters to both Novacom and Dr. Blackgaard's company, two groups that had tried to take over the world.

Actor Jimmy Weldon, voice of Perry Browning, editor of *Home and Country* magazine

Sound Bites with Christopher Diehl

The *Odyssey* writers are always putting in scenes with Bart Rathbone eating pork rinds. There was a scene like that in "Suspicious Finds." So, being the diligent sound designers that we are, we have to be authentic and get the sounds of the real thing. A potato chip just wouldn't sound the same going into the mouth. I think I've gained five pounds doing the sound effects for those pork rinds scenes!

My Take: Marshal Younger

I had to do a lot of research for "License to Deprive." First, I researched old buildings to find out what year the "oldest building in the state" would have been built. It helped a little that we've never announced in which state Odyssey is located. Then, I read a few books about life in the 1700s. The questions Abraham peppers Ed with (about macadam roads and mud wagons) are all from that research.

Sound Bites with Nathan Jones

"License to Deprive" included a scene where Abraham, the history specialist, ate hot beet casserole. Since we didn't have any around—and we had to get the sound effects—we made a slimy concoction of oatmeal and raisin bran. It sounded just right and was healthy too . . . yum!

BTS: Accidental Dilemma

Jason Whittaker tried to keep his secret-agent identity a secret. But Jack Allen found out in "The Final Conflict" (album 25), Eugene learned about it in "The Search for Whit" (album 27), and even Leonard Meltsner got in on the truth in "The Top Floor" (album 48).

Connie finally found out in album 50. No wonder she always complains that she's the last to know anything!

My Take: Paul McCusker

In "Accidental Dilemma," Jason is struggling to remember the secret code to disarm a rigged computer. The Whisperer says, "I always use my birthday." Actor Chris Edgerly ad-libbed this line, my favorite ad-lib of the album.

The Geography of Odyssey

The mountains and landmarks around Odyssey have been inspired by a number of places around the United States. In "Accidental Dilemma," Tasha Forbes mentions Gold Camp Road that leads into the mountains from Odyssey but has been closed for years. The real Gold Camp Road is in Colorado Springs, Colorado.

Cut Scenes

Occasionally, we put jokes into our scripts that only the team will read . . . except this once. Here is an example from the climax of "Accidental Dilemma":

```
CARSON: (hugs Grady) Are you all
right?

GRADY: I am . . . now.
[Tasha charges in with her team,
the police, the fire depart-
ment, ambulance personnel, the
city sewer repairmen, the elec-
tric utilities service personnel,
an agent from OSHA, an ice-cream
truck, and a short man with a
large utility belt who happened
to be walking by while attempting
```

The cast and crew of "The Triangled Web"

to catch the last bus to
Connellsville for his night shift
at a tool shop. (Sadly, he missed
the bus and was later fired from
his job, causing him to hate Whit
and Whit's End. He will eventually concoct a scheme to exact his
revenge on them all.)]

TASHA: (*charges in*) All right—
weapons down—nobody move.

My Take: Nathan Hoobler

I always thought that actor David Griffin's story (see opening paragraph, album 11) about how he saw the director and producer whispering in the control room as he waited to hear from them in the studio was heart-

breaking—but also hilarious. We had a similar incident happen to Edwin Blackgaard in "A Class Reenactment" when Eugene and Connie weren't sure what to tell him about his play.

BTS: A Class Reenactment

The character of Duncan Banquo is named after two characters in seventeenth-century William Shakespeare's tragedy, *Macbeth*.

BTS: A Class Reenactment

This script originally ended with Edwin Blackgaard's closing narration about the founding of Odyssey. Upon reading the script the day before recording, the team felt that another ending was needed. We quickly wrote a scene where Edwin embarrassed himself in front of the much-discussed theatre critic. Actor Will Ryan stepped in to play the critic.

Sound Bites
Usually we bring all of the actors into the studio at the same time to record our shows. However, several of the actors in "The Triangled Web" were in different locations around the country. We recorded actress Katie Leigh calling them on the phone, just like her character does in the show. So we actually called Brandon Gilberstadt (Jared DeWhite), and Sage Bolte (Robyn Jacobs) at their homes from the studio.

My Take: Marshal Younger
"The Triangled Web" was inspired in part because we noticed that Lucy always seemed to hang around with different boys in the older *Odyssey* shows. We thought, "What if all of those boys actually had crushes on Lucy?" After this show, I think we'll have to refer to her as Lucy Cunningham-Schultz-Davis.

BTS: The Triangled Web
There was a real energy in the studio during the recording of "The Triangled Web." Jonathan Crowe remembers, "There was something special about bringing all those beloved characters back to life. And we were all surprised that Genesis Long's voice hadn't changed a bit, even after so many years." Actor David Griffin remembers, "I was floating on clouds for a few weeks after the recording . . . like I always am after a session."

Sound Bites: Rights, Wrongs, and Winners
In keeping with Wooton's favorite song, his cell phone plays "Camptown Races."

BTS: Rights, Wrongs, and Winners
Magazine editor Perry Browning mentions that the town of Klamath Falls, Oregon, was last year's Best Small Town winner. We added that line because cocreator Phil Lollar always imagined Klamath Falls when writing about the town of Odyssey.

Sound Bites: The Imagination Station, Revisited
John Mark is played by Chad Reisser, who played Digger Digwillow in the original Imagination Station adventure.

Album 51?
Look for even more exciting adventures in the next album. Whit would say, "The best is yet to come."

I Haven't Heard You Since. . .

The Best Small Town included appearances by a number of characters who hadn't been heard on the show in a long time. Here they are, organized by their last appearance, starting with the longest time away from the series.

Character	Previous episode appearance	Album
Curt Stevens	"It Takes Integrity"	13
Robyn Jacobs	"Pen Pal"	15
Jack Davis	"A Call for Reverend Jimmy"	22
Lawrence Hodges	"Subject Yourself"	24
Philip Glossman	"The Final Conflict"	25
Tasha Forbes	"The Search for Whit"	27
Lucy Cunningham-Schultz	"It's a Wrap"	28
Jimmy Barclay	"Living in the Gray"	42
Jared DeWhite	"Split Ends"	42
Jack Allen	"And That's the Truth"	43
Edwin Blackgaaard	"The Power of One"	44
Harlow Doyle	"Odyssey Sings!"	45
Walter Shakespeare	"Odyssey Sings!"	45

The Lost Episodes

Rediscovered!

Okay, the obvious question must be asked . . . How did *The Lost Episodes* get lost in the first place? When we ventured into the vault to find them, we felt a little like Indiana Jones in some forbidden temple; hence Whit and the action-adventure cover.

Ever since the beginning of *Adventures in Odyssey*, some programs didn't fit into our regularly released albums for one reason or another. Sometimes we left them out because of timing. For example, we didn't want to place a Christmas show in an album we were releasing in the middle of the summer. Or, we wanted to save some episodes for other special collections. In other cases, we decided that the content might be a little too mature or controversial to be included with our normal episodes. All of these reasons led to a group of several episodes that simply didn't appear in our normal collections. That is until *The Lost Episodes* released.

Episode Information

8: Dental Dilemma
Original Air Date: 1/9/88
Writer: Susan McBride
Sound Designer: Bob Luttrell
Scripture: Psalm 27:1
Themes: Teasing, dealing with fear
Summary: Middle-schooler Mark Forbes plants fear in the heart of his younger sister, Emily, as she anticipates her first dental appointment.

15: My Brother's Keeper
Original Air Date: 2/27/88
Writer: Paul McCusker
Sound Designer: Bob Luttrell
Scripture: Proverbs 12:18
Theme: Sibling conflict
Summary: A boy named Phillip Callas wants to get rid of his younger brother, and his wish might come true—permanently.

16: No Stupid Questions
Original Air Date: 3/5/88
Writer: Susan McBride
Sound Designer: Bob Luttrell
Scripture: Proverbs 18:15
Themes: Respect for the handicapped, the value of seeking knowledge
Summary: Young Meg Stevens asks a constant stream of questions, which annoys a cranky man named Chris Gottlieb.

22: A Simple Addition
Original Air Date: 4/16/88
Writer: Susan McBride
Sound Designer: Bob Luttrell
Scripture: Romans 12:10
Theme: Sibling rivalry
Summary: Elementary-schooler Nicky is upset that his baby sister is taking his parents' attention away from him.

30: Honor Thy Parents
Original Air Date: 6/11/88
Writer: Phil Lollar
Sound Designer: Bob Luttrell
Scripture: Exodus 20:12
Theme: Respecting parents
Summary: Ten-year-old Laura Fremont is ashamed of her parents because she thinks they are "hicks."

44: It Sure Seems Like It to Me
Original Air Date: 9/17/88
Writer: Phil Lollar
Sound Designer: Bob Luttrell
Scripture: Psalm 19:14; Ephesians 4:29
Theme: Exaggerating
Summary: Leslie, a young girl with a reputation for exaggeration, tells her most outrageous story yet.

45: What Are We Gonna Do About Halloween?
Original Air Date: 10/22/88
Writer: Paul McCusker
Sound Designer: Bob Luttrell
Scripture: Romans 12:2
Themes: Halloween, bringing light from darkness
Summary: Two boys, Brad and Leonard, try to come up with an alternate way to celebrate Halloween at Whit's End.

55: Auld Lang Syne
Original Air Date: 12/31/88
Writer: Phil Lollar
Sound Designer: Dave Arnold
Scripture: Revelation 22:13
Themes: The importance of memories, reflecting on your life
Summary: Whit and his friend Tom Riley look back at their adventures over the last year.

116: Isaac the Benevolent

Original Air Date: 6/23/90
Writer: Phil Lollar
Sound Designer: Dave Arnold
Scripture: Matthew 7:12; Luke 6:31
Theme: The Golden Rule
Summary: Isaac Morton tries to put the command to "do unto others" into action, but it always seems to backfire.

117: The Trouble with Girls

Original Air Date: 6/30/90
Writer: Paul McCusker
Sound Designer: Bob Luttrell
Scripture: 1 Corinthians 13
Themes: Crushes, puppy love
Summary: Jimmy Barclay has to deal with puppy love when he starts getting love notes from a classmate named Jessie.

134: Pamela Has a Problem

Original Air Date: 12/1/90
Writer: Paul McCusker
Sound Designer: Dave Arnold
Scripture: Psalm 82:1-4
Themes: Abortion, the sanctity of life
Summary: Connie's friend Pamela arrives from California with a surprise—she's pregnant.
PARENTAL WARNING:
This story deals with the concepts of the sanctity of life and abortion in an open and frank way. While the issues are handled sensitively, the subject matter may be too mature for younger listeners.

142: Train Ride

Original Air Date: 1/26/91
Writer: Phil Lollar
Sound Designer: Bob Luttrell
Scripture: Matthew 5:44
Themes: Pranks, breaking up the daily routine
Summary: Whit and Eugene get caught up in a mystery on a train ride back from Chicago.
PARENTAL WARNING:
Although the story is told tongue-in-cheek, this murder mystery may be too intense for younger listeners.

161: Isaac the True Friend

Original Air Date: 8/3/91
Writer: Phil Lollar
Sound Designer: Dave Arnold
Scripture: 1 Samuel 20; Proverbs 18:24
Themes: Bible story of David and Jonathan, friendship
Summary: Isaac takes an Imagination Station adventure to see two of the greatest friends in history—Prince Jonathan and a shepherd named David.

435, 436: A Look Back, I and II

Original Air Dates: 12/18/99 & 12/25/99
Writer: Phil Lollar
Sound Designer: Rob Jorgensen
Themes: Remembering the past, salvation
Summary: Cocreator Phil Lollar takes a peek back at the first 13 years of *Adventures in Odyssey*.

500: 500

Original Air Date: 7/13/02
Assembled by Nathan Hoobler
Sound Designer: Jonathan Crowe
Theme: The behind-the-scenes story of *Adventures in Odyssey*
Summary: Five hundred episodes of *Odyssey* are remembered with highlights from hundreds of Odyssey clips and never-before-heard material.

501: Inside the Studio

Original Air Date: 11/23/02
Writer: Nathan Hoobler
Sound Designer: Jonathan Crowe
Theme: A behind-the-scenes talk with the *Odyssey* actors
Summary: Take an exclusive look inside the production studio in honor of the 15th anniversary of *Adventures in Odyssey*!

Why These Episodes Were "Lost"

- "Dental Dilemma," "My Brother's Keeper," "No Stupid Questions," and "A Simple Addition" were originally created for *Family Portraits*, the pilot series that preceded *Adventures in Odyssey*.

- As you may know, celebrating Halloween is one of those subjects that challenges Christian parents. "What Are We Going to Do About Halloween?" was written to give parents a few alternative ideas to Halloween, hoping to find middle ground. Or so we thought. As it turned out, parents holding differing views about all aspects of Halloween didn't approve of the position we took in the episode, so we put the program aside.

- "Isaac the Benevolent" and "The Trouble with Girls" are not so much "lost" as "displaced" episodes, thanks to Officer David Harley (see "The Trouble with Harley," album 1). Some of the Officer Harley episodes were rewritten and rerecorded (see "The Officer Harley Remakes," album 8), and these are two of those episodes. But they became more of an anomaly when they appeared in a collection called "The Early Classics," replacing the original episodes. They were completely out of chronological order. Eugene Meltsner appeared in these two episodes in that album, though he wasn't actually introduced as a character until two albums later. So we removed them from that early album and put them in *The Lost Episodes*.

- "Honor Thy Parents," "It Sure Seems Like It to Me," and "Isaac the True Friend" were odd little episodes in which our usual hope of good writing, directing, and acting fell a little short of our high standards, so we simply refused to include them in our albums. We include them here as interesting curiosities and as a glimpse into the dynamics and pressures of creating a weekly radio series.

- "Train Ride" was a mystery/adventure that captivated many listeners, but it also dismayed some because of a violent moment on the train. As it turned out, that moment was not what some listeners thought it was—but the impression was made and we respected the critical letters we received.

- We've also done a number of retrospectives that were never released in a collection. These included "Auld Lang Syne," a retrospective on the stories from 1988; "A Look Back," an end-of-millennium perspective hosted by *Odyssey* cocreator Phil Lollar; "500," a celebration of our first 500 programs; and "Inside the Studio," which included the actors' perspectives on the 15th anniversary of the series. Listeners can finally enjoy these shows on *The Lost Episodes*.

Behind the Scenes: My Brother's Keeper

This was Paul McCusker's first script contribution to the world of *Odyssey*. Phil Lollar wrote the story, which Paul turned into a full-fledged script.

50 E. Foothill Blvd., Arcadia, CA 91006 • (818) 455-1579

August 10, 1987

Mr. Paul McKusker
236 Greenlea Place
Thousand Oaks, California 91361

Dear Paul:

Enclosed please find the guidelines for our new "Odyssey" program you requested.

I think you'll find these useful. They contain condensed biographies of our main character "Whit" and some of the other semi-regulars, as well as a brief history of "Whit's End" and the town of Odyssey.

I do hope that we can work together in the future. We have placed you on our roster of freelance writers and consider your contributions to be a valuable asset to "Odyssey, USA." (By the way, if you ever change your mind, you know where to find us!)

Thanks again for your interest in our program, and I wish you all the best in your writing projects.

Sincerely,

Phil Lollar
Senior Writer, "Odyssey, USA"

PL/st

P.S. I'm looking forward to receiving the publishing information you mentioned in our phone conversation!

Dedicated to the Preservation of the Home • James C. Dobson, Ph.D., President

The first of many letters between the two most prolific *Odyssey* writers

Goof Alert!

In "The Trouble with Girls," Curt Stevens says that his mom packed his lunch. However, in "Home Is Where the Hurt Is," Curt says that his mom left the family when he was little.

Goof Alert!

Toward the end of "Train Ride," Whit tells Inspector McGreavy, "You showed me your manuscript . . ." However, Whit and the inspector never got a chance to look at the roughs of the book. Seeing the "murder" at the back of the train interrupted them.

BTS: Train Ride

We learned a little bit about Odyssey's geography in this episode. Apparently, it is between Chicago, Illinois, and Cincinnati, Ohio, and a day's train ride from the former. However, later episodes introduce geographical "facts" about Odyssey that seem to contradict this information.

Sound Bites

Dave Madden made his debut performance in "Honor Thy Parents." He later played Chester in "Family Vacation" (album 2) but was eventually cast as *Odyssey*'s favorite window washer, Bernard Walton.

BTS: Isaac the True Friend

This story introduced the character of Sam Johnson, who was for a time one of *Odyssey*'s central kids. He was played by actor Kyle Ellison. Kyle's mother later became the tutor for the child actors when they were at the *Adventures in Odyssey* studio.

Actor Chad Reisser, voice of Mark Forbes

BTS: *Dental Dilemma*

Actor Chad Reisser played Mark Forbes in this episode. Chad later played the recurring role of Whit's grandson, as well as Digger Digwillow, the young man who meets Jesus in the Imagination Station, and many other characters. Emily Forbes was played by actor Sage Bolte, who later played character Robyn Jacobs.

Goof Alert!

"A Look Back" was recorded with host Phil Lollar to commemorate the end of a year, decade, century, and millennium. After the show aired, several listeners wrote in to inform us that the millennium actually ended December 31, 2000, not 1999. But, honestly, did any of you celebrate at the end of 2000?

The Problem with "Pamela Has a Problem"

by Paul McCusker

The story behind "Pamela Has a Problem" started back in 1990. At the time Dr. Dobson asked the entire ministry of Focus on the Family to make a special effort to find ways to support the ministry's position on a variety of social issues. For example, one of Focus on the Family's core beliefs is the sanctity of every human life, whether born or unborn. So the *Odyssey* team decided to produce a program that would look at the issue of abortion in a way that children would understand.

While we knew that some parents might object to a program about abortion, we thought it was important to show dramatically the Christian side of the debate—something you don't often get in movies or on television.

The episode aired in December 1990. We received a lot of good initial responses from people who appreciated how we handled the issue. But we also received letters from parents who questioned the appropriateness of talking about such a thing in what's considered a kids' show. As time went on, we decided to air the episode only on the radio for special occasions. We also decided not to include it in one of our regular albums, but we hoped to include it in a special collection someday. And now we have.

Liz Horton

Clubhouse magazine circa 1990: Can you find all the items in this picture that begin with the letter S? So far, we've found 37. (Here are two examples of harder ones: scream and stripe)

Special Section: The Dusty Episodes

Still Lost?

Every series has episodes that didn't work out for one reason or another. *Odyssey* has a few that have been pushed to the back shelf and are gathering dust. Why aren't these episodes included in any of our packages? Here's the inside story:

- "Doing Unto Others," "Bobby's Valentine," "Missed It by That Much," "The Case of the Missing Train Car," "The Quality of Mercy," "Gotcha!" "Harley Takes the Case," and "The Return of Harley" were all episodes that prominently featured Officer Harley, who was banned from *Adventures in Odyssey* (see "The Trouble with Harley," album 1). However, all of these episodes were rewritten to replace Officer Harley (see "The Officer Harley Remakes" in album 8).

- "Lights Out at Whit's End" and "Addictions Can Be Habit-Forming" were also Officer Harley episodes. Since we didn't feel that they were quite up to *Odyssey* standards, we decided not to rewrite them. (Whit and Tom rapping the song called "Communicate!" in "Lights Out at Whit's End" will have us cringing for years to come.)

- "You Go to School Where?" was scrapped because it portrayed home schools inaccurately. Phil Lollar recalls: "The home schooling movement became large and sophisticated in a very short time,

In the creative frenzy of production, the team sometimes produces an episode that doesn't fit the needs of our albums.

thus outdating the episode more quickly than any of us could have imagined. Some scripts you're proud of . . . some you wish you'd never written. 'You Go to School Where?' definitely falls into the latter category, and that's why it's unreleased."

• "Christmas Around the World" is being saved for a future Christmas package, which hasn't yet materialized.

• "The Telltale Cat" was deemed to be too violent because David threw his sister's cat into Trickle Lake.

• The script for "B-TV: Grace" was supposed to be humorous, but some people considered it offensive to the Amish.

• In the process of teaching a lesson about name-calling, the producers worried that "Sticks and Stones" would give young listeners a new arsenal of names to call their classmates.

• "Career Moves" was a "split episode," meaning that it was a 10-minute half story that was originally paired with another episode to make a whole episode. The other half of the show ("The Bad Guy") was paired with another episode for *In Your Wildest Dreams* (album 34). So we had an extra 10-minute episode that didn't fit. We had to choose half a show to remove, and we dropped "Career Moves."

Unreleased Episode Information

3: Lights Out at Whit's End
Original Air Date: 12/5/87
Writers: Steve Harris & Phil Lollar
Sound Designer: Bob Luttrell
Scripture: 1 John 1:7
Themes: Communication, fellowship
Summary: A power failure leaves the kids at Whit's End without anything to do. That is, until Whit shows them what life was like without electricity . . . and how much fun it could be!

9: Doing Unto Others
Original Air Date: 1/16/88
Writer: Phil Lollar
Sound Designer: Bob Luttrell
Scripture: Matthew 7:12; Luke 6:31
Theme: The Golden Rule
Summary: Sixth-grader Johnny Bickle tries to figure out how to practice the Golden Rule.

11: Addictions Can Be Habit-Forming
Original Air Date: 1/30/88
Writers: Steve Harris & Jim Adams
Sound Designer: Bob Luttrell
Scripture: 1 Corinthians 6:12
Theme: Addictions
Summary: A young girl named Joey tries a variety of bizarre methods to get her friend Stefanie to go on a diet.

13: Bobby's Valentine
Original Air Date: 2/13/88
Writer: Paul McCusker
Sound Designer: Bob Luttrell
Scripture: 1 Corinthians 13
Themes: Crushes, puppy love
Summary: Young Bobby gets a note from Amy, who thinks that he's the cutest boy in school. Bobby, however, wants to stay as far from Amy as possible.

14: Missed It by That Much
Original Air Date: 2/20/88
Writer: Paul McCusker
Sound Designer: Bob Luttrell
Scripture: Matthew 25:1-13
Theme: Tardiness
Summary: Middle-schooler Rachel Weaver is late for everything. But when Connie threatens to kick her off the volleyball team, Rachel tries her very best to be on time.

21: The Case of the Missing Train Car
Original Air Date: 4/9/88
Writer: Phil Lollar
Sound Designer: Bob Luttrell
Scripture: Matthew 18:21-35; 1 Corinthians 13:7
Themes: Forgiveness, unconditional love
Summary: When a model train car goes missing from Whit's End, many kids suspect Michelle Terry, a girl with a bad reputation.

23: The Quality of Mercy
Original Air Date: 4/23/88
Writer: Paul McCusker
Sound Designer: Bob Luttrell
Scripture: Matthew 18:21-35
Theme: Mercy
Summary: Ten-year-old troublemaker Scott Williams is let off the hook when he is caught trying to steal apples from Tom Riley. Unfortunately, Scott doesn't extend the same mercy to others.

24: Gotcha!
Original Air Date: 4/30/88
Writer: Phil Lollar
Sound Designer: Bob Luttrell
Scripture: 1 John 4:1-6
Theme: The occult
Summary: Middle-schooler Philo Sanderson loves pulling practical jokes, but Whit is disturbed when Philo says that his lucky rabbit's foot keeps him safe.

25 and 26: Harley Takes the Case, I and II
Original Air Dates: 5/7/88 & 5/14/88
Writer: Paul McCusker
Sound Designer: Bob Luttrell
Scripture: Luke 15:11-32
Theme: You can't run away from your problems.
Summary: Officer David Harley tries to find a missing boy named Steve Larson.

70 and 71: The Return of Harley, I and II
Original Air Dates: 4/29/89 & 5/10/89
Writer: Phil Lollar
Sound Designers: Bob Luttrell & Dave Arnold
Scripture: Proverbs 14:7, 25
Theme: Controlling your imagination
Summary: Officer Harley returns to Odyssey and is caught up in a mystery involving bootleggers and hidden caves!

85: You Go to School Where?
Original Air Date: 9/16/89
Writer: Phil Lollar
Sound Designer: Dave Arnold
Scripture: Proverbs 22:6
Theme: Home schooling
Summary: It's back-to-school time in Odyssey. But Esther Langford doesn't go to Odyssey Elementary. Her parents teach her at home.

370 and 371: Christmas Around the World, I and II
Original Air Dates: 12/14/96 & 12/21/96
Writer: Paul McCusker
Sound Designers: Dave Arnold & Mark Drury
Scripture: Luke 2
Theme: Christmas
Summary: The Imagination Station gives Eugene, Tom Riley, Sam Johnson, and Erica Clark a tour of Christmas celebrations around the world.

438b: The Telltale Cat
Original Air Date: 3/11/00
Writer: Jim Ware
Sound Designer: Jonathan Crowe
Scripture: Numbers 32:23
Theme: Your sin will find you out.
Summary: David Straussberg resorts to desperate measures to get rid of his sister's cat.

439: B-TV: Grace
Original Air Date: 3/18/00
Writer: Jim Ware
Sound Designer: Todd Busteed
Scripture: Ephesians 2:8-9
Theme: Grace
Summary: Take a modernized version of the prodigal son, add free hot dogs and lemonade, and voilá—you have a menu for teaching B-TV viewers a lesson about getting things we don't deserve.

442b: Sticks and Stones
Original Air Date: 4/15/00
Writer: Marshal Younger
Sound Designer: Rob Jorgensen
Scripture: James 3:1-12
Theme: The impact of hurtful words
Summary: The Rathbone family is determined to keep the Petersons from opening a competing electronics store. Doing his share to deter the newcomers, Rodney Rathbone decides to attack their son, Matthew, with mean names.

444a: Career Moves
Original Air Date: 4/29/00
Writer: Marshal Younger
Sound Designer: Jonathan Crowe
Theme: Honesty
Summary: Nathaniel Graham works at the Electric Palace for a day, and Bart tries to teach him to be a crooked businessman.

Original Novels

Like the Radio Show . . . Only Different

If you're familiar with the radio series, you might be surprised to find that most of the audio characters don't appear in the *Adventures in Odyssey* novels. That was done on purpose. The radio show is produced on a weekly basis, and the characters change much more quickly than is possible in the published books. A book that covers only a few weeks of a character's life takes at least a year to write, edit, and publish. By the time a few books are in print, a kid from the radio show might have graduated from middle school, grown up, gotten married, and moved away! We decided to place the novels in an *Odyssey* time period prior to the arrival of characters like Connie and Eugene. Most of the original novels take place in a pre-radio-show time period. Only one of the novels, *A Carnival of Secrets,* overlaps the time period of the *Odyssey* radio show.

Still, we felt it was important to include some familiar elements from Whit's End so the novels didn't feel completely different. One example is the Imagination Station. But how could the Imagination Station appear in several of the novels when, technically, that invention wasn't introduced until *after* the arrival of Connie and Eugene? Author Paul McCusker answers: "I decided when I wrote the novels that Whit—being the compulsive tinkerer that he was—had worked on early prototypes of the invention before presenting it to the public. That's why in the novels the Imagination Station is hidden away in the basement."

The Imagination Station also works differently in the books than it does in the radio series. For example, book character Mark Prescott goes back into his own past, which no one in the radio show did until "The Mortal Coil" (album 16). And when Mark gets into the invention in *The King's Quest*, he winds up in a fictional world—which is something that didn't happen in the radio series until much later.

Novel Information

Strange Journey Back
(Four Books in One Volume)

1. Strange Journey Back
Original Publishing Date: 1992
Writer: Paul McCusker
Themes: Friendship, responsibility
Summary: After his parents separate, Mark Prescott arrives in Odyssey with his mother and finds adjusting to the quirky small town hard to do. When he discovers the Imagination Station at Whit's End, he wonders if it's the solution to reuniting his parents.

2. High Flyer with a Flat Tire
Original Publishing Date: 1992
Writer: Paul McCusker
Themes: Friendship, family ties
Summary: A local bully accuses Mark Prescott of slashing his bicycle tires, so Mark sets off to prove his innocence—encountering more suspects than he was prepared for.

3. The Secret Cave of Robinwood
Original Publishing Date: 1992
Writer: Paul McCusker
Themes: Faithfulness, forgiveness
Summary: Mark Prescott learns a hard lesson about friendship as he betrays the secret of a good friend in order to impress the Israelites—a gang he wants to join.

4. Behind the Locked Door
Original Publishing Date: 1993
Writer: Paul McCusker
Themes: Trust, honesty, purity of thought
Summary: While his mother is away, Mark Prescott stays at Whit's home where secrets seem to abound behind locked doors. Keeping his curiosity under control is nearly impossible, and a chance opportunity allows Mark to encounter a painful truth from Whit's past.

Danger Lies Ahead
(Four Books in One Volume)

1. Lights Out at Camp What-A-Nut
Original Publishing Date: 1993
Writer: Paul McCusker
Themes: Friendship, helping others
Summary: While attending a summer camp, Mark Prescott is paired with his nemesis, Joe Devlin, in a treasure hunt that leads them both into danger.

2. The King's Quest
Original Publishing Date: 1994
Writer: Paul McCusker
Theme: God's control in difficult circumstances
Summary: The good news is that Mark Prescott's parents have reconciled. The bad news is that Mark must now move away from Odyssey. To show Mark how to trust God in any situation, Whit sends him on an adventure in the Imagination Station to a place of brave knights, evil wizards, and a quest for a precious ring.

3. Danger Lies Ahead
Original Publishing Date: 1995
Writer: Paul McCusker
Theme: Trust
Summary: Jack Davis befriends the new kid at school—but soon finds himself caught up in the boy's many stories. Are they true or not? Jack nearly loses his closest friends—and finds himself in peril—trying to find out.

4. A Carnival of Secrets
Original Publishing Date: 1997
Writer: Paul McCusker
Theme: Trust, honesty
Summary: Patti Eldridge disobeys her parents and listens to a fortuneteller at a traveling carnival. Strange events soon follow, and Patti is quickly caught up in a web of intrigue and mystery.

Point of No Return
(Four Books in One Volume)

1. Point of No Return
Original Publishing Date: 1995
Writer: Paul McCusker
Themes: Counting the cost
Summary: When Jimmy Barclay becomes a Christian, he is certain that his life can only get better as a result. But when everything goes wrong, he wonders what his faith is all about.

2. Dark Passage, Part I of II
Original Publishing Date: 1996
Writer: Paul McCusker
Theme: The sanctity of life
Summary: Jack Davis and Matt Booker take an amazing journey back to the 1850s. Matt is captured as a slave and Jack joins the abolitionists to rescue him.

3. Freedom Run, Part II of II
Original Publishing Date: 1996
Writer: Paul McCusker
Theme: The sanctity of life
Summary: To keep a promise to a young slave, Jack Davis and Matt Booker step back into the Imagination Station and return to the Underground Railroad.

4. The Stranger's Message
Original Publishing Date: 1997
Writer: Paul McCusker
Theme: Following Jesus in every situation
Summary: A homeless man's arrival in Odyssey challenges Whit and the kids to consider what it means to answer the question: "What would Jesus do?"

From top: *Strange Journey Back*, *Danger Lies Ahead*, and *Point of No Return*

Behind the Scenes: Behind the Locked Door

In this book, we find out that Whit has kept a room for his son Jerry set up in the attic. Whit and his family had moved to Odyssey while they were mourning Jerry's death.

Goof Alert!

The cemetery worker in *Behind the Locked Door* says that Jenny Whittaker is buried in California. However, in the radio episode "The Decision" (album 28), Jack Allen says that she is buried in Odyssey.

BTS: Lights Out at Camp What-A-Nut

Mark Prescott and Joe Devlin get stuck in a bomb shelter in this book. In the radio episode "Connie Goes to Camp" (album 5), Lucy Cunningham-Schultz and her friend Jill are caught sneaking out at night heading for this same shelter.

Release Dates

The *Adventures in Odyssey* novels were originally scheduled for release in 1991. But the first *Odyssey* videos were also scheduled to come out then, and some members of the team were concerned that releasing two new products would confuse our audience. As a result, we decided to delay the release of the book series so that they would not compete with the video series. However, in an unexpected twist, a publisher asked for permission to release the novels in England. So the first three novels came out in England (with different covers) several months before they were available in the United States.

The release schedule wasn't the only conflict between the videos and the novels. Mark Prescott's name in the original manuscripts for the book series was David Prescott. But the producers of the videos didn't want their audience to confuse David with the character of Dylan, so the name in the novels was changed.

The 1991 British covers

BTS: The Stranger's Message

Originally outlined as a four-part radio episode, this book was a modern-day retelling of the 1896 Charles Sheldon book *In His Steps*. In every situation, the book's characters considered the question, "What would Jesus do?" Around the time *The Stranger's Message* was being written, the same question caught on in the Christian market and led to the popular WWJD? campaign.

BTS: Danger Lies Ahead

This book is told from Jack Davis's perspective. Though we never heard much of Jack's parents in the audio series, this story explores his home life. The book also features Oscar and Lucy Cunningham-Schultz, popular kid characters from the audio show. Paul McCusker dedicated the book to "Genni, Donald, and Joseph," the actors who played Lucy, Jack, and Oscar, respectively.

Goof Alert!

In *Point of No Return*, Mary says that Grandpa Barclay died when Jimmy was five. But he appeared alive and well in the radio episode "And When You Pray . . ." (album 4), which takes place later in the chronology than this book. Maybe it was "Grandpa Barclay" from another side of the family.

Goof Alert!

The first printing of *Dark Passage* and *Freedom Run* included a pastor named "Ferguson," though the same character was named "Jamison" in the corresponding radio episode, "The Underground Railroad" (album 24). Subsequent printings corrected this error.

BTS: Freedom Run

Dark Passage and *Freedom Run* are two parts of the same story. However, *Dark Passage* is told in the third person and *Freedom Run* is in the first person—or, rather, "first-persons," since the chapters alternate between Jack Davis and Matt Booker as our narrators.

BTS: The Stranger's Message

This book bridged the gap between the book series and the radio show. The final chapter of the book retells the opening scene of the radio episode "Connie Comes to Town" (album 1).

BTS: A Carnival of Secrets

Oscar's last name was never revealed in the audio series or the previous novels. *A Carnival of Secrets* finally puts the mystery to rest. His last name is "Peterson."

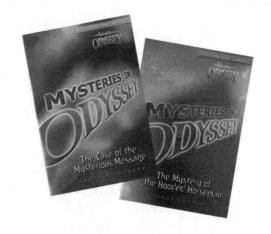

Mysteries in Odyssey!

Two *Adventures in Odyssey* mystery novels were released in 2002. *The Case of the Mysterious Message* was written by Marshal Younger and featured Cal Jordan and Sarah Prachett discovering a lost bag of mail from the 1960s. *The Mystery of the Hooded Horseman* was written by John Beebee and told a story about one of Whit's contacts in the National Security Agency who hid some government information in an old violin.

Passages Novel Information

Where in the World Is Marus?

The Passages novels begin with a mystery involving a series of manuscripts that claim to be true stories about another world called Marus. Each manuscript is written by a different author and chronicles the adventures of several kids from *Odyssey*, in different times, who travel to an alternative world.

Through each novel, Whit and Jack Allen investigate, unearthing yet another story—six in all. The stories themselves may seem very familiar since they're all taken from Scripture. But the readers are left to guess which Bible stories the kids from *Odyssey* are experiencing. (Note: Read about the *Adventures in Odyssey* radio episode titled "Passages" in album 34.)

Darien's Rise: Manuscript 1
Original Publishing Date: 1999
Writer: Paul McCusker
Theme: Belief
Summary: Kyle and Anna, two kids from 1950s Odyssey, find themselves transported to a strange new world called Marus. They are immediately caught up in a struggle between a power-mad king and his valiant young general.

Arin's Judgment: Manuscript 2
Original Publishing Date: 1999
Writer: Paul McCusker
Themes: Trust, obedience
Summary: Wade Mullens, a young boy who lives in post-World War II Odyssey, enters the world of Marus when the nation is in rebellion. Some believe that Wade Mullens is the pivotal player in a battle for weapons that could destroy the world.

Annison's Risk: Manuscript 3
Original Publishing Date: 1999
Writer: Paul McCusker
Theme: Justice
Summary: A game of hide-and-seek takes Maddy Nicholaivitch to Marus where she is taken in by a beautiful princess who has just married the conquering king. After overhearing the secret plans of the king's most trusted advisor, Maddy must decide if her loyalty to the princess is worth the price of her life.

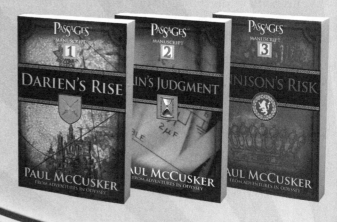

Glennall's Betrayal: **Manuscript 4**

Original Publishing Date: 2000
Writer: Paul McCusker
Theme: Loyalty
Summary: In Depression-era Odyssey, James Curtis runs away from home and joins a mysterious group of gypsies. Along the way, he is kidnapped and sold into slavery where he meets a young man named Glennall. Together, James and Glennall journey to the capital in Marus and discover that there is a higher purpose to the random events of their lives.

Draven's Defiance: **Manuscript 5**

Original Publishing Date: 2000
Writer: Paul McCusker
Theme: Standing up for what's right
Summary: Knocked unconscious in a railroad tunnel, Scott Graham finds himself in a land where a cruel king and queen rule with fear and hopelessness. Time itself seems to have stopped. An encounter with a man who claims to speak for the Unseen One takes Scott to corridors of power and a life-threatening confrontation.

Fendar's Legacy: **Manuscript 6**

Original Publishing Date: 2000
Writer: Paul McCusker
Theme: Faith
Summary: Carried along by a wild crowd, Danny Taylor, his brother, Wayne, and Michelle Brewer tumble head over heels into Trickle Lake and emerge in a fountain in Marus. Michelle is seized by the police and taken to the palace, while brothers Wayne and Danny wind up in the company of a man who is determined to lead his oppressed people to freedom.

Map of the "other world" of Marus

The Creation of Passages
by Paul McCusker

A few years ago I was involved with efforts to create stories that would communicate a Christian point of view in a way that would influence people who may not be Christians. *Focus on the Family Radio Theatre* was the first effort. The Passages series was the second.

Passages was the result of a wild idea I had to take Bible stories and retell them plot point for plot point in an alternative world. I thought that approach would allow people who were overly familiar with the Bible stories to get a fresh perspective on those events and characters. And I believed that those who didn't know the stories were from the Bible would still enjoy the books and might just go back to the Bible to read the originals.

To start, I had a picture in my mind of King David as a swashbuckling hero living in a nineteenth-century-type country where steam locomotives cut across the landscape and horse-drawn wagons still took produce to the village marketplaces. Or, in fact, it was like England—a country where I once had the pleasure of living. Astute readers have noticed that the name of my country—"Marus"—is actually the ancient name for England, "Sarum," turned inside out.

I pitched the idea to Focus on the Family's publisher Al Janssen and editor Larry Weeden. They liked the idea and suggested that I write the stories in the context of the *Adventures in Odyssey* series, which seemed like a pretty good idea. We discussed which stories to tell, and I worked out the prologues and epilogues with Whit and Jack, writing them in such a way so that those who didn't know *Odyssey* could still appreciate the stories.

I never wanted readers to know the stories were based on the Bible stories to the extent that I resisted putting in any disclaimers or explanations in the books themselves. I wanted to follow in the footsteps of writers like C. S. Lewis and others who told their stories without overtly pointing to their source material. I had hoped readers would figure it all out along the way and perhaps even identify *which* Bible story I was telling. It seemed more fun that way. And, as was true with Jesus' parables, I wanted readers to have their own "Aha!" moment when they finally figured out what I was doing.

What's the Title?
These books went through several name changes. Originally, they were titled Corridors, reflecting the idea of "halls" between one world and another. Then the name Tesseracts was suggested. (In geometry, a tesseract is a "four dimensional cube," where the fourth dimension represents the change of the cube through time.) Finally, we settled on Passages, a word that evoked a journey and also hinted that the books paralleled passages of scripture.

Behind the Scenes: Glennall's Betrayal
The original title for this book was *Glennall's Revenge*. But, since this novel was based on the biblical account of Joseph and that story didn't include revenge as a theme, we decided to change it. To fit an established page count for the series, nearly one third of the original *Glennall* had to be cut. However, some sections were restored for the rerelease of the series in 2006.

July 2000
Breakaway
magazine

is Wade, and he meets others named Oshan (ocean), Pool, Riv (river), and Thurston (thirsty). Arin is an anagram of "rain." Finally, the bad guy's name is Tyran, which is not a water word, and was intended to evoke the word "tyrant."

Q & A with Paul McCusker

Q: Passages contains elements similar to the Chronicles of Narnia. Were these similarities intentional?

PM: I think it's impossible to create stories about people from our world going into other worlds without comparisons to the Chronicles of Narnia series. Similarly, it's impossible to write any fantasy stories without thinking of the Lord of the Rings trilogy. So I knew there was no doing Passages without readers thinking about Narnia. (Ironically, after I'd started the Passages series, I was able to adapt the Narnia books for *Focus on the Family Radio Theatre*.)

There are important differences, of course. Passages doesn't have the mythological elements that Narnia has. No nymphs or dryads. No talking animals. And my storylines are meticulously based on Bible events (whereas Lewis alluded to the Bible without always paralleling it). Lewis also assumed that Narnia is real. In our series, the mysterious notebooks leave a question about the reality of Marus. Maybe it is real, or maybe it's just a place that some guy made up.

BTS: Darien's Rise

Portions of this book were included in the June and July 2000 issues of *Breakaway* magazine.

Goof Alert!

The beginning of *Arin's Judgment* mentions Wade Mullens's father as Henry. However, in the epilogue, his name is Ronald.

BTS: Darien's Rise

Characters in this book visit a town named Door. The scene parallels the biblical story of David when he visits the priests in Nob.

My Take: Paul McCusker

Since *Arin's Judgment* paralleled the story of Noah and the flood, I gave many of the characters water-sounding names. The boy's name

Kidsboro Information

A Small World

Kidsboro is a small town in the woods behind Whit's End in Odyssey. It's a nice little place. It has a church, a store, a police station, a bakery, a weekly newspaper, and a total of zero citizens over the age of 14. It's a town run by kids. Ryan Cummings, the mayor, helps enforce the laws, create new job opportunities, and in general, keep the peace in a town where he seems to have lots of friends and only a few enemies. Kidsboro not only teaches moral and biblical principles, but the series also teaches concepts of government, politics, economic principles, the judicial system, United States history, and Bible stories. (Look on whitsend. org for information about three "Kidsboro" radio episodes that were released spring 2008.)

1: **Battle for Control**
Original Publishing Date: 2008
Writer: Marshal Younger
Themes: The importance of rules, the Ten Commandments
Summary: Ryan Cummings votes not to allow Ashley to become a citizen of Kidsboro. As a result, Ashley's friend Valerie Swanson decides to run against Ryan in a recall election for the role of mayor.

2: **The Rise and Fall of the Kidsborian Empire**
Original Publishing Date: 2008
Writer: Marshal Younger
Themes: Selflessness
Summary: Kidsboro experiences a "Golden Age" where businesses are prospering. But the era is cut short by one selfish act, causing Kidsboro to experience a Great Depression. It may take one unselfish act to make things right again.

3: **The Creek War**
Original Publishing Date: 2008
Writer: Marshal Younger
Themes: Loving our enemies
Summary: Max Darby, the richest, most powerful kid in town (and Ryan's mortal enemy) gets kicked out of Kidsboro and decides to create his own town across the creek—Bettertown. Tempers flare between the two towns, and they soon find themselves in a war.

4: **The Risky Reunion**
Original Publishing Date: 2008
Writer: Marshal Younger
Themes: Standing up for what's right
Summary: While Ryan Cummings deals with some dangerous trouble at home, in Kidsboro he has to make decisions that set up friend against friend, making Kidsboro into an equally dangerous place.

Through the Closing Credits. There was a scene in the script where a bunch of kids made a movie together. Robert thought that the whole script was going to be about kids creating their own world. When the screenplay went another direction, he was disappointed. But I found the idea of kids running their own world intriguing enough that I created the book series.

I wrote four Kidsboro books, each illustrating moral lessons and teaching in subtle ways about economics, government, and politics. The first book of the series was published in March 2000. At the time, the novels didn't have anything to do with *Odyssey*. Later, Focus on the Family asked me to take the books and "Odyssey-ize" them. I added Whit, Eugene, Rodney Rathbone, and some other *Odyssey* characters to the existing storylines, and now they're part of the *Adventures in Odyssey* canon.

The Creation of Kidsboro
by Marshal Younger

The inspiration for Kidsboro came from an unusual source. I often bounce my creative ideas off a fellow writer and friend of mine named Robert Skead. (*Odyssey* listeners will know that name because it's been mentioned on the show.) In the late 1990s, I gave Robert a screenplay I had written titled *Staying*

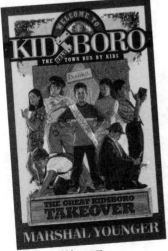

The original *Kidsboro* cover

521

Character: Sherman
Quote: "Rawf"
Something you may not know about Sherman:
Whit owned him before Dylan did.

Videos

In the late 1980s and early 1990s, Focus on the Family created a best-selling series of part live-action, part animated films titled *McGee and Me!* To follow up on this success, a series of animated videos based on the *Adventures in Odyssey* radio dramas was developed.

To adapt a radio series to a visual medium is a difficult task. When the first *Odyssey* videos were created in 1989 and 1990, the only visual representations of the characters and world of Odyssey had been a few album covers. Each listener imagined his or her unique version of what every character and place should look like. The *Odyssey* videos adopted a visual style reminiscent of classic Disney, and the radio series art soon morphed to match this new style.

Alongside the existing characters of Whit and Eugene, the videos introduced a new cast of characters, including Dylan Taylor, his parents, and his younger sister, Jesse. While the radio program was aimed at 8- to 12-year-olds, the videos were geared for a younger audience.

Video Information

1: The Knight Travelers
Writer: Ken C. Johnson
Directors: Mike Joens & Ken C. Johnson
Theme: What is truly important
Summary: Dylan and Whit set out to retrieve the Imagination Station from the clutches of the evil Fred Faustus. Along the way, Dylan discovers what is truly important in life.

2: A Flight to the Finish
Writer: Ken C. Johnson
Directors: Mike Joens & Ken C. Johnson
Theme: Caring
Summary: The race is on! Dylan bolts from the starting line, determined to win Odyssey's super-hot soap-box derby. But when Holly's car careens out of control, Dylan's faced with a tough dilemma—helping her or winning the race.

3: A Fine Feathered Frenzy
Writer: Ken C. Johnson
Directors: Mike Joens & Ken C. Johnson
Theme: Responsibility
Summary: After mowing down Mrs. Harcourt's prized rose garden, Dylan tries to make amends by agreeing to watch her treasured parrot Napoleon. When the bird escapes, it's a chase against time to retrieve the pet before Mrs. Harcourt returns.

4: Shadow of a Doubt
Writer: Mike Joens
Directors: Mike Joens & Ken C. Johnson
Theme: Loyalty
Summary: There's a cat burglar on the loose in Odyssey and the trail of clues leads to . . . John Avery Whittaker! It's up to Dylan to prove Whit's innocence before it's too late.

5: Star Quest
Writers: David N. Weiss & Rob McFarland
Directors: Robert Vernon & Stephen Stiles
Theme: Jealousy
Summary: When Dylan and Sal Martinez learn that their favorite sci-fi TV show is filming in Odyssey, they are determined to get in on the action. But they wind up getting the ride of their lives when a robot goes out-of-control.

6: Once Upon an Avalanche
Writer: Paul McCusker
Directors: Robert Vernon & Stephen Stiles
Theme: Brotherly love
Summary: A hair-raising toboggan ride lands Carter, Dylan Taylor, and his sister, Jesse, into the bottom of Avalanche Canyon. They must work together to overcome the many obstacles in their path to safety.

7: Electric Christmas
Story: Robert Vernon
Writer: Stephen Stiles
Directors: Robert Vernon & Stephen Stiles
Theme: The true meaning of Christmas
Summary: Sparks fly when Dylan and his scheming neighbor, Doug Harding, both enter Odyssey's yard-decorating contest. While Dylan and Doug go all-out with a flashy, larger-than-life exhibition, Jesse's humble manger scene seems to pale in comparison.

8: Go West, Young Man
Writers: Paul McCusker & Robert Vernon
Directors: Robert Vernon & Stephen Stiles
Theme: Responsibility
Summary: Strap on yer chaps, grab yer hat, and get ready for a rip-roarin' ride to the Wild West, where Dylan and Eugene face off with the Dalton gang.

The Knight Travelers

Shadow of a Doubt

9: Someone to Watch Over Me

Story: Phil Lollar
Writers: Phil Lollar & Robert Vernon
Directors: Robert Vernon & Stephen Stiles
Theme: God's protection
Summary: Dylan has had some wild times in the Imagination Station before, but never one like this! He finds himself in the battle to end all battles, encountering one life-threatening struggle after the next.

10: In Harm's Way

Writer: Robert Vernon
Directors: Robert Vernon & Stephen Stiles
Theme: Friendship
Summary: Dylan finds it hard to see past Elliot's "nerdy" appearance to the true kid inside, until Whit takes him on a unique trip in the Imagination Station.

11: A Twist In Time

Story: Robert Vernon
Writer: Stephen Stiles
Directors: Robert Vernon & Stephen Stiles
Theme: Responsibility
Summary: Whit is working on a secret new invention. Dylan and Sal sneak into his workshop and inadvertently trigger a surprising series of events that could lead to disaster for Whit's End and the future of Odyssey!

12: A Stranger Among Us

Writer: Robert Vernon
Directors: Robert Vernon & Stephen Stiles
Theme: Jumping to conclusions
Summary: Connie and Dylan watch a mystery movie and before long *every* visitor to Whit's End looks suspicious to them. Then the situation intensifies when an inmate escapes from a nearby prison!

13: Baby Daze

Writer: Ken C. Johnson
Directors: Robert Vernon & Stephen Stiles
Theme: The sanctity of human life
Summary: A baby shows up on the doorstep of Whit's End, and Eugene wants to study the child's behavior in the name of "science." But the baby's short history catches up to him when an evil scientist and runaway robots follow him to Whit's End!

14: The Last Days of Eugene Meltsner

Writer: Robert Vernon
Directors: Robert Vernon
Theme: Living each day as if it were your last
Summary: Through Whit's new invention, the Micro-Simulator, Eugene takes a fantastic voyage into his own circulatory system. What he finds there forces him to reevaluate how he'll spend the remaining days of his life.

15: Escape from the Forbidden Matrix

Writers: John Beebee, Jeffrey Learned, & Robert Vernon
Director: Robert Vernon
Theme: The folly of wasting time
Summary: Dylan and Sal are invited to play their favorite video game—*Insectoids*—from *inside* the game. But when they enter the "forbidden matrix," they face an even more dangerous foe.

16: The Caves of Qumran

Writer: Jeffrey Learned
Director: Ed Olson
Theme: The Bible is the greatest treasure.
Summary: When a mysterious old treasure map shows up in Odyssey, Whit, Dylan, Connie, and Eugene embark on a perilous journey that leads them to the Caves of Qumran in the Middle East.

17: Race to Freedom

Story: Paul McCusker & Marshal Younger
Writer: Marshal Younger
Director: Chad Morgan
Theme: The sanctity of human life
Summary: Dylan and Carter stumble upon an Imagination Station adventure that takes them back to pre-Civil War days. Carter discovers that he is a slave in Kentucky, and it's up to Dylan to rescue him.

A Fine Feathered Frenzy

A Flight to the Finish

Behind the Scenes

Several of the videos are based on *Adventures in Odyssey* radio episodes. *Someone to Watch Over Me* closely parallels the radio show of the same name (album 10), but removes the battle at sea. *Escape from the Forbidden Matrix* was based on "Gloobers" (album 32). *The Caves of Qumran* is very loosely based on "The Treasure of LeMonde" (album 6), while *Race to Freedom* parallels both "The Underground Railroad" radio episodes (album 24) and the *Dark Passage* and *Freedom Run* novels.

A Twist in Time

BTS: A Stranger Among Us

While Eugene and Whit appeared in the videos from the beginning, Connie Kendall and Bernard Walton weren't introduced until #12 and #14, respectively.

BTS: Go West, Young Man

In the video "Go West, Young Man," Angus Dalton says, "You boys have had your fun. Now you'll pay for it!" The coachman from Disney's 1940 movie *Pinocchio* says the same line.

Goof Alert!

In *Escape from the Forbidden Matrix,* the Master Brain says, "Mr. Taylor, Mr. Martinez . . . welcome to my world." The pair wonder how he knows their names, and he says that their names are printed on their uniforms. However, their *first* names are printed on their uniforms and the master brain calls them by their *last* names.

BTS: A Twist in Time

For many years, the *Odyssey* team discussed an idea that we gave the code-name "Odyssey of the Future." The basic story featured kids who get into the Imagination Station and accidentally wind up in the future—but it's a bleak one, where Whit's End is a derelict building, Whit has disappeared, and Dr. Blackgaard is in charge of a corrupt and oppressive regime. Paralleling the King Arthur legends, Whit eventually emerges as a Merlin-type, living in the secret tunnels beneath Whit's End, waiting for the "promised ones" who will lead Odyssey to freedom. Eventually the kids take on that mantle and play decisive roles in the rescue of Odyssey.

In Harm's Way

The Hunchback of Notre Dame (1996), and Galactus on the animated series for television *The Fantastic Four* (1994–1995).

BTS: Shadow of a Doubt

Animation producers Ken C. Johnson and Mike Joens appear in *Shadow of a Doubt* reading a *Marmaduke* comic strip.

Sound Bites

Eugene sings "Seasonal Felicitations" in *Electric Christmas*. He also sings it in the radio show "Caroling, Caroling" (album 15) and the music album *Eugene Sings! Christmas*.

Sound Bites

Whit hums the theme song to the *Last Chance Detectives* in *Go West, Young Man*. The *Focus on the Family* radio theme song can be heard on the Taylors' radio in *A Flight to the Finish*.

We had discussed the idea for years as a series on the radio program, but eventually decided against it. Some elements of this idea would appear in the *Passages* novels—the concept of the kids playing critical roles in the outcome of events—and other elements were incorporated into *A Twist in Time*.

Sound Bites

Dr. Fred Faustus, the villain who appears in *The Knight Travelers* and *The Caves of Qumran*, was played by the late Tony Jay. Tony also played the voice of Shere Khan the tiger in the movie *The Jungle Book 2* (2003) and television's *TaleSpin* (1990–1994), Judge Claude Frollo in the animated movie

Eugene Sings!

Two music albums featuring *Odyssey*'s boy genius were released in 2005. *Eugene Sings!* and *Eugene Sings! Christmas* took singing and ukulele playing to places few had dared to go. *Eugene Sings!* includes classics like "Have You Ever Been to Odyssey?" "I Just Met a Girl Named Katrina," and the delightful ballad "The Moonlight, a Tuba, and You." *Eugene Sings! Christmas* presents the oft-requested "Seasonal Felicitations," "Jingle Jangle Jungle," and "I Went and Told It on the Mountain."

A SPECIAL MESSAGE FROM EUGENE:
Here are a few of my comments on these calliphonic cantabulations:

My Dog Has Fleas
I always use this song to tune my Kokomo Ukulele. Some "ukesters" (my latest neologism) employ pitch pipes, but I find this tune is much catchier. You can tell I didn't write this song because the lyrics include the word "ain't."

I Just Met a Girl Named Katrina
This song is dedicated to my very own Katrina (and all Katrinas everywhere who have a periwinkle-eyed Eugene who loves them).

The Only Thing Missing Is You
I trust you appreciate the concept of a Time-Saving Alphabet, as heard in this song. Personally, I would consider the removal of the letters C and Q from the alphabet before I would ever dream of eliminating U!

Lift Up Your Heads!
The fact that this may be the most exhilarating track on this CD has very little to do with me. But it has very much to do with everybody else, especially The Jubilo Singers with featured soloists Elaine, Janine, and Francine Martin! People always like to quote Psalm 23. I just thought it was time to move on . . . to the next psalm!

Alphabetical Episode Index

Through episode #642, album #50

Index Key

- A#– Album number
- AA– Action adventure episode
- Barc– Barclay family episode
- Camp– Camp episode
- C-mas– Christmas episode
- Comedy– Comedies
- E#– Episode number
- FP– *Family Portraits*
- Hist– History episode
- Int'l– International adventures episode
- IS– Imagination Station episode
- L– Love story episode
- LE– *The Lost Episodes* album
- Myst– Mystery episode
- N– No episode number or no album number

Title	*Number*	*Album Number*	*Categories*
A			
A . . . Is for Attitude	E#110	A#08	
Accidental Dilemma, I	E#634	A#50	AA
Accidental Dilemma, II	E#635	A#50	AA
Act of Mercy, An	E#115	A#08	
Act of Nobility, An	E#187	A#13	AA
Addictions Can Be Habit-Forming	E#11	A#N	
Adventure in Bethany, An, I	E#226	A#16	IS
Adventure in Bethany, An, II	E#227	A#16	IS
Adventure of the Adventure, The	E#138	A#08	
Afraid, Not!	E#261	A#20	
All the Difference in the World	E#303	A#23	
All Things to All People	E#522	A#40	
All's Well with Boswell	E#125	A#08	Comedy
All-Star Witness	E#578	A#45	
Aloha, Oy!, I	E#256	A#19	Comedy, Barc
Aloha, Oy!, II	E#257	A#19	Comedy, Barc
Aloha, Oy!, III	E#258	A#19	Comedy, Barc
Always	E#579	A#45	
Amazing Grace	E#384	A#29	Hist
American Revelation, The, I	E#508	A#39	IS, Hist
American Revelation, The, II	E#509	A#39	IS, Hist
And That's the Truth	E#556	A#43	
And the Glory	E#240	A#17	Comedy
And When You Pray . . .	E#60	A#04	Barc
Angels Unaware	E#325	A#25	AA
Another Chance	E#332	A#25	AA
Another Man's Shoes	E#419	A#33	
Arizona Sunrise	E#402	A#30	Hist
Around the Block	E#593	A#46	Comedy
Aubrey's Bathrobe	E#504	A#39	
Auld Lang Syne	E#55	A#LE	
B			
Back to Abnormal	E#573	A#45	Comedy
Back to Bethlehem, I	E#135	A#10	C-mas, IS
Back to Bethlehem, II	E#136	A#10	C-mas, IS
Back to Bethlehem, III	E#137	A#10	C-mas, IS
Back to School	E#43	A#03	
Bad Company	E#65	A#04	Barc
Bad Guy, The [Split]	E#444b	A#34	
Bad Hair Day, The	E#252	A#19	Comedy
Bad Luck	E#107	A#08	
Barclay Family Ski Vacation, The	E#99	A#07	Barc
Bassett Hounds	E#516	A#40	Comedy
Battle, The, I	E#83	A#05	AA
Battle, The, II	E#84	A#05	AA
Benefit of the Doubt, The	E#507	A#39	
Bernard and Esther, I	E#165	A#11	
Bernard and Esther, II	E#166	A#11	
Bernard and Jeremiah	E#601	A#47	IS
Bernard and Job	E#399	A#30	
Bernard and Joseph, I	E#130	A#09	
Bernard and Joseph, II	E#131	A#09	
Bernard and Saul	E#541	A#42	
Best Face Forward	E#379	A#29	Comedy
Best Intentions	E#213	A#16	Comedy
Best Laid Plans	E#455	A#35	
Best of Enemies	E#614	A#48	Comedy
Bethany's Flood [Split]	E#444c	A#34	Comedy
Better Late than Never	E#119	A#09	
Between You and Me	E#503	A#39	
Big Broadcast, The	E#114	A#09	Comedy
Big Deal, The, I	E#449	A#35	IS
Big Deal, The, II	E#450	A#35	IS

Here Today, Gone Tomorrow? III	E#525	A#40	AA
Heroes	E#48	A#03	Barc
Hidden in My Heart	E#321	A#26	Comedy
Hide and Seek	E#404	A#31	IS
Highest Stakes, The I	E#628	A#49	
Highest Stakes, The II	E#629	A#49	
Hindsight	E#521	A#41	
Hold Up!	E#169	A#12	AA
Home Is Where the Hurt Is	E#150	A#11	
Home, Sweet Home	E#364	A#28	
Homecoming, The	E#159	A#10	
Honor Thy Parents	E#30	A#LE	
Hymn Writers	E#242	A#18	Hist

I

I Slap Floor	E#440	A#34	Comedy
I Want My B-TV	E#298	A#23	Comedy
Ice Fishing	E#100	A#07	
Idol Minds [Split]	E#441b	A#34	
Ill-Gotten Deed, The	E#92	A#06	AA
Imaginary Friend [Split]	E#428b	A#33	Comedy
Imagination Station, The, I	E#66	A#05	IS
Imagination Station, The, II	E#67	A#05	IS
Imagination Station, Revisited, The, I	E#641	A#50	IS
Imagination Station, Revisited, The, II	E#642	A#50	IS
Impossible, The	E#589	A#46	AA
In All Things Give Thanks	E#411	A#32	
In Memory of Herman	E#N	A#FP	
Inside the Studio	E#501	A#LE	
Into Temptation	E#236	A#17	Barc
Invisible Dog, The	E#569	A#44	
Isaac the Benevolent	E#116	A#LE	
Isaac the Chivalrous	E#184	A#13	AA, IS
Isaac the Courageous	E#108	A#07	
Isaac the Insecure	E#86	A#07	
Isaac the Procrastinator	E#148	A#10	
Isaac the Pure	E#180	A#13	
Isaac the True Friend	E#161	A#LE	IS
It Began with a Rabbit's Foot . . .	E#266	A#20	L
It Ended with a Handshake	E#267	A#20	L
It Happened at Four Corners	E#277	A#21	AA
It Is Well	E#221	A#16	Hist
It Sure Seems Like It to Me	E#44	A#LE	
It Takes Integrity	E#181	A#13	
It's a Pokenberry Christmas, I	E#385	A#31	C-mas, Comedy
It's a Pokenberry Christmas, II	E#386	A#31	C-mas, Comedy
It's a Wrap!	E#369	A#28	
It's All About Me	E#517	A#40	Comedy

J

Jesus Cloth, The	E#222	A#18	
Joke's on You, The	E#391	A#30	Comedy
Just Say Yes	E#377	A#29	

K

Karen	E#50	A#03	
Kids' Radio	E#36	A#02	Comedy

L

Lamb's Tale, A	E#557	A#43	C-mas
Last "I Do," The	E#562	A#44	Hist
Last Great Adventure of the Summer, The	E#42	A#02	AA
Last in a Long Line	E#157	A#10	
Last Resort, The	E#333	A#25	AA
. . . Last Shall Be First, The	E#151	A#11	
Leap of Faith	E#388	A#30	AA
Lesson from Mike, A	E#412	A#31	
Let This Mind Be in You	E#62	A#04	
Letter, The	E#N	A#FP	
Letting Go	E#344	A#27	
License to Deprive	E#633	A#50	Comedy
License to Drive, A	E#194	A#14	Comedy
Life of the Party, The	E#02	A#01	
Life Trials of the Rich and Famous	E#451	A#35	Comedy
Life, in the Third Person, I	E#626	A#49	
Life, in the Third Person, II	E#627	A#49	
Lights Out at Whit's End	E#03	A#N	
Like Father, Like Son	E#216	A#16	
Like Father, Like Wooton	E#604	A#47	Comedy
Lincoln, I	E#104	A#07	Hist, IS
Lincoln, II	E#105	A#07	Hist, IS
Little Credit, Please, A	E#323	A#25	
Live at the 25	E#502	A#09	Comedy
Living in the Gray, I	E#535	A#42	Barc
Living in the Gray, II	E#536	A#42	Barc
Living Nativity, The	E#214	A#16	C-mas
Long Way Home, The [Split]	E#437b	A#34	
Look Back, A, I	E#435	A#LE	
Look Back, A, II	E#436	A#LE	
Lost by a Nose	E#561	A#44	
Love Is in the Air, I	E#335	A#26	L, Comedy
Love Is in the Air, II	E#336	A#26	L, Comedy
Lyin' Tale, The [Split]	E#438a	A#34	Comedy

M

Mailman Cometh, The	E#529	A#41	Comedy
Making the Grade	E#264	A#20	Barc
Malachi's Message, I	E#406	A#32	
Malachi's Message, II	E#407	A#32	
Malachi's Message, III	E#408	A#32	
Mandy's Debut	E#448	A#34	Comedy
Marriage Feast, The	E#229	A#18	
Matter of Manners, A [Split]	E#446a	A#34	
Matter of Obedience, A	E#58	A#04	
Mayor for a Day	E#153	A#11	Comedy
Meaning of Sacrifice, The	E#152	A#11	Barc. Comedy
Melanie's Diary	E#139	A#10	
Member of the Family, A, I	E#17	A#01 & FP	
Member of the Family, A, II	E#18	A#01 & FP	
Memories of Jerry	E#352	A#27	
Merchant of Odyssey, The	E#359	A#28	Comedy
Midnight Ride, The	E#197	A#14	Hist
Mike Makes Right	E#20	A#03	
Missed It by That Much	E#14	A#N	
Missing Person	E#121	A#08	AA
Mission for Jimmy, A	E#91	A#06	Barc
Missionary: Impossible	E#452	A#35	
Model Child, A	E#163	A#12	
Modesty Is the Best Policy	E#192	A#13	Barc
Monty's Christmas	E#97	A#07	C-mas
More Like Alicia	E#401	A#30	
Mortal Coil, The, I	E#211	A#16	
Mortal Coil, The, II	E#212	A#16	
Moses: The Passover, I	E#190	A#14	Barc, IS
Moses: The Passover, II	E#191	A#14	Barc, IS
Most Extraordinary Conclusion, A	E#566	A#44	AA
Most Intriguing Question, A	E#564	A#44	AA
Most Surprising Answer, A	E#565	A#44	AA
Moving Targets	E#327	A#25	AA
Muckraker	E#143	A#11	
Mum's the Word	E#602	A#47	Comedy
My Brother's Keeper	E#15	A#FP & LE	
My Fair Bernard	E#246	A#18	Comedy
My Favorite Thing	E#598	A#47	Comedy
My Girl Hallie	E#537	A#41	
Mysterious Stranger, The, I	E#244	A#18	Myst
Mysterious Stranger, The, II	E#245	A#18	Myst
Mystery at Tin Flat, The	E#520	A#40	Myst

N

Name, Not a Number, A, I	E#290	A#22	AA
Name, Not a Number, A, II	E#291	A#22	AA
Natural Born Leader	E#409	A#31	

Naturally, I Assumed . . .	E#260	A#19	Comedy, L
Nemesis, The, I	E#77	A#05	AA
Nemesis, The, II	E#78	A#05	AA
New Era, A, I	E#619	A#49	AA, Int'l
New Era, A, II	E#620	A#49	AA, Int'l
New Era, A, III	E#621	A#49	AA, Int'l
New Kid in Town, The	E#N	A#FP	
New Year's Eve Live!	E#387	A#31	Comedy, Hist
No Bones About It	E#390	A#30	Comedy
No Boundaries	E#445	A#34	
"No" Factor, The	E#199	A#15	
No, Honestly!	E#189	A#13	Comedy
No Stupid Questions	E#16	A#FP & LE	
No Way In	E#547	A#42	AA
No Way Out	E#546	A#42	AA
Not One of Us	E#129	A#09	
Nothing But the Half Truth	E#543	A#42	Comedy
Nothing to Fear	E#10	A#01	
Not-So-Trivial Pursuit	E#417	A#32	
Nova Rising	E#460	A#35	AA
Now More Than Ever	E#592	A#46	
Nudge, The	E#600	A#47	

O

O. T. Action News: Battle at the Kishon	E#477	A#37	
O. T. Action News: Jephthah's Vow	E#389	A#30	
Odyssey Sings!	E#572	A#45	Comedy
On Solid Ground	E#210	A#15	
One About Trust, The, I	E#380	A#29	
One About Trust, The, II	E#381	A#29	
One Bad Apple	E#128	A#07	
Only by His Grace	E#615	A#48	
Opening Day	E#418	A#33	
Operation Dig-Out	E#94	A#06	AA
Opportunity Knocks	E#457	A#35	AA
Other Side of the Glass, The, I	E#616	A#48	Myst
Other Side of the Glass, The, II	E#617	A#48	Myst
Other Side of the Glass, The, III	E#618	A#48	Myst
Other Woman, The	E#368	A#28	
Our Best Vacation Ever	E#79	A#05	Barc
Our Daily Bread	E#234	A#17	Barc
Our Father	E#230	A#17	Comedy, Barc
Out of Our Hands	E#597	A#47	
Over the Airwaves	E#141	A#09	Comedy

P

Pact, The, I	E#511	A#39	Myst
Pact, The, II	E#512	A#39	Myst, Camp
Painting, The	E#378	A#29	Myst

Scripture Index

2 Samuel

11:1–12:23; 16	B-TV: Envy	A#24

1 Kings

17:1–19:2	Elijah, I & II	A#06
21	B-TV: Envy	A#24

1 Chronicles

16:8	Thanksgiving at Home	A#07

2 Chronicles

15:7	My Fair Bernard	A#18
20:15	Shining Armor, I & II	A#37
32:7-8	The Courage to Stand	A#13

Nehemiah

8:10	Count It All Joy	A#18

Esther

	Bernard and Esther	A#11

Job

	Bernard and Job	A#30
	Worst Day Ever	A#35

Psalms

1:1-2	The Good, the Bad, and Butch	A#23
1:1-5	When Bad Isn't So Good	A#20
18:2	Cover of Darkness	A#47
19:14	It Sure Seems Like It to Me	A#LE
20:7	Box of Miracles	A#38
22:27-28	Columbus: The Grand Voyage	A#16
23	Karen	A#03
27	The Right Choice, I & II	A#28
27:1	Dental Dilemma	A#LE
27:5-6	A Name, Not a Number, I & II	A#22
33:11-13, 16	East Winds, Raining	A#13
33:12	The Midnight Ride	A#14
33:12-22	By Dawn's Early Light	A#12
33:18	Timmy's Cabin	A#14
37	Opportunity Knocks	A#35
37:4-7	The W. E.	A#36

Psalms (continued)

39:4	Rescue from Manatugo Point	A#06
46:1	The Nemesis, I & II	A#05
51:17	A Test for Robyn	A#13
55:22	Life, in the Third Person, I & II	A#49
56:3	Blood, Sweat, and Fears	A#47
68:5	Our Father	A#17
68:6	Aloha, Oy!, I, II & III	A#19
73:23-26	Memories of Jerry	A#27
82:1-4	Pamela Has a Problem	A#LE
82:3	The Underground Railroad, I, II & III	A#24
	Home, Sweet Home	A#28
89:14	The Scales of Justice	A#13
90:12	Rescue from Manatugo Point	A#06
91:11-12	Someone to Watch Over Me	A#10
96:1-2	Hymn Writers	A#18
103	Stormy Weather	A#02
104	Wonderworld	A#15
106:23	Nova Rising	A#35
118:24	It's a Wrap!	A#28
119:11	Hidden in My Heart	A#26
130:7	Prisoners of Fear, I, II & III	A#45
133	B-TV: Behind the Scenes	A#40
139:13-14	The Pushover	A#29
	Ice Fishing	A#07
139:14	Isaac the Insecure	A#07
146	Pen Pal	A#15
147:3	Letting Go	A#27

Proverbs

1:5	The Fundamentals	A#21
1:19	It Happened at Four Corners	A#21
3:5	The One About Trust, I & II	A#29
3:5-6	A . . . Is for Attitude	A#08
	Between You and Me	A#39
	Passages, I & II	A#34
	The Decision	A#28
3:11-12	A Member of the Family, I & II	A#01
4:5-9	Blackgaard's Revenge, I & II	A#33
	Two Roads	A#34
6:16	Connie Goes to Camp, I & II	A#05
6:16, 19	Muckraker	A#12
10:4	A License to Drive	A#14
	Isaac the Procrastinator	A#10
10:29	It Takes Integrity	A#13
	Treasure Hunt	A#14
11:3	By Any Other Name	A#08
11:12	Broken Window	A#36
12:1	Making the Grade	A#20

Jeremiah (continued)

| 17:9 | Hold Up! | A#13 |
| 29:11 | Here Today, Gone Tomorrow? I, II & III | A#40 |

Daniel

1-3	Deliver Us from Evil	A#17
3	V.B.S. Blues	A#02
4:35	A Time for Action, I & II	A#46

Micah

| 6:8 | Blind Justice | A#27 |
| 7:5 | A Question of Loyalty | A#13 |

Habakkuk

| 2:19 | My Girl, Hallie | A#41 |

Malachi

2:13-17	Whit's Visitor	A#FP
2:14-16	Father's Day	A#14
2:16	Monty's Christmas	A#07
4:6	While Dad's Away	A#FP

Matthew

1:18-2:1	Back to Bethlehem, I, II, and II	A#10
1:18-25	Gifts for Madge and Guy	A#01
2:1-15	The Star, I & II	A#13
5:8	Isaac the Pure	A#13
5:9	Peacemaker	A#14
5:21	Where There's Smoke	A#33
5:23	Seeing Red	A#41
5:23-24	Red Wagons and Pink Flamingos	A#22
5:33-37	The Sacred Trust	A#03
5:43-48	The Reluctant Rival	A#07
5:44	Exactly as Planned	A#38
	Tornado!	A#30
	Train Ride	A#LE
6	Fifteen Minutes	A#36
6:1	It's All About Me	A#40
	Rewards in Full	A#24
6:10	Thy Will Be Done	A#17
6:12	The Homecoming	A#10
6:13 (KJV)	The Power	A#17
6:14-15; 18:21-22	Welcome Home, Mr. Blackgaard	A#26
6:19	Treasures of the Heart	A#16

Matthew (continued)

6:19-20	The Long Way Home	A#34
6:19-21	Tales of Moderation	A#13
	The Fifth House on the Left, I & II	A#21
6:24	The Case of the Secret Room, I & II	A#02
6:25-34	The Y.A.K. Problem	A#33
	W-O-R-R-Y	A#26
6:28-29	Bethany's Imaginary Friend	A#33
6:31-33	Our Daily Bread	A#17
7:1-2	A Book by Its Cover	A#21
	Like Father, Like Son	A#16
7:12	Doing Unto Others	A#N
	Isaac the Benevolent	A#LE
10:30	Coming of Age	A#12
10:42	The Chosen One, I & II	A#47
13:1-23	Scattered Seeds	A#07
14:1-12	The Big Deal, I & II	A#35
18:10	Someone to Watch Over Me	A#10
	Someone to Watch Over Me	A#11
18:12-13; 20:1-16	The Last Shall Be First	A#12
18:15	All-Star Witness	A#45
18:21-22	Call Me if You Care	A#43
18:21-35	An Act of Mercy	A#08
	Arizona Sunrise	A#30
	B-TV: Forgiveness	A#32
	Buried Sin	A#32
	The Case of the Missing Train Car	A#N
	The Painting	A#29
	The Quality of Mercy	A#N
	What Happened to the Silver Streak?	A#09
19:5-6	The Vow	A#09
19:13-14	Forever . . . Amen	A#17
19:26	The Impossible	A#46
	The Power of One	A#44
20:25-28	Mike Makes Right	A#03
20:34	The Invisible Dog	A#44
21:28-46	Over the Airwaves	A#09
22:1-14	The Marriage Feast	A#18
22:21	A Single Vote	A#03
22:39	A Cheater Cheated	A#46
24:36-42	The Second Coming	A#10
	The Second Coming	A#11
25:1-13	Better Late than Never	A#09
	Missed It By that Much	A#N
25:14-30	The Buck Starts Here	A#33
25:23	Chain Reaction	A#33
	Mandy's Debut	A#34
25:29	Switch	A#46
25:31-46	The Visitors	A#07

Romans

3:10, 23	It Began with a Rabbit's Foot . . .	A#20
3:23	Hold Up!	A#13
	Preacher's Kid	A#23
	Promises, Promises	A#01
3:29	Not One of Us	A#09
5:3-4	Around the Block	A#46
5:8	It Began with a Rabbit's Foot . . .	A#20
	Karen	A#03
6:1	Rights, Wrongs, and Reasons	A#15
6:23	Not-So-Trivial Pursuits	A#32
	That's Not Fair	A#06
	The Marriage Feast	A#18
8:18, 28, 31	The Battle, I & II	A#05
8:28	Black Clouds	A#41
	Exit	A#38
	For Thine Is the Kingdom	A#17
	Pokenberry Falls, R.F.D., I & II	A#26
	Poor Loser	A#30
	You Win Some, You Lose Some	A#33
	Thank You, God	A#03
	Whit's Flop	A#01
8:38	Pink Is Not My Color	A#41
10:8-10	It Began with a Rabbit's Foot . . .	A#20
10:14-15	A Mission for Jimmy	A#06
12:1	The War Hero	A#20
12:2	Heatwave	A#06
	What Are We Gonna Do About Halloween?	A#LE
	With a Little Help from My Friends	A#27
	A Different Kind of Peer Pressure	A#FP
12:10	A Simple Addition	A#LE
	Just Say Yes	A#29
	A Simple Addition	A#FP
12:10, 15	The Joke's on You	A#30
	The Potential in Elliot	A#19
12:17-21	Silver Lining	A#41
12:18	Best of Enemies	A#48
12:19-21	A Case of Revenge	A#30
	The Ill-Gotten Deed	A#06
13:1	Subject Yourself	A#24
13:1-5	Lincoln, I & II	A#07
13:1-7	Mayor for a Day	A#12
	The Living Nativity	A#16
15:1-3	The Truth About Zachary	A#23
15:2	The Winning Edge	A#08

1 Corinthians

2:9	The Mortal Coil, I & II	A#16
6:12	Addictions Can Be Habit-Forming	A#N
6:12-13	The Twilife Zone	A#21
9:14, 16	A Prayer for George Barclay	A#19
10:13	B-TV: Temptation	A#49
	Into Temptation	A#17
	The Devil Made Me Do It	A#32
10:24	Something's Got to Change	A#42
12	B-TV: Behind the Scenes	A#40
	The Mystery at Tin Flat	A#40
12:11	For Trying Out Loud	A#39
12:12	Viva La Difference	A#29
12:13	Not One of Us	A#09
13	Bobby's Valentine	A#N
	The Trouble with Girls	A#LE
13:5	Buried Sin	A#32
13:5, 7	Emotional Baggage	A#10
	It Ended with a Handshake	A#20
13:7	Arizona Sunrise	A#30
	B-TV: Forgiveness	A#32
	The Case of the Missing Train Car	A#N
	The Painting	A#29
	What Happened to the Silver Streak?	A#09
13:12	A Glass Darkly	A#43
15:51-52	Gone . . .	A#21
15:51-57	The Very Best of Friends	A#07
	Where Is Thy Sting?	A#24

2 Corinthians

1:10-11	Expect the Worst	A#38
3:17	The Day Independence Came	A#02
3:18	A Change of Hart	A#01
	Thy Kingdom Come	A#17
4:18-5:2	The Mortal Coil, I & II	A#16
5	The Perfect Witness, I, II, & III	A#23
5:16-17	A Change of Hart	A#01
5:17	The Highest Stakes, I & II	A#49
	The Undeniable Truth	A#47
5:20	The Pact, I & II	A#39
6:14	First Love	A#08
	The Turning Point	A#24
6:14-18	A Question About Tasha	A#27
10:5	Think on These Things	A#43
13:14	Family Vacation, I & II	A#02

Theme Index

D

Theme Index

R

S

Bible Story Episode Index

Jeremiah (Jer.)	Bernard and Jeremiah	A#47
Daniel's refusal to eat royal food,		
the king's dream (Dan. 1–2)	Deliver Us from Evil	A#17
The Fiery Furnace (Dan. 3)	V.B.S. Blues	A#02
	Deliver Us from Evil	A#17
Daniel and the Lion's Den (Dan. 6)	Hallowed Be Thy Name	A#17
	B-TV: Thanks	A#31
Jonah (Jonah)	Return to the Bible Room	A#02
	Hide and Seek	A#31
	B-TV: Obedience	A#39
The birth of Christ (Matt. 1; Luke 2)	Back to Bethlehem, I, II, & III	A#10
	Unto Us a Child Is Born	A#22
The visit of the Magi (Matt. 2)	The Star, I & II	A#12
Jesus' baptism (Matt. 3:13-17)	Hide and Seek	A#31
Jesus is tempted by Satan (Luke 4:1-13)	The Devil Made Me Do It	A#32
Jesus calls Peter and Andrew (John 1:35-51)	Hide and Seek	A#31
The healing of the centurion's son (Matt. 8:5-13; Luke 7:1-10)	Run-of-the-Mill Miracle	A#48
Jesus eats with sinners (Matt. 9:9-13)	B-TV: Grace	A#N
John the Baptist's last days and death (Matt. 11:2-19)	The Big Deal, I & II	A#35
Parable of the Four Sowers (Matt. 13:1-23)	Scattered Seeds	A#07
Parables about the kingdom of heaven (Matt. 13:24-52)	Thy Kingdom Come	A#17
Jesus feeds the five thousand (Matt. 14;		
Mark 6; Luke 9; John 6)	Share and Share Alike	A#22
Parable of the Good Samaritan (Luke 10:30-37)	The Big Broadcast	A#09
Parable of the Unmerciful Servant (Matt. 18:21-35)	An Act of Mercy	A#08
	B-TV: Forgiveness	A#32
Parable of the Workers (Matt. 20:1-16)	. . . The Last Shall Be First	A#11
	B-TV: Grace	A#N
The healing of Bartimaeus (Matt. 20:29-34)	B-TV: Compassion	A#27
Parable of the Two Sons (Matt. 21:28-32)	Over the Airwaves	A#09
Parable of the Wicked Tenants (Matt. 21:33-41)	Over the Airwaves	A#09
Parable of the Marriage Feast (Luke 14:15-24, Matt. 22:1-14)	The Marriage Feast	A#18
Parable of the Prodigal Son (Luke 15:11-32)	The Prodigal, Jimmy	A#04
	B-TV: Grace	A#N
Parable of the Lost Coin (Luke 15:8-10)	B-TV: Grace	A#N
Jesus heals ten lepers (Luke 17:11-19)	The Pretty Good Samaritan	A#26
	B-TV: Thanks	A#31
The raising of Lazarus (John 11–12)	An Adventure in Bethany, I & II	A#16
Jesus's arrest (John 18:1-11)	Hallowed Be Thy Name	A#17
Peter's denial of Jesus (Mark 14:32-42)	The Devil Made Me Do It	A#32
Crucifixion and resurrection of Jesus Christ (Mark 11–12)	The Imagination Station, I & II	A#05
	Hide and Seek	A#31
	The Imagination Station, Revisited, I & II	A#50
Ananias and Sapphira (Acts 5)	I Want My B-TV	A#23
	The Devil Made Me Do It	A#32
The apostle Paul (Acts)	The Power of One	A#44
Paul's conversion (Acts 6:8-8:1; 9:1-31)	Saint Paul: The Man from Tarsus	A#23
	Saint Paul: Set Apart by God	A#23
	Hide and Seek	A#31
Paul's last journey (Acts 24–28)	Saint Paul: Voyage to Rome	A#26
	Saint Paul: An Appointment with Caesar	A#26
Philemon (Philem.)	A Prisoner for Christ	A#06

Adventures in Odyssey Collector's Checklist

For a full selection of the latest *Adventures in Odyssey* products: Log on to our official Web site WhitsEnd.org, call Focus on the Family at (800) A-FAMILY, or visit your local Christian bookstore.

Unless otherwise noted, *Adventures in Odyssey* products are intended for ages 7 and up.

Adventures in Odyssey Audio Series

Each audio drama album contains 12 (or more!) exciting episodes, plus a booklet that takes you behind-the-scenes. Enjoy over 4 hours of entertainment in each 4-CD set.

- ❏ Volume 1: The Adventure Begins
- ❏ Volume 2: Stormy Weather
- ❏ Volume 3: Heroes
- ❏ Volume 4: FUNdamentals
- ❏ Volume 5: Daring Deeds, Sinister Schemes
- ❏ Volume 6: Mission: Accomplished
- ❏ Volume 7: On Thin Ice
- ❏ Volume 8: Beyond Expectations
- ❏ Volume 9: Just in Time
- ❏ Volume 10: Other Times, Other Places
- ❏ Volume 11: It's Another Fine Day . . .
- ❏ Volume 12: At Home and Abroad
- ❏ Volume 13: It All Started When . . .
- ❏ Volume 14: Meanwhile, in Another Part of Town
- ❏ Volume 15: A Place of Wonder
- ❏ Volume 16: Flights of Imagination
- ❏ Volume 17: On Earth as It Is in Heaven
- ❏ Volume 18: A Time of Discovery
- ❏ Volume 19: Passport to Adventure
- ❏ Volume 20: A Journey of Choices
- ❏ Volume 21: Wish You Were Here
- ❏ Volume 22: The Changing Times
- ❏ Volume 23: Twists and Turns
- ❏ Volume 24: Risks and Rewards
- ❏ Volume 25: Darkness before Dawn†
- ❏ Volume 26: Back on the Air
- ❏ Volume 27: The Search for Whit
- ❏ Volume 28: Welcome Home!
- ❏ Volume 29: Signed, Sealed, and Committed
- ❏ Volume 30: Through Thick and Thin
- ❏ Volume 31: Days to Remember
- ❏ Volume 32: Hidden Treasures
- ❏ Volume 33: Virtual Realities
- ❏ Volume 34: In Your Wildest Dreams
- ❏ Volume 35: The Big Picture
- ❏ Volume 36: Danger Signals†
- ❏ Volume 37: Countermoves†
- ❏ Volume 38: Battle Lines†
- ❏ Volume 39: Friends, Family, and Countrymen
- ❏ Volume 40: Out of Control
- ❏ Volume 41: In Hot Pursuit
- ❏ Volume 42: No Way Out
- ❏ Volume 43: Along for the Ride
- ❏ Volume 44: Eugene Returns!
- ❏ Volume 45: Lost & Found
- ❏ Volume 46: A Date with Dad (and Other Calamities)
- ❏ Volume 47: Into the Light
- ❏ Volume 48: Moment of Truth
- ❏ Volume 49: The Sky's the Limit
- ❏ Volume 50: The Best Small Town
- ❏ The Lost Episodes†

†Parental preview recommended

Adventures in Odyssey Novels

Original Novels
Original stories set in a time before the audio series.

- ❏ #1: Strange Journey Back
- ❏ #2: Danger Lies Ahead
- ❏ #3: Point of No Return

KIDSBORO™ Series

What will happen in a town run entirely by kids? Find out in Kidsboro, where kids make, and sometimes break, the rules.

- ❏ #1: Battle for Control
- ❏ #2: The Rise and Fall of the Kidsborian Empire
- ❏ #3: The Creek War
- ❏ #4: The Risky Reunion

Passages™ Series

A group of pre-teens in Odyssey stumble into another world where new discoveries await. For ages 10 and up.

- ❏ Manuscript 1: Darien's Rise
- ❏ Manuscript 2: Arin's Judgment
- ❏ Manuscript 3: Annison's Risk
- ❏ Manuscript 4: Glennall's Betrayal
- ❏ Manuscript 5: Draven's Defiance
- ❏ Manuscript 6: Fendar's Legacy

Adventures in Odyssey Animated DVD Series

These half-hour adventures feature fun stories and character-building lessons—just like the audio series! Now even young children can discover essential truths in the town of Odyssey. For ages 5 and up.

- ❏ #1: The Knight Travelers
- ❏ #2: A Flight to the Finish
- ❏ #3: A Fine Feathered Frenzy
- ❏ #4: Shadow of a Doubt
- ❏ #5: Star Quest
- ❏ #6: Once Upon an Avalanche
- ❏ #7: Electric Christmas
- ❏ #8: Go West, Young Man
- ❏ #9: Someone to Watch Over Me
- ❏ #10: In Harm's Way

❏ #11: A Twist in Time
❏ #12: A Stranger Among Us
❏ #13: Baby Daze

ANIMATED DVDs: NEW SERIES

❏ #1: The Last Days of Eugene Meltsner
❏ #2: Escape from the Forbidden Matrix
❏ #3: Caves of Qumran
❏ #4: Race to Freedom

Games for the Whole Family

Award-winning, family-friendly games teach virtues with fun!

❏ Answer That!™ The Family DVD Trivia Game: *Adventures in Odyssey* Edition
❏ The Great Escape
❏ The Sword of the Spirit
❏ The Treasure of the Incas

Musical Albums

Tap your feet (and lift your spirit) with Eugene's clever tunes—featuring his famous ukulele, keyboards, and more. For ages 4 and up.

❏ Eugene Sings!
❏ Eugene Sings! Christmas

Special Audio Collections

Note: These CD sets contain episodes that are included in the Audio Series (Volumes 1-50).

❏ Bible Eyewitness Collector's Set
❏ Bible Eyewitness: The Hall of Faith
❏ Christmas Classics
❏ A Christmas Odyssey
❏ Discovering Odyssey
❏ For God and Country
❏ A Maze of Mysteries
❏ The Novacom Saga
❏ Platinum Collection

Stay in Touch with Focus on the Family . . . so you don't miss out on the next adventure!

- *WhitsEnd.org*—Go behind the counter at Whit's End with news, discussion questions for episodes, podcasts, and much more!
- **Clubhouse** *magazine*—Get games, comics, and an exclusive story from *Odyssey* every month in this magazine for 8- to 12-year-olds.
- *Family.org*—Discover other Web sites and products designed for your life stage, whether a teen, young adult, or parent.

FOCUS
ON THE FAMILY

**Where Will
Adventures in Odyssey
Take You Next?**

The first 20 years were only
the beginning. Look for new
adventures that will be filled
with the same valuable life
lessons, just as much wonder
and discovery, and more
excitement and imagi-
nation than ever. You
never know what will
happen when you
visit the world of
*Adventures in
Odyssey!*

MEET THE

CAST AND CREW

WHO BRING

THE SHOW

TO LIFE

ADVENTURES IN ODYSSEY
TWO DECADES OF IMAGINATION

"Odyssey Sings"
by John Fornof and Marshal Younger

Okay, Mr. ...ts.
Listen to ...ll sing my
...ra...ght...

The *Odyssey* kids, circa 1989. *From left:* Chad Reisser (Monty Whittaker-Dowd and Digger Digwillow), Kyle Fisk (Artie Powell), Azure Janosky (Donna Barclay), Genni Mullen (Lucy Cunningham), Donald Long (Jack Davis), David Griffin (Jimmy Barclay), Joseph Cammaroto (Oscar)

Oh, W...

Am I ...

No, ...

Chris Anthony, host of *Adventures in Odyssey*, with her ever-present smile, circa 1988

WHIT:
...made a couple of
...ppears to be
...The auditions
...be on TV and the
...get a recording

From left: Fabio Stephens (Curt Stevens), and Donald Long (Jack Davis) during the recording of "Elijah"

Everyone ...

WHIT:

Hal Smith, the original voice and personality of John Avery Whittaker

From left: Parley Baer (Uncle Joe Finneman) and Walker Edmiston (Tom Riley and Bart Rathbone). Both actors enjoyed recording biblical episodes.

Sage Bolte (Robyn Jacobs), a good sister on and off the show

Aria Curzon in 2006, voice of
Mandy Straussberg

Lauren Schaffel (Liz Horton) and Corey Padnos (Trent
DeWhite) are friends in real life and on the show.

Odyssey cast and crew members outside a North Hollywood studio. *From left:* Will Ryan (Eugene), Alan Young
(Jack Allen), Dave Madden (Bernard Walton), sound designer Jonathan Crowe, executive producer Dave Arnold

The *Odyssey* team at the recording of "The Triangled Web" (album 50). *Standing, from left:* Sound designer Jonathan Crowe, executive producer Dave Arnold, sound designer Nathan Jones, actors Fabio Stephens (Curt Stevens), Genni Long (Lucy Cunningham-Schultz), Donald Long (Jack Davis), Katie Leigh (Connie), David Griffin (Jimmy Barclay), producer Marshal Younger. *Sitting, from left:* Actors Will Ryan (Eugene), Dave Madden (Bernard Walton), Paul Herlinger (Whit), and host Chris Anthony

Actor Corey Burton (Bryan Dern) holds a candid interview with actor Will Ryan (Eugene)

Jess Harnell, voice of Odyssey's favorite mailman, Wooton Bassett

CURT:
You know, let's not bother
him. He's busy.

...fulness...

Actor Mary Mouser, voice of
Grady McKay's sister, Sam

Jac

Mr. Walton

Some stirring from inside.

Actor Katie Leigh behind the mike as
Connie Kendall

From left: Writer Paul McCusker, writer/director Phil Lollar, coordinator Joyce Blaine, sound designer Bob Luttrell, sound designer Dave Arnold

Davi

Be
and

andy and
hat are

LUCY:
We heard about the Best

Actor Paul Herlinger, voice and personality of Whit from 1996 to the present

Sound designer Nathan Jones with actor Mark Christopher Lawrence, voice of Ed Washington

The *Odyssey* creative team uses (and abuses) the Foley room in 2007. *From left:* Sound designer Nathan Jones has the keys to Whit's End. Coordinator Carol Rusk prepares to slide down a snow-covered hill with Alex Jefferson ("Snow Day," album 36). Producer Marshal Younger makes the sound of a miniexcavator ("A New Era," album 49). Jonathan Crowe uses a makeshift hula skirt ("Something Blue," album 41). Writer Kathy Buchanan is a prisoner ("Something Significant," album 49). Executive producer Dave Arnold uses a hula skirt and a suit of armor ("Something Blue"). Sound designer Chris Diehl puts out a fire ("B-TV: Behind the Scenes," album 40). Writer Nathan Hoobler answers the Whit's End phone ("Two Friends and a Truck," album 44).

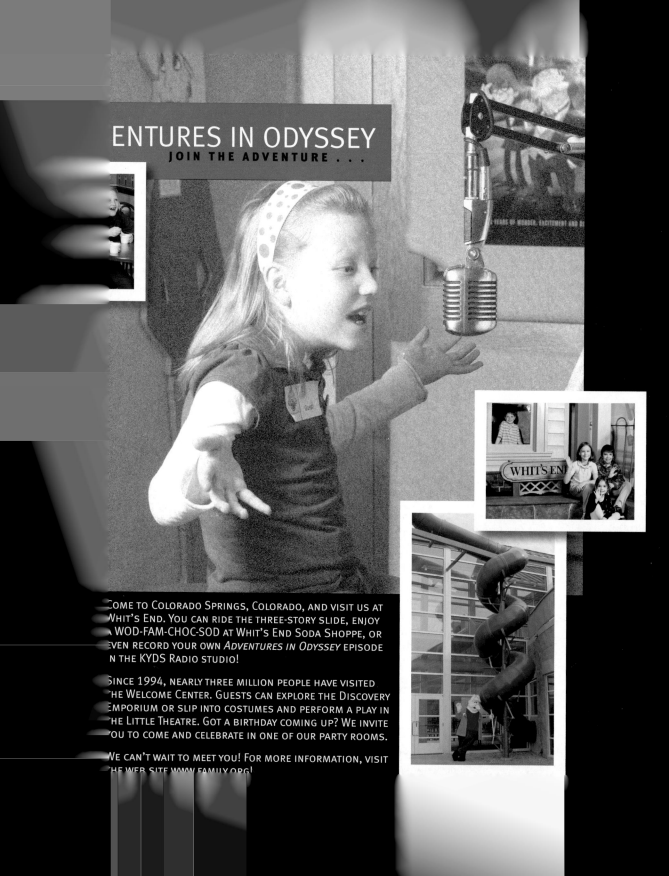

ENTURES IN ODYSSEY
JOIN THE ADVENTURE . . .

COME TO COLORADO SPRINGS, COLORADO, AND VISIT US AT
WHIT'S END. YOU CAN RIDE THE THREE-STORY SLIDE, ENJOY
A WOD-FAM-CHOC-SOD AT WHIT'S END SODA SHOPPE, OR
EVEN RECORD YOUR OWN *ADVENTURES IN ODYSSEY* EPISODE
IN THE KYDS RADIO STUDIO!

SINCE 1994, NEARLY THREE MILLION PEOPLE HAVE VISITED
THE WELCOME CENTER. GUESTS CAN EXPLORE THE DISCOVERY
EMPORIUM OR SLIP INTO COSTUMES AND PERFORM A PLAY IN
THE LITTLE THEATRE. GOT A BIRTHDAY COMING UP? WE INVITE
YOU TO COME AND CELEBRATE IN ONE OF OUR PARTY ROOMS.

WE CAN'T WAIT TO MEET YOU! FOR MORE INFORMATION, VISIT
THE WEB SITE WWW.FAMILY.ORG!